A MATTER OF NEED

"You'd better have a care. This is the second time someone in the vicinity has taken a shot at you. First he missed, now he's wounded you. The next time, he may finish the job."

"Actually, 'tis the third such attempt. There was one in London as well."

She sucked in her breath. "My regard for you grows apace, m'lord. To inspire irritation is common. To engender murderous hatred is remarkable. Who might wish you dead?"

"With the possible exception of yourself, I can think of no one . . . at least, no one this side of the Atlantic."

"Pray cease your foolish banter. Much as I might wish my father and the marquess had not hatched their cork-brained scheme, I have not attempted to shoot you."

"As you have already assured me, you would not have missed." He sighed and combed his fingers through his hair. "I have a friend in London looking into the matter. There's little else to do now."

"As difficult as it might be for you, you could exercise a bit of judgment and not ride alone through woodlands where anyone with a musket can make a target of you," she replied heatedly.

"Why, countess, I'm touched. 'Twould seem that you care."

"Indeed I do, m'lord dolt. As I thought I had made clear this afternoon, we need each other. . . ."

YANKEE EARL

SHIRL HENKE

LEISURE BOOKS NEW YORK CITY

A LEISURE BOOK®

October 2003

Published by

Dorchester Publishing Co., Inc.
200 Madison Avenue
New York, NY 10016

ISBN 0-8439-5241-5

The name "Leisure Books" and the stylized "L" with design are trademarks of Dorchester Publishing Co., Inc.

Printed in the United States of America.

Visit us on the web at www.dorchesterpub.com.

Chapter One

"Jason Edward Beaumont, American nobody, is now Earl of Falconridge," Rachel Fairchild huffed to herself in disgust. The gossip circulating about London had reached Harleigh Hall within a fortnight of his presentation at court. And now he was expected to arrive for an inspection of his estate. She simply had to catch a glimpse of him, to take his measure before being formally introduced to him in London next month.

Not bad enough that nasty little Mathias would have been the next earl. At least he was Cargrave's proper English heir. But with Mathias's demise, the marquess had now bestowed the title on some colonial upstart. Just her ill fortune that Harleigh and Falconridge adjoined. At least she would have known how to handle Mathias had he been the new earl. She'd bested him at every childhood game, even given him a thrashing with a hackamore she seized off the stable wall after she caught him abusing one of his grandfather's horses.

1

They had been eight years old at the time, and he'd been in mortal terror of her ever since.

Rachel was forced to admit she had that unfortunate effect on most men. At five feet six inches, with an athletic body, hazel eyes and dark hair, she was hardly the epitome of English beauty. Petite blue-eyed blondes with softly voluptuous figures were all the rage, but even if she'd fit the physical mold, there was no way the Honorable Miss Rachel Fairchild would ever have been able to flutter her eyelashes and play flirtatious games to win a husband as her younger sisters had.

Ugh, the vapid, simpering conversations, the idle gossip, the utter frivolity of their lives appalled her. Rachel knelt down and ran a handful of rich brown dirt through her fingers, smelling the ripeness of summer on the early morning air. How she loved the land, the rhythm of the seasons from planting to harvest time. "All I ask of life is to work this fertile soil in peace," she murmured.

Just then the sound of a shot echoed from upstream, followed by the pounding of horse hooves, splashing down the creek. She could hear the clatter of dislodged stones as some fool rode his mount far too swiftly in such treacherous footing. Why, the horse would most probably break its legs! If there was anything Rachel could abide less than a fool, it was a rider who abused his mount. She reached for her bay's reins, then started to swing into the saddle just as another shot rang out, combined with loud male cursing.

"I'll give that sapskull better cause for those oaths," she declared, intent on delivering a fine tongue-lashing to the approaching rider. Rachel was certain he was one of her neighbors, who were much given to riding down innocent animals for sport, but before she could get her seat on the skittish bay, a big black stallion burst through a willow thicket headed directly toward her.

2

His rider, as big and dark a brute as the horse, attempted to swerve around her. He might have succeeded, but her bay nickered in terror and hopped sideways, hooves flailing as it slipped in the mud at the stream's edge. Rachel was caught with one foot in the stirrup and one long leg halfway over the saddle when the horses collided. Suddenly she found herself sailing backwards, straight into the muddy bank, where she landed with a thunk. The sound of a gravelly male voice muttering dire imprecations registered as she floundered in the muck. If only she could gather enough wind in her lungs to screech at the imbeciles, equine and human!

"Reddy, if you weren't already gelded, I'd prune you myself," she muttered through gritted teeth as the bay nickered nervously, backing into the creek, ready to bolt at further provocation. Unlike her skittish horse, the big black stood his ground, awaiting a command after its rider dismounted. As the intruder's high black boots strode toward her, she crouched on all fours with her hair hanging in oozing clumps around her face. She peered through what felt like wet moss hanging on a tree branch. Unwillingly her eyes traveled up the long legs attached to the boots, strong horseman's legs. She raised her head and flipped her sodden hair over her shoulder. It landed with a nasty plop as her inspection settled on a most indelicate portion of his anatomy.

Oh, and his anatomy was a splendid one indeed, she was forced to admit. Tall, broad-shouldered and narrow-waisted, he wore a pair of tight buckskin riding breeches that left little to the imagination, and a shirt of fine white linen, open halfway down his chest, scandalously revealing a mass of thick black hair. Her perusal was interrupted by a low, rumbling chuckle.

The cheeky devil was laughing at her while she hunkered like some sow in a mud wallow! "You want for manners as much as for common sense," she snapped, "knocking me from my mount, then daring to make sport of your handiwork."

"My apologies, but I had another matter in mind as I rounded the bend in the creek," he replied, looking over his shoulder warily before returning his attention to the woman at his feet. "Someone was shooting at me. As I was unarmed, it didn't seem sporting to remain a stationary target."

She snorted in derision. "You chucklehead, no one was shooting at *you*. 'Twas just some local chawbacons poaching game."

"I don't know how you judge a man's intent in England, but in America we deem one shot to be an accident. When a second whizzes past a man's head, he takes it quite personally . . . unless he resembles a deer."

"In your case, more like a braying ass," she muttered beneath her breath, now recognizing his peculiar accent. He had to be Cargrave's heir. She must stand and take his measure. Her height gave her an advantage over most men, but she feared he would not be one of them. His strong brown hand reached down and took her arm, but before he could assist her, another shot suddenly rent the soft sounds of the woodland.

"Down," he grunted, squashing her back into the mud and falling atop her. "You wouldn't happen to have a pistol about, would you?"

Rachel saw stars for a moment as the air once again rushed from her lungs. The great oaf must weigh over twelve stone! Before she could reply, he was rolling toward a thicket of mulberry bushes, dragging her with him.

"Still think our friend is out for venison?" he whispered.

"If you knock every person you meet insensate, then

4

try to squash them like insects, I should imagine many might resort to firearms in self-defense," she hissed. What the deuce was going on here? Surely whoever was shooting meant no harm. She called out in the general direction from which the shot had come, "Halloo, this is Rachel F—"

"Quiet, you little fool! You'll give our position away."

His hand, now covered with mud, smothered her greeting. She bit him, then spit the creek slime from her mouth.

He jerked his hand away with a faint oath, then seized her by her sodden shirt and began to tromp deeper into the most overgrown part of the brush beside the stream, dragging her along pell-mell. "I am only going to say this once. You will either do precisely as I say or I really will knock you insensate and carry you—is that clear?"

Another shot rang out, and a slender sapling a few feet from them was sheered in half. Still holding on to her shirt, which now had pulled from its mooring inside her riding breeches, he plunged further into the brush, moving with surprisingly quiet deliberation, following the twisting course of the creek. Now her mouth was dry with fear. Someone was deliberately trying to hit them—or, more likely, the charming fellow glowering at her as they halted behind a stout oak tree.

"Well?" he asked with one black eyebrow raised.

Odious American. She nodded grudgingly.

"I'm going to whistle for Araby. He'll follow the creek until he reaches us."

She scoffed. "A horse trained to come at your whistle?"

Ignoring her dubious smirk, he continued, "As I jump out and mount, I'll reach down for your arm. I want you right behind me so I can kick him into a gallop and

5

take off while I'm pulling you over the saddle. No time to dawdle."

He was not jesting. "I'm dressed to ride astride. Just let me jump behind you," she replied. His eyes skimmed over her hips and down her long legs with what she might have taken for male appreciation if not for his reply.

"Thank God you're a country wench, not some damned countess, but I don't want a female covering my back in any case. I'll pull you in front of me. Be ready."

Then he raised his fingers to his mouth and gave a shrill, ear-piercing whistle that drowned out her retort, after which he began dragging her along the bank of the stream again. The sound of horse hooves splashing through the water quickly followed. Damned if the black was not obeying! As the horse drew close, its owner broke from cover and jumped across the rocky stream bed, leaping on the big stallion's back in one fluid movement, a deed which a horsewoman such as Rachel would have admired under other circumstances. But just then another shot echoed across the water. She simply clawed for his outstretched arm, allowing herself to be flung over his saddle while the big horse took off like a cannonball.

She hung across his thighs like a sack of turnips. Every bounce jarred her belly and further winded her as they sped down the creek, then cut into an open meadow several dozen yards ahead. When he finally slowed the black and checked the perimeter of the woods, assuring himself that they were out of firing range, she squirmed from his grasp and slid unceremoniously down his leg to the ground, still disconcertingly able to smell the faint aroma of male musk combined with horse. Oddly, it unsettled her, but she

6

attributed the reaction to her aching stomach and the wild ride.

Rachel had never felt at such a disadvantage in her life as she did at that moment, looking up at the arrogant Yankee Doodle. In spite of his muddy appearance, he merely looked ruggedly handsome, not slimy and unkempt as she did. He had a dimple at one side of his mouth when he grinned, which he was doing now, as if he understood exactly how she felt. Never one to allow an opponent the first move, she raised her chin proudly and faced the insufferable devil.

"You must be the one they're calling the Yankee Earl in London."

"Jason Beaumont, at your service, Countess," he replied with a mocking toss of his head. The sunlight danced off the blue-black highlights in his shaggy hair.

Does he know? She stood frozen for a moment as he slid effortlessly from the black.

"How are you privy to what goes on in the ton? This is quite a rustic place for gossip about the Quality."

"And, of course, you assume I'm a rustic wench," she replied sweetly. She was dying to know if giving him her name would elicit any response, but decided it would be better to take him by surprise at the ball next month.

He cocked his head and crossed his arms over that broad naked chest. "You speak like a countess and possess the arrogance of one, but I vow I've never seen a female this side of the Atlantic dressed in britches."

She enjoyed the puzzled expression in his dark blue eyes. "Oh, but you have seen females in britches in America?"

"Yes . . . among my blood brother's people."

"Blood brother?" she echoed. What sort of barbarian society did he come from?

"The Shawnee. They're Indians."

7

"Savages! You compare me to savages!"

"Not at all," he replied. "They have far better manners than you."

She raised her hand to slap his face, but he caught her wrist, enveloping the slender bones in one big hand. "Tut, don't tempt fate, m'dear. My Shawnee brothers may have better manners, but I don't."

"Let me go," she gritted out, suddenly aware of how isolated they were and how big he was, towering over her not inconsiderable height. She knew how to defend herself and had done so against her fair share of country ruffians over the years, but this fellow was unsettling in a far different way.

He was holding her much too near that bare, hairy chest. Rachel seemed unable to take her eyes from one small droplet of perspiration as it wended its way down his throat into that black forest. *How would it feel to touch that hair, feel the crisp spring of it? To feel the hard muscles beneath?* Before she could stop herself, she blurted out, "You're a fine one to cast aspersions on my manners, going about half naked. At least my body is decently covered."

He released her, chuckling as he said, "Covered, yes, but as to decently . . ." His eyes roamed slowly over her curves, which were far more tantalizingly revealed by her soaked shirt and pants than she could have imagined. In spite of the voluminous cut of the shirt, the mud and creek water had molded the soft cloth like second skin to breasts, belly and hips.

She preferred riding astride in britches when working on the estate, but Rachel knew it was not acceptable for any woman, least of all one of Quality, to wear men's apparel. Flushing because of that—certainly not because of *his* opinion, or the way he affected her— she replied, "A pity that poacher was such a poor

8

marksman. A few holes in that thick colonial hide might let some of the wind out."

With that, she spun on her heel and stalked across the meadow toward home, feeling his mocking blue gaze burning a hole in her backside. She felt compelled to place some distance between them. Just for now. *I'll exact my revenge when next we meet,* she consoled herself, refusing to admit how the Yankee lout upset her equilibrium.

Suddenly his black pulled up beside her and he leaned down, murmuring to her, "Crude colonial that I am, I should not leave a woman stranded without her horse."

"I shall manage famously," she said without looking up. "My home is but a short distance."

"Ah, but I must accompany you," he insisted. "Indeed, we can ride as we did before. You make a fine baggage, Countess."

"What marvelous flash of wit . . . and you need not even pick your nose to prime your brain pan. A marvel for so great a lobcock!"

With his mocking laughter echoing in her ears, she plodded doggedly toward Harleigh Hall. It was only a mile or so distant, no difficult walk . . . if only her boots did not squish with every step she took. That wretched Reddy would by now be munching hay in his stall, all safe and dry.

She cursed the horse . . . and the Yankee.

But she would never ride in any fashion with her body pressed against any portion of his, especially that bare chest. Just thinking of it made her shiver in spite of the heat. She ignored him when he reined in and sat, leaning on the saddle, watching her stomp toward the manor house nestled in the valley below. "Stubborn

9

wench," he called out after her retreating figure. "We'll meet again, Countess."

A threat or a promise? She smirked. *If only you knew, you crude colonial clod*. Rachel Fairchild would have a surprise or two up her lace-covered sleeve when next they did meet.

Chapter Two

Alvin Francis Edward Drummond was a small man with light tan hair and piercing green eyes that missed nothing. He was possessed of a wicked wit, a fierce sense of loyalty and an absolute aversion to the state of matrimony.

Reclining on a lyre-back chair in the dressing room of the eminent tailors Schwartze and Davidson, he observed as Jason was fitted for the clothing a new earl would need to carry him through the end of the Season. "No, no, that won't do a'tall, good fellow," he said, waving away a bolt of fine woolen cloth.

As the clerk scurried away, Drum emitted a sigh, then turned his attention back to his newfound friend, picking up their conversation where they had been interrupted. "You mean to say that you actually *lived* with Red Indians—and you without a dram of their blood?" the dandy inquired with one slim eyebrow raised to indicate amazement.

11

"Yes. They're a remarkable people," Jason replied with a grin, imagining Drum's reaction if confronted by six feet four inches of Shawnee warrior with a shaven head and roached scalplock.

"I have a good friend from the col—er, the United States," Drum corrected himself, "who is right now somewhere belly deep in a swamp with his cousins, who happen to be . . ." He paused and put a pinch of snuff on the back of one pale hand, inhaled and sneezed delicately into a snowy linen handkerchief. "Ah, yes, Muskogee—I do believe that is what Alex's tribal brothers are. I say, you would not by any chance be acquainted with Alex Blackthorne or any of those Muskogee chaps, would you?"

Jason threw back his head and laughed. "I'm afraid you underestimate the size of the United States. The Muskogee reside in Georgia, nearly a thousand miles south of Maryland, where I lived. But I've heard of Blackthorne Shipping. The family has one of the largest and most successful merchant operations in the country."

"A pity you never had the opportunity to meet Alex. Lud, the times the three of us could have had," Drum said with a sigh. Then, peering at Jason through his quizzing glass, he shook his head. "Odd, that. With your black hair and all that sun-darkened skin, you more resemble an Indian than Alex does. We really must do something about giving you a fine English pallor, my boy. Perhaps a touch of arsenic, eh? It's all the crack to whiten one's complexion."

Jason shuddered. "There are many things I will do for my grandfather, but poisoning myself is not among them," he replied as the tailor entered the room buried beneath half a dozen bolts of kerseymere.

Drum's impeccable taste in fashion had induced Jason's grandfather to overlook the young rapscallion's reputation as a duelist and gambler who lived well beyond his means. In spite of his faults, he was well received at all the best clubs, including White's and Watier's. George William Beaumont, ninth Marquess of Cargrave, was determined that his grandson be accepted by the ton. There was no one better equipped to make over an American privateer into an English gentleman than the Honorable Mr. Drummond.

When the ordeal was finally over and Drum announced that Jason had sufficient finery to last him until the Season ended, the two men repaired to the library of the Beaumont city house just off Grosvenor Square.

"Grandfather is expecting me to attend a recital tonight." Jason sighed as he handed Drum a brandy, then raised his own glass.

"At Chitchester's?" Drum inquired. Jason nodded, and his companion shuddered. "Zounds, 'twill be the duke's younger sister Theodosia torturing the pianoforte."

Jason chuckled. "You are most unchivalrous for a gentleman, sirrah."

"The gel's on the marriage mart." He studied Jason over the rim of his Waterford tumbler with merry green eyes.

Now it was Jason's turn to shudder. "No, thank you. *If* and when—note the emphasis on the first word—I decide to marry, I shall choose a woman for her personal allure, not her dowry or bloodlines." Suddenly the hoyden in britches from Falconridge flashed into his mind, and he grinned.

"Thinking about that allure, are we, hmmm?"

"Just a rather unusual female I encountered last week in the country. No one of account. But she possessed a sharp wit. Claws to match, too."

13

"Just like Alex. Always chasing a skirt," Drum said with a chuckle.

"No skirt."

"No skirt? Egad, was she running about mother naked?"

Jason smirked. "She wore britches."

"Britches?" Drum choked on his brandy.

"Is there an echo in here?"

Ignoring the taunt, Drum asked sourly, "Is there to be nothing left sacred for us poor males? Women in britches, indeed. We need a night of diversion sans female company, in skirts or otherwise attired. Heigh-ho, we're off to the Haymarket Room. Two of Domenico Angelo's pupils are putting on a demonstration with foils."

"Personally, I've always preferred a good sturdy cutlass."

"Being a retired pirate, you would . . . regrettably," Drum replied. "But you shall learn better under my most excellent tutelage."

The room was not all that large, considering the crowd. Drum had been right. Unlike gambling hells, dog fights and horse races, where ladies of the evening were always in evidence, the fencing demonstration drew an all-male audience. Most were from the upper ten thousand, but a few wealthy Cits were present as well. The low murmuring of fencing enthusiasts filled the smoke-laden air as gentlemen puffed on expensive cigars and wagered.

"I say to hell with that Mediterranean mediocrity," a nasal voice announced from a corner of the room as Jason and Drum entered. The speaker stood surrounded by a gaggle of sycophants. His blond hair was cut a la Brutus, framing a pale angular face with a long

14

patrician nose and deeply set yellow eyes that skimmed the crowd with restless energy.

As the fellow continued to hold forth, it was apparent to Jason that he had imbibed too much, but no one seemed inclined to notice. "Who is that pompous ass?" he asked Drum, sotto voce.

"Ah, Forrestal, an insufferable lout. Drinks too much and has execrable taste in fashion," Drum replied, shaking his head at the man's waistcoat, which was embroidered with a garish floral design. "If the sot ventured into the countryside in that flowered monstrosity, he'd be suffocated by amorous butterflies."

"His companion's sensibilities don't appear offended," Jason replied dryly.

"That's because Forrestal is Etherington's heir. Currently he's waiting for the old man to kick the bucket so he can ascend to the dukedom. Well known as a skilled duelist."

"Displaying such manners, he had better be."

"Ah, but he'll be a duke one day. Most of the ton is willing to overlook a fault or two for that. Of course, in the meanwhile he's perpetually out at heels."

"Why doesn't his father give him an estate to run for himself? Surely a duke has several to spare."

"Heigh-ho, you've seen what a charming creature he is—would you gift him with aught before absolutely forced to do so?"

"You have the right of that," Jason replied thoughtfully, feeling the future duke's eyes fasten on him with inexplicable hostility.

"Come, they're about to begin," Drum said, moving through the press.

Jason was passing by Forrestal and his entourage when one of the duke-in-waiting's companions seized hold of his arm and said, "Wouldn't care to place a wager on Arless, would you? We have a purse-proud

15

Cit over there who's taking all bets. Demned tradesmen don't know how to behave in the presence of their betters."

Jason looked over the shorter man's head and met those disquieting yellow eyes, almost certain the future duke had put his friend up to this. "If you're wagering for Arless, I should like to place my money on his opponent. Say, one hundred pounds?"

Suddenly the conversation about them quieted as heads tilted in Jason's direction. Few men in the room were as tall as Beaumont, but he and Forrestal were of a height. The Englishman uncoiled his body from the wall and quite literally shoved his short, rotund companion out of the way.

"My, my, chaps, what have we here, hmmm?" He circled Beaumont like a shark, gliding smoothly in spite of his advanced state of inebriation. "Speaks like a foreigner."

Beaumont felt Drum's cautioning hand on his arm but shrugged it off. "I was raised in America."

One thin pale eyebrow arched sardonically. "Ah, you must be Cargrave's heir. The Yankee earl," he said with a sneer.

Jason's patience was about at an end. "Do you take my bet or not?" he asked the short fellow, ignoring Forrestal.

Before his companion could reply, Forrestal purred, "Of course he will, and how about another with me? Something a bit headier . . . just to make it interesting. Say a monkey? That is, five hundred pounds . . . if you have it?"

"Oh, I have it. Unlike your father, my grandfather trusts me with the purse strings," Jason replied with a wolfish grin. "Five hundred it is." As he turned away, he was pleased to see an angry flush darken the Englishman's face. "I have the feeling that His Almost-

Grace arranged for that fellow to waylay me," he murmured to Drum.

"Perhaps. But Forrestal would resent any foreigner inheriting Cargrave's extensive titles. Xenophobic, don't you know?"

Jason chuckled. "What Englishman isn't? Arless's opponent had better be good or Grandfather will cane me for squandering six hundred pounds."

"It was not politic to cross swords with Forrestal, even though he is a stiff-rumped lout," Drum replied.

"I know little about politics—but I'm skilled enough with a sword."

Drum harrumphed and corrected his companion. "Cutlass. Forrestal would cut you to fishbait with a foil."

"Don't place any wagers on that," Jason said softly as the exhibition began.

The two combatants were evenly matched, both highly skilled with foils, but Arless's foe began to steadily outpoint him. By the time the contest was over, sterling flasks of spirits were being upended all around the room in celebration or consolation.

"It would be wise to send a servant to collect your winnings on the morrow," Drum advised.

"Recall, I'm not a politic fellow."

Sighing, Drum followed his impetuous American charge. He did not like the glint in Forrestal's eyes when they alighted on Beaumont. *What the deuce put the bee in his britches over Jason?*

"Ah, the Yankee earl come to collect his winnings," Forrestal slurred, taking a long pull from a pocket flask embossed with his family crest. "Just like the rest of the tradesmen . . . crass moneygrubbers, the lot of you. But I forget myself. After all, you're to be excused, being raised in a land without nobility."

"There are many definitions of nobility, sir. In America, one of those is a man who pays his debts without whimper."

Several of the Englishman's companions shuffled nervously, exchanging whispers behind their hands. Forrestal made a swift, cutting gesture with his arm and all fell silent. "Do you intimate that I would default on a debt of honor?" he purred to Beaumont.

Jason simply held out his open palm. Unsmiling, he said, "Do you whimper? Pay me."

"I shall repay you, sirrah!" With that Forrestal raised his arm and delivered a resounding slap to Beaumont's cheek.

"As the challenged, my friend, you have the choice of weapons. I, of course, shall stand your second," Drum said smoothly to Jason, then turned and handed Forrestal his card. "I shall discuss the particulars of this matter with your man on the morrow. Have him call at my residence. And please be civilized . . . no earlier than twelve."

Rachel had only been in London two days and already had heard more than enough about that American upstart Jason Beaumont. The maids at her father's city house sighed about how handsome he was, the footmen gossiped about his exploits among the demimonde, and even the dour cook chuckled about his wild colonial antics as if he were her own special charge.

Worst of all, Rachel's younger sister Harriet, now Baroness Widmere, insisted on reading aloud from the scandal sheets in which he was featured. A man as exotic as the Yankee earl, for that was what the broadsides had dubbed him, sent the baroness into fits of sighing. Although her baron was a pleasant enough young chap, he was very staid and deadly dull. Being timid herself, Harriet had chosen him for precisely that reason, but she loved to dream about dashing princes riding off with fair maidens.

Wed when she was but seventeen after a Season when no less than five young bucks offered for her, Harry was a pretty, plump little blonde, resembling their mother, who had been delicate and flighty in the same way. Rachel took after their maternal grandfather, a big, bluff man who spent his life working the land. If given her way, she would have done the same, but here she was in London, awaiting that accursed ball tomorrow night.

Her sister gushed breathlessly, "Can you imagine it, Rachel—they say he has lived with Red Indians in America."

"Oh, I can well imagine it," Rachel replied tartly.

"I wonder, are all Americans so impetuous? He's cut quite a swath in the card rooms and gaming hells. Also . . . ah, I should not mention it with you still unwed, of course . . ."

When Harriet's round little face pinkened, Rachel sighed and replied as her sister had hoped she would, "But of course you will tell me anyway, won't you, Harry? I do understand country matters, after all."

"Well, you should never admit *that*," Harry admonished. For a moment it appeared as though she were the elder, but her giggle quickly dispelled the notion as she warmed to her subject once more. "His reputation with the Cyprians is become legendary, and there have been rumors regarding a liaison with the Marchioness of Shrewsbury. He's only been here a fortnight, and already the ton is quite agog with his exploits. Imagine challenging Forrestal!"

"If you read correctly from the broadsheets, my dear, 'twas Forrestal who issued the challenge," Rachel replied dryly, pretending interest in the array of ball gowns spread across the bed.

19

"Oh, bother the silly rules. The thing is that Falconridge was ever so brave. Forrestal has quite the reputation with foils," she added worriedly, chewing on her plump lower lip. "He might have killed the earl."

"So much the better," Rachel replied. *It would certainly have solved one problem.*

"Never say it!" Harry cried. "I thought you could not abide Forrestal. And the earl did make quite a cake of him. 'Tis rumored he studied under some French fencing master in America."

The thought of the American slicing the shirt and pants from Forrestal's body was gratifying, even if he was only a shade less detestable than Etherington's heir. Rachel could not resist a small smirk.

Harry tittered. "I would love to have seen him with his clothing in tatters, holding up his unmentionables with one hand while trying to wield a blade with the other." At that picture, both women burst into laughter, and it seemed for a moment that they were girls at home in the country once more.

Then Rachel sobered. "The Yankee has made a deadly enemy. He'd best watch his back. The next Duke of Etherington will never forgive such a humiliation."

"You could have been a duchess," Harry said slyly, moving across the room to consider the ball gowns on the bed.

Rachel shuddered. "And have to take Frederick Forrestal in the bargain? Let us not discuss men any further, Harry."

"As the eldest, 'tis your duty—"

"Bugger my duty," Rachel blurted out. "Oh, I am sorry, Harry. I did not mean to take out my frustrations on you."

"Best not let Father hear such language, m'dear," her prim younger sister said in a hushed voice. For all her addlepatedness, Harry genuinely loved Rachel and wanted her to be happy. For any proper English lady, that meant a husband. "You've been spending too much time in stables and not enough in ballrooms," she scolded.

"That has always been my choice, Harry. I want nothing more than to spend my life at Harleigh Hall, to raise livestock and crops."

" 'Tis most unnatural, Rachel, which is why Father has done what he did. Although I may never forgive him his methods of handling things. Imagine, not informing me until the day you arrived! The whole of it has been much too sudden, and I worry about all the secrecy! What will our friends say? Why, the Dowager Duchess of Chitchester shall positively swoon with shock."

Seeing that her sister was working herself into a fine taking, Rachel diverted her with the one foolproof method she knew. "No remedy for any of that, Harry, but I require your help now. Which of these gowns should I wear?"

"Well, you simply must look your best, that is for certain. Father—"

"I know what is going to happen," Rachel said in grim resignation. "Now, let us dispense with further discussion of it and select the gown I shall wear to the guillotine."

The music of a twelve-piece orchestra lilted from inside the Cargrave city house. Outside, the press was quite magnificent with carriages queued up for blocks in either direction, each disgorging its elegantly attired passengers by turns. Footmen in Cargrave livery directed the flow of vehicles and assisted guests up the flower-strewn front stairs, where they were announced as they entered the ballroom.

Lords and ladies sparkled as brilliantly as the crystal chandeliers hanging from the arched ceiling. A rainbow of color and the babel of conversation filled the room. Gentlemen with stiffly starched cravats bowed over bejeweled ladies in softly clinging gowns of silk and mull. Flowers overflowed huge Meissen vases, blending their heady perfume with that worn by both men and women.

No one who was anyone would fail to attend when George William Beaumont, ninth Marquess of Cargrave, gave one of his exceedingly infrequent and always lavish festivities. Even the Prince Regent had promised to put in an appearance later in the evening. Rumors abounded regarding what had occasioned the gala, since the Season was almost over.

To add to the titillation, Viscount Harleigh's eldest daughter—who most considered already on the shelf—was to be in attendance. That alone was occasion for gossip. Rachel had always avoided socializing with the upper ten thousand, even going so far as to cut short her one Season and return to the country, leaving her father furious and several would-be suitors nursing wounded egos. She had returned for her younger sisters' Seasons. Both Sophie and Harriett had wed advantageously, and in short order Rachel hied herself back to Harleigh Hall, where it was rumored that she rode about the countryside like a hellion and grubbed in the dirt like one of her father's tenant farmers.

She made men nervous. No doubt about it. In spite of her striking looks, Harleigh's eldest was possessed of too much stature, too little decorum and far too cutting a wit. She looked men straight in the eye and said precisely what she thought. It simply was not the done thing for a young lady of Quality. These were traits more appropriate to the wild Cargrave heir, whom the scandal sheets were calling the Yankee earl. Was it not positively delicious that he was to be in attendance as well?

From the moment he set foot in the ballroom, Jason knew he was the source of gossip. It happened everywhere he went, especially at haut ton events such as this. His grandfather had insisted he attend, mentioning that he would at last have the chance to meet the marquess's best friend, Viscount Harleigh. In truth, Jason was curious about Hugh Fairchild, since his estate adjoined Falconridge and they would soon be neighbors. He had wanted to call at the viscount's seat last month when he'd been in the country, but since it was the height of the Season, Hugh was in London.

However, neither the viscount nor Jason's grandfather was in evidence. Probably closeted away with brandy and cigars, he thought, wishing he could join them. But that was not to be; an assortment of matrons with marriageable daughters in tow bore down on him like sparrow hawks on a robin. He quickly found himself dancing and making interminably boring small talk.

Then the oddest sensation overcame him. The hairs on his nape prickled, an experience more familiar when he was raiding with the Shawnee than dancing in a lavish ballroom. *Someone is watching me.* Smiling at the birdlike twittering of the girl in his arms, Jason surreptitiously scanned the crowd. When the waltz ended, he bowed over his companion's hand and returned her to her chaperone.

He expected his stalker to be a man, judging by the calculated boldness of the perusal. When he saw his newfound nemesis, Frederick Forrestal, lounging against a column near the entry, surrounded by his usual entourage of slavering young nobs, Jason was certain he'd solved the mystery. But the future duke appeared to be assiduously ignoring him. It was not surprising that Frederick would avoid a contretemps that would remind everyone about the humiliating outcome of their recent duel.

But damned if the malaise plaguing Jason did not persist. Feeling it again, he turned in the opposite direction . . . and locked eyes with *her*. Surely it could not be his hoyden from the country? But there was no mistaking that long-legged, purposeful stride as she cut a path through the assembly, headed directly toward him. He would have recognized the way her body moved anywhere, but little else about her.

She was a vision in peach silk. The low-cut gown revealed the soft swell of lush breasts and clung lovingly to those slender hips and incredible legs. Great masses of gleaming chocolate-colored hair were artfully arranged in curls atop her head and trailing in soft tendrils over one shoulder. Her complexion was unfashionably touched by the sun but clear and smooth as butterscotch, a perfect foil for the elaborate filigreed gold necklace and earrings set with tiger's eyes. Unconventional stones for a most unconventional lady. And lady she must be, for everyone in the ballroom deferred to her as she passed by.

Jason was aware of the growing silence as she approached him. All conversation seemed to melt away, leaving only the strains of the orchestra as it began playing another sweeping waltz. Every person in the room watched avidly, waiting to see what would happen next. He noted that a low buzz of whispering resumed behind fans and hands. Did they know something he did not?

Her wide-set hazel-green eyes shot sparks at him. He was not surprised, considering the way he had treated her when first they met. Grinning in spite of himself, he thought, Let the ton speculate. No one but he and his "countess" knew the cause of her animosity. As soon as she reached him, he swept her into the waltz before

24

she could say a word. Every eye in the room was on them as they whirled around the floor.

Rachel fought the urge to stamp on his feet. Would this crude colonial always keep her off balance? She had wanted to shock him, see him flummoxed and gaping just as she had been on their first encounter, not smirking as if he were . . . was . . . a bloody earl!

I will not *lose my temper.*

She detested the advantage his height gave him. Her high-heeled dancing slippers normally allowed her that advantage. Forcing herself to look up into his laughing blue eyes, she said smoothly, "I will give you high marks for consistency, sirrah. You are unchangingly rude."

"You, on the other hand, are most agreeably change-able—at least in regard to costumes, Countess. I'll not speak of manners."

"How gallant you are now that you know I am no rustic wench," she replied scathingly.

"Ah, I am still not entirely certain of that, but perhaps we could begin again," he said, tilting his head closer to hers as his arm tightened about her incredibly slender waist. She stiffened and tried to pull away. A faint flush was visible on her sun-kissed face. He smiled to himself with satisfaction. "It would seem I have the same effect on you as you do on me," he whispered conspiratorially in her ear, inhaling the heady fragrance of honeysuckle.

Her thoughts scattered in panic. If only her step did not fit so well to his. Their bodies moved in time to the lilting music as if they had been made to dance to-gether, an exercise she normally detested since she towered over most of her partners. Physically, he was her perfect match. Rachel tamped down that exceed-ingly disquieting thought, the very last she wished to consider now or ever. With a scathing smile, she said,

"If by the same effect you mean immoderate loathing, then I imagine 'tis true."

He threw back his head and laughed, once again pulling her closer. "What m'lady says and what m'lady feels are not at all the same. Let us not argue, but begin as if we had just met for the first time. I am Jason Beaumont, Earl of Falconridge, at your service."

When he smiled at her, she felt her head spin. Attributing her reaction to the way they were whirling about the floor, she calmly replied, "Ah, yes, the scandal sheets are filled with your exploits, m'lord *Yankee earl*."

"You are determined to be a disagreeable baggage. But since you are the one who sought me out, the very least you can do is to give me your name."

"I shall be delighted. I am Rachel Fairchild of Harleigh Hall." She waited a beat to see if her name registered in his mind. When it did not, she added with a falsely sweet smile, "And your future wife."

Chapter Three

Jason stopped dead in the center of the dance floor, releasing her as if she had suddenly burst into flames. "Pardon?" His mind went blank. He could think of nothing better to say as she began to grin like a prison guard on the hulks where he and his crew had been held captive.

"Are you deaf as well as boorish?" she asked rhetorically, warming to her explanation. He truly did not know anything of what had been arranged for them—and the announcement was to be made tonight! "I am the eldest daughter of Hugh Fairchild, Viscount Harleigh, whose estates adjoin those of Falconridge. My father and your grandfather have decided that we are a proper match. So much so that the highlight of this ball—indeed, the sole reason for holding it—is to announce our betrothal just prior to the midnight supper."

Jason stood rooted to the floor, mutely staring at her.

"My, my, and they did not inform you," she tsked.

" 'Tis customary for the groom to be apprised of the matter long before the bride."

The viper-tongued wench was enjoying this altogether too much. Jason felt a sudden urge to wipe the superior smirk from her face by kissing those pouty pink lips and then turning her over his knee and paddling that shapely little rump. The idea might have merits, but not before they straightened out this absurd talk of marriage. Instead, he offered her his arm, bowing gallantly as he said, "We had best continue this discussion elsewhere, do you not agree?"

The orchestra chose that moment to cease playing. Feeling everyone's eyes fixed avidly on the two of them, Rachel nodded, although she did not accept his arm. Instead, she charged toward the opened double doors leading to the interior courtyard gardens, assured that the odious American would follow, hoping dearly that no one else would dare.

Jason watched her forge ahead like Moses parting the Red Sea. There was no recourse but to let her lead the way. When she reached the seclusion of a boxwood hedge, she whirled about, ready to continue her patronizing diatribe, but he cut her off without preamble, saying, "My dear Miss Fairchild, we have only met twice, and to the best of my knowledge, I have not made you a marriage proposal. You have made it abundantly clear at both encounters that you detest me. It would certainly seem that a mistake of catastrophic proportions has been made."

"I could not agree more, but our wishes do not signify." Rachel could not keep the bitterness from her voice. She hated the weakness it betrayed to this arrogant stranger who had such an unsettling effect upon her. Her voice was brittle as she continued, "I do not know how such matters are handled in your country—

28

er, pardon, I mean your former country—since there is no peerage."

"You mean that my grandfather and your father wanted to merge their estates, so they concocted this insane scheme and thought I would agree without protest, like a lamb at slaughter?" His expression was as dark as the clouds scudding across the moon.

"Precisely so. The price of being an earl has just gone up, has it not?" she retorted, feeling a totally irrational surge of hurt when he likened marriage to her with being led to slaughter. After all, this was exactly what she had hoped to achieve. He wanted the match no more than she did, so he would be her ally. She moistened her lips, working up her courage to outline her plan. "The marquess and the viscount have arranged everything, but—"

Jason interrupted her angrily. "We will see about that! Since you seem so well apprised of things, would you happen to know where I might find the old bas—my grandfather?"

He was livid. Good! "The old bas—your grandfather is most probably in the library with the old bas—my father, drinking a toast to our betrothal. Shall we go see?"

Jason spun on his heel and headed toward the house without another word.

"My, my, I do believe we shall," she murmured to herself, hastening to catch up with him.

George William Beaumont, ninth Marquess of Cargrave, was feeling just the least bit apprehensive as the evening wore on, not that anyone observing him could tell it as he puffed on a fine cigar, blowing out a cloud of pale gray smoke. Although smoking was not in fashion, nothing tasted better to him than a cigar. He let the pleasure of tobacco soothe his nerves.

With less than three hours to midnight, he had just sent a servant to summon Jason to meet with them. His grandson must be informed of the betrothal announcement and made to see that there was no way out. How would the lad take it? Would the old man have to move his last chess piece onto the board, the one he had concealed until now? And if so, would it work?

The marquess could not be certain. Jason gave every appearance of adjusting to the lifestyle of a peer. He had the address of an earl, no doubt of it. He was intelligent enough to manage all the vast holdings and titles to which he was now heir. But he was also headstrong and damnably . . . American. No matter that by an accident of fate he'd been born here in England.

Just then Harleigh interrupted, as if echoing his troubling ruminations. "I must confess I still have reservations about this match, George. My gel is dead set against it, and you know how headstrong she is."

Cargrave smiled. "I was just thinking the same thing about my grandson. They will both come up to scratch, never fear. Rachel may be no conventional miss, but she will settle Jason down."

Harleigh harrumphed nervously. "Yes, but who will first settle *her* down? Heaven knows, I've had no luck in that direction," he added with a sigh.

"They shall settle each other down, of course." The old marquess's eyes, usually so cold and penetrating, took on a warm glow for a moment as he remembered his life with Mathilda, his marchioness. *Twenty years and still I miss her.*

"Where the deuce do you think that grandson of yours could have gotten off to? Must be a quarter hour since we dispatched Winters to fetch him," Hugh said, still not reassured about their plans.

Cargrave shrugged with studied casualness. "Saw

him from the balcony earlier, dancing with some baron's daughter. Can't have gotten far."

"Are you certain it was wise not to inform him until now? I know how impetuous these Americans can be. He *was* raised in the colonies."

The marquess waved his cigar dismissively. "I know the lad. If he had time to brood on it, he might hatch some nervy scheme to thwart me. He's awake on every suit, no doubt of that. Which is why I have handled matters this way. Once he realizes the announcement will be tonight . . . and we introduce him to your beautiful daughter, he will have to go along."

"Rachel may be a striking young woman, but I say again, she can be . . . difficult," the viscount replied, repressing a shudder as he remembered the porcelain-smashing, furniture-bashing scene she had created back at Harleigh Hall when he'd first informed her of the betrothal.

The marquess knew about Rachel Fairchild's famous temper and penchant for riding astride across the countryside. The gel had spirit to match his grandson's. If only the young fools would see it. "Have no fear, my friend. Jason shall deal famously with her."

Harleigh sighed. "I certainly hope he can handle her. Lud, I have never had any luck. My younger gels were both biddable. You know Rachel is not."

"All the better. Jason likes nothing so much as a good challenge."

The two men sat in the library, a magnificent mahogany-paneled room lined with bookshelves which stretched to the top of the fourteen-foot ceiling. Cargrave studied his old friend over the rim of a Waterford brandy snifter. Mercifully, like himself, Harleigh had spawned far better looking offspring than either of them had a right to expect. While Cargrave was tall with a great beak of a Roman nose and deep-set eyes, Harleigh

31

was slight of figure, pop-eyed and stooped with age in spite of being over a decade younger than the marquess. Ah, but Jason and Rachel were tall and strong, long of leg and fair of visage. What splendid children they would have!

As if reading Cargrave's thought, Harleigh raised his glass in a toast. "To the next generation of Beaumonts and Fairchilds!"

"Here, here," Cargrave replied, keeping his eye on the ormolu clock that sat on the carved marble mantel across from the deep leather chairs in which they sat facing each other. *Where is that boy?*

Just then the heavy walnut door crashed open and "that boy" strode in, slamming it behind him with a resounding crash. Neither of the old men noticed Rachel, who had slipped in before its closing, taking a seat in the shadows behind a potted palm to watch the combat.

Always one to take the offensive, the marquess stood up and turned to face his grandson. "That is scarcely the proper way for a gentleman to respond to a summons, sirrah!"

Jason advanced on the tall old man. "But we both know, don't we, Grandfather, that I'm no bloody gentleman. I'm an American."

"No longer," Cargrave snapped back. "By the grace of God and His Majesty, you are now the sixth Earl of Falconridge, and with such title comes responsibility."

"Responsibility for a wife?"

"Just so, m'boy, just so. Mind your manners now while I present you to my old friend and your neighbor, Hugh Fairchild, Viscount Harleigh."

Jason barely spared a nod in the direction of the slight figure standing across from his grandfather. From her place behind the palm, Rachel studied the contrast between the two Beaumont men and her quiet, mild-mannered father. Hugh Fairchild seemed to fade into the rich dark woodwork of the library as Jason and the old marquess stood glowering at each other.

In spite of the disparity in their ages, one could easily see that they were related. George's slate-gray eyes locked with the dark blue of his grandson's, both deep-set, boring into each other with palpable intensity. They faced off like two wolves preparing to dispute ownership of a kill. The marquess's rages were legendary, and everyone in England from royal dukes to street sweeps quaked in terror when the old man's wrath was aroused. Yet Jason Beaumont not only appeared utterly uncowed but equally as dangerous.

In spite of herself, Rachel was impressed. She valued courage greatly and had sent many milk-and-water suitors scurrying away during her season. Her own father, although she loved him dearly, was ineffectual in any confrontation. He carried the day only by doggedly pursuing his agenda behind an opponent's back—and in regard to marriage, she had become his opponent.

Crude Yankee, Jason Beaumont might be, but he was every inch a man. She could still remember the length of his self-assured strides, the arrogance of his manner the first time they'd met. He would never concede defeat to any man. Or woman.

"I consented to your blackmail in order to rescue my crew from a prison hulk. I gave my word to be the next Marquess of Cargrave. I did *not* agree to be Rachel Fairchild's husband," Jason ground out.

"Do you find something amiss with the gel?" Cargrave had reined in his temper. A satisfied gleam in his eyes betrayed his confidence. He waited, crossing his arms over his chest as he studied Jason.

Rachel found herself tensing as she waited for his reply. She certainly did not want to marry Jason Beaumont . . . yet for some perverse reason she found it important that he not find her undesirable. Her fingers dug into the brocade of the chair arm as she leaned forward to hear his reply.

"Oh, you mean some fault other than her temper, which would make a treed bobcat's seem mild? Or perhaps her manners, which are equal to those of a drunken tar?" If Jason heard the faint gasp of outrage coming from the corner, he ignored it. "The lady"—he paused for ironic emphasis—"wants no more of this arrangement than do I."

"Small wonder she would not, sirrah! You are behaving abominably in front of the gel's father. Rachel is Harleigh's firstborn."

Jason turned to Fairchild and snapped, "You have my condolences, sir."

"I realize my daughter can be . . . a bit difficult from time to time, but—"

"A bit difficult!" Jason interrupted. "That is like saying the North Atlantic in January is a bit choppy!" he roared.

At that rejoinder, the viscount subsided as young Beaumont turned his attention back to his grandfather, stating flatly, "*If* and when I decide to marry, 'twill be on my terms, to a woman whom I choose."

The marquess curled his lip and leaned forward. "I think not."

"You think not?" the younger Beaumont echoed, his own wide mouth curving into a parody of a smile. "What would you do—de-earl me?"

"No, I most certainly would not, you ungrateful whelp. That would quite defeat the purpose of freeing you from the prison hulks and concealing the fact that you were an American privateer," the marquess replied. "Not to mention all the strings I was forced to pull with the Admiralty to have you made over into His Majesty's latest naval hero," he added dryly. Cargrave strolled back to the chair from which he had risen upon his grandson's angry entrance and once again took his seat, steepling his gnarled fingers in front of him. A contemplative expression veiled his face, as if he were considering his next move on a chess board.

Jason knew the signs, and a knot of dread began to tighten deep in his gut. *What is the old bastard up to?* "And your purpose is?"

Ignoring the question, the marquess began to speak once more. "During the tragic cholera epidemic which took your father's life, I believe the lives of two young people were also lost—your estate manager and his half-blood Indian wife. They left behind a young son whom your family took in. Cameron Edmund Barlow, or Fox as he is known among his mother's people . . ."

"Yes, Fox, who, you undoubtedly know, stowed away on my last voyage and was captured with my ship." The fist in Jason's belly clenched tighter. "He was to be repatriated to America. You gave your word."

Ignoring the fury in his grandson's voice, Cargrave replied with utmost reasonableness, "Ah, and I kept my word. Your crew were all sent safely home. But young Fox was not a member of your crew. By your own admission, he was a stowaway."

"And you have him. Your winning chess piece," Jason said bitterly.

"Precisely." The old man's tone was clipped and businesslike now.

"Everything is a bloody game to you, isn't it, Grandfather?"

"And I always play to win. You, of all people, should know that by now."

"Yes, I should," Jason replied softly. "You cheat when necessary. If you left my foster brother on that hulk—"

Cargrave shot up from his seat, all the calm self-assurance of a moment ago evaporated. "Damn you!

35

Grandson or no, if I did not need an heir so desperately, I should call you out for such an insult!"

"If Fox is still on the *Laurel*, you shall not need to call me out," Jason replied in a deadly tone.

At this point, the viscount, sunk frozen in his chair, stood up once more and interposed himself between the two larger men. "Gentlemen, gentlemen, please," he beseeched. "You are grandfather and grandson. Do not even think of such an absurd thing as calling each other out." He waved his hand vaguely. "I am certain George would not have left a child to languish in prison." His pale eyes moved worriedly from the younger to the elder Beaumont, hoping for confirmation.

"It seems you have a better opinion of me than my grandson does," the marquess replied sternly, glaring at Jason. "Young Master Barlow has been safely tucked away while you were cutting a swath through the ton this past month. A pity I cannot name him my heir. He demonstrates considerably greater intelligence than the foster brother he so idolizes. One might hope he'll outgrow that," the old man muttered beneath his breath.

At this point, Rachel could hold her peace no longer. The marquess had blackmailed the hateful Yankee lout into assuming the title. That perhaps spoke well of Jason's integrity, she was forced to admit, remembering her insinuations about his having betrayed his country for an earldom. But she brushed that matter aside as the realization sank in—now the marquess intended to use the boy to blackmail his heir into marrying *her*!

"I believe this whole charade—or is it a chess match?—has gone far enough," she said imperiously as she walked into the center of the room, her peach silk gown swishing with every step.

"Rachel, child—good God, how long have you been listening?" the viscount croaked.

"Long enough to plot three murders, Father," she replied sweetly, without taking her eyes from Jason's. "Let me assure you, m'lord earl, this treed bobcat is every bit as furious over being forced into marriage as are you."

Cargrave watched her dark eyes flash with fury, meeting Jason's startled blue ones. *Lud, what splendid children they will have! She is the perfect match for that wild hellion. Now all he has to do is tame her. A bit easier said than done.*

"We may be in perfect accord on the issue, Countess, but I suspect my grandfather will not agree." Jason turned, lifting one black eyebrow at the marquess.

"Young Fox calls my daughter-in-law 'Mama,' and she considers him her second son; hence he is a member of my extended family . . . over here on a visit," Cargrave added slyly.

"And how long will this 'visit' last?" Jason asked.

"I imagine even one with your gravely challenged mental capacity should be able to deduce the answer to that," Rachel interjected acidly.

Jason glowered at her, but the marquess grinned now, thoroughly enjoying himself once again. "I'm certain Fox will not wish to return to America until after witnessing the nuptials of his foster brother. I suspect he'd be hurt if you did not ask him to stand as witness." Without waiting for Jason's reply, he stepped to the wall and yanked upon a bellpull, summoning the footman waiting behind the adjoining door.

"Bring Master Fox," the marquess instructed the servant.

The door to the library once again burst open, but this time a footman was there to carefully close it behind the boy who dashed toward Jason with a cry of utter delight. "Jace! Grandfather said you were here!"

Jason hugged the black-haired youth with copper-dark skin and midnight eyes as the others observed. The viscount looked mildly startled at such a noisy interruption. The marquess looked smugly self-satisfied. But Rachel was utterly nonplused by the arrogant American's display of affection for the boy. Here was a side of the earl that she would never have suspected. She watched keenly as he listened to Fox chatter about his new life.

"Grandfather has given me a horse of my very own— Little Chief! And all sorts of wonderful teachers, not at all like the ones at school in Baltimore. I have a riding instructor and a fighting teacher—oh, I mean he's teaching me how to shoot pistols and how to fence with swords and—"

"Whoa, Fox," Jason said, laughing and tousling the lad's straight black hair, which he noted had been cut in the latest fashion. The boy was also dressed in proper English attire. "You've been busy indeed, it would seem. Life at Cargrave Hall must be a great adventure."

"Oh, yes!" The boy paused, noting for the first time that the marquess and a second gentleman were standing behind Jason. "Oh, I have not minded my manners, have I?"

Rachel stood back out of his line of vision, taking in the whole scene. The lad bowed like a most proper court gentleman toward the viscount, then looked up at Cargrave, saying, "Good evening, Grandfather."

"Grandfather?" Jason echoed, raising his eyes to meet those of the marquess questioningly.

"And, pray, why not?" the marquess said fondly, patting the boy's back.

"Grandfather said that since he was your grandfather and I was your foster brother, it was only logical that

38

he was my foster grandfather." Fox's large black eyes shifted worriedly between the old man and Jason.

Jason could read the self-satisfied smirk in the marquess's eyes. "Yes, Fox, our grandfather is a most logical man . . . and a devious one."

Fox nodded, once more at ease. "Does that mean he cheats at chess? He does, you know," the lad blurted out, then flushed with embarrassment and stammered, "I'm sorry, Grandfather. I did not mean that to sound badly."

The Marquess of Cargrave struggled to smother his guffaw with only partial success as Jason fixed him with a baleful glare, saying, "Truth is truth, Fox. He always cheats."

By this time Cargrave had controlled his brief spurt of mirth. Taking the lad by his shoulder, he directed Fox's attention to Hugh Fairchild. "We must mind our manners, son. This is Viscount Harleigh, my very good friend, Hugh Fairchild."

Fox bowed again with the smoothness of a trained courtier. But when the marquess turned the boy to face Rachel, Fox's polish evaporated like mist in sunlight. His eyes, already large and glowing, seemed to grow to twice their size and his mouth opened in wonder as he beheld the gleaming vision in peach silk who now stood before him. In her high-heeled slippers and with a mass of curling chocolate hair piled high atop her head, she was almost as tall as his hero, Jason. And she was so very beautiful that when she smiled at him as Grandfather made introductions, all he could do was stammer and gape until Jason prodded him gently into making his bow.

Rachel studied the beautiful child whose sinuous long-legged body and finely chiseled features gave a hint of the striking man he would one day be. Another arrogant American like Jason Beaumont? She hoped not as she smiled warmly and said, "Master Fox, I am delighted to meet you."

Fox's face once again flushed hotly as he blurted out, "You must be the most beautiful lady in all England! And America, too!"

The two older men smiled indulgently at the boy, but only Jason noted the way the compliment seemed to affect Rachel. She looked startled, and he detected a faint flush steal up her throat to stain her sun-gilded face. Did she not know she was beautiful? He observed her with interest as she spoke to Fox. She was not conventionally pretty, certainly. Her features were more strong and handsome than the round-eyed, dainty sort currently in favor. Her coloring was off, too, by the standards of the ton, but her skin glowed like honey and her thick chocolate-brown hair begged for a man to run his fingers through it.

Jason caught himself in horror. He was falling right in line with his scheming grandfather! Damned if he would wed the she-cat, even if he did fancy those long legs wrapped around him. Need of a woman was certainly no cause for matrimony. His troubling ruminations were cut short by his grandfather's announcement to Fox.

"Miss Fairchild is to be your brother's bride."

"You mean you're going to marry her, Jace?" Fox asked in awe, still staring at Rachel.

She and Jason exchanged troubled looks. What could they say that would not disappoint or confuse the boy?

"That is a matter for the adults to decide, young man, and I happen to know it is well past your bedtime," Jason said, giving the lad's shoulder an affectionate squeeze.

Cargrave caught the quelling expression in his grandson's eyes and nodded. "So it is, you young rascal," he said, ringing for a servant to take the lad up to his room.

A brawny man missing half an ear and possessing a nose squashed flat as a run-over turnip answered the summons. He was dressed in a cutaway jacket and old-fashioned knee britches that strained over massive shoulders and bulging thighs. His small piggy eyes swept the room, settling almost insultingly on Jason, as he bowed before the marquess. "Come along, Master Fox," he said with forced joviality.

After bidding everyone good night, Fox departed with the battered fellow who the marquess said was the boy's bodyguard. Jason fixed the old man with a shrewd stare, murmuring, "You would have done better to choose a bodyguard more adept at guarding his own body."

"Mace Bings will serve to keep the lad safe, considering that the only one he need be protected from is you," Cargrave replied.

"You mean I might steal him away and sail home to America?" Jason suggested.

"You have given your word to be my heir," the marquess replied sternly.

"But not to wed the woman of your choice," Jason shot back.

"Young Master Fox has infinitely better taste than do you, young nodcock. He appreciates Miss Fairchild's worth," Cargrave snapped.

"Then let him marry her!"

"If either of you say one more word as if I were absent or an imbecile incapable of speaking for myself, I shall be forced to dash your thick heads together," Rachel interjected in a deceptively mild tone.

The viscount's eyes nearly popped from their sockets as he laid a trembling hand on Rachel's arm, trying to deflect her ire. "Now, my dear—"

"Shush, Papa," she said, patting his hand dismissively, then turning back to the marquess. "M'lord, I believe your grandson and I should become better acquainted. Perhaps there is some way to smooth out this frightful coil." She bestowed a blinding smile on him before offering her hand to Jason. "Do let us be civil and join the dancing. As I recall, you do dance, do you not? Or need you paint your body first?"

"Oh, I dance, m'lady . . . even without war paint," he replied, then whispered low in her ear as he took her hand, "on occasion, even without clothes."

Rachel stifled her angry retort, gliding from the room serenely after nodding good evening to the marquess and viscount.

Fairchild shuddered as the young couple departed. He knew what that unholy light in his daughter's eyes presaged, and he did not like it one bit. What devilment was the gel up to now?

Chapter Four

"You've made quite a conquest." Jason said as they headed toward the sounds of music in the ballroom at the opposite end of the corridor. "The lad is decidedly smitten."

Rachel looked up at the wry smile curving his lips. "And you, of course, are decidedly not," she said with more tartness than she intended. What was it about this accursed Yankee that raised her ire so quickly? And why did it bother her that he did not find her attractive? Was that not exactly what she wanted? Nonetheless, she could not stop herself from blurting out, "Temper of a treed bobcat and manners of a drunken tar, indeed! With such sugary words 'tis small wonder you could only find a wife if one were forced to wed you."

He stopped and looked at her in frank disbelief. "I just witnessed the exchange between you and your father. Give me leave to doubt that the viscount could force you to do anything you didn't wish."

She felt the heat climbing up to her face and fought the urge to claw at him just like the bobcat he had named her. *Damn the man!* She clenched her fists in the folds of her skirt to conceal her trembling, vowing not to feel the slice of pain. Her voice was cool when she replied, "I do not wish to be your countess, a title you so sarcastically bestowed upon me when first we met. In spite of my father's docile nature, when he sets his mind on an idea, nothing can dislodge it. He has worn me down with reminders of my duty . . . something with which you appear to have only the slightest acquaintance."

Jason stiffened. "I understand duty all too well, *Countess*. It was my responsibility to my crew which led me to this sorry plight."

"Oh? And was it not your peerless leadership, Sir Privateer, which caused your worthy crew to languish on a prison hulk in the first place?"

He sighed in resignation. "Our bickering solves nothing."

"I could not agree more. Neither of us wants this marriage, so it is incumbent upon us to find a way to escape it."

"And how do you think we might do so with my grandfather holding Fox hostage?"

She looked up and down the long corridor, then headed for a door halfway to the ballroom. "Come. We would be wise to discuss this matter in private."

Jason followed her into an elegantly appointed sitting room furnished with beautiful Chippendale chairs and sofa. She stood behind one delicate gold brocade chair and waited as he closed the door. He turned and crossed his arms over his chest, then said, "Pray continue. What do you have in mind that could free us?"

Ever since her father had explained about her betrothal, Rachel had been desperate to foil him and Car-

44

grave. She had known that the earl was American, but until tonight, she had believed the fabrication the marquess put about—that Jason was a secret agent for the Admiralty. She'd had no idea he had been a prisoner, forced to become Cargrave's heir . . . and now blackmailed into wedding her. Armed with this new knowledge, she now knew precisely how they should proceed.

The dancers swept about the huge ballroom floor in a blur of brilliant color and glittering jewels. Laughter punctuated the strains of the orchestra as ladies flirted with their partners. Jason and Rachel had vanished for well over an hour. When they reappeared, they were the cynosure of the crowded room. Their abrupt departure from the dance floor earlier had ignited all sorts of delicious speculation. Were they to be affianced? Or had Harleigh's termagant daughter drowned the American in the garden fishpond? With a gel such as Rachel Fairchild and a Yankee earl, anything was possible.

Jason noted the way Rachel studiously ignored the whispers and stares as they passed through the crowd. She looked as regal as a queen, smiling politely to acquaintances but pausing to speak with none. He leaned down and said softly, "They shall be quite titillated by what is about to occur."

"I shall be happy to lend a small measure of excitement to their vapid lives," she replied.

"So you are not overly fond of the ton?"

"Is that faint approval I detect in your voice?" she asked with irony.

"Merely puzzlement. Most young women of my acquaintance both here and in America love nothing so much as dressing in the latest fashions and having a gaggle of men dance attendance on them."

"I am not most women."

"Assuredly not," he replied dryly. "You prefer riding about the countryside in men's britches."

"I have overseen my father's estates since I was but fifteen. There is real work to be done . . . if one has the wit and the will to do it."

"A very American way of thinking, Countess. Before the war I ran a large shipyard. Built the fastest clippers on the seas."

"So much the better for piracy when hostilities broke out." Her tone was deceptively sweet. "Let us see how soon we can arrange for your return to the high seas. But in the meanwhile, we must play out this charade. Come, let me introduce you to your cousin Roger. If all goes as planned, *he* shall soon be the next Earl of Falconridge."

"Roger Dalbert? I met him several times when I visited my grandfather."

She led him toward a paunchy balding man with a round ruddy face who stood beside a plump woman dressed rather unflatteringly in puce satin. As Rachel made the introductions, Dalbert shook Jason's hand heartily, slapping him on the back.

"I say, dash it all, but it is good to see you again, Jason." Roger beamed as he drew the lady at his side forward. "May I present m'wife, Garnet. Never thought I'd be so happy leg-shackled, but I am."

Garnet Dalbert made her curtsy, smiling up at Jason. She had a plain face with a weak double chin and a little shapeless nose, but her eyes shone with keen intelligence when she spoke. "I'm given to understand that you were a shipbuilder in America, m'lord."

"Yes, in Baltimore."

"Those sharp-built ships can maneuver circles about our lumbering scows," she replied.

"You know about Baltimore clippers, then?" he asked

with surprise. In spite of her execrable taste in clothing, she seemed quite intelligent.

"Garnet owns a shipping line in Gravesend. Runs it herself, right well. She'll talk all night of tall masts and topsails," Roger interjected with an indulgent chuckle.

"Really, that is splendid. There is nothing so enjoyable as discussing one's occupation with another who has the wit and the will to work," Jason replied, casting a swift glance Rachel's way. He was pleased to see the barb strike home.

Without waiting for her rejoinder, he asked Mistress Dalbert to dance as the orchestra played a country reel, leaving Rachel with his cousin Roger. Good chap, Roger, but a bit of a bore, he thought as he and Garnet discussed the fine points of ship construction and the deplorable effects the war was having on trade between England and the Continent as well as with her former colonies.

As he and the plump little matron talked, he could feel Rachel's eyes following him from across the room. For some damnable reason, he could not rid himself of the thought of peeling that sheer peach silk from her lush body. Forcing the distracting image aside, he decided that a visit to one of the city's better bawdy houses was in order at the end of this disastrous evening. Surely a skilled bit-o'-muslin could make him forget about bedding a hellion like Rachel Fairchild.

In spite of his resolve, when he returned Garnet to her adoring husband, he could not help watching from the corner of his eye as his nearly betrothed danced with a young baron. Roger droned on about the stag he had taken the previous winter and what a splendid trophy it made on his study wall while Jason made appropriate nods of agreement, even though his mind was focused utterly on Rachel.

As soon as the quadrille was over, she returned to

his side. When she approached, her cheeks were flushed and her hazel-green eyes glowed with pleasure. From the dance? . . . or was she anticipating what was to come at the stroke of twelve? *The little witch.* He'd bet anything it was the latter.

"Let's keep the gossips off balance, Countess." Without giving her a chance to say anything, Jason reached out and swept her into the waltz as the orchestra began playing again.

"Are all Americans such impulsively ill-mannered louts, or is it just you?" Although her tone dripped disdain, she found herself matching her steps to his with increasing pleasure as they spun about the floor.

"Ah, but, Countess, I am no longer American," he countered.

"But still an ill-mannered lout," she shot back.

Jason threw back his head and laughed, then replied, "But now an *English* ill-mannered lout, remember?"

"As if anyone in the ton could forget that," she replied. "When the announcement was made that Cargrave had petitioned for his Yankee grandson to be named his heir, half of London thought he'd taken leave of his senses. I'm amazed it has come to pass."

"I wondered myself if Grandfather could get away with his scheme, but things appear to be working out smoothly."

"The marquess is a most powerful man, accustomed to getting what he wants."

"You mean he's utterly ruthless and will use any means, fair or foul, to get his way," he corrected.

"You say that, yet I detect a fondness for him in spite of the blackmail."

He looked down at her appraisingly as the waltz ended. "Are you such a shrewd judge of human nature, Countess?"

She met his eyes steadily. "Yes, I do believe I am."

"Aside from my lack of manners, how would you judge me?"

She appeared to consider this while they made their way to the refreshment table. "Reckless at times. Stubborn always. Loyal to your friends, I suppose, else you would not have agreed to your grandfather's terms for freeing your crew," she added grudgingly.

"I appreciate your honesty." His expression was wry as he offered her a glass of champagne.

Rachel took the delicate crystal and sipped while eyeing him with amusement. She could feel those around them watching with avid curiosity and felt her blood race in a peculiar way. Normally, she detested being on display, having the gossips speculate about poor Harleigh's eldest, that hoyden who preferred horses to men.

But this man is different. Where on earth had that thought come from? Rachel almost choked on her wine. Jason Beaumont affected her in ways no other man ever had. If she were not so strongly opposed to marriage and the end of a way of life she loved, she might actually have accepted his suit . . . but then she sternly reminded herself that he had not paid suit. He possessed as little interest in marriage as she.

They danced several times more as the evening wore on, a shocking breach of social decorum, adding to the speculation about a match. Both were careful to say nothing that might betray their plans.

At midnight Cargrave and Harleigh made their way to the center of the room and the orchestra played a fanfare. The crowd fell silent as the marquess prepared to speak.

"It is with great pride and pleasure that my old friend Viscount Harleigh and I announce the betrothal of his daughter, the Honorable Miss Rachel Fairchild, and my grandson, the Earl of Falconridge." He and Harleigh raised their glasses in celebration as the crowd broke into polite applause.

A babel of soft murmuring and tittering laughter filled the room as everyone's eyes swept in the direction of the young couple, who were standing near the wide arched doorway to the main foyer. Jason could see the look of smug accomplishment lighting his grandfather's face. He turned toward Rachel and whispered something.

A shocked gasp ricocheted through the assembly when she replied by dumping her glass of champagne over his head and stalking furiously from the room. Jason watched her departure for an instant, then turned back to the now hushed crowd. Wiping his face with a handkerchief, he smiled stiffly. Then Jason Beaumont, sixth Earl of Falconridge, made a formal bow and quit the room.

An expression of abject horror whitened the viscount's face. Jason did not pause long enough to see the marquess's slow grin.

The smell of tobacco and gin blended with the smoke from poorly trimmed candlewicks which cast their flickering light around the crowded gaming hell. Rough looking men with broken noses and missing pieces of ears presided over the green baize tables scattered around the large, low-ceilinged room. Faro. Whist. Macao. Hazard. Whatever game of chance a sporting blood wished, Wheatie offered. Cold-eyed professional gamblers played alongside rowdy young toffs from the better part of town. The laughter of garishly dressed females punctuated the low murmur of men placing bets.

Drum had brought Jason here after the debacle at the ball earlier that evening. The little dandy insisted that it would take his friend's mind off his troubles and related how he and Alex Blackthorne had met at Wheatie's tables. The aura of danger appealed to Jason. He gambled recklessly, with Drum watching his back and rationing the amount of blue ruin he consumed. Always lucky at cards, Beaumont found himself winning steadily before the night was over. But the pile of blunt on the table in front of him did nothing to assuage his restlessness.

"I'm becoming afflicted with what you English call the Lombard fever," he said to Drum.

" 'Tis nearly dawn," his companion replied, studying the whites of Jason's eyes, which by this time resembled red ink on a bankruptcy ledger. Several of the gamesters around the table muttered about the American toff quitting while he was so far ahead, but one quelling look from Drummond made them subside in surly acquiescence.

Stuffing several guineas into the cleavage of his blond companion's gown, Jason whispered, "With thanks for bringing me luck."

"Aw, luv, if you goes 'ome wi' me, I promise yer luck ain't goin' ta run out anytime soon," she cooed, brushing her large white breasts against his arm.

He shook his head. "Sorry, Ginnie," he said, hoping that was her name. It was late, and he was well on his way to being foxed. Besides, in addition to giving him luck that wouldn't "run out anytime soon," he suspected that if he went with her, the wench would probably give him something else that wouldn't "run out anytime soon." *One night with Venus, a lifetime with mercury!*

"Let us depart, then," Drum interjected, taking his much larger charge's arm; he was used to squiring brash young foreigners about the dangerous haunts of London.

Shortly they were on the narrow, dark street in front

of Wheatie's, ready to walk until they could find a
jarvey to take them home. Hack drivers seldom ventured into such dangerous parts of the city. It proved to
be a long and sobering walk. As they neared the more
civilized confines of the West End, Drum described
how his friend Joss's fighting dog had once knocked
Alex Blackthorne across a marble foyer, riding his chest
like a sled. Jason threw back his head to laugh just as
a shot whistled past his nose. Instantly both men
crouched, weapons drawn as they moved quickly into
the shadows.

"A near thing, that," Drum whispered, his eyes scour-
ing the dark alleyway. "Be still. There may be another
lurking," he cautioned.

"He'll get away—and I'm bloody tired of being used
for target practice," Jason replied, shaking off his
friend's hand and running toward the alley.

"Little wonder your ship was all but shot out from
under you," Drum murmured softly. He had his Egg pistol in one hand and a deadly sword cane in the other.

Within moments, it became clear that the attacker
had escaped into a warren of old buildings housing
several hundred of the city's poorest inhabitants. They
made their way back to more familiar territory, where
Jason flagged down a jarvey and gave directions to
Drum's lodgings.

The little dandy was not to be deterred from learning
about the earlier attempt on Jason's life in the country.
"It would appear you have made an enemy who wants
to see you dead."

"Forrestal already tried that, if you recall. I don't kill
so easily."

"Ah, yes, Etherington's heir. He might be the one hiring these assassins. I did a bit of looking into his affairs
after your duel. You were right in assuming that he
staged the confrontation at the Haymarket Room."

"Whatever for?" Jason asked, perplexed, leaning back against the musty-smelling squabs of the coach.

"Well, you know how far in dun territory Forrestal is," Drum said with relish. "Since his creditors have become rather persistent of late, most particularly those who own his gaming vowels, he's been casting about for a way out. Man's obviously quite desperate. Set his sights on marrying an heiress."

There was something in Drum's tone that brought Jason's heavy eyelids wide open once again. "An heiress . . . has he any particular one in mind?"

Drum's thin lips curved in an elegant smile. "Why, none other than your very own dearly beloved Miss Fairchild."

"And she refused, I take it?"

"Didn't even get to the gel. He approached her father, but the viscount had already set his mind to the match with his old friend Cargrave's heir. Told Forrestal that the matter of his daughter's future—and her very considerable fortune—had already been arranged."

Jason stroked the beard beginning to bristle his jaw. "So, you think he'd try to get rid of me so that he could resume his suit for Rachel?"

"She has quite a reputation as an irascible ape-leader now. If you were not there to come up to scratch, her father would be rather desperate. Might figure he could do worse than make an alliance with the heir to a dukedom."

Jason shook his head in weary amazement. "I will never get used to the way you English speak of marriages as alliances or arrangements. Sounds rather like politics or high finance to me."

"Or war," Drum replied with a chuckle.

The scandal sheets went wild the following morning with reports of the debacle at Cargrave's ball. By that night there was scarcely a soul in all of London who had not heard about the betrothal and Rachel Fairchild's reaction to it. Not that her prospective husband had appeared much happier when he strode from the room. And was it not most intriguing that earlier they had danced together with seemingly perfect civility four times? After all, if a lady allowed a gentleman to partner her more than twice during the course of an evening, gossip always ensued if they were not betrothed. Would she defy her father's wishes and reject the Yankee earl?

Inside their private coach en route to Harleigh Hall the following morning, Rachel's sister Harry was determined to have an answer to that very question. "You have not said more than three words since we departed, Rachel. We simply must talk, sister to sister."

"I do not feel like making idle conversation," Rachel replied dismissively.

"How could you do such a despicable thing to the earl? To Father and the marquess as well! Why, poor Papa was pale as milk. 'Tis a wonder he did not collapse in a fit of apoplexy after the hoydenish display you put on at your own betrothal. Whatever could Falconridge have said to so overset you?"

"As I told you this morning when you arrived, I will not discuss the earl."

The mulish tilt of Rachel's chin indicated all too well to Harry that she would gain no further satisfaction from her sister for the time being. However, like their father, the baroness was infinitely patient and doggedly determined. "I rather thought he was handsome . . . in that bold, reckless manner American men seem to possess."

Rachel snorted. "And how many American men have you in your acquaintance?"

"Well, I have heard stories . . ."

"You've read the scandal sheets, most especially the

adventures of the infamous Yankee earl. Give over, Harry. I do not wish to dwell on him."

"But you must marry him, Rachel. Better to talk about any . . . difficulties you foresee now." Harry's cheeks pinkened, and she fidgeted nervously with the draw-strings of her bonnet as she worked up courage to ask, "Did he whisper something . . . suggestive to you before you threw the champagne at him? I mean, I could un-derstand your behavior if he was licentious or at-tempted to treat you like one of the demimonde."

As she warmed to her topic, Harry's self-conscious-ness gave way to self-righteousness. "If you would but explain to Papa, I am certain he would be willing to cry off the arrangement."

Rachel gritted her teeth and sighed for patience as her sister chattered on inanely. Once Harry's mind took hold of an idea—no matter how unlikely—she held to it with the tenacity of a pit dog and jumped to conclu-sions with the speed of a cutpurse outrunning a charley. Interrupting her disquisition regarding her friend Lady Julia's misalliance with an Italian count, Rachel finally said, "It would signify nothing if Father broke the be-trothal with Falconridge. He would only find another candidate."

Harry babbled on about several most suitable men in her husband's acquaintance, but Rachel only pre-tended to listen. Her thoughts turned instead to what she would do after Jason Beaumont was gone. *And he will be gone.* The thought elicited a most unexpected feeling of . . . discomfort. Pushing that aside, she con-sidered her essential problem: getting herself off the marriage mart permanently.

Jason watched Fox stroke Araby's neck and croon to the big black in Shawnee as the marquess approached them, smiling fondly. They had all journeyed to Falconridge the morning after the ball so that Fox and Jason would have time for a brief visit. Jason also knew that the Fairchilds were expected to arrive at Harleigh in a day or two, which would give him and Rachel time to mend the rift before any further social events. At least, that was the crafty old marquess's plan.

Well you should be pleased, Grandfather. You think everything is going your way. "Good morning," Jason called out to the old man. "Fox and I were just out for a ride . . . along with Mace and Bradley," he added with the appropriate frown. The old man was keeping a close watch on the boy.

"Oh, Grandfather, Araby is as splendid as Little Chief. We jumped seven stone fences just as if we were flying," Fox said excitedly.

Placing a hand proprietarily on the lad's shoulder, Cargrave nodded, eyeing Jason as he said, "Fox, we're off to Cargrave Hall shortly. Go with your tutors now and prepare to depart. You may bid Jason farewell at the coach." At the boy's crestfallen look, the old man added, "Your foster brother has work to do here at Falconridge, but after he and Miss Fairchild are wed, you shall come to visit as often as you like."

Fox turned to Jason. "It won't be long until then, will it?" he asked hopefully.

"Why is it I suspect that you're more interested in seeing Rachel than me, hmmm?" he said, ruffling the boy's thick black hair. "And, no, it won't be long until we're together again. Go along now. I'll be at the coach to say goodbye."

Jason and the marquess watched the boy attempt to match his strides to those of his two "tutors" as they herded him toward the manor house.

Falconridge, unlike Cargrave Hall, was not a vast granite monstrosity. Jason had always disliked the pretension of the marquess's seat, but his own was quite different. Built of lime-plastered sandstone and timber, it sprawled across a pretty glade in the midst of rolling woodlands. Because additions had been made to it helter-skelter since the seventeenth century, it was eclectic in style, with many large windows overlooking the verdant countryside.

"You seem to be dealing well here," Cargrave said. "I knew you'd like this, since it more nearly resembles what you were used to back in Maryland."

"There are similarities," Jason replied grudgingly, "but I was not responsible for the daily running of the plantation."

"And so you shall not be for Falconridge, either. Use that much vaunted Yankee business sense to select a reliable man of affairs to handle the estate. Remember, one day you shall have not only this place but Cargrave, Chatfield, Montrose and, of course, Harleigh."

"If my countess does not cry off," Jason replied, testing the waters.

The marquess waved that possibility aside, chuckling. "She does have a bit of a temper, I grant you. Best not to arm her with champagne at the wedding breakfast."

"I suspect I should be more concerned about her bashing in my brains with a fireplace poker on the wedding night than about a splash of wine in my eyes at the wedding breakfast."

"Surely you do not doubt your ability to handle a strong-willed woman? I was given to believe that American men prided themselves on such matters."

"Do not attempt to pique my Yankee vanity, Grandfather. This is not America, and Rachel is more than just strong-willed."

"What the deuce did you say to her to set her off?"

" 'Tis a personal matter between the lady and myself, as I've already told you."

"Just so you straighten it out shortly. Hugh is expecting you for dinner on Friday next. Do not disappoint him."

"And to make certain that I do not, Fox will remain with his 'tutors' at Cargrave Hall."

The marquess's gray eyes flashed triumphantly. "His tutors are eminently qualified for their work."

"I don't know about Bradley or LaFarge, but Mace looks to be an unsavory sort. I wouldn't trust him with the boy, were I you."

"Ha, 'tis you whom I dare not trust with young Master Fox, lest you take him and run for the nearest seaport."

Jason shrugged in resignation. "Come, Grandfather. I shall walk you to your coach."

As Jason watched the Cargrave coach turn down the circular drive in front of the manor, he smiled to himself. *Yes, Grandfather, remain well pleased with yourself . . . until Fox and I escape your net.*

After the marquess and Fox had departed, Jason spent the duration of the morning closeted with the estate steward, then decided to take a long ride across Falconridge to clear his head of the fog caused by reading dusty ledgers. Being the heir of the ninth Marquess of Cargrave was quite a bit of a bother.

At the shipyards in Baltimore, he had relied upon his old friend Morton Riggs to handle office matters while he devoted his efforts to designing and building beautiful clippers. But he had always taken his responsibilities to his employees seriously. He fancied himself a good judge of men and intended to find someone here in the countryside who could be trusted to fill Morton's role—that was, once he returned from taking his foster brother safely to America.

The old marquess would have ample time to stew and then give his word not to "arrange" any further betrothals for his heir. Once they had that singularly important matter settled, Jason would return to fulfill his duty to the Beaumont family name. If the old man refused, well then, so be it. Jason would never set foot on English soil again.

Comfortable with working people, Jason hoped to learn the names and duties of all his tenants. Good lord, if he indeed did become Cargrave's heir, he would have to do the same at four other estates! Just contemplating the exercise gave him a headache. He had a groom saddle Araby, who was eager for another outing after a rubdown and long midday rest. Soon they were sailing across the rolling hills through dense stands of woodland.

Without quite realizing how, Jason found himself nearing the border with Harleigh where he and Rachel had first met with such disastrous consequences. Not that much had changed for the better on their second encounter, he thought wryly. What was it about the chit that got under his skin? He reined in Araby as he approached a small, secluded pool hidden behind a stand of elms. The stream dividing Falconridge from Harleigh must feed this small lake, he surmised.

The enchantment of the spot led him to dismount and turn the stallion to grazing on the lush grass around the water's edge while he found a rock shaded by several overhanging branches which afforded him an excellent view of the water. Taking a seat, he stretched out his long legs and considered the enigma of Rachel Fairchild. He lay back on the warm rock's smooth surface and laced his fingers behind his head, staring up through the sun-mottled leaves at the brilliant azure of the sky.

She was an intelligent woman, and that was good. He desired her, and that was bad. To act on such a base physical urge would lead to permanent consequences. The very thought of it made him shudder. He was certain the war between England and America would end in a year or two, but marriage with that viper-tongued wench would be akin to living the rest of his life under siege. Odd, though, for after the ball when he had intended to seek out one of the elegant courtesans of his acquaintance, the idea had lost all appeal. Instead he'd ended up gambling until dawn at Wheatie's. Why had none of the Cyprians taken his fancy?

The thought had troubled him over the past three days. He could not seem to get Rachel out of his mind. Her transformation at the ball had certainly been startling, but she was hardly the first striking woman of good family he'd met. His mother had been playing matchmaker for years, to no avail. Of course, now she, too, was allied with his grandfather in the desire to marry him to Rachel.

Visions of long sleek legs and masses of thick chocolate hair danced behind his eyelids as he closed them and started to doze in the afternoon heat. Suddenly a loud noise roused him. Disoriented, he sat up and looked across the water. Two huge mastiffs bounded down the hillside. Circling around the pool, they headed directly toward him at a dead run, barking furiously. Their open mouths revealed large, sharp, yellow fangs.

Chapter Five

Rachel had let the mastiffs get too far ahead of her. They were always boisterous and eager for a run after being confined in the Hall while she was in the city. She heard their loud baying and the sound of a man's voice and at once kicked Reddy into a gallop, heading through the woods to the pool. Good lord, they might tear the fellow into pieces if he panicked and tried to run from them!

Of course, the interloper was most probably another pesky poacher, but she still did not want the fool's death or injury on her conscience. Rachel kneed Reddy into the water, cutting across the pool to reach the dogs before they cornered their prey. The worthless horse shied as soon as the water grew deep enough to require that he swim. She forced him to obey, but in the process he splashed her with enough water to drench her and blur her vision. "Venus! Helen! Come!" she commanded loudly as she heard the sound of the man's voice. They did not obey, which was most unusual . . . and ominous.

Then she recognized that voice and almost reined in. If they did tear Jason Beaumont to bits, she would not have to marry him. But of course, that was utterly ridiculous. Guiding Reddy up onto the bank, she blinked the water from her eyes and beheld a sight that made her blood run cold. Jason was on the ground with both dogs on top of him! "Oh, please, God, no," she murmured, then jumped from the gelding's back, shrieking at the mastiffs. "Venus! Helen! Come!"

Then it dawned on her why they had not obeyed her commands. Jason's laughter echoed across the clearing. The accursed man was playing with her girls! They were rolling and flopping about like a pair of puppies. Striding up angrily, she stood over them, glaring as Jason got to one knee, casually thumping Venus on a haunch.

He looked up at Rachel with a big grin splitting his face. "Now, be good girls and sit." When they both obeyed the command, he could see her bristle with anger. Smothering a good hearty laugh, he turned his attention back to the mastiffs, saying, "You are beautiful young ladies but too forward by half. Rolling about on the grass with a strange man is simply not the done thing, I'm given to understand." He tsked scoldingly at them, and they obliged by falling on their sides and fawning adoringly at his feet.

"Next time I shall bring Adonis and Paris instead of these two worthless beasts," she said sweetly. "I doubt you'd charm them quite so easily."

He raised one eyebrow at her and answered, "No, not males of any species . . . but as to rolling about on the grass with a beautiful female . . ." He eyed her appreciatively, enjoying it when she looked down with horror at the way her sheer white linen shirt had molded to her breasts.

Rachel realized that she was once again at a disadvantage with the lout thanks to Reddy. Her shirt and britches were soaked, and her hair had come unfastened from its plait in her headlong gallop from the woods. Great masses of damp brown curls hung down her back and spilled over her shoulders. She started to smooth her shirtfront and tuck it back into the waistband of her pants, but caught herself just in time. Instead she tossed her head, sending the heavy hair flying backward as she said, "If you had whispered that lewd comment to me at the ball, I should have been well justified in dumping champagne over your head."

"A pity I didn't think of anything half so improper," he replied.

"My sister is convinced that you're a fearful lecher and that my father should break the engagement at once."

"She's correct about my lechery. Perhaps you could cry off. But then, do you think it possible that your father would make another match, with some fellow even more odious than I?"

Rachel started in surprise. That probability had plagued her for weeks before she'd met the Yankee. He was quite bright even if he was an insufferable sapskull. "Although I am loath to admit it, there are men in London worse than you—but only one or two," she quickly added.

He found it difficult to concentrate when she reached up to replait that magnificent chocolate-colored mane. The wet cloth of her shirt clung lovingly to the curves of her breasts, leaving little to his imagination—and Jason had a most excellent imagination. "Men such as Forrestal?"

She blinked and pinned him with those clear hazel-green eyes. "What do you know of Etherington's heir, other than that you are the better fencer?"

Jason shrugged. "Only that he offered for you and your father turned him down. A wise move, that. Forrestal gambles to excess and is so deep in dun territory 'twould take your whole dowry to pay his vowels."

"How fortunate that my father and your grandfather concocted our match instead," she said ironically. Of course, it would never occur to Jason Beaumont that any man would want her for aught but her dowry. Deep inside, she feared that he was right.

"And how ·fortunate that the viscount has such a clever daughter who has concocted the perfect way to thwart them." He watched as she began to pace nervously, unable to tear his eyes from the delectable curve of her derriere. Who would ever have imagined a woman could look so inviting in a pair of twill britches?

She let him fall in step beside her, the two mastiffs sniffing adoringly at his heels. *Fickle creatures.* As they walked around the water's edge, Rachel noted the way his long legs perfectly matched her own stride, remembering the way they had danced together at the ball. Forcing her thoughts from such disquieting musings, she reminded him, "You agreed that the best way to approach this problem was to appear resistant to the match at first. My father would have suspected something was amiss if I'd done what was proper at the ball, and I'm equally certain that crafty old marquess would have assigned someone to watch your every move if you'd pretended to agree to their plans."

"You could have warned me that you intended to drown me in champagne," he said with wry amusement.

"It had to look convincing, did it not? I could have

broken the Waterford punch bowl over your thick skull."

"I shall attempt to be suitably grateful," he replied dryly. "When I answer your father's summons to dinner on Friday next, should I be perfunctorily polite to you?"

"That would test your acting ability to the extreme. A bit of residual anger is a better idea. I warrant that after your display in the library and what transpired at the betrothal announcement, Papa will expect you to be in a howling rage."

"That I can manage, but gradually we shall have to act civil to each other in their presence if we are to convince them to let down their guard."

"Very gradually. Remember, they know us well and would not believe for a moment that we'd simply capitulate. 'Twill take me a bit of time to arrange ship's passage in Bristol, too."

Jason hated having to rely on Rachel's connections in this country to enable him and his foster brother to board a ship bound for America. Hell, if his grandfather had not resorted to using Fox as a pawn, Jason would have been honor-bound to stay. Now all certainty about his future as an earl was in grave doubt. As to wedding Miss Fairchild, he had no doubts at all . . . or did he?

Where the deuce did that come from! Pushing the horrifying notion to the very back of his mind, he turned to her and asked, "How soon do you believe I'll be able to free Fox and return him to America?"

Rachel frowned in concentration. She had been considering further ramifications of their plan. En route to Harleigh Hall with Harry, it had become abundantly clear to her that merely foiling the plot to blackmail Jason into marriage would do nothing but postpone the inevitable. Her father would only find another candidate. No matter if she had two heads, with the size of the Harleigh inheritance, someone would agree to marry her, and it could be Forrestal.

"It will take several months to work matters out," she replied cautiously. She dared not reveal her thoughts until she had considered them very carefully. "You must pay social calls at the Hall. Act interested in crops and livestock management. Father will expect that of you, since you will have all the Cargrave properties to run as well as mine.

"Oh, and when you discuss merging the estates, do not forget that I shall have to be included in the conversations," she continued. "Father would be very suspicious if I were not, since I am the one who has run Harleigh for the past six years. There has been a movement gaining some support in Parliament for repeal of the tariffs on wheat . . ."

Jason smiled as she chattered away, making no reply. When she paused and looked up at him, bemused, he said, "You remind me of my mother."

Was that flattering or not? Rachel was uncertain how to take it. But then, why did she give a jot whom he reminded her of? "Oh, and how is that?" she asked levelly.

"After my father died, she took over running the plantation. Did a splendid job of it, too, until my sister Margaret married Terrance and he assumed control."

"Isn't that always the way? No matter how competent a woman may be, once a man appears on the horizon, she must, of course, give way and let him take control of everything she's worked so hard to achieve."

He could hear bitterness in her voice . . . and vulnerability. "My brother-in-law did not take anything away from my mother. She still keeps her hand in running the plantation and gives advice to Terrance. That rapscallion Irishman has been wise to heed it, too. In addition, she has other interests which she prefers to devote her time to now, especially since she's become a grandmother."

"You must miss them," Rachel said, surprisingly touched by the obvious love he showed for his family.

"Aye, I do. God knows, I would that I were with them now, with this earl business well and truly settled."

His tone indicated to her how little he cared for the trappings of the peerage. Rachel felt forced to make a grudging confession. She owed it to him. "When I first heard about the marquess investing you as his heir, I thought you a crass opportunist." She almost lost her nerve when he looked questioningly at her. Moistening her lips, she continued, "I assumed you'd leaped at the chance to become an earl."

"And betrayed my country to make the bargain?" His voice held an edge.

"Yes," she admitted, meeting his cool blue gaze. "I owe you an apology for that assumption. After I learned that you'd been forced to become Cargrave's heir, I knew I was wrong."

"A handsome apology indeed, Countess. Thank you," he replied sincerely.

When he smiled so honestly at her, without a trace of mockery, her heart turned over. "I must confess, however, when I learned the lengths to which the marquess had gone, blackmailing you into marrying me, it did smart a trifle." *Why on earth did I say that?* The man had the most disconcerting effect on her!

Her wry chuckle did not entirely cover the embarrassment she must have felt. For once, Jason could not think of a teasing retort. Instead, he stopped walking and looked at her intently, saying, "I should be quite surprised if anything could shake the self-confidence of a remarkable woman such as you, Countess."

She reached down nervously and gave Venus a pat as the dog nudged her leg affectionately. "Ah, but our goal is that I never become your countess, is it not?"

With horror, he detected the faint flush of pleasure his words had elicited. Best to play the boorish Yankee sapskull she expects, lest you end up leg-shackled to the chit, he reminded himself. "That is most certainly true," he replied, taking a seat on a nearby rock. He leaned back casually and added, "I'd never dream of taking Harleigh Hall away from you."

"Do not be so certain you *could* take it away, m'lord earl," she retorted.

There was more than a hint of that old imperiousness in her tone. Better that than exchanging further compliments! "If I have learned anything since my most unwilling induction into the peerage, 'tis that men control all lands and titles. Earls outrank countesses—perhaps even duchesses, since, after all, we had the good sense to be born males."

Helen chose that moment to take off after a rabbit, racing into the thickest part of the woods bordering the pool.

"Helen, no! Come!" Rachel called out. The mastiff pivoted in mid-bound, but the damage was already done. She had jumped belly deep into a patch of brush and was now obediently retracing her path to her mistress. Rachel backed away, commanding the dog to sit.

"What's wrong? You're surely not a tenderhearted female who'd swoon because a dog feasts on a rabbit?" Jason asked, reaching down to thump the dog who sat beside him.

Rachel smiled, allowing plenty of time for Helen to nuzzle his face and neck while he petted her. Venus approached, eager for a share of the attention that Jason was lavishing on Helen. Grinning like a rider who has just been awarded the brush at a fox hunt, Rachel replied, "Helen may take all the rabbits she wishes. We're quite overrun with them, and they eat the gardens. However, it is quite a nuisance when she wallows in poison oak. The brush to the south of the pool is quite infested with it, I fear."

With an oath, he jerked his hand from Helen's shiny coat as if she'd burned him, backing away and ordering her to sit.

"I have some special soap in my saddlebag to wash the poison from her fur. Unfortunately, it does nothing to relieve the itch once one is afflicted," she said, strolling leisurely back to Reddy. "Would you care to help me bathe Helen?"

Jason's only reply was another snarled oath as he pulled off his boots and dived into the water, scrubbing his hands and face furiously with sand. "Damn you. I'll make you pay for this, Countess, believe me," he yelled.

Rachel's laughter echoed across the still water of the pool, filling the afternoon air.

"I say, old chap, you don't look a'tall the thing," Drum said, grimacing delicately and keeping his distance from Jason, who sat digging at his hands and face, which were smeared with an evil-smelling salve. "Your fingers more closely resemble sausages than digits. I shall refrain from commenting upon your visage, *alors.*"

"How charitable of you, *old chap,*" Jason snarled.

"A pity, but that's what comes of rustication," Drum replied with a shudder of distaste.

"This is what comes of spending an afternoon with a hellion such as Rachel Fairchild," Jason retorted, gritting his teeth at the infernal itching.

"Whatever is that ghastly smell? Stinks like a Thames garbage scow in August," Drum said, wrinkling his nose as he lifted a faultlessly snowy handkerchief to cover it.

"A most-difficult-to-come-by home remedy to cure my poison oak," Jason replied. "I brought most of the necessary herbs with me from America, but do you have any idea how difficult it is to find bear grease in England?"

"Bear grease? Do not tell me. This is one of your Shawnee medicinals."

"And I thank God for it. The first time I went on a raid with them I was in far more danger from skin rash than Cherokee arrows. Kettle Keeper brewed up this concoction for me. I never went anywhere in the woods without covering my body with it. Who in the hell would've thought I'd require it in jolly old England?"

"Bear grease." Drum shook his head. "Little wonder that your red Indians are said to be able to slip through the woodlands noiselessly. They must be slippery indeed."

"That is not amusing, Drum."

The little dandy shrugged. "You could have easily prevented this injury had you remained sensibly in the city." Alvin Francis Edward Drummond seldom ventured outside London unless dire penury loomed, forcing him to take a coach to his father's seat in Berkshire.

"Need I remind you that I have duties at Falconridge which necessitate my spending time here?"

They were seated in a large sunny room in the manor house. Light spilling through the mullioned windows cast red and gold patterns over a deep blue carpet and the two leather chairs the men occupied. Drum continued to edge discreetly back in his seat whenever his companion leaned too close. "Do have a care. I should hate to get bear grease on my best jacket, dear fellow," he admonished when Jason stood up and walked past him to pour a glass of hock for himself.

Gesturing to the cool, foamy pitcher, Jason said, "I shan't pour for you, lest I contaminate you, but feel free to have some."

Eyeing the handle of the pitcher where Jason had

touched it, Drum shook his head. "That is quite all right. Not thirsty, thank you." As Jason returned to his seat, Drum took snuff, watching his friend resume scratching.

Once his ritual with the snuff box had been completed, the little dandy got down to the business that had drawn him most unwillingly into the countryside. "Forrestal was definitely in London when the shots were fired at you here. Odd; I would have thought he would do the deed himself. A bit craven, even for him, to lie in wait and fire from cover. But he is so vain about his marksmanship, I wonder that he would hire it done."

"A blessing if he did hire someone. Whoever it was, he was no marksman."

Drum shrugged. "Some country bumpkin from Etherington's estate perhaps."

Jason left off scratching long enough to ask, "What of the night at Wheatie's?"

"That Forrestal could have done himself. No one could account for his whereabouts after he left the ball at Cargrave Hall."

"Perhaps he shares your aversion to leaving London," Jason said.

"Perhaps, but there is the other possibility we discussed. Your dear cousin Roger."

"*You* discussed. Roger Dalbert could no more kill a man than he could lift the Tower of London."

"Tut, he would be Cargrave's heir if you were dead. Of course, when I checked on his whereabouts during the attempts on your life, all times were accounted for. But anything is possible if one has the blunt to hire enough men."

Jason shook his head stubbornly. "Roger is one of the most gentle and least rank-conscious men I've ever met. Titles mean nothing to him. Look at the woman he married. Garnet is from the merchant class. No pretension whatever in her. She's more interested in ship-building than being a marchioness. And she's quite wealthy to boot—not that Roger has ever been one to live high."

"I must confess, having met them, I'm inclined to agree with you. He seems more content sitting in front of a fire with his hounds than socializing. And Mistress Dalbert has a reputation for choosing the most wretch-edly unflattering wardrobe of any lady of the ton. But women are always a dicey lot."

"Believe me, I could not be more painfully aware of that fact," Jason said glumly, forcing himself to ignore the maddening itch, which the salve was only margin-ally successful in curbing. "I swore I'd take revenge for Rachel's perfidy . . . if only I could think of anything dire enough with which to afflict her."

"She is not subject to poison oak, I take it?"

Sighing, Jason shook his head.

"You could drown her in that pool. That would solve two problems at once," Drum suggested helpfully.

"She is an excellent swimmer."

"I have every faith that you will think of some suitable chastisement for the chit," Drum replied cheerily.

"Strangling her with my bare blistered hands does hold a certain charm," his friend said as he gave in once more and resumed digging.

Drum beat a hasty retreat back to London the following day, promising to keep a sharp eye on Frederick For-restal and his companions. He also mysteriously al-luded to investigating some financial matters, but would say nothing further. Jason spent the duration of the week plotting revenge on Rachel Fairchild . . . and itching.

By the end of the week, his infestation of poison oak had all but cleared up, thanks to the Shawnee salve.

After being cooped up in the manor house with nothing to take his mind off his misery but bookkeeping ledgers, Jason was eager to go for a ride on Friday morning. That night he was to dine at Harleigh Hall with his nemesis and her father. He still had not thought of a suitable punishment for her, but arriving in a "howling rage" for the meal would not tax his acting ability in the least.

He pushed Araby hard, riding across the rolling fields and woodlands of Falconridge until both he and the great black stallion were sweat-soaked. The day was warm, and thoughts of a dip in that pool enticed him. Now he knew to avoid the thicket where the poison oak grew.

Reining in, he unsaddled the black and gave him a brief rubdown, then turned him loose to graze near a stand of white birch. Pulling off his boots and clothing, Jason dived into the water and swam with strong, clean strokes back and forth across the pool until he felt cool and relaxed. Moving into the shade of a low-hanging willow, he floated silently, considering how he would behave at dinner with the Fairchilds that evening.

Gradually his thoughts drifted. Visions of a great mane of chocolate-colored hair falling over a smooth body the color of warm butterscotch danced in his mind. Rachel wore nothing but a smile, beckoning him to come closer. Like a man in a trance he stalked her, but for every step he took forward, she took one back, until at last she evaporated in a blur of mist.

He splashed and broke the reverie, then realized he was hard as a board, aching with sexual longing. Wiping a lock of wet hair from his eyes, he stood up in the shallow water. Damnation, the very least she owed him was to allow his fantasy to continue to its fruition before vanishing! Perverse woman, she was amazingly consistent, frustrating even his daydreams. He started to move, then froze as the sound of hoofbeats reverberated over the meadow on the opposite side of the pool.

Someone was coming, but because of the trees, whoever it was had not spied Araby or his rider's clothing. Jason himself was hidden deep in the shadows of the willow. After several attempts on his life, and with his pistols on Araby's saddle, he was intent on using extreme caution. Best to see whether the rider was friend or foe before revealing himself. There was also the small matter of being stark naked.

" 'Tis probably some local farm boy come to cool himself and his mount with a drink," he murmured as the horse drew closer.

Jason squinted through the dense willow branches, blinking water droplets from his eyes as the horseman reined in and dismounted. As recognition dawned, he smothered a gasp of amazement. There was absolutely no way he could ever mistake that tall, slender body or long, sure stride.

Rachel led her horse to drink at the edge of the water.

She was not riding Reddy today but a dainty white mare, which somehow seemed incongruous. Such a strong-willed, reckless woman as Rachel Fairchild should always ride a big, powerful horse . . . or a big, powerful man. Cursing, he quashed the disquieting thought. The very last thing on earth he needed to do was think of bedding a woman like Rachel. He'd be leg-shackled for life, and it would be hell on earth every moment they were out of bed.

The most sensible thing he could do was to retreat to his side of the pool, dress, and saddle Araby, then ride like hell for Falconridge. But then Rachel began to strip off her clothing just as he had earlier, obviously eager to dive into the water. Jason stood stock-still in the shadows, wishing devoutly that he had a glass so he might get a closer view of the show she was unwittingly putting on.

And some show it was.

She pulled off her boots, then peeled the blousy linen shirt and fitted trousers from her body. He had believed that he'd seen every inch of her curves when she had appeared before him mud-soaked, then later on, water-soaked. Oh, my, but he'd been mistaken. She was even more long-limbed and lithe than he'd imagined, with high, pointed breasts and slender thighs. Unable to stop himself, he moved through the water quietly, drawing closer to gain a better view. Her skin was gilded by the sun all over, indicating that she spent long hours outdoors letting its gentle rays caress every delectable inch of her.

As he studied the patterns of light and darker golden skin, the ache in his nether region grew even more intense. Not enough that she taunted him in dreams, now she had come to do so in person. He watched as she waded waist deep into the pool, then began to cut through the water with clean strokes. She was headed for a cluster of rocks close to his hiding place. A perfect spot for sunbathing?

Sure enough, she slid graceful as a sylph onto one moss-slicked rock and reclined with an audible sigh. Probably dreaming about poisoning me at dinner tonight, he thought. Grinning wickedly, he began moving across the shallows toward her, keeping under cover of low-hanging trees as he drew nearer. Two could play at this game . . .

Chapter Six

Rachel lay back, letting the warm sun soothe her frazzled nerves. Tonight he would once again invade her world. She had to think, to plan how to handle her maddening attraction to him. The object was to get free of the rogue, not entangle herself further. That would lead only to disaster for both of them. The only way she could convince Jason Beaumont to agree to her revised plan was to approach him coolly, dispassionately, showing him the ultimate reasonableness of it all.

Ah, but the Yankee earl was able to make her spitting mad at every encounter—or worse yet, make her feel insecure and inadequate, emotions she had suppressed since childhood. She regretted the poison oak. It had been petty and vindictive, and would no doubt cause him to be suspicious of her proposal . . . if she ever worked up the courage to broach it.

She stretched languidly, trying to relax her tense muscles, then lay back, only to be startled from her peaceful idyll by the sound of a sudden splash. At the same instant as she tried to sit up, a large hand encircled her ankle and a disturbingly familiar voice said, "What have we here, a mermaid?"

Rachel let out a shriek of horror, attempting to cover herself as his lascivious gaze swept over her naked body. "Release me at once, lest my dogs tear you apart," she commanded in the steadiest tone she could muster while holding her hands over her privy parts and shaking her hair over her breasts.

Jason chuckled, not relinquishing his hold. While he tugged gently on her ankle, pulling her down the moss-slicked rock, he replied, "You will forgive my doubts that Venus and Helen would harm a hair on my head. At least intentionally," he added, remembering the poison oak.

"I'm not referring to those fickle females. I brought Paris and Adonis today. I doubt they'll succumb to your masculine charms so easily."

He could not resist letting his eyes roam over her golden flesh, butterscotch-soft and inviting. One rose-brown nipple peeked tantalizingly through the dark chocolate screen of her hair. It was a good thing he was half submerged in the pool or else she would be able to see positive proof of the effect she had on his body, which was rigidly at attention and throbbing wickedly. He struggled to concentrate on her words . . . something about Paris . . .

"If you were a gentleman, you would never spy on a lady's bath, much less accost her this way," she said icily, much calmer as she saw the large tan heads of her mastiffs appear at the top of the hill.

"How often, Countess, have you yourself said I'm a Yankee impostor, no true gentleman at all, hmmm?"

His fingers stroked the instep of her foot tantalizingly. She felt like curling her toes with the pleasure of it.

Fighting the urge, she shot back, "I said *if* you were a gentleman. No one knows better than I that you are not, but that does not mean you can take advantage of a lady without consequences."

"I fail to see any ladies about," he said, tugging more insistently on her ankle. She tried to kick him with her free foot, emitting a startlingly unladylike oath as she did so, but he ducked and seized her other ankle, tsking at her as he pulled her into the water with a loud splash. "Ladies don't possess such vocabulary, Countess."

"You'll shortly be treated to more than a demonstration of my vocabulary," she gritted out, watching the dogs playfully bounding down the hill to join in the watersport.

Jason wrapped one arm around her and drew her body flush against his, oblivious to impending doom. All blood feeding his brain was in use elsewhere at the moment. "And," he gasped in spite of himself, "you may be treated to a demonstration of the effects of your hoydenish behavior, Countess."

Having grown up on a large country estate, Rachel was conversant with the aroused male of any species. Suddenly the dogs in the meadow were forgotten, as were propriety, her schemes to be free—everything but the heat and hardness of the man holding her so closely. Her breasts tingled where they encountered the thatch of dark hair on his chest. She could feel his heart pounding in rhythm with her own, hammering out frantic beats of awakened passion. Her hands had somehow taken hold of his shoulders, and her fingers dug into the sleek curve of powerful muscles. Below the water, his erection pressed at the juncture of her thighs, incredibly hot in the cool water.

Rachel was saved from utter madness by loud splashing and whoofing as the mastiffs made their way clumsily toward her to join in the game. The noise of her rescuers galvanized her into action. She pressed her palms against his chest and gave a hard, sudden push while at the same time bracing her back against the rock so that she could kick out with one foot.

Jason felt her heel connect sharply with his knee and stumbled backward on the slippery bottom just as the mastiffs' loud snorting and splashing registered in his consciousness. Thrashing in the water to regain his balance, he suddenly remembered what she had said earlier—these were not his "girls" but the males, Paris and Adonis.

Rachel swam quickly to the mastiffs and positioned herself between them, then said, "Fetch," pointing to Jason as if he were a twig floating on the current! And with those massive jaws and pointy yellow teeth, the beasts could crunch his bones as easily as if he were indeed no more than a bundle of sticks.

He had never moved so swiftly in his life as he did at that instant, scrambling up on the slippery rocks and climbing to the peak of the tallest one, where he wedged himself in a narrow crevice. The dogs tried but could not get a purchase on the mossy surface. Jason watched with horror as Rachel moved behind the behemoth she called Adonis.

"I could boost him up out of the water so he could reach you . . ." She let her words trail off. He deserved to be frightened out of his wits for what he had nearly done to her . . . or what, in truth, she had nearly done to herself, although she was loath to admit it.

"Killing me or dismembering me, as it were, would serve neither of us, Countess," he replied coolly, hoping she could not see the sweat beading his brow. It was devilish difficult to maintain a facade of calm while one's private part was hanging out like a puckered sausage dangled in front of a ravenous dog.

He wriggled sideways as inconspicuously as he

could, continuing, "You yourself admitted that if you fail to wed me, your father will only come up with another suitor, most probably Forrestal. We need to reach some sort of accord that will protect both of us from the machinations of that pair of old tyrants. Damn it, grab that dog—it's climbing up here!"

This was better than she could have hoped. He was playing directly into her hands. "Reluctantly, I am forced to agree that you are correct about the need for an accord, but you have behaved quite badly. I must administer some sort of punishment," she replied blithely, pulling Adonis away from the rocks.

" 'Tis you, witch, who deserves punishment for the poison oak. I was merely exacting a bit of revenge for that trick."

"You seem to have recovered without a trace," she said, letting her eyes stray from his face to his hands, then lower. Indeed he was recovered . . . breathtakingly! "What you did just now was far more heinous. I should let you rot until you starve on that rock, but I shall be merciful. Guard," she instructed the mastiffs, then turned and swam toward the willows, where Araby and Jason's saddle were hidden.

His saddle . . . and his clothes! Suddenly he realized what she was about. There was nothing he could do to stop her. He eyed the dogs, whose energy in the water appeared boundless as they circled the rocks. After making a few utterly futile overtures to them, he concluded they were made of sterner stuff than Venus and Helen. They snapped at his fingers and growled at the sound of his voice.

Rachel appeared on the opposite bank several minutes later, having retrieved her own clothing and donned it in the cover of a willow. She waved his pants and shirt like banners from across the water as she called out, "I left you your boots."

"Most generous of you," he replied sardonically.

" 'Twouldn't do to try riding barefoot. As to the rest . . . I would give a great deal to be present when you arrive at your stables clad only in riding boots. I do hope the saddle leather does not geld you."

He could see her grin even at that distance. "I shall manage, Countess. My Shawnee friends ride bareback . . . I recommend we try it some day."

A faint grin tugged at the corner of his mouth as she stomped toward her mare. Uttering a sigh of relief when the mastiffs swam toward the shore to rejoin their mistress, he slipped from his perch on the rocks and made his way to where Araby grazed patiently. Dinner that evening should prove most interesting indeed.

Jason considered with wry amusement that his arrival at the stables dressed in nothing but boots and buckskin breechclout would be bandied about the manor house and surrounding countryside in shocked whispers for weeks to come. As he rode toward Harleigh Hall that evening he murmured, "Well, why not?" Such a peccadillo fit his image as Yankee earl, and since there was no way he could ever dispel that, he might as well play the part to the hilt.

Of course, Miss Rachel Fairchild had contributed significantly to his scandalous reputation as well, first dumping champagne over his head, then stealing his clothes. It was just as well that the chit had no idea he carried a few "necessaries" from his days with the Shawnee in his saddlebags. If she'd taken the breechclout with the rest of his clothes, he might have been too sore to ride to dinner this evening. For all his sly innuendo regarding bareback activities, he'd always found it damnably uncomfortable to have nothing between his person and a horse's bony spine.

He grinned, remembering the way she had yielded

to him in the water before the untimely arrival of those hounds from hell. He had tried to sort through his feelings about her ever since their afternoon encounter, but was no closer now to deciding exactly what his feelings were than he had been four hours earlier.

It had been many a year since he'd felt such intense desire for a female, perhaps not since his first sexual adventures as a green lad. Rachel was highly unconventional, stubborn, opinionated and choleric. But she also possessed a razor-sharp wit and keen sense of humor, not to mention all those perfectly marvelous physical attributes which he had only begun to explore in the water. But Jason was far too young to marry. He had, in fact, never given it serious thought during his seagoing days, ignoring his mother's subtle hints about settling down.

After all, his sister Margaret had provided three children who could one day take over the family estates and shipping firm. But now, he was forced to concede, the situation was different. If he and his grandfather reached an accord and he returned to England to live, he would one day have to wed and provide Cargrave an heir. But that whole issue was still far from settled. "I'd be well served if Grandfather refused to negotiate and Roger Dalbert inherited," he muttered to Araby. Then he could stay in America and never have to face matrimony.

Gwendolyn Beaumont had been wise enough not to force the issue or try to be a matchmaker for her son. Perhaps therein lay the problem. If his grandfather had not attempted to manipulate his life so arrogantly, he might have found Rachel Fairchild quite appealing— that is, if she, too, had not been infuriated by her father's determination to see her wed to his old friend's grandson. But as things stood now, the only thing he and the lady shared in common was a resolute determination to thwart two scheming old men.

She was a hellion when crossed. He shuddered to think of what Paris and Adonis might have done to him if they'd been able to climb up on those rocks. Who knew if she'd have been able to call them off once they had the blood scent? Who knew if she would have tried? No, it was decidedly wiser to forget the interlude in the water and concentrate on outsmarting the marquess.

"You're not the only chess player in the family, Grandfather," he murmured to himself. Feeling a bit of satisfaction with his resolve, he reached down to give Araby a pat.

Just then the crack of a shot rent the bucolic quiet of the country evening. Jason felt a sharp, burning pain in his right arm, but took no time to consider it as he kicked the stallion into a swift gallop. He stretched out low on the big black's neck to present a smaller target. Within a few dozen yards a second shot rang out, whistling past his ear. Whoever was firing at him was not only a damn good marksman, but could reload with considerable skill as well. Of course, there could be more than one attacker. In any event, if he had not leaned down when he did, he would be a dead man now.

Jason rode hard for several miles, rounding a bend in the road and then pushing Araby over the rise of a hill before he slowed the big stallion to a brisk trot. Whoever had fired at him did not appear to be giving pursuit. Still, Jason planned to take no further chances. He removed one of his Hawken pistols from his saddlebag and clenched it in his fist. The familiar feel of the American weapon was a comfort. Thank heaven the marquess had been able to retrieve his grandson's sea chest. For the second time that day, Jason felt a surge of gratitude toward his conniving grandfather.

By the time the rambling manor house came into view, he was starting to feel light-headed. The wound in his upper arm was bleeding copiously. When he slipped from the saddle at the front entry, the footman paled, his eyes nearly popping from their sockets as he observed the widening red stain on Jason's sleeve.

"If you'd be so kind, my dear fellow," he said, handing the reins to the servant, who took them mutely.

By this time the front door had opened and a tall, cadaverously thin man with the officious air of an upper servant made his way down the stone stairs to where Jason stood. Taking in the situation with one haughty glance, he summoned two additional footmen from the house. Jason waved them away and succeeded in climbing the steps unaided. He had no more than set foot inside the foyer when Rachel and her father appeared in response to the commotion of the servants.

"My apologies for bleeding on your carpet, m'lord," he said to the viscount.

"Dear heavens, whatever has happened?" Hugh Fairchild croaked, staring with disbelief at the gory mess of Jason's sleeve.

"Don't be a cake, Father. 'Tis obvious someone has shot the earl," Rachel said, calling out for one of the maids to have someone called Beatty fetch her medicinal basket and a pot of water.

"Egad—shot?" Harleigh echoed. "What possible reason would someone have for doing such a thing?"

Rachel cocked one eyebrow, studying Jason as she replied, "Father, I can think of legions of reasons."

"Now, daughter, there is no reason to be uncivil."

"Come, before you utterly ruin the carpet," she instructed Jason, ignoring her father's remonstrances. She took his uninjured arm and guided him into a small sitting room off the foyer. The viscount trailed behind them, wringing his hands.

"Was the villain planning to rob you?" Hugh asked.

"Since he, or they, shot without first demanding that I hand over my purse, I somehow doubt it, although 'tis always possible that he, or they, simply intended to strip my corpse and steal my horse as well," Jason replied.

"You do seem to possess an extraordinary talent for getting yourself into trouble," Rachel said tartly as she shoved her patient into a lyre-back chair.

"I fear 'tis a lifelong talent," he replied.

"But not one conducive to long life," she retorted.

Just then a short, squat woman with a huge wart on her chin waddled through the door bearing a basket of medical supplies. "Here's yer basket, m'lady. Farley'll be about with the water anon," she said with obvious disapproval in her voice as she watched Rachel removing the injured man's jacket. "Ye'd best be letting me tend to him."

As the servant placed the basket on a Pembroke table beside the chair, Rachel replied, "That is all right, Beatty. I can manage." She moved in front of the much heavier woman and opened the lid.

"It is not proper, Rachel," the viscount interjected. "You are an unmarried lady and should not be viewing a gentleman who is not fully clothed."

"Might I remind you that as per the connivance of Cargrave and yourself, this 'gentleman' is my betrothed? Besides, I am the best doctor in seven counties."

"You doctor animals, not men," the viscount reminded her with a worried frown.

Rachel looked down at Jason, but before she could retort, he cautioned, "Don't say it."

"Whatever could you imagine I might say, m'lord?" she replied primly, but the unholy gleam in her eye when she removed a scissors from the basket was apparent to him. "I must cut away that shirt before I can assess the damage."

The blood had begun to clot, and the sheer lawn fabric was fused to an ugly long gash sliced deeply into his biceps. Jason used his good hand to unfasten the studs in his shirt. " 'Tis ruined anyway," he murmured as he shrugged it from his good shoulder, wincing when he inadvertently moved his injured arm.

Rachel tried not to look at the broad, hard planes of his chest or the pattern of black hair dusting the muscled surface. "Here—you'll be about it all night," she said, using impatience to cover the disquietude his nearness evoked. "Do try not to faint when I cut the cloth from your skin."

He looked dispassionately down at the seeping wound. "I have survived far worse . . . unfortunately for you, Countess." His dark blue eyes lit with faint amusement as he said, "Perhaps I should inquire of the stablemen if you have just returned from a hard ride."

"If I were the one shooting at you, I would not have missed. Now hold still. This will hurt like the dickens."

"How considerate of me, making your evening such a delight," he groused, but did not make a sound when she inserted the scissors beneath the shirtsleeve and slowly began cutting it free of the long gash.

" 'Twill require at least a dozen stitches," she said, forcing her hands to remain steady in spite of the way his nearness caused her heart to pound.

"I doubt that you acquired skill in plying a needle while doing genteel embroidery."

"I acquired my skill while sewing up the hurts of animals too stupid to avoid doing themselves harm. Rather like you." She tossed the bloody cloth into a Wedgwood bowl sitting on the table, then turned to

Beatty, saying, "Where is Farley? I need to cleanse the wound before I can see to stitch it."

As if conjured up, the old servant entered, carefully carrying a large bowl and pitcher filled with water. She directed him to place the bowl on the table and pour, then dismissed him and turned to her father. The viscount was by this time as white as parchment and dabbing at his sweat-beaded brow with a handkerchief. "Father, you know how this oversets you. Perhaps it might be best if you were to wait for us in the study."

"Quite so, m'dear," he replied, moving to the door with great alacrity. "I shall order Perkins to break out my best port. Nothing better to revive an injured man," he said to Jason before he beat a hasty retreat.

"The last time he attempted to help me, when his prize mare was foaling, he passed out, poor man," she whispered to Jason.

"I shall endeavor to remain conscious, if for no other reason than to keep you from stitching my arm to my leg or some other such mischief."

When Beatty snorted in amusement, Rachel cast a sharp look at the servant, then turned her attention to bathing the wound. The gash was long and jagged, bleeding freely once more now that she had removed the shirtsleeve. Once she was satisfied that she had gotten rid of every tiny bit of fabric, she dusted the wound with yarrow powder and turned her attention to threading a needle with which to suture.

Keep your hands steady. She focused on the eye of the needle, trying not to think of the man sitting so close to her and of the considerable pain that she would soon be inflicting upon him. She could feel his body heat, smell the now all too familiar male musk emanating from him. And his eyes. She knew those cool blue eyes were studying her intently. She refused to meet his mocking gaze. 'Twould serve the lout right if she did stitch his arm to his leg—or some other far more sensitive part of his anatomy! Doggedly she set to work.

Jason was growing increasingly dizzy from blood loss, but willed himself not to fall into a vaporish faint in front of this very unvaporish female. After all, he had given her his word that he would not do so. The sudden sting of the needle puncturing his flesh served to clear his head. He must also, at all costs, not let her know she was causing him discomfort. To distract himself, he studied her hands.

Although she had long, slender fingers, her nails were short, the joints innocent of any rings. These were the capable hands of a woman used to performing manual labor, not those of a finely bred English aristocrat. "You are quite good at stitchery, Countess," he said softly as she tied off the thread.

"I've little appetite for embroidery, as you surmised. Fortunate for you that I have had a deal of practice stitching up injured dumb animals." Giving him no time to retort, she turned to Beatty. "Please fetch one of my father's shirts for His Lordship."

Nodding sourly, the servant waddled from the room.

" 'Twill be a bit small, but you shall have to make do," Rachel said to Jason, measuring the breadth of his shoulders and comparing them to the thin viscount's.

Suddenly she realized that they were alone and he was but a foot from her, half dressed. The episode in the water flashed through her memory, causing her breath to catch as she recalled the crisp texture of the hair on his chest and the way her nipples had felt when they came into contact with it. She could feel again the hardness of his muscles . . . and the hardness of that other place, so masculine and demanding. She had nearly succumbed—would have if not for the mastiffs dashing to her rescue.

What am I thinking? Rachel chastised herself. She bit

her lip, turning away from his probing gaze to extract a length of gauze from the basket. "I'll have to wrap your arm—"

"What's happened to that cool doctorly air, Countess?" he asked, raising his good arm and taking her hand in his. As he raised it to his lips, he could feel her tremble.

Chapter Seven

Jason expected her to jerk her hand away and berate him for being a lecher, but she surprised him. When he raised his eyes from her hand, she met his gaze without so much as a flutter of her lashes. Reading what lay beyond those luminous hazel-green eyes was quite another matter. "A physician without words of advice?"

"You'd not heed one thing I said, so why should I bother?" she replied, still not withdrawing her hand from his. The cheeky devil was casting a spell, trying to intimidate her. She fought the impulse to pull away abruptly and instead slowly let her fingers disengage, teasing his large palm with her fingertips as she did so. *You are playing with fire,* she admonished herself.

"You might be surprised at how much I do heed you, Countess," he said, starting to rise.

Rachel knew that if she let him tower over her, she would be at a disadvantage, so she placed her hand on his uninjured shoulder and pressed him back into his seat. Best to turn this brief period while they were alone to practical considerations. "You'd better have a care. This is the second time someone in the vicinity has taken a shot at you. First he missed; now he's wounded you. The next time he may finish the job."

"Actually, 'tis the third such attempt. There was one in London as well."

She sucked in her breath. "My regard for you grows apace, m'lord. To inspire irritation is common. To engender murderous hatred is remarkable. Who might wish you dead?"

"With the possible exception of yourself, I can think of no one . . . at least, no one this side of the Atlantic."

"Pray cease your foolish banter. Much as I might wish my father and the marquess had not hatched their cork-brained scheme, I have not attempted to shoot you."

"As you have already assured me, you would not have missed." He sighed and combed his fingers through his hair. "I have a friend in London looking into the matter. There's little else to do now."

"As difficult as it might be for you, you could exercise a bit of judgment and not ride alone through wood-lands where anyone with a musket can make a target of you," she replied heatedly.

"Why, Countess, I'm touched. 'Twould seem that you care."

"Indeed I do, m'lord dolt. As I thought I had made clear this afternoon, we need each other to avert a mutually distasteful fate. In spite of the inestimable strain of doing so, please try holding that in mind. Perhaps if you wear a cap, it might help."

"See there? I knew you would offer words of advice," he said with no particular rancor in his voice.

Rachel was even more concerned, now that she knew without doubt that someone was actually trying to kill him, although why she should be, she refused to consider. Instead she said, "I must bandage your arm."

"As you wish," he replied, his voice low and husky.

She turned away from his penetrating blue eyes as conflicting emotions warred within her. Still uncertain, she took a long strip of linen from her basket and reached for his stitched arm. "Hold the end of this while I wrap it," she said, placing his good hand over the bandage to secure it in place as she began to wind the material around and around his arm.

Jason could smell the perfume in her hair—a subtle, honeysuckle sweetness quite at odds with her characteristically sour disposition, he thought wryly. She leaned down, biting her lower lip in concentration as she applied the bandage. Now that the sharp pain from the stitching and the light-headedness had faded, he was increasingly aware of how fetching she looked in a simple gown of dark green mull. The gently rounded neckline was demure by the standards of the ton, but when she leaned forward, reaching around his arm as she did now, he could see the deep vale between the swell of her breasts. Stifling a groan, he looked away, knowing that she would soon be able to discern a telltale bulge in his britches if he did not avert his eyes.

Rachel was keenly aware of his nearness as she concentrated on completing her task. She did not realize that her breasts were so splendidly revealed, and would have been horrified if she had known. Seduction was an art which she had never practiced. Harry had tried, without any success, to give her all sorts of instruction on how to enthrall a man, but Rachel had not listened to her younger sister.

Yet she began to sense something humming between herself and Jason. Irrationally, she hoped that he was as affected by their intimacy as was she. Then she looked down at his lap and could not resist a tiny, only slightly embarrassed, smile. Jason Beaumont might well have been blackmailed into this betrothal, but he did not find her unappealing. That was some balm for her wounded ego. She almost laughed. She hoped the swelling in his britches was as uncomfortable as the stiches in his arm.

As she finished tying off the bandage, he was sure he would not be able to withstand any further enticement without acting on his pressing needs . . . and they were pressing. Why in hell had he not availed himself of some of the lovely Cyprians in London before his exile here in the hinterlands? For that matter, why had he not taken that fetching young dairy maid up on her coy offer yesterday? Damned if he knew. But just as he stood up, intent on taking his tormentor in his arms, Beatty waddled through the door.

The old hag seemed to possess sharp instincts, glaring at him as if she was well aware of the gross impropriety he had been considering. "Here's His Lordship's shirt," she said to Rachel. "Though I cannot see how that one'll be able to get even his unbandaged arm in a sleeve of it."

"We shall make do, Beatty," Rachel replied, dismissing the servant with thanks.

Gifting Jason with one last gimlet-eyed look, Beatty quit the room. Rachel took the shirt and held it up. " 'Tis an old one, made before Father lost so much weight two years ago when he had the ague. Let me help you with it."

He stood and turned, putting his good arm through the sleeve and allowing her to work the other one up his injured arm. She was finally able to ease it over his shoulder, but when he faced her, it was quite apparent that there was no way on earth the shirt could be fastened in front. A six-inch gap stretched over his bare chest.

Standing back to survey the problem, Rachel said,

"Well, if you were to dine in the same scandalous manner in which you ride, with your shirt draping open to your navel, this would suit."

He chuckled. "Remember, I rode truly 'bareback' only this afternoon."

The image of him astride that great black beast stark naked stirred emotions in her which were totally new and confusing in the extreme. "We shall have to devise some means of covering you decently."

"I agree. Even if your father did not object, I'm quite sure Beatty would drop a scalding tureen over my head during the soup course at dinner."

"You have the right of that. Turn around," she commanded, taking the scissors from her basket again.

He eyed them with misgivings. "Dare I take the chance?"

"The dogs are in the kennel. You're safe." she replied impatiently. When he turned, she slid the blades into the fabric and sliced it from the collar halfway down the back. "Now try closing it."

He turned to her with a smirk, holding the two sides of the shirt together with his good hand. "I'm decent."

"Not that I have been able to detect thus far. Here, fasten your shirt studs," she said, reaching down for the sapphire jewelry glittering in a pile on the table. "Your coat, although somewhat stained, will give you the illusion of propriety."

He took one stud and worked it through the shirt placket, but when he tried to raise his injured arm to complete the task, he grimaced and lowered it once more. "I'm afraid I shall require some assistance."

She could see the dare gleaming in his eyes. "I could send for Father's valet," she said, then added, "but we would not want to keep Father waiting any longer, would we?"

As she began to fasten his shirt, he grinned down at

94

her. "Perish the thought, Countess," he murmured softly, noting the way her hands had begun to tremble.

Dinner went smoothly enough. The food was plain country fare, which Jason complimented fulsomely, explaining that he had tired of the endless courses of heavily sauced food in London. The three of them discussed livestock, crops and legislation pending in Parliament which would affect them. Jason was not surprised at Rachel's knowledge of estate management, but he was impressed by how keenly she understood politics. He was happy that she was on his side in the matter of breaking this damnable betrothal. She would make a most formidable opponent if she set her mind to having him to husband.

Yet, at times during the meal, not to mention during the earlier interlude in the sitting room, he would have sworn she was trying to entice him. And there was also the disturbing news that the date for their nuptials had been set—a scant two months hence. Grandfather was taking no chances, it would seem. Both he and Rachel made ineffectual protests when the viscount broached the subject. The normally diffident old peer proved surprisingly stubborn, saying only that he and the marquess had agreed, and the banns were being posted that very week. Then he had abruptly changed the subject.

Owing to Jason's injuries, a servant had been dispatched to Falconridge to inform the staff that the earl would be spending the night at Harleigh Hall. As they said their good nights, Jason vowed that he would find a way to have a serious talk with Rachel before the sun rose. The sooner they settled on a plan for getting Fox to his estate, the sooner he and the lad could escape the marquess.

He waited up until the whole household was asleep,

which was not all that difficult, considering that his arm throbbed wickedly and he had refrained from taking the laudanum the housekeeper had brought him. With someone trying to kill him, he was not about to dull his senses with an opium infusion. At the stroke of one, he finally slipped from his room, listening in the dark hallway for any sounds of stirring. All was dead silence but for the soft night sounds outside an open window and the gentle ticking of the case clock.

Jason had learned from a pretty upstairs maid that Rachel's room was the last door at the end of the corridor. Not surprisingly, he also learned she slept without a maid in attendance. Now he made his way past pier tables and chairs, being careful not to overturn urns filled with summer flowers. Their subtle fragrance reminded him of Rachel, and that now familiar ache in his groin plagued him once more.

Just as he was halfway down the long hallway, creaking floorboards sounded at the opposite end. Flattening himself behind a walnut column which protruded from the wall, he waited silently. He cursed when he recognized the waddling gait of Beatty, making her way down the rear servants' stairs from the third floor. *No doubt the old harridan's on her way to the kitchen to filch a hind quarter of beef to tide her over until morning.*

Once he was certain she had passed, he approached Rachel's room. The smooth ivory knob turned silently. With a slight creak, the heavy walnut door swung open. He slipped inside and closed it, then allowed a moment for his eyes to adjust to the darker interior.

"I was just about to give up and go to your room. Did you get lost in the hallway?" Rachel stepped from an alcove near the window, over which heavy velvet drapes had been drawn.

Jason blinked his eyes as the brightness of the candle she lighted filled the room. She was clad in a plain blue cotton robe belted over a white lawn night rail. "I would have imagined you sleeping in something a bit less missish," he said, eyeing the high neckline against her slender throat. "Perhaps nothing at all ... but then I suppose that would scandalize the maids."

The lout always seemed to grab control of every conversation, no matter the circumstances. "I don't require a maid unless I'm being tricked out for a ball."

"How very American of you, Countess," he said dryly. Then walking closer to her, he asked, "Why did you expect me to come to your room tonight?"

"Do not flatter yourself that I planned seduction."

He studied her appraisingly. "No, I warrant not, else you would have dressed—or undressed—differently. Still, after the way you responded this afternoon in the water ... not to mention tonight when you were tending my wound ... well, a man might draw conclusions."

"And they would be as sapskulled as he is," she replied sweetly. "You heard my father at dinner. The banns have been posted. We have but two months to find a solution to this tangle."

"I must admit, you were right about the old boy. Never would've credited he could be so stubborn."

Rachel gave an elegant snort. "In his own way he's as devious as the marquess, just with less flair. But remember, he did remark on how fond your grandfather has become of Fox. Write your foster brother a letter, inviting him to visit when the Mountjoys' are having their annual summer ball. The marquess always attends, and we shall be expected to as well. Once Fox has spent time here and all goes smoothly, we shall be able to lull your grandfather into a false sense of security. Then you should be able to have the boy return for another visit, not too long before the wedding."

Jason watched as she began to pace back and forth

across the floor, intent on her scheme. The robe was ugly in the extreme, but when it gapped open, the white lawn night rail revealed her considerable charms. *Does she have any idea how very sheer that prim little gown is?* he wondered, already imagining his hands caressing soft golden skin through the gauzy fabric. His eyes swept her from head to toe, hungrily. *Hell, I'm as gluttonous as old Beatty!* Rachel's feet were bare, long and slender with an elegant arch to them. Was there nothing about the wench that he did not find appealing?—other than her temperament and the fact that he could be forced into marrying her, he quickly reminded himself.

"I've dispatched a groom I can trust to secure passage for you and Fox on a ship bound for Canada. Once you're there, how you get to the United States is your problem."

"I'm nothing if not resourceful, Countess," he chided her, trying to concentrate on the plan instead of thoughts of bedding her.

"The ship will sail out of Bristol. The marquess and my father will both be certain you've headed for London or one of the port cities to the south in Hampshire or Sussex. They'll never believe you'd risk riding all the way to the western coast. With really swift horses, we might just make a dash for it, but that is leaving much to chance, for there is no way of guaranteeing the ship will sail immediately after we arrive. 'Twould be wiser to don disguises, perhaps pose as traveling tinkers—"

"Wait a moment," he cut in abruptly as her words finally registered. "What do you mean by 'we'?"

She looked at him as if he'd grown a second head, then sighed at the density of the male cranium. "Without me to act as guide, how do you propose to find your way quickly to Bristol? Good lord, it took you half the night to find your way from your room to mine. At that rate, Fox will be a man full grown before you could stumble upon Bristol unaided. 'Tis a long and arduous ride, well over a hundred miles through rough terrain."

"All the more reason not to have a woman along."

"I can ride as long and hard as any man alive," she snapped. "I'll outride you."

He cocked one eyebrow and grinned, studying her flushed, angry face. "A promise, Countess?"

Rachel gritted her teeth at his sheer male arrogance. He stood there, arms crossed over his chest, leaning casually against a sturdy maple bedpost, grinning lecherously at her. She fought the urge to pull the lapels of her robe together and instead fisted her hands at her sides. "I would love nothing better than to give you a good facer, but I suppose if you appeared at breakfast with a blackened eye, it would raise questions."

"You had no such concern about giving me poison oak."

"You were not spending the night under my roof then, you clunk-headed ass!"

Jason wanted to laugh aloud but repressed it lest they awaken servants. "Here we stand in your bedchambers, you dressed in your night rail and I most, er, casually." He wore the open shirt and old riding breeches she had stolen from him that afternoon.

"I fail to see anything amusing in that. If we were discovered, we'd be compromised into the very marriage we're plotting to avoid."

"Ah, Countess, therein lies the rub. Everyone would think we were trysting instead of going at each other like a pair of pit dogs," he said, unfurling his body and stepping toward her. "I believe trysting would be far more entertaining," he murmured.

She did not like the slumberous look in his eyes or the heat emanating from his body as he drew closer, yet she refused to back away. "I would not do anything rash were I you, m'lord. It could seal our doom."

"Only if we're caught," he said hoarsely as he curled his good arm around her waist and pulled her against him.

This is madness! her mind cried out, but she went silently into his embrace. What might have happened at the pool that afternoon had the mastiffs not intervened? This time there would be no one to rescue her but herself. *But first . . . let me see just what this man-woman thing is all about . . .*

His lips brushed hers ever so softly, like the lightest touch of butterfly wings. Her eyelids closed as her head dropped back, cupped in his palm. As he brushed kisses against her lashes, his fingers kneaded through her heavy hair, caressing her scalp. She could feel the pounding of his heart—or was that her own? She could not tell as his hot, seeking mouth moved down the column of her throat, then back up to her lips, which now were parted, emitting small panting noises.

His tongue made a swift foray inside her mouth, dancing lightly against her own, and she gasped with surprise. When he deepened the kiss this time, pressing his lips hard against hers, she could feel the fierce hunger inside him. It was as if he were infusing her with the same blazing heat, a dizzying desire for something she could not recognize. She kissed him back, awkwardly at first, then with growing confidence as his lips and tongue taught hers how the game was played.

Before she realized it, he had somehow unfastened the belt of her robe and pushed the heavy cotton aside so that one large hand had unrestricted access to a breast. Her nipple tingled and throbbed, pebbling hard through the sheer fabric of her night rail as he massaged and teased it. Then he broke the kiss and moved his head lower, taking the aching bud in his mouth, suckling it while he prepared the other one for the same magic.

Rachel was spinning out of control as she arched against his caresses. Her arms were pinned partially to her sides by the robe he'd pushed down to her elbows. Their lower bodies were fused together, and his erection pressed insistently against the barriers of cloth. She knew nothing of kisses sweet and hot or the incredible sensations a man's mouth on her breasts could evoke, but she was well aware of the purpose of his hard male staff. And fear mingled with desire.

He began to lower her to the carpet. Rachel knew she would be utterly lost if she did not do something at once. Almost inadvertently, she pushed against him, trying to back away, but her hands could not reach his chest, confined as they were by the robe. Instead they slid up his forearms and connected with his biceps. When her fingers dug into the fresh stitches, he grunted with pain and stumbled backward, releasing her with a mild oath of surprise.

Rachel backed away, panting and breathless, her face crimson with shame. "What a mutton-headed, addlepated, bird-witted . . ." All words failed her as her pulse throbbed madly, robbing her of coherent thought.

Jason stood watching her with bare comprehension, holding his aching arm to his chest. "You seemed willing enough a moment ago, Countess. All you needed to do was turn your head away and ask me to stop."

How could she admit that she had been so caught up in their passion, she was powerless to think rationally, much less get her body to obey? A tiny pulse in her throat continued to hammer as she drew in a deep, calming breath. "I will admit the fault was mine as well

101

as yours that things grew so . . . so out of hand."

"Most generous of you, but as I recall, *things* were growing quite well in hand," he replied, watching her pull her robe closed over the two large wet spots on her night rail.

She stiffened at his suggestive comment, hissing angrily, "If we had been caught doing what we were about to do, Father would have been importuning the marquess to secure us a special license immediately. We'd have been before a priest within a day's time, make no mistake about that—or do you wish to be leg-shackled to me for the rest of your life?"

"Countess, there is nothing on this earth I would less rather do than spend the rest of my life with a mercurial hellion like you." Just as he had on the night of their betrothal announcement, Jason executed another stiff, angry bow and turned to leave the room, pausing only long enough to add, "I shall do as you ask and extend an invitation for Fox to visit. Please be certain we have passage on that ship to Canada."

Rachel stood frozen as the door closed with soft finality. She felt suddenly cold in spite of the warm summer air. Jason Beaumont was the most dangerous man she had ever met.

Jason was relieved when he came downstairs the following morning and found that Rachel had already ridden out with her steward to check on a blight in some outlying wheat fields. The viscount was not yet about, preferring to take his morning tea and biscuits in bed while reading. Jason penned a brief note of thanks, begging his host's pardon for his early departure by explaining that duties at Falcon's Crest demanded his immediate attention.

He kept a weather eye out for possible ambushes as

he rode home via the longer but more open public roads. Both Hawken pistols were loaded, primed and thrust into his belt. He had spent the remainder of the long night cursing his own stupidity. Whatever had made him take leave of his senses, he was happy that Rachel had possessed the good judgment to stop him, even if his ego did smart at the abrupt method she had chosen to use. Who could understand the mind of a woman?

Especially this woman.

Rachel Fairchild was like no other female of his acquaintance. There was no denying that. She could be cool and logical, discussing the foibles of Lord Liverpool's government, the brilliance of Wellesley's strategy on the Peninsula or the genius of J. M. W. Turner's new exhibition at the Royal Academy. She cared nothing for female fripperies, dressed in men's clothing, and worked her land as diligently as the most industrious Maryland planters of his acquaintance. A most competent woman, yet one who was frightened of her own sensuality.

She was utterly unconcerned about what the ton thought of her, yet seemed genuinely surprised and confused that a man could find her physically attractive. If not for the Damoclean sword of matrimony poised over his neck, Jason would have relished the opportunity to teach her just how desirable she was to a man unafraid of a strong, intelligent woman. But she had been right about the folly of pursuing their mutual attraction. Inevitably, it would lead to a fate neither of them wished to embrace.

He arrived back at his own estate without incident. Whoever had taken the shot at him yesterday had given up for now, but he could not let down his guard. The assassin had tried three times, and there was no reason to believe lack of success thus far would cause him to give up. Summoning his head stableman, a shrewd old Scot named Lurey who had worked for the marquess for over forty years, Jason described the attempts on his life. He asked the man to select half a dozen servants he could vouch for and assign them to patrol the estate, watching for strangers.

Next he wrote and posted a letter to Fox and another to his grandfather, asking that the boy be allowed to pay a visit, since the marquess could collect him when he arrived for the Mountjoys' summer ball.

During the following days, Jason occupied himself with estate matters, learning the names and duties of all the servants. When he was not poring over ledgers and reviewing plans for livestock and crop sales, he rode tirelessly around his vast holdings, asking questions of his steward and tenants. There was much to learn about this earl business.

He tried not to think about Rachel Fairchild.

But at night, when he dropped exhausted into his solitary bed, she would haunt his dreams. Several of the more comely female servants had made it abundantly clear that they would welcome the new lord to their beds, but he politely ignored their invitations, something the old Jason Beaumont, with a woman in every port, would never have done. If memories of Rachel had anything to do with his self-imposed celibacy, he refused to think about it.

A week after their disastrous encounter, a servant from Harleigh brought a note from her indicating that passage for him and Fox had been arranged with a Captain Harting from Bristol, bound for Canada. The following day he received a missive bearing the impressive Cargrave crest. He tore it open and read, to his delight, that the old marquess agreed to send Fox for the proposed visit. Of course, he would be accompanied by his "tutors," Mace and company.

Jason grinned in anticipation. "Not long, Grandfather, and I will checkmate *you.*"

Chapter Eight

"I really don't know why you're in such a taking, Rachel," Harry fussed as she tried to smooth her sister's heavy hair into a neat roll at the back of her neck.

"Oh, bother the stupid hair," Rachel replied snappishly. "Just let me plait it and get it out of the way." She yanked the pins from her sore scalp and shook her long tresses over her shoulder, then began braiding them into a fat, gleaming plait. As she worked, memories of being naked in the water with Jason Beaumont and covering her breasts with her hair returned to haunt her. That, and the night following in her room . . . the kiss . . .

How could she ever forget that kiss, his hands and mouth on her breasts? She had nearly tumbled to the floor in a haze. Every night since, she had tossed and turned in her bed, restless and achy, unable to sleep. Each time she closed her eyes, visions of what had transpired between them would rise and her body would begin to throb in the most disturbing places, secret places known to no man . . . before Jason Beaumont.

Jason Beaumont. He would be arriving momentarily with Fox. Their plan was proceeding smoothly. If all went well over this weekend visit, her prospective bridegroom and his foster brother would be on a ship bound for the New World when Fox visited next. And she would return to Harleigh Hall alone. That was what she wished—was it not?

Harry's voice interrupted her confusing thoughts. "I know why you have been behaving so crustily. The earl is bringing that wild red Indian boy with him!"

"Cameron Edmund Barlow is not a wild red Indian. He's been raised quite properly, and even the marquess finds him utterly charming." Rachel did not mention that Fox had pronounced her the most beautiful lady in England. "I am looking forward to seeing him again."

"Then it must be the earl himself, the Yankee ruffian. Why, I have a mind to tell Father to send him packing. He's quite overset you with his lecherous innuendos. He—"

Rachel's snort of derision interrupted her sister's diatribe. "I've never been 'overset' in my life. Enraged, yes. Overset, no. And as for our father sending the likes of Jason Beaumont packing—even if he desired to do so, which he most certainly does not—'twould be like a field mouse challenging a mastiff."

"I scarcely think Father would approve of your calling him a field mouse," Harry said reprovingly. "Rachel, if you are so afraid of this marriage—"

"I am not afraid of Jason Beaumont." Rachel bit off each word, knowing that she was lying even as she spoke them. She was afraid, very much so, only not in the way Harry thought. What would her prim sister think if she knew Rachel was every bit as hot blooded as the wild Yankee? She would die before admitting

107

her weakness. "He is detestably arrogant and boorish, but I have a deal of skill in handling that sort of man, considering they make up the majority of the gender."

"If you can 'handle' him that easily, then why have you been so waspish the past weeks? I declare, if I had known the earl was such a dreadful fellow, I would not have tarried with dear Melvin at Brighton but rushed back to your side. You should have written me."

Rachel smiled fondly at her sister. "You and the baron were overjoyed by the Regent's invitation to the gala. I would not have you give it up. Besides, there really was nothing you could do." That, at least, was the truth.

"Nonsense. If he is a hectoring ruffian, I shall have Melvin speak most firmly with him. We will not have you wed to anyone unsuitable."

The idea of her brother-in-law speaking firmly to anyone, least of all the Yankee earl, amused Rachel. Melvin Chalmers, third Baron Widmere, made their father seem a veritable lion by comparison. His facing down Jason Beaumont was downright laughable, although she would never hurt Harry's feelings by saying so. "You really must forget the idea that the earl has intimidated me. I shall deal with the betrothal in my own way."

Harry looked up from the girondale looking glass where she had been adjusting her bonnet. "Rachel, I recognize that tone. What mischief are you planning?"

"Why, dear sister, whatever do you mean? I am planning nothing at all."

"There's a clanker if ever I heard one," Harry replied, studying the gleam in Rachel's eyes. "Before you do something precipitous and most improper, I shall take this man's measure for myself."

"Do you think Miss Fairchild's family will like me?" Fox asked Jason nervously as they rode to Harleigh Hall.

Keeping a close eye on them, Mace, the body servant and Bradley, the riding instructor, followed right behind.

The boy had been questioning Jason about Rachel since he arrived at Falconridge two days ago. He was still smitten with puppy love of the highest order. "I'm certain her sister and brother-in-law will like you, Fox," he replied, smiling. "The viscount, you've already won over."

"Yes, he was ever so nice to me when he visited Grandfather last month. I wish he had brought Miss Fairchild along, though."

"You shall see her soon enough," Jason replied.

"Grandfather says you shall be married in the early fall. I can hardly wait for the ceremony, Jace."

Fox had not asked directly about being in the wedding, but Jason knew that the boy was hoping to be included. How could he explain the situation without giving the lad too much information this soon? If Fox's infatuation with Rachel had not complicated matters, he might risk explaining their plan for escape now. But the boy had also become quite attached to the old marquess as well. What if Fox accidentally let something slip to their grandfather? Jason had tried to avoid the topic as much as possible. What a tangle this had grown into, he thought, rubbing his arm. The injury was almost healed, but if he lived to be one hundred, Jason would never forget Rachel tending it.

Searching for some way to shift the topic, he said, "Do you ever miss home?"

Fox shrugged. "Sometimes I miss Mama Beaumont and my Shawnee cousins, but there is so much to do here, and to learn. Grandfather still cheats at chess, but sometimes he lets me win. One day I suppose I shall return, but . . ."

Jason waited as the boy's voice faded away. "You're thinking of your parents, aren't you?"

"Aye. Do you still miss your father?"

Jason nodded. "You never forget those you love, but the pain of the loss fades with time. Only be patient, Fox, and you will heal."

Most of Fox's family, white and Indian, had died in the epidemic. The boy had been rootless and melancholy for the year after. It was small wonder he had stowed away on Jason's ship, looking for a grand adventure. What did surprise Jason was the bond that had grown so quickly between the boy and the marquess.

If you're only using Fox to control me, pretending to care about him, Grandfather, you shall pay dearly, dearly indeed, Jason vowed grimly, as the boy began to chatter about the brusque old marquess. Fox believed the sun rose and set on George William Beaumont.

"See ahead, there is Harleigh Hall," Jason said, pointing to the sprawling stone manor house set in the valley below them.

"Oh, it is beautiful—just perfect for Miss Fairchild," Fox replied in a hoarse whisper.

Jason watched the boy's eager face light up at the prospect of seeing his angel again. What in hell was he going to do about this whole damn mess? Just then Fox kicked his horse into a gallop, yelling, "I'll race you, Jace!"

"You're learning to cheat just like Grandfather!" Jason yelled back, allowing the boy the advantage since his small gelding was no match for Araby. As Jason spurred the big stallion after Fox, he watched his foster brother ride, bending low over the horse's neck, moving as one with the big animal. Bradley must be teaching him well, he thought. The boy had had little opportunity to ride while his parents were alive.

From the portico on the east wing of the house, Rachel and Harry watched the two riders coming down the meadow pell mell, followed by two others who did not appear to be participants in the contest. Those must be the "tutors" she and Jason would have to deal with, Rachel thought.

"They are riding quite recklessly," Harry said with a delicate shudder. She was terrified of horses and always lagged behind during a hunt, hugging her saddle in white-faced misery, although she would not miss the socializing for the world. Rachel seldom participated because she felt it a bloody unfair contest with two dozen hounds and even more riders charging after one poor beast.

" 'Tis Jason and Fox racing," Rachel said, shielding her eyes from the sun. Her heart began to drum hard, keeping cadence with the hoofbeats as the riders drew near.

"Oh, they are going too fast," Harry murmured worriedly.

Melvin came up behind his wife, placing his hands reassuringly on her shoulders as he said, "Tut, m'dear, nothing to worry about."

"I'm not so sure," Rachel said. "That stretch is overgrown with warrens. The dogs are forever chasing and digging there for rabbits." She walked swiftly to the steps and started down, muttering about sapskulled males and their recklessness. The two riders were neck and neck now, nearing the end of the drive. She yelled for them to rein in, but before either of them could respond, Fox's mount stumbled suddenly, pitching the boy over his neck. The horse went down, but rolled to its side and regained its footing. The boy did not move.

Jason turned his horse instantly and slid from his back in one smooth movement, racing to where Fox lay. He fell to his knees and reached for the boy, crying his name over and over.

111

"Don't move him!" Rachel yelled as she picked up her skirts and raced toward them. "You might make any injury worse."

Jason looked up at her, and the anguish on his face squeezed the breath from her body. As she knelt beside them, she could see his large, strong hands trembling. "Here, let me check his pulse," she said gently, moving his hand away from the boy's head so she could touch his throat. " 'Tis good and strong." She gently examined his limbs and most especially his neck. "He seems to have no broken bones, although a hard blow to the head can often cause loss of consciousness. His neck is not broken."

"I never should have let him ride so fast. He's not used to handling such a large mount. He's inexperienced, and I raced him," Jason murmured to himself, every syllable tortured.

"From what I saw, 'twas Fox who instigated the race. There is no way to keep boys from being boys, Jason," Rachel said with compassion.

"But I—"

Just then Fox emitted a weak cough and opened his eyes, blinking as he stared up into Jason's pale face.

"Fox, you're awake! Thank God!" Jason whispered hoarsely as the boy sat up.

"Sorry I fell, Jace. Is Little Chief all right?" the boy asked worriedly, looking over to where his gelding stood munching on tall meadow grasses.

"Bugger Little Chief. He's fine. 'Tis you I was worried about," Jason choked out.

Rachel watched in surprise as he took the boy in his arms and rocked back and forth, holding him as tenderly as any mother would. There were tears of relief glistening in his eyes as he finally released the lad. As was the foolish way of men, he turned his head to blink back the evidence while Fox spied Rachel and stammered embarrassed greetings, apologizing for his poor horsemanship. As she assured him that being tossed over the head of a falling horse did not in any way make him a poor rider, Mace and Bradley reined in a respectful distance away.

Bradley leaped from his horse and walked over to them, his concern apparent. The former boxer remained in the saddle wearing a bored scowl. As the riding instructor chastised the boy about the need to study the terrain over which one was galloping, Rachel studied Jason. His face was still ashen. Memories of that night in Cargrave's library flashed into her mind once more, of Jason hugging the lad with such fondness. He loved Fox as if he were his own flesh and blood.

To rescue Fox, Jason would even marry me. The thought stung. Repressing it, she stood up, brushing grass stains from her rumpled skirt. She looked a positive fright, rumpled and sweating in the noon heat. Before she'd met Jason Beaumont, her appearance never bothered her in the least.

Fox, too, jumped up, looking at her with worshipful eyes. "I apologize for causing you distress, Miss Fairchild," he said gravely. "May I escort you to the house?"

Rachel nodded, smiling at the boy and giving him her hand. "I would be honored, Master Fox."

"For someone lying stretched out like the dead moments ago, you've recovered nicely," Jason said with mild irritation kindled by concern.

"I just had the wind knocked out of me, Jace."

"It might be wise for you to spend a day or so close to the house and off of horses, just to be certain there are no lingering effects from your fall," Rachel cautioned. The boy sighed in resignation, agreeing reluctantly.

As they started to walk, her eyes met Jason's for a

113

moment and she sensed his disquietude. *He knows that I saw what he perceives to be weakness.*

Men were such beetleheads.

Her irritation was forgotten when she realized that she had to attend to Fox's "tutors." She gave them instructions about gathering the horses and taking them to her head stableman, who would escort them to the servants' quarters and see that they were fed and given a place to sleep for the night.

By this time Harry and Melvin had made their way from the portico to the edge of the garden. As hostess, Rachel made introductions between her family and her guests. She had been certain that once Fox saw her much prettier sister, he would forget about her. That did not turn out to be the case at all.

All through dinner he was unfailingly polite to Harry, but kept his attention fixed on Rachel. So did Jason. The boy's adulation was balm to her confidence—always lacking in social situations—but the man's disturbing blue eyes on her were unnerving in the extreme. Was he pleased or unhappy with her? She wished she had let Harry fix her hair and select a more flattering dress than the simple tan cambric she had insisted was good enough. Until she met Jason Beaumont, Rachel Fairchild had never given a fig about her looks.

What was happening to her?

A rooster crowed loudly at the fuzzy gold ball of the sun inching its way over the treetops beyond the stables. It was going to be another sweltering day, Rachel thought as she made her way to Reddy's stall. She had dressed for the heat, wearing her oldest breeches and shirt, and had pinned her hair up off her neck, covering it with a perfect horror of a straw hat given her by a retired stableman. The frayed brim kept the sun at bay on days such as this one.

The big bay greeted her with a friendly snort, eager for a romp before the heat set in. No one was about. Even the stablemen did not begin their labors this early, but it had always been the best time of the day for Rachel. She had several fields to check on and wanted to get the chore done before anyone else was awake in the manor house.

Like their father, Harriet was a late sleeper, as was the baron—not that they would present any particular problem. Melvin would bury his nose in the London newspapers and her sister would spend hours on her toilette. Rachel had checked on Fox and found him sleeping peacefully. His breathing was regular and his color good, so the tumble yesterday, while frightening, had apparently done no serious harm. She intended to keep a close watch on the boy for the duration of his visit just to be certain.

But what of Jason? Somehow she could not imagine him lazing away a beautiful morning abed. They would have to spend some time together during this visit. After all, the reason for this charade was to convince her father that the two of them were becoming resigned to the match, and even attracted to each other. How could she pretend such a thing?

Because it is true, a voice inside her head whispered.

The disquieting image of Jason holding Fox in his arms filled her mind. He was more than a smooth seducer, and nothing like the title-hungry Yankee she had imagined him to be. But he did not want to marry her. That was one fact she surely knew—but did she want to marry him? Her thoughts whirled about in her head until the big bay nuzzled her, hoping for an apple.

"You great beggar, you," she said, giving the horse's nose a pat as she pulled the treat from her pocket and

115

fed it to him. "Let's see about getting you saddled up so you can earn your apples."

She stepped outside the stall and reached for a bridle hanging on the wall, but just as she took hold of it, an unfamiliar voice broke the dawn stillness with the guttural harshness of the London slums. "Wal, wot 'ave we 'ere now? Ain't ye a fine-lookin' farm gel. That arse is prime, specially in them breeches."

Rachel turned to see the large, battered face of Fox's "body servant," Mace, leering at her. He advanced with swaggering steps and placed one huge meaty paw on her arm. She yanked free with a snarled oath. His ugly slash of a mouth opened in a wide grin that revealed blackened and broken teeth. "I likes 'um that fights, yes I do," he said, seizing her again and yanking her against his huge body.

" 'Tis a good thing, for you will rue this day," she gritted out, nearly gagging from the stench of his rotten teeth. He obviously did not recognize the viscount's daughter from yesterday, much less the splendidly tricked-out woman she had been at Cargrave's ball. "I am Harleigh's daughter," she said in an iron voice.

Mace laughed, fondling her breast as his scarred fist ripped the fabric. " 'Arleigh's gel dressed like th' sorriest stable 'and? Ye takes me fer a bloody fool. I seen 'er, and she don't look nothin' like ye."

She twisted in his grip, angling toward the center of the stable where the saddle rack stood three feet high. There would be no reasoning with the half-witted swine. *If only I can—*

Her thoughts were cut short as Mace's body suddenly crumpled forward, nearly carrying her down with him. Rachel jumped clear as Jason landed another kidney punch to the boxer's back. Incredibly, Mace managed to stay on his feet, though he was gasping in agony as he turned to face his attacker. But before he could put up those menacing fists to deliver a blow, Jason seized his left arm and twisted, pivoting on one foot while slamming the other into Mace's knee.

The giant's knee buckled, and he went down in an ungainly heap. Then with blurring speed the earl used the toe of his boot to deal a sharp kick to his opponent's temple. Mace flopped over as limp as a wet rag, out cold.

Just as Jason turned to Rachel, Bradley entered the stable and froze at the sight before him. The marquess had made it clear to the riding instructor that Jason might attempt to kidnap Fox. He and Mace had been charged with preventing that at all costs.

Bradley dashed forward, attempting to draw a pistol from his coat pocket, but the earl was too quick for him. Before Bradley could pull back the hammer, Jason was across the stable floor, knocking the weapon from his hand and delivering a sharp punch to his midsection, followed by another to his jaw, sending him sprawling into the hay.

The entire sequence of events had taken but a few seconds. The Yankee stood between his two felled opponents, not even winded from the exercise. Ignoring the obviously unconscious riding instructor, he made his way over to the boxer to be certain the far larger man would not be getting up any time soon. Rachel was slack-jawed with amazement as he stepped over Mace's prostrate form and his eyes swept her from head to toe.

"Dear God, did he hurt you?" He could see that her shirt was torn and an ugly bruise would soon form on her shoulder. He wanted to kick the bastard lying on the floor another time just for good measure, but the string of oaths issuing from his damsel in distress stopped him cold. "Are you all right?" he asked again, growing uneasily certain that her ire was directed at him, not Mace.

"You brick-headed, maggoty-brained, addledpated Yankee! I could have handled that ox myself!"

Her hands were fisted at her sides, her breasts heaving with the exertion of excoriating him, and her face was flushed with fury. She was utterly magnificent. Jason looked at her in consternation, alternately angry that she would be so ungrateful, and bemused because he found her so attractive. "You could have handled him, could you? Ah yes, how foolish of me not to have realized. What I mistook for brutish pawing was really a quaint form of British cowering, by Jove!"

She stepped closer to him, her eyes still blazing. "Don't mock me, you—you—oh!" she gasped suddenly, doubling over and starting to fall to the stable floor.

Had the hellion fainted? It would certainly not be in character for the Rachel Fairchild he knew. She must have been hurt in the struggle, he thought as he bent down to catch her in his arms. Then he froze.

"Now, Sir Jason the Bold, Rescuer of Damsels, I would advise you to straighten up very slowly," she purred, holding a great fistful of his hair with one hand.

Jason looked down to where her other hand held a small, wickedly sharp stiletto to his throat. When he did not move quickly enough, she applied a bit of pressure, and a tiny bead of blood rolled down his neck.

Chapter Nine

Jason did as she ordered.

"I shall talk. You will listen."

Although his eyes blazed back at her, he remained silent.

"Good, you possess a few shreds of common sense," she said, releasing her tight grip on his hair but keeping the dagger to his throat. "I do not require rescuing. Not today, not ever. I had my own 'fight instructor,' a canny old groom who used to be a Whitechapel cutpurse before my mother gave him respectable work in an attempt to reform him.

"But that is neither here nor there. The plain fact is that your precipitous method of handling this stupid affair has just destroyed any hope we had for you and Fox to slip away to Bristol. After this buffoonery, the marquess will see that he's guarded by someone significantly more adept than yon ox."

As she slipped the knife back into her boot, Jason

seethed. "Might I suggest that 'yon ox' here would not have accosted you in the first place if you dressed the part of lady of the manor instead of stable hand?"

"Leave it to a marplot such as you to trowel on insult after slopping on injury," she snapped, angered as much by his low opinion of her as by the ruination of their scheme.

"Speaking of injury, Countess, that ox would not have given a fig for your fainting spell. Tricks like that only work on men who care about women."

She stilled for a moment; then all her indignation evaporated. "All right, Jason, I confess you are right. I was careless, and once he seized me with those great tree-trunk arms, I most probably would have had a difficult time reaching my knife."

A crooked grin spread over his face. "You do keep a man off balance, Countess. I give you that."

As he smiled at her, her heart turned over. "I've nicked you. Damn my temper!" Without realizing what she was doing, Rachel reached up to his neck where a bead of blood trickled toward his shirt collar. She blotted it with her finger, then sucked on the fingertip as she stared into his eyes.

Jason groaned and pulled her into his arms, kissing her with a hunger he was unable to hide. Rachel returned the heated kiss, opening her lips to his questing tongue, letting her own tongue dart inside his mouth and taste of him. Soon she, too, was moaning low in her throat as their bodies fused together. This kissing business was getting easier and more pleasurable with practice. In fact, there was nothing she would love half so much as continuing it, but Bradley chose that moment to loose a faint groan of his own, one decidedly not from passion.

Rachel and Jason broke apart, breathless and dazed by the sudden return to grim reality. *What was I think-*

ing? she castigated herself, unable to meet his burning blue eyes.

Jason considered what he had just done. Damn it all to hell, she had bewitched him. What else could account for his grabbing her and kissing her right in the middle of a stable filled with his grandfather's men? He stepped away from her and checked on Bradley, who had lapsed once again into full unconsciousness. When he turned back to her, Rachel had composed herself as well.

Ignoring what had just passed between them, he said, "Now 'tis my turn to confess, Rachel. You're right about my blunder. The marquess will never let Fox return here once he learns what I did to Mace. He'll be watching me like a falcon searching for field mice." He cursed, combing his fingers through his hair as he paced beside Mace's still form. "We could take Fox and head for Bristol right now."

Rachel swallowed the hollow ache welling up deep inside her and replied matter-of-factly, "We cannot. The ship on which I booked passage for you is en route to Dublin and not scheduled to return for weeks."

"I was afraid you'd say something like that," he said glumly. The date of the wedding was drawing uncomfortably close.

"I shall simply have to come up with an alternate plan," she said.

"Well, until you do, let us revive poor Bradley so he can help me throw Mace Bings on a wagon and send him as far from here as possible."

As Rachel rode about the fields later that day, she mulled over the change in their plans. It would be impossible to wrest Fox from the old marquess's clutches as things stood. Her father had just received a note that morning from Cargrave announcing his safe arrival at

Falcon's Crest. The Mountjoys' ball was tonight. As soon as Bradley and his young charge returned to Jason's manor house, the riding instructor would be duty bound to inform his employer that Jason had easily bested him and the boxer.

What else could she do to prevent the marriage from taking place?

Niggling at the back of her mind was an alternate possibility, one so shocking that Rachel had been loath to consider it . . . until now. She preferred to remain unwed. Failing that, she required a husband whom she could control. A man who was the polar opposite of Jason Beaumont.

And yet she could not deny the intense attraction she felt toward the arrogant Yankee earl. He was just as obviously attracted to her. If not for being blackmailed into marriage, he would have tried to bed her, she was certain. Unfortunately, she was equally certain that once he accomplished the seduction, he would move on to his next conquest without giving her another thought. Rachel realized that his side of their physical attraction was just that—purely physical. But what did she feel?

"Damnably confused," she muttered in reply to her own question. For all his faults, Jason could be trusted to keep his word if he gave it. He was not the boorish lout she had first believed him to be. Besides being strikingly handsome, witty, and charming when he chose to be, the earl possessed deeper qualities. He was loyal to his friends, for whom he had sacrificed the seafaring life he loved. He was devoted to a half-caste orphan, caring for Fox as if the boy were his own brother. He had even been willing to honor his bargain with the duplicitous marquess if the issue of their marriage could be resolved.

One way to resolve it was . . . to go through with it.

There, she had admitted the idea to herself. "I must be taking leave of my senses." She patted Reddy absently, deep in thought about her undeniable attraction to Jason. What if they could reach some accommodation? She turned the thought over and over as she rode aimlessly through the fields, waving absently to her tenants, totally unaware of the condition of the crops she was supposedly inspecting.

If they did wed, his grandfather would believe he had won. He would relax his guard over Fox and it would be easy for them to spirit the boy away. Jason could take him back to America, leaving her behind. She would be free of her father's endless matchmaking and separated from her husband by an ocean. She could live her life as she chose, and he would enjoy the same freedom.

There were many complications to this daring idea, not the least of which was mustering the courage to suggest it to Jason. It was likely he would laugh in her face if she did so. Still, the thought would not leave her. So many problems would be solved. She did not let herself consider how many others would be created.

Fox patted Little Chief as his horse ate an apple from his hand. "You deserve a fine reward after such a great ride," he said, recalling the thrill of sailing over several low hedge rows during the early-morning ride he and Jason had taken under Bradley's watchful eye. Both adults had been exceedingly cautious about letting him jump the gelding after his spill the day before, but he had cajoled them until Jason agreed.

Convincing his riding instructor was a more difficult matter, but he had finally carried the day. Odd, but there seemed to be a bit of antagonism between the men. Bradley had a swollen jaw, almost as if someone had given him what Grandfather called a right proper facer. Had the riding instructor and Jace fought? He wondered if it had anything to do with Mace's leaving. When Fox came downstairs that morning, he had been informed that the man had been discharged by the earl. Jace refused to explain why, and since Fox disliked the boxer, he had not pressed the issue. But he did rather like Bradley and hoped the riding instructor would not be let go as well.

Little Chief distracted him by nuzzling his cheek, hoping for another treat. "That's enough for you, you rascal. We have to ride back to Jace's house to meet Grandfather soon, and you don't want to be so full that you pop your saddle girth, do you?"

"That would not be good, for certain," Rachel said as she walked her big bay into the stable.

"Oh, good afternoon, Miss Fairchild," Fox said shyly. He was surprised to see her dressed in men's breeches and shirt, but even so, she was still the most beautiful lady he could ever imagine. When she began to unsaddle Reddy herself, he rushed over. "M-may I help you?"

Rachel smiled. "I'd appreciate that very much." The boy placed the stirrups over the saddle and reached for the cinch strap to unfasten it. "You seem to know your way about horses."

"Until I came to England I never had much chance, but I always loved horses. Jace took me riding a few times, but he was away at sea a lot by the time I grew old enough to really ride. All because of this stupid old war. I want it to be over."

"Do you miss your home in America?" she asked.

"Oh, I want to go back some day, but now that you and Jace are getting married, I'm just as content to stay in England. Grandfather says I can spend part of the time with him and part of the time with you . . . that is, if you don't mind."

His expression was so wistful, it squeezed her heart.

How could she tell him that his beloved Jace did not wish to marry her? Best to allow Jason to explain the situation to his young charge during their voyage back to America. "I would love to have you spend as much time with me as you wish, whenever you wish," she replied honestly.

"Then . . . we're friends, Miss Fairchild?"

"Yes, we are," she replied with a big smile. "And just to prove it, I give you leave to call me Rachel."

Fox gulped in surprise. "Do you mean it, Miss Fair— Rachel?" he asked, daring to do as she bade him.

She smiled again. "Yes, I most certainly do, if I can call you Fox? Now, you grab the blanket when I swing the saddle off Reddy's back."

As they worked, putting away the tack and rubbing down the horse, she drew out the shy boy, getting him to talk about his life in Maryland. Of course, he could not describe any event without mentioning his hero Jason. He boasted of his foster brother's exploits on land and sea.

"My mother's people call Jace the Moccasin. It's a name of high honor among the Shawnee."

"Really?" she questioned, puzzled. "I shouldn't imagine being called a shoe to be much of an honor."

Fox laughed. "No, not that kind of moccasin. A water moccasin." At her blank look, he explained, "That's one of the most deadly snakes in the wilderness. Poisonous and swift as lightning when it strikes."

"Oh, and he earned this name, did he?" She could think of a number of occasions when he'd behaved like a snake, no doubt about it!

"Yes, he did." Fox warmed to his tale. "When he was fifteen, Jace came to live with my mother's sister and her husband for a season. You see, he wanted to learn the Shawnee way just like his father had before him. One day while the men and older boys were off hunting, a band of Cherokee raided our village and carried off my aunt Singing Wind because my uncle Otter is a great chief and they wanted to lure him into a trap. But Uncle Otter was too smart for them.

"Instead of leading all his warriors into an ambush, he waited and sent out scouts to learn where they were holding her. Then he and Jace sneaked past the sentries into their camp while the foolish Cherokee slept. My brother cut my aunt free, while my uncle signaled his men to attack as soon as she was safe. But one of the enemy awakened and attacked Jace. Jace buried his hatchet in the warrior's head as fast and clean as could be. Uncle Otter told me it split his skull in half right down to his neck," the boy said with relish.

Rachel turned pale green. The image of brains and blood flashed before her eyes. She'd seen a man's skull burst open in a riding accident when she was little older than Fox. It had not been a pretty sight.

"And Jace took three more scalps before the raiders were driven into the woods by my uncle's warriors."

"Scalps?" she gulped, swallowing her gorge. Perhaps she had better reconsider the idea of actually going through with this marriage.

"Yes. He struck with such deadly speed that my uncle gave him the name Moccasin. They sing about him around the campfires to this day," the boy said proudly.

Not wanting to crush his enthusiasm, Rachel squelched her repulsion and changed the subject. "Soon I shall have to get ready for the Mountjoys' ball tonight, and you—"

"Will have to ride back to Falcon's Crest with Bradley and me," the subject of the boy's paean said as he sauntered into the stable. "Why don't you go find Bradley and have him help you saddle his horse?"

"All right. I was just telling Rachel how you got your Shawnee name. Maybe after you're married and you

126

come to America for a visit, you can take her to meet Aunt Singing Wind and Uncle Otter."

"Perhaps," Jason replied, amused by the greenish cast of Rachel's complexion. "Now off with you, or I shall be late for the ball tonight." As soon as Fox dashed out the door, he turned to Rachel with a grin. "Now you are utterly convinced that I belong back with people your fine English sensibilities consider savages."

"You were just a boy. Not to be blamed for . . . for . . ." She swallowed, remembering Amos Chidley's brains smashed against the paving bricks after that riding accident. "Fox possesses considerable skill as a storyteller."

"All boys that age are bloodthirsty little savages, red and white. A pity you never had brothers, else you'd have learned that."

"I scarcely possess a weak stomach," Rachel said, raising her chin a notch.

"And you're exercising great Christian charity toward me," he replied, chuckling. Odd, but instead of being angered by her "civilized" prejudices, he found her willingness to excuse him endearing. "Allow me to give you some reassurance regarding the scalps."

"Oh, and what, pray, could that be?" she asked, proud of the steadiness of her voice.

"Contrary to what Fox believes, I did not take them," he whispered conspiratorially. Rachel blinked. He suddenly wondered if telling her the rest of the story was such a wise idea. *I must be growing soft in the head over this witch.* That was the only place he grew soft while in Rachel Fairchild's presence, he realized wryly. "You see, I was so concerned with getting Singing Wind out of the enemy camp that I never even thought about . . . er, exercising my warrior's prerogatives. Fortunately, or unfortunately, Otter took care of that. After the battle, he collected the trophies for me."

127

Rachel was beginning to see a bit of humor to the grisly tale in spite of her earlier revulsion. He appeared to be embarrassed by the whole thing. "Oh? And what did you do with these trophies?"

"Remember, I was only fifteen and didn't want to appear any less than a full-fledged warrior."

Now she was certain of his discomfiture. "So?" she prompted.

"Like an idiot, I told the warriors my mother would not let me keep them." When Rachel burst out laughing, he felt his face heating. How had he managed to turn the tables on himself so completely? "I am so pleased my story amuses you. I explained that my mother had a dream warning her that if I kept scalps, it would bring her misfortune."

"And they believed this?"

"The Shawnee are great believers in medicine dreams—with some good reason. Only a couple of years ago, a great Shawnee chief predicted not only the appearance of a comet but an earthquake as well."

"And both occurred?" she asked incredulously.

"Within weeks of when Tecumseh said they would, yes. Anyway, our band respected my mother's wishes, and Otter kept the scalps for me."

"I trust you have not had cause to take any others since?" she asked, only half jesting.

He fingered her long plait of chocolate-colored hair consideringly, holding it fast when she tried to move back a step. "Not until recently, Countess."

As soon as Jason and Fox returned to Falconridge, the boy excitedly dashed to the house to greet his "grandfather." Jason still could not help wondering at the bond that had formed between the old man and the boy. He was also alarmed, for a number of reasons. It greatly complicated his plans for returning Fox to America, but more importantly, he feared that the marquess could be using Fox as a mere pawn on his chessboard. Once he'd achieved his endgame, he might discard the lad without a care.

If appearances were to be believed, that was not so, but no one knew better than Jason just how devious the old man could be. He tried to reassure himself that in the long run it would not signify, since Fox would be sailing home in a matter of weeks. Children had short memories, and once he was reunited with "Mama Beaumont" and his Shawnee relations, "Grandfather" would quickly be relegated to the past.

Jason had no more than set foot in the foyer of his manor house when a servant announced in tones of hushed awe that the Marquess of Cargrave wished to see him in the study. Commanded his presence was what the old goat really meant. Without bothering to change from his riding clothes, Jason strode to the study. He could hear Fox explaining about his adventures at Harleigh Hall. Standing quietly in the doorway, Jason observed the exchange, paying particular attention to the way the marquess listened, interjecting questions now and again, but mostly just enjoying the lad's youthful enthusiasm. Genuine affection shone from those harsh gray eyes, no doubt of it.

Clearing his throat to make his presence known, Jason strode into the room. "You summoned me, m'lord?" he asked without preamble.

"Ah, Jason, good to see you, too, lad." Then turning to Fox with a jovial wink, he said, "Your brother has not a fragment of your fine manners. You really must tutor him."

"Allow him to remain with me at Falconridge and he can do so," Jason said with a gleam of a dare in his eyes, but the old man responded just as he expected.

"Balderdash! I have plans for Master Fox at Cargrave

Hall. His new French tutor has just arrived, and Lady Belmot has just whelped." Lady Bel was the old man's water spaniel. "Six puppies, and," he added, turning to Fox, "you shall have pick of the litter."

"Oh, Grandfather, really? I love Lady Bel already. One of her puppies for my very own would be wonderful." Collecting himself, he bowed politely and said, "Thank you, Grandfather."

Giving the boy's hair a fond tousle, the marquess laughed. "Well done, lad, well done. Now off with you. Your brother and I have business to discuss."

As soon as Fox had closed the door behind him, Cargrave fixed his grandson with a shrewd stare. "Fox informs me that I shall have to find a new bodyguard. Since I was the one who employed him, I cannot credit that Bings would have allowed you to dismiss him so easily."

"He couldn't argue. He was unconscious. I'll let Bradley impart the details, but suffice it to say the fellow was every bit as unsuitable as I warned you he would be. He attacked Rachel in the stable, thinking her to be a serving wench."

The old man stood up abruptly. "Good God! The gel wasn't harmed, was she?"

"No, but it was probably better that I dealt with him than she. The 'gel' carries a stiletto in her boot," Jason said dryly.

Cargrave laughed heartily. "She does have spunk, that one. Always liked her best of Hugh's daughters. The other two are flibbertigibbets, but Rachel has a head on her shoulders. Reminds me of Mathilda."

Considering that the late marchioness had been scarcely five feet tall and in her youth had possessed pale red hair, the comparison did not seem apt to Jason, but he knew the marquess had doted on her. "Rachel scarce has Grandmother's sweet disposition."

130

"Ha! Just shows what the young know. In her day, my lady wife was known far and wide for the sharpness of her tongue as well as her mind. Took some taming, she did, but in the end, 'twas well worth it. Ah, the battles we had," he said fondly.

Ignoring the old man's reverie, Jason said, "I assume you intend to hire another 'bodyguard' for Fox. This time, at least have his references verified, lest he shoot the majordomo and steal the family silver."

"Eh, speaking of shooting, what is it I hear about someone mistaking you for a deer?" Cargrave's impassive expression did not completely mask his concern. "I'm given to understand you were fired upon right here on Falconridge land."

Jason shrugged. "The first time, I was with Rachel. The assassin could have been aiming at her."

"That is not amusing—and what do you mean by 'the first time'?"

The old man was awake on every suit. Jason cursed himself for his careless slip of the tongue. He did not want to be encumbered by yet more bodyguards watching over him as well as Fox. "I chanced upon Rachel in the woods adjoining our properties the first week I was here. The shots probably came from poachers with dreadful aim."

"Hugh informed me you arrived at his home for dinner one evening bleeding like a stuck hog. Are you telling me that was a poacher, too?" His keen gray eyes skewered his grandson as he waited for a reply.

"No. Most probably, someone intended to shoot me that time," he conceded. "I suspect Forrestal. He was rejected in his suit for Rachel and has taken a strong dislike to me over it. Drum is looking into the matter for me now. I'm certain we can handle it discreetly, and no more will come of it."

Cargrave snorted. "Etherington's heir is as worthless

131

as teats on a bull. Hugh and I laughed over his suit, and he dismissed it out of hand. Boy runs with a worthless crowd. Gambling and carousing without a care for their family names. Surprised the Mountjoys allow their youngest to spend time with them."

Jason lifted an eyebrow with interest. "Do they, now?" He remembered Robin Mountjoy from the summer he'd spent in England. The two of them had been cast together because they were close in age, a year or two apart. The youngest of six siblings, he was thin, quiet and easily led.

"They may have taken him in hand. At least, the boy's safely ensconced here in the country until the fall Season. He'll be in attendance at the ball tonight. Speaking of which, I expect you and Hugh's gel to do us proud. No more of this exchanging insults and dumping glasses of champagne . . . else I shall hire a dozen more like Mace Bings and set them to guarding you as if you were the bloody crown jewels!"

Jason sighed. The old man always knew when and how to apply coercion.

"He is most charming, I must say, especially considering he was raised in America," Harriet said, giving her toilette a final inspection at the cheval glass in her sister's bedroom. "They do all manner of strange things over there. 'Tis what comes of not having an hereditary peerage to ensure that society is held to its proper course."

Rachel wondered what Harry would say if she related the tale of the scalps to her sister, but, not wanting to revive her after a fainting spell, she decided against it. "The earl is . . . unusual, to say the least."

"Ah, and ever so handsome. Is that why you have taken such pains with your appearance for a change?" Harry inspected her tall, elegant sister who was wearing a new gown. The dressmaker had brought it for a final fitting only yesterday. The deep moss green mull was a perfect foil for her sun-tinted complexion, and she had consented to wear the family emeralds, or at least a small portion of them, a pair of delicate earbobs and the lightest of the three necklaces in the collection.

Rachel shrugged, not wanting to admit even to herself that interest in Jason Beaumont had motivated her to order new clothing. "The mull is far cooler than the old taffeta I usually wear to the Mountjoys' ball. Come, 'tis past time we were leaving. Father and Melvin are most likely pacing downstairs."

"Well, I believe you have done quite splendidly for yourself. An earl, heir to the Cargrave title and charming enough to lure birds from the trees. He could not take his eyes from you last night at dinner, you know."

"Do not be ridiculous. He did nothing of the kind."

"You would have taken note of it had you paid him the slightest attention. 'Twas really quite rude, Rachel, devoting exclusive attention to the boy. What an odd American notion, allowing children to eat at table with adults, but none the less, the Yankee earl will certainly come up to scratch."

"Jason wants this match no more than do I," Rachel snapped.

"Then I would say that the banns have been posted none too soon a'tall," Harry replied with a titter, following as her sister stalked from the bedroom.

During the long ride to the Mountjoy manor house, Rachel ignored the banal conversation among her family members, nodding when her agreement was solicited. As the Fairchild coach bounced and swayed over rutted roads in the dusty heat of early evening, she grew increasingly preoccupied. Everyone would expect her to dance frequently with the earl now that their betrothal had been officially announced. She would have to endure hours of smiling and posturing.

And dancing with *him*.

Was Harry right? Had she taken extra pains with her appearance to impress Jason? No, she decided; certainly not. After all, he had made it clear that he was quite interested in her when she wore muddy riding togs . . . or nothing at all. Yet she could not forget how it had felt to whirl about the floor in his arms, their steps so perfectly matched. Almost as perfectly as their heartbeats.

She shifted nervously on the plush seat cushion, trying to suppress the heated memories of other times when she had felt his heart beat in time with hers. Being in his arms tonight was not a good idea at all. Whenever she was close to him, whenever he touched her, she lost her ability to think coherently. A perfect example of her weakness was this afternoon, when he had reeled her in by her plait, then looked deeply into her eyes and made such an insulting comment.

Scalp her, indeed! And she, ninny that he reduced her to, had been unable to think of a single setdown. If he had tried to kiss her instead of releasing her, she was quite certain she'd have allowed it—nay, have participated eagerly as she had done before. But he'd at least saved her that indignity. Instead he had initiated a discussion about how they were to proceed with their plans to convince the marquess and the viscount that they would go through with the marriage. They'd agreed to be civil tonight.

That meant he would have to touch her.

And she would have to allow it.

When the coach pulled into the Mountjoy drive, Rachel was immersed in her troubling reverie, no surer of how she would manage the evening than she had been hours earlier. The driver reined in the horses, and the

lumbering old vehicle lurched to a halt. Blinking in surprise, she collected herself and waited as her father and
brother-in-law climbed from the coach to assist the ladies, but when she leaned out the door with gloved
hand outstretched, it was not the viscount or the baron
who took it, but the earl.

"I recognized the Harleigh crest and came to pay my
respects, Countess," Jason murmured. "Might as well
make our entrance together and get on with it."

She could feel the heat of his hand through her
gloves! Ignoring the catch in her throat, she allowed
him to help her from the coach with a regal tilt of her
head. He released her and assisted Harry, who began
chattering immediately, allowing Rachel to collect her
thoughts.

"How kind of you, m'lord. I was just saying to Melvin
what a delight it was to make your acquaintance during
dinner last night, was I not, my dear?" Melvin got in no
more than a nod before Harriet turned back to the earl.
"Do note how fashion-conscious you have made our
dear Rachel. I have tried for years and years, but you
have—"

"I do not think the earl is in the least interested in
fashion, Harry," Rachel interjected with a telling look
directed at her sister. When she turned back to Jason,
the amused smile on his face made her wish him and
her garrulous sister to perdition.

He offered her his arm with a gallant flourish, then
bent to whisper in her ear, "You did not have to go to
such a bother for me, Countess, as I know how much
you detest fashion fallalls."

"Do not preen yourself. I did nothing whatever to
please you," she replied through gritted teeth as they
ascended the stairs and waited their turn to be announced.

"Ah, how you disillusion me. Or should I believe your

sister, hmmm? Dear Harriet is quite knowledgeable about matters of the heart."

Rachel scoffed. "But one must first possess a heart, an organ you lack."

"Then why, when I hold you close, does something in my chest beat so fiercely? Or is it perhaps yours responding to me?"

Rachel was saved from an indelicate reply by a footman, who announced the Earl of Falconridge and his betrothed, the Honorable Miss Rachel Fairchild of Harleigh. As faint sounds of the orchestra wafted on the summer air, they made their first entrance as a couple.

Chapter Ten

Balls in the country during summer were far less formal affairs than those given in London. The marriage mart was ostensibly closed between the "Season" in the spring and the "Little Season" in the fall. Not that many a mother who'd been disappointed during her daughter's come-out would fail to keep a sharp eye out for eligible bachelors at any summer affair. But the frenetic tension of the city gave way to more casual merriment. Oswald and Edwina Mountjoy, Duke and Duchess of Kensington, always gave the first and best-attended soiree of the summer, inviting all their neighbors for miles around, from the highest-ranking members of the peerage right down to the local gentry. Dressed in summer finery, no one ever missed it.

The orchestra played gaily as ladies chattered and waved their fans in vain attempts to move the thick summer air. Those fortunate enough to have spent spring in the Great Wen shared the juiciest gossip with

137

their country sisters. For the gentlemen, talk turned from politics to horse racing. Jason only half listened to the conversation between his cousin Roger and Squire Abingdon as they discussed the merits of the squire's new thoroughbred, which would be racing in an upcoming local contest. The two men, friends since childhood, droned on about gait and body conformation and the merits of adding wheat bran to the oats in equine diet.

Jason's attention kept drifting across the room to where his "countess" stood talking animatedly with a paunchy old man who had the sun-blistered face and callused hands of a serious farmer.

She would rather discuss crops than gossip with her sister and her friends, he realized. At the opposite side of the room he could see a group of young matrons and their younger charges clustered around Harriet, giggling and whispering delightedly. Rachel's choice of conversation topic appealed to him. He had always appreciated women with level heads and a strong dose of practicality. No one would ever accuse her of "having apartments to let," Drum's quaint way of describing vacuity. Even so, Jason was forced to admit that it was not solely her unconventional mind that drew him, but her unconventional beauty as well.

He studied her while she was unaware of his perusal, a habit he had caught himself falling into of late. Whether she had tended to her appearance to please him or not, she looked especially delectable tonight. The deep mossy green of her gown complemented the healthy golden glow of her skin—and a great deal of skin was revealed by the low-cut neckline and short cap sleeves. Some women resorted to dampening the cloth to make it cling to their curves, but she did not require the artifice. Her slightest movement revealed the curve of full breasts, slim hips, delicious long legs.

She was of a height with the majority of the men in the room, towering over many in her high-heeled slippers. That heavy mane of dark hair added more inches, arranged in a simple Grecian coil at the crown of her head. A few curling tendrils caressed her nape and cheeks. His fingers curled at his sides as he fought the urge to walk over to her and touch the silky wisps.

Before he could reconsider, Jason turned to Roger and said, "If you'll excuse me, I believe Miss Fairchild favors waltzes."

"Eh? Ain't they playing a reel?" the squire bellowed to Roger.

Leaning close so his hard-of-hearing companion could understand him, Dalbert replied in a loud voice, "It don't matter what they play or if they play a'tall. My cousin's bewitched by his bride-to-be."

Jason could hear them as he wended his way through the dancers. In fact, he was certain half the room could. *Was* he bewitched? The question had been bothering him ever since that interlude in the water. His dreams had been plagued by visions of Rachel wet and naked, returning his kisses with hesitant ardor. And there was little hesitance in her ardor the other night in her bedroom. That had been a near disaster. He was reluctantly grateful that she had possessed the good sense to stop it before they were both ensnared in the marquess's trap.

Yes, he desired her. But that hardly meant he was besotted with the wench! He pushed the disturbing images aside, reassuring himself that if Roger and the others believed he and Rachel were smitten, it would help convince her father and the marquess that it was so. And that was the ultimate goal. Was it not?

When he reached her side, the older man she had been conversing with excused himself with a self-conscious grin, leaving the two young people to themselves. "I told Cousin Roger you loved to waltz."

"But they aren't playing a waltz," she replied.

"So said Squire Abingdon," he said with a grin. "But they will sooner or later. In the meanwhile . . ." He extended his hand to her.

Rachel did not want to take it, really she did not. Or so she kept telling herself. Every touch had become torture . . . but such sweet torture that she could not resist. And, after all, they had to convince the marquess of their acquiescence. That was the ultimate goal. Was it not?

As they walked to the edge of the dance floor, waiting their turn to join in the next set of the reel, he murmured in her ear, "The emeralds match your eyes."

Rachel blinked. "Have you gone muzzy-brained, m'lord? My eyes are hazel brown, not green." His breath so close to her cheek sent a tiny shiver down her spine.

"Tonight they are as green as this," he said, brushing his fingertips past the teardrop-cut stone dangling from her earlobe. "The jewelry complements you."

"It has been in the Fairchild family for generations. Part of my dowry. Would you marry me for a pile of emeralds, m'lord?" She was flirting! What on earth had come over her? What would he think?

Jason grinned at her as they swung into the dance. "Perhaps. You know I was a privateer. I've a weakness for booty . . . and beauty."

"Flummery," she replied, caught off guard by his response. He was flirting back! But that was the plan, she reminded herself, looking over to where the old marquess watched them with gleaming slate-colored eyes. Her father had gone into the card room for a game of whist, leaving his crafty co-conspirator behind to observe. Cargrave looked very well pleased.

They finished the set, flushed and breathless from swift-moving exertion in the hot, stuffy room. French windows on two sides of the huge ballroom were opened to let in the cooling night breezes, but with the press of people the fresh air did little but cause the candles on the chandeliers overhead to flicker. Rachel could feel her heart racing as a tiny bead of perspiration trickled between her breasts. Was Jason as affected by this dangerous game they were playing as she?

"I do believe I saw Grandfather's foot tapping in time to the music," he said to her.

For Rachel it was like a dousing with cold water. Of course. The plan. Jason was only playing at being a suitor for Cargrave's benefit. She had to keep reminding herself of that fact. "I noted it, too," she replied coolly, grateful that she had not yet had to endure the intimacy of waltzing with Jason. But before the evening was over she would have to do so. " 'Tis a bit warm. Let's go out into the garden," she suggested as the orchestra prepared to resume playing.

He nodded, offering her his arm. Together they strolled out onto a flagstone patio lit by torches. Scattered in the dim light, small clusters of people laughed and talked while servants bustled about delivering cooling liquid libations to them. Here and there in the shadows, couples lingered, whispering and stealing kisses when they thought no one was looking.

The fresh air was a blessed relief, even if it was heavy with mist from the nearby river. Rachel could feel her hair beginning to curl from the dampness and reached up to smooth it, but Jason surprised her as his own fingers brushed back a tendril from her cheek.

"Let it curl. I've wanted to touch it ever since you emerged from the coach," he said in a husky voice. His hand remained at her throat, barely touching the pulse point beneath her ear.

The tiny caress robbed her of breath, but she fought the weakness. "You need not play the swain with quite

141

so much ardor, m'lord. Cargrave is no longer watching."

"Who says I must act only to please him, hmmm? Can I not please myself? And you?"

"You do not please me, Jason."

He tsked at her. Then as a servant passed by, he motioned the man over. "Please bring the lady a sherry, and I shall have rum punch." Turning back to Rachel, he asked, "Are you quite certain that I do not please you?"

"As certain as I am of your enormous hubris," she replied tartly.

He threw back his head and laughed, letting the tension between them ease. She was right to put a period to their dangerous games, no matter that she enjoyed them as much as he. They bantered for a few moments, discussing Drum's thus far unsuccessful attempts to learn who might be attempting to kill Jason. Then a different servant returned with the drinks Jason had requested.

He took a deep swallow and grimaced. "Odd flavor. Whoever mixed it certainly would be better employed stirring sheep dip."

"Great evening, ain't it though?" Roger Dalbert asked as he and his wife strolled toward them. "Oh, you remember m'wife, Garnet?"

She was tricked out like a Bartholomew baby once again, this time in a ghastly shade of purple trimmed with scarlet lace. "Ah, yes, we met at your betrothal ball," Mrs. Dalbert said, curtsying to the earl and his future countess.

Roger harrumphed, red-faced as he recalled the way the ball had ended. "Raised a bit of a breeze that night, eh, what?" he said, grinning sheepishly at Jason.

Jason laughed and winked at Rachel. "We've been

rubbing on together quite a bit better here of late, haven't we, pet?"

The double entendre brought a hint of color to her face. Rallying, she replied, "Ah, but, *pet*"—she paused to emphasize the word—" 'twas you who did all the rubbing."

Garnet dabbed at her damp forehead with a scarlet handkerchief. " 'Tis awfully warm tonight," she said, raising her wineglass.

Rachel murmured at the same time to Roger, "Poor fellow rubbed muzzles with one of my mastiffs and caught a frightful case of poison oak. One must be careful where one bestows kisses."

Roger let out a great bark of laughter, then slapped Jason heartily on the back, causing him to spill the remainder of his drink. "Terribly sorry, old chap. Cowhanded in the extreme. Didn't get yer gown, did it, m'dear?" he asked Garnet, who stood nearest to Jason.

"No harm, dearie," she said, masking her vexation as she brushed away a few spots from the purple horror she was wearing.

"As long as Mistress Dalbert's gown isn't ruined, there's no loss with the drink. Worst rum punch I ever tasted," Jason replied to his cousin. Poor old Roger had always been a clunch of the first water. Signaling a servant bearing a tray laden with glasses of champagne, Jason set their empties on the tray, took two crystal flutes and offered them to the ladies. Then he took two more for his cousin and himself.

Responding, Roger raised his glass in a toast. "Here's wishing you a felicitous union such as we have." He patted Garnet's shoulder fondly, and she smiled at him.

Jason leaned close to Rachel and chimed his glass against hers. "This time you might drink it."

She peered at him over the rim of the flute. "Easy, my *pet*. This time I might spit it."

143

Roger and Garnet did not know exactly how to take the exchange, but guffawed nervously when Jason roared with laughter. "You would, wouldn't you?"

"Is that a rhetorical question?" she shot back, holding the glass to her lips.

"What, pray, is so amusing, you young scamp?" Cargrave asked, strolling onto the terrace to check on them.

Jason turned to his grandfather, but before he could reply he felt a sudden surge of dizziness. Everything around him began to spin. He could not breathe, and his heart was pounding in his chest as if he had just run miles on a hot Maryland afternoon.

"What's wrong, Jason?" Rachel asked, stepping to his side to help the marquess hold him up. His face was as red as Garnet's handkerchief, and his knees were starting to buckle.

"I say, old man, you don't look quite the thing," Roger said with alarm in his voice.

"I—I may have seen these symptoms before," Garnet interjected, staring at Jason's flushed face. "Does the young lord have a weak heart? Does he take medicine—?

The marquess interrupted. "Preposterous! The lad's as healthy as a young bull."

Undeterred, the dowdy little woman reached toward Jason, but his grandfather attempted to seize her wrist. She slapped away the old man's hand and placed her fingertips on Jason's throat, then placed her hand flat against his chest. She turned to Rachel, taking her hand and pressing it to Jason's chest. Rachel's eyes widened. "Mother of God! His heart is hammering so fast it will tear his chest asunder!"

Garnet nodded. "You're right about that, dearie. We must sit him down someplace quiet."

By this time a crowd had begun to gather around.

The marquess bellowed at two footmen, "Get over here and carry him indoors at once!" Turning to the gawking spectators, he physically shoved the elegant assemblage back. "Clear the way here, quickly."

As the servants carried Jason's unconscious body into the house, Rachel seized hold of a squire who lived nearby and said, "Send for the nearest physician. Your fastest horse and rider, please!"

Then Rachel picked up her skirt and dashed after Garnet, who was following Cargrave and the footmen carrying Jason. "What did you mean about recognizing the symptoms?"

"My father, dearie. He had a bad heart, took foxglove for it, but once he overdosed himself. A terrible mistake. Speeds up the heartbeat like mad."

"But how could Jason have gotten hold of foxglove?" The instant she asked the question, Rachel gasped. "He's been poisoned!"

"Poisoned!" Garnet echoed in horror. "Good heavens, here? Who would—"

" 'Tis no matter now—all that is important is Jason. What can we do to save him?"

Garnet patted Rachel's arm and replied, "Never fear, dearie. Your betrothed is young and strong, not like my elderly father. If 'tis foxglove, there are ways to deal with it. Come along," she said calmly as the duchess directed her servants to take Jason into a sitting room just off the ballroom.

Garnet took charge without anyone giving her leave to do so. Her no-nonsense practicality seemed to reassure everyone, even the imperious old marquess. "First of all, keep him sitting upright. There's a good chair—that one with the footstool. Place his feet upon it, just so," she said, herself raising his legs and positioning them.

Rachel and Cargrave stood to the side, both frankly

145

terrified by Jason's flushed face and gasping breath. At Garnet's command, Rachel loosened his stock and helped a footman remove his jacket and shirt studs. His face was still beet red, and he had begun to perspire fiercely.

"We must get him cool," Garnet said. "Send for some of that ice on the buffet table, a large block of it. Bring a pick to chisel it into smaller pieces, and some linens to hold it. Also, I shall require a sharp knife and several large bowls."

In moments Garnet had devised ice bags and had directed servants to press them against Jason's body. "Be especially sure to keep that large one over his heart. Cooler blood pumps less swiftly," she explained in her sensible tone of voice as she took the sharp knife from the footman who had brought it and tested its razor-keen edge.

Garnet looked at Rachel appraisingly. "You seem to have a level head, dearie. I'll need your help with this. Here, you hold the bowls in place as I open his veins, and mind you don't faint, else we'll ruin the duchess's fine Turkey carpet."

"Never approved of the damned leeches bleeding a man. Makes him weaker," Cargrave said, stepping forward.

Rachel placed her hand on his arm. "I think Mistress Dalbert knows what she's doing, m'lord." Turning to Garnet, she added, "I shall not faint."

"Good. Hold that bowl while I let blood. You see," she explained as she worked, "his heart is beating overswiftly, pounding blood through his body. If 'tis not slowed, he will perhaps die, or at the least lapse into a coma as happened to m' father. We lower the pressure by lessening the amount of blood the heart must pump."

Rachel held the first bowl, positioning it beneath the

146

incision. Bright red blood spurted into it—Jason's life's blood. Would he die? She could not bring herself to think of it. Swallowing the acid burn of terror climbing up her throat, she set the bowl so it could catch the precious fluid, then picked up the second one as Garnet moved to Jason's other arm.

As they worked, Cargrave stood back. He had served with His Majesty's forces in the colonies fighting the French and their Indian allies and had seen a great deal of blood shed on both sides. But that was war, and the people were all strangers. This was his own son's son, his last remaining close family member, and never had he realized how very much he loved the boy.

He watched Rachel work at Garnet's side, as brave and cool-headed as any man could wish. What a perfect match they made. That was why he had chosen her for Jason, all lands and titles be damned! She was cut of the same cloth as Mathilda. *Ah, my dear one, how proud you would be if only you could see them together . . .*

"Don't you dare die on me, Jason Beaumont. I shall never forgive you, you inconsiderate Yankee lout," Rachel whispered low in his ear as she bathed his flushed face with icy cold cloths. Did she imagine it, or did his eyelids flutter open for a second? Rachel held her breath and reapplied the cloth to his face once more, dabbing it around his eyes, which suddenly opened.

"J-Jason?" she croaked, only then realizing that she had been holding back tears all the while she worked.

He stared up at her blurred face. The world was still spinning but not quite so fast as it had earlier. He shook his head and blinked. "Rachel? Where . . . what . . . holy God Almighty!" he rasped, looking down at what appeared to be buckets of blood—*his* blood, still seeping in a steady stream from both arms!

"Lie back, m'lord, calm yourself," Garnet said soothingly. "I shall have these bound up in no time, and you'll be just the thing again."

Rachel and the marquess held him back in the chair while the servants struggled with the ice bags he had dislodged from his neck, chest and thighs. "No further need for those, I warrant," Garnet said, flicking one stubby hand to the ice. "Remove them."

"You've been poisoned, Jason," Rachel said.

He stared at her dumbly for a moment, then collected his thoughts as his head gradually began to clear. He was sweat-soaked, but no longer burning up, and his heart had stopped its frenetic pounding. "Poison, you say? I've eaten nothing since early afternoon. It must have been in my drink—the one good old Roger spilled, bless him."

"Apparently 'twas a massive dose of foxglove. If it had not been for Mistress Dalbert, you might have died," Rachel said, blinking back tears of joy.

"Is that a touch of concern I detect in your voice? And what are these, hmmm?" he asked, wincing as he raised a bandaged arm to trace the silvery trickle down her cheek.

"It would quite spoil everything if you were to go and do something as untoward as dying. That would leave me at the mercy of every greedy fop in London," she said, taking his hand in hers and holding it tightly.

"I think it would be best if His Lordship were to have a bit of bed rest now," Garnet said to the marquess, who beamed at the young couple with a trace of tears glittering in his own eyes.

Cargrave responded, issuing commands for a bed to be prepared and servants summoned to carry Jason to it.

As for Jason and Rachel, she knelt in front of him holding his hand. Neither said a word, oblivious to the commotion surrounding them.

* * *

"Take this, please. I've eaten until I'm fair bursting," Jason said, pushing away the remains of a huge bowl of porridge.

He lay in a large bed in one of the Mountjoys' guest rooms, propped up with pillows. In the early-morning light streaming in from an open window, his sundarkened skin appeared bleached nearly as pale as the sheets. Rachel took the tray as the physician rubbed his hands nervously, saying, "I insist you take more nourishment to fight off the bad humors in your blood."

Jason scoffed. "Bugger my blood—my bad humor comes from nearly being poisoned."

"You *were* poisoned. Garnet was right. 'Twas foxglove," Rachel said sharply.

The leech nodded his bald head in agreement. "I fear she is correct, Your Lordship. Very fortunate Mistress Dalbert knew to bleed you . . . although I am not at all certain about the ice," he added, stroking his receding chin in perplexity.

Ignoring him, Jason considered what had transpired the preceding evening. "Yes, I most probably owe her my life." The old doctor had not arrived until the middle of the night, summoned from the bedside of a merchant in a distant village. After observing the old fool, Jason was grateful he had been unavailable earlier.

After the physician had excused himself, saying he would return to check on his patient that evening, Cargrave asked, "What thrice-damned blackguard has done this?" He paced across the carpet like a caged wolf, too furious and frightened about Jason to give in to fatigue. He and Rachel had spent the night at his grandson's bedside. "Must be the same bastard who took those shots at you in the woods."

Jason looked about the room, making sure no servants remained, then said, "I'm certain the poison was

149

put in the rum punch I drank. The footman who brought it was not the same fellow I sent to fetch it."

"I recall it being a different man," Rachel said. "I shall make discreet inquiries with the majordomo to see if we can locate him."

"No, I shall do that. I'm betting we'll find young Mountjoy had a hand in it. You remain here with this headstrong pup and keep him abed," the marquess instructed Rachel.

With that, he was off, leaving Jason and Rachel alone. She placed a linen over the tray and reached for the bellpull to summon a servant to take it, but Jason stopped her, wrapping his hand around her wrist. "Roger's wife is not the only one to whom I must be grateful, Countess," he said softly. "You assisted her most ably."

"I'm not the vaporing sort, Jason," she said, pulling away from his grasp. She needed distance between them to think straight. "I've delivered foals and overseen the butchering of cattle and hogs at Harleigh."

"Always so calm and practical, Countess . . . but was I hallucinating last night or were those tears on your cheeks when I awakened?"

She snorted, pulling the bellrope. "You were daft with foxglove fever. Now get some rest. You're still quite ill."

"You look to be the one who needs rest," he said, studying the dark circles beneath her eyes. She was still wearing the green gown, now blood-spattered and badly wrinkled, and she looked ready to fall asleep on her feet.

"We cannot leave you at the mercy of the servants here after what's happened. I shall wait until the marquess returns," she replied.

He pulled a small pocket pistol from beneath his pillow and said, "Grandfather thinks of everything. I shall

150

be able to protect myself adequately in your absence. Now go get some rest."

She was about to refuse when a rapping sounded on the door and Roger Dalbert poked his head inside. "I say, old fellow, you look all the crack compared to last time I saw you. Garnet said you were out of the woods. Had to come make certain for m'self."

"I'm most grateful to your wife, Roger—and to you. Had you not spilled that rum punch, I would most likely be laid out at Falcon's Crest awaiting burial."

Roger harrumphed, "Well, for once, seems my cow-handedness worked for the better, eh, what?"

"So it did, coz, so it did," Jason agreed with a grin.

Chapter Eleven

The marquess's inquiry revealed that the servant who had brought Jason's rum punch was missing. He had been newly hired only days before the ball, but when they went to the nearby village where his references indicated he had been previously employed, they found the fellow had used another man's name. That man professed to know nothing about the matter. Fuming, the marquess conceded that it was probably true.

Two days later, the recalcitrant patient got up and dressed himself over the dithering protests of the Mountjoy bodyservant assigned to him. Jason ordered his coach brought around, and he and his grandfather returned to Falconridge, where Fox waited, eager to see for himself that his brother was all right. Immediately Cargrave posted a letter to the Hon. Mr. Drummond in London, requesting that he take on some additional duties. From here on, until they determined who was behind the attempts to kill Jason, Drum was to be his bodyguard.

Rachel had slept for most of the first day after Jason's brush with death, too exhausted to brood over her undeniable reaction to it. This morning after his departure, she sat alone in the study, staring blankly at a huge stack of bills and tenant records that required her immediate attention. She sighed and plunked her pen back in its holder, unable to concentrate. The skies outside were leaden with impending rain, matching her mood. She stood up and began pacing back and forth across the carpet, then gazed out the window, thinking about the earl.

" 'Tis all his fault," she sighed, blaming Jason for her inability to work. Just then fat raindrops began splattering against the panes, as if the very heavens were echoing her malaise.

He had noted her tears and teased her about them, the clodpole, but when he had taken hold of her wrist, she had felt such a surge of tenderness that it had left her shaken to the core of her soul. Over the past weeks she had become resigned to the unsettling physical attraction she felt for him, assuring herself repeatedly that it was perfectly natural and would pass with time. After all, she was a healthy young woman who understood country matters, even though she had never felt the slightest stirring of interest in a male before.

Ah, but Jason Beaumont was not just any male, she conceded disconsolately. He was so intensely virile that all other men of her acquaintance were virtual eunuchs by comparison. From the first moment she had watched him striding up to her in the mud of the creek, she had been undone. And just when she had convinced herself that she could withstand the delicious onslaught of his sexual appeal, he had turned the tables on her once again. How inconsiderate of him to nearly die that way!

Rachel was terrified that she was falling in love with the earl. The lout. How dare he come crashing into her carefully ordered life and destroy the plans she had made since she was a fifteen-year-old girl? *And he does not want to wed you.* She pressed her face against the cold glass and closed her eyes, willing away the horrifying thought. "Well, I do not wish to wed him either!" she whispered against the steady patter of raindrops.

But she feared that it was no longer true.

"You are certainly Friday faced," Harry said, entering the study carrying a tray laden with tea and scones. "I thought you might be brooding all to yourself. At least you had the decency to remain indoors and not hide in the stables as you did when we were children. I declare, Rachel, if I had to muddy the Belgian lace on the hem of this gown to reach you, I warrant I'd be in quite a taking."

Rachel turned with a weak smile on her face as her sister fussed with the tray. Soon the room was filled with the heady fragrance of freshly poured tea and warm scones ladled generously with apricot preserves. "I remember that when we were young you would hide in the attic when you were upset—not that I'm upset," she quickly added.

Harriet scoffed. "Come and sit. We must discuss the earl."

Rachel knew that when her sister got that look in her eyes, there was no arguing with her. She took a cup and inhaled the aromatic steam rising from it. "Ah, that is good."

"Have a scone. You've not been eating properly these past weeks. Why, just yesterday I remarked on it to Father. You'll be a wraith by the time your trousseau is completed, and then nothing will fit!"

Dutifully Rachel took one of the heavy pastries and bit into it, forcing down food for which she had no appetite. "All this talk of trousseaus is upsetting in the extreme, Harry. I would prefer not to discuss it."

"Faddle. I am not talking about your wedding clothes—although heaven knows you have not paid the least attention to what that seamstress in London is doing," Harry upbraided her. Wiping a crumb from the edge of her mouth, she continued, "You must tell me how you feel about Jason."

"I find him arrogant, irritating and annoying in the extreme. Is there anything else you wish to know?" Rachel said, turning her attention to sipping tea.

"Then it must be love."

Rachel spit hot tea into her saucer. "Where ever did you get such a crack-brained notion as that?" She had been certain her sister was convinced that Jason was a horrible lecher who repelled his bride-to-be.

"From watching the two of you together these past days," Harry replied shrewdly. "When it seemed the earl would die, I feared you might expire with him."

Rachel blinked, studying her sister as if she had never seen Harriet Chalmers before. "Since when have you grown so wise?"

"Since when have you grown so chuckle-headed that you cannot see what is plain as the nose upon your face? You are in love with Falconridge, and he with you."

Rachel shook her head and set her tea aside. "You are mistaken. He does not love me, nor does he wish to wed me. Only to . . ."

"So, my first assessment of his character was not terribly far off the mark after all," Harry said dryly. "Well, no matter. He shall come up to scratch, and you shall win him over. The earl is the only man strong enough to match you."

"I do not wish for a husband who will command me," Rachel said stubbornly.

"Oh, you would have one *you* can command? I know you have always harbored the silly idea that if you were forced to wed, you would somehow convince Father to choose a jelly-kneed fellow. But that would never work. The Yankee will make you happy."

"I do not think so. He is being blackmailed into the match. His grandfather is holding Fox and will refuse to release him until Jason has done his duty." She wondered if this new, more sophisticated Harry would understand what she was going through.

"Cargrave is using that innocent boy as a cat's-paw?" Harry said indignantly. "Well, that certainly does not speak well of either the marquess or the earl, for being such a cake that he does not know what is good for him. So, we shall just have to give them both what they wish."

The impish light in Harry's eyes worried Rachel. "I mislike your tone. How can we give two men what they wish when they wish opposites on the matter?"

" 'Twill be a brace of snaps, trust me. All you need do is get Falconridge to the altar, and 'twould appear the marquess already has that matter well in hand."

Should she confide in Harry? Rachel hesitated only a moment. For all her flightiness, Harry was loyal to a fault and had always been willing to distract their father when he tried to take his eldest daughter to task for her hoydenish behavior. "The earl and I have concocted a plan to rescue Fox and spirit him from England. Then Jason will not be forced to wed me—and that is for the better, considering his feelings toward me."

"Pah! Men never know what is best for them, especially reckless rogues like Falconridge. He's enjoyed cutting a swath through the London Cyprians too much to give over to domestic bliss easily. But reformed rakes make the best of husbands . . . or so I have it on quite good authority."

"I do not want to marry a man who does not love me," Rachel said, surprising herself with the plaintive cry in her voice.

"As I said, I have been observing him as well as you for some time now, and I believe he does love you. He simply does not know it yet. Men are such simpletons about the truly important matters in life." Seeing Rachel's highly dubious look, Harry pressed on. "He follows you with his eyes. There is such a . . ." Harry coughed delicately in her handkerchief, then continued, "Well, a hungry look in them—as if he might try to devour you whole."

Rachel snorted indelicately as she replied, "Indeed, he has tried. And I have nearly succumbed, God help me. But that is lust, m'dear, not love."

"For men, that is the beginning of love. Without it, we would never land them, and England would be in a sorry state indeed. You feel a deal more than simple lust for Jason Beaumont. Do not even attempt to deny it."

Rachel did not.

"I thought so," Harry crowed with a self-satisfied smirk. "Well and good. You have fallen in love with him, and he desires you. Now all we need do is see that your plan goes off smoothly . . . with a few minor . . . er, alterations. Now, here is how we shall play this suit . . ."

Jason stood in the library of the Cargrave city house, holding a note written in Rachel's tall, graceful penmanship. It matched the woman quite well—long, lithe, elegant yet bold. He crumpled the missive unread, balling it up in his fist. He felt angry with himself for being unable to get her off his mind, as if he were a mooncalf in the throes of first infatuation. How dare she send reminders to ensnare him?

His grandfather had left Falconridge, taking Fox with him, as soon as he was assured that his grandson was recovering well from his brush with death. Cargrave had informed Jason that he would see the lad the week of the nuptials, which were to be held at St. George's in the alarmingly near future. In the meanwhile, Jason was saddled with Drum as his shadow. The little dandy was not only deadly with a rapier, but a crack shot with a pistol as well. If he had not enjoyed Drum's company, Jason might have been annoyed with this further high-handedness on the marquess's part. As it was, he was resigned to being guarded as if he were the Regent himself.

Since Rachel had not deigned to visit during his convalescence, he had been bored to distraction, able to think of nothing but how she had looked at that moment when he awakened in the Mountjoys' bedroom. Did she genuinely care for him? That was dangerous. Almost as dangerous as if he cared for her.

"I say, old fellow, if you don't want to read it, just toss it away. No need to squeeze it thus, unless you're attempting to make a diamond of it." Drum strolled into the book-lined room and took a seat on one of the massive cordovan leather chairs, which dwarfed his small frame.

Jason looked down at Rachel's letter, balled up in his fist as if he were indeed pulverizing it into a gem. Why had she written him? He was a fool for not reading it, as it most likely contained information on how they were to proceed in spiriting Fox away. *Perhaps that is why you don't wish to read it.* Scowling, he tossed the note onto his grandfather's large desk and sprawled in the chair opposite Drum.

"Have you found any connection between Forrestal's

chum Mountjoy and that footman who nearly did me in?"

Drum cocked his head, stroking his chin consideringly. "No luck. You had the right of it about the duke's youngest. He's as deep in dun territory as Etherington's heir. Gives 'em something in common, I warrant," he said dryly. "That and their love for cards. Mark me, I said 'love for', not 'skill at'."

"But no way to link them to what happened to me at His Grace's soiree?" It was a rhetorical question. Drum had experienced no more luck in finding a trace of the footpad who had shot at them in town than Jason had had in establishing the identity of whoever had attacked him in the country.

"Best to lie low until we are able to spirit young Master Fox away from the clutches of the marquess," Drum advised. He had been brought in on Jason's plans, and having such an aversion to matrimony himself, had quickly been won over to assisting his friend and Miss Fairchild, whom he had yet to meet. "At least if these attacks cease once your engagement is broken, you shall know Forrestal was the guilty party."

Jason stiffened at the thought of Frederick Forrestal anywhere near Rachel. "Rachel would never have him."

Drum studied his fingernails intently, murmuring, "But would she have you, m'lord earl?"

"Don't be ridiculous. I've already explained how we're going to outwit my grandfather. 'Twas her plan."

"And you appear all cock-a-whoop over it," Drum replied. "I ain't some chawbacon fresh out of Surrey, my good fellow. You've been blue-deviled ever since you returned to the city, and the cause is Rachel Fairchild."

"The cause is nearly being poisoned," Jason shot back, unable to keep his eyes from straying to the wadded-up ball of paper lying on the desk.

"Go read it," Drum dared him.

"How the hell would you know 'tis from her?"

Inhaling a pinch of snuff from the back of his wrist, Drum sneezed, then replied, "I possess a keen nose. The perfume is far too subtle for a Cyprian. Must be your betrothed's. Wish I had as much skill at detecting who the devil is trying to kill you, but never fear. I shall continue to keep that most excellent nose of mine to the ground until I solve the puzzle." He cocked an eyebrow at the earl and waited. "Well . . . ?"

Jason gave in and stalked over to the desk. Seizing the balled-up paper, he unwadded it carefully, then broke the seal and read it. Drum watched as an odd mixture of scowl and smile played about his lips.

"She is in London. For the fitting of her trousseau." As he said the word, visions of Rachel swathed in lace flashed into his mind. Yards and yards of sheer ivory lace through which he could see the rich butterscotch of her skin.

"And she wants to meet with you," Drum supplied as his friend stood staring at the leather-bound first editions on the walnut bookshelf in front of him without seeing them at all. The little dandy had a fair idea of whom Jason was seeing inside his mind.

"Honestly, Harry, I feel like a Bartholomew baby in this." Rachel squirmed as the itchy taffeta chafed her skin. She stood in the fitting room of the most elegant mantua maker's shop in the Burlington Arcade, surrounded by day gowns, afternoon gowns, ball gowns and riding habits, not to mention piles of soft lacy undergarments and night rails. The dress she was trying on was a deep shade of maroon, which she detested. "I look dreadful in this color. It clashes with my complexion."

"It would do no such thing if you would allow me to

apply whiteners to your skin. You simply must stay out of the sun. I warrant you're as dark as Jason."

At the mention of his name, Rachel felt her face heat even darker until she was certain she must perfectly match the shade of her dress. She could still recall the sun-stained splendor of his big, muscular body with its patterns of black hair covering chest, forearms and . . . lower.

She had sent a missive at her sister's urging yesterday morning, as soon as they arrived in the city. Thus far she had received no word back from Jason. Yankee clodpole! The least he could do was favor her with a reply of some sort. He was probably off with his latest bit-o'-muslin having a fine time while the day of their nuptials drew closer and closer. If they actually went through with the marriage, would he continue to take lovers? In the ton, most men did, she knew.

The thought did not sit well. Then she realized that Harry was speaking to her. "Oh, no, I will never bleach my skin with any of your poultices. 'Twould do no good anyway, since I plan to continue running the Hall, which requires that I be outdoors."

"Have you considered that your husband may not wish to have you riding about in men's clothing?"

"He liked me well enough in them before," she snapped. He had practically undressed her with his eyes on both occasions. Then there was the time when she had undressed herself before his eyes—unknowingly, she hastened to remind herself.

"But that was before you were to became his countess," Harry replied primly.

I'm already his "countess." How ironic that he had chosen to taunt her with that title. Angry with the direction of the conversation, and Jason's lack of response to her note, she wanted nothing so much as to yank off the gown. "Let us be quit of this place before I go mad."

"Not before you try on the night rails," Harry replied with a note of finality.

Madame Louvois came bustling in, a measuring tape in her hands and the gleam of avarice in her eyes. "*Mais oui, ma petite,* you must see how beauteous they are," the gnarled old woman gushed.

Rachel was anything but petite, towering over the emaciated little Frenchwoman. However, one look from Harry convinced her to give in with a sigh of resignation. She seized an armload of the filmy creations, quite a bit different from the plain cool muslin she normally slept in, and headed for the fitting room.

All the regular fitting rooms had been filled when she and Harry had arrived fashionably late for their appointment. That was Harry's fault, but since Rachel had not wished to come in the first place, she had not complained about her sister's habitual tardiness.

She had been assigned a small sewing room at the end of the hall. Madame had wanted to evict a Cit's daughter from a fitting room, but Rachel's sense of fairness would not tolerate such rudeness. The sewing room was crowded with pincushions and dressmaking forms, for which the Frenchwoman's assistant had apologized profusely. That made no difference to Rachel. If it would help get this ordeal over with more quickly, she would have been content to use a broom closet.

The assistant, a mousy little thing with a pinched face and tiny, deft hands, helped her out of the elaborate maroon ball gown. Rachel basked in a shaft of sunlight streaming in from a high window, trying to forget the purpose of the lacy confection she was donning.

His mouth suddenly went dry as dust.

Jason stood rooted in the doorway, the curtain in his hand pulled halfway back as he expected to enter the gentlemen's waiting room. Obviously, he had chosen the wrong door at the end of the hallway . . . or was it the soft sound of Rachel's voice that had lured him, seductive as a siren's song? He had thought he heard her, but since the witch had been invading his dreams, waking as well as sleeping, he had convinced himself that it was merely his imagination.

He had delayed responding to her note, not trusting himself alone with her. But, as Drum had pointed out before dropping him in front of the Burlington Arcade, if he wished to avoid the very thing he feared, he had to meet with her in response to her request. When they had arrived at the Fairchild city house that morning, he was irritated to learn that his fiancée was at Madame Louvois's shop for a fitting . . . of the trousseau for their wedding.

It was as if he had conjured her up dressed in silk and lace so sheer it matched his fantasies of yesterday. What was happening to him? Damn and damn again, but he had to get out of here before she caught him spying on her a second time! Yet his feet seemed incapable of obeying the commands his brain cried out. He watched, mesmerized, as the silk slid over her skin. Every lush curve of her body was bathed in soft sunlight, enriching the chocolate hue of her hair, unbound and falling down her back. The loosely draped night rail plunged to a deep vee, showing the hollow between her high breasts to fine advantage. Yards of pale bronze lace dripped from the neckline, wrists and hemline.

All he could think of was stalking into the room and tearing it off her, then laying her over the long, narrow sewing bench in the corner and making fierce, desperate love to her. *Think, dammit, think!* He certainly could not act on the base urging of his stone-hard body, no matter the ache in his loins. That would give Grandfather exactly what he wanted. He dropped the curtain as if it were a sheet of flame and stepped back into the hall, dazed. Sweet heaven, what had he almost done?

His first impulse after he recovered his wits was to leave immediately, forget about waiting for Drum to return and simply hire a hackney, all the assassins in England be damned! He felt like kidnapping Fox and riding to Bristol right now, taking his chances on finding a ship bound for anywhere outside England. The woman was making him a candidate for Bedlam! Then he remembered that he had given his card to Madame Louvois's assistant, who had instructed him to wait in the gentlemen's room until his betrothed had completed her fitting. It would be remarked upon if he vanished.

Somehow he intuited that Rachel would know the reason why. He would be damned if he'd give her the satisfaction. When she had sat at his bedside after the poisoning, he'd sensed that her feelings for him had changed.

That frightened him far more than bullets or foxglove.

What if she had decided to go through with the marriage? This whole charade could be a ploy on her part to lure him into her oh-so-silken snare. After all, he was certainly a more desirable candidate than Forrestal or any of his ilk. Her unusual beauty combined with her outspokenness obviously drove conventional suitors away. He had introduced her to physical desire, and now he would pay the ultimate price: leg-shackling.

He cursed silently, then stalked down the hall in search of the gentlemen's waiting room, determined to face her and discuss their situation honestly. He had been bullied, blackmailed and badgered enough. He was damned if he would be deceived one more time.

He did not see the small blonde standing at the other end of the long hallway, observing him silently, a tiny smile wreathing the Cupid's bow of her lips. The Baroness Widmere was well pleased with how matters were progressing. Now if only Rachel could steel her nerve to do what she must . . .

Rachel wiped her damp palms against the soft muslin of her gown, an old one she had worn during her Season five years ago. A bit tight in the bodice now, but it fit well enough—or did it? She had been in such pique at having to endure a morning at the modiste's that she had grabbed the first thing that came to hand. Only now did she pause to realize that compared to the finery for which she had just been fitted, this gown was frayed and the yellow color faded. Why was she thinking about her gown, for pity's sake?

Because I want to make a good impression on Jason so he will be agreeable to my bargain. Harry had been exceedingly certain that he would be. Her sister had smiled behind her fan, rather like a cat genteelly burping canary. Was his unexpected arrival at Madame Louvois's part of some scheme? Rachel had been preparing herself for this interview for several days, but now that it was upon her, she felt her resolve wavering.

What if he refused? Then she would simply have to go back to searching for some malleable fool who would be acceptable to her father. The thought did not sit well at all. Could Harry possibly be right about Jason's feelings for her? There was only one way to find out. She stepped into the room where he waited.

Chapter Twelve

Jason stood with his back to her, giving her time to study him as he stared glumly out the window. They were alone, and Harry had made certain that none of Madame's employees would interrupt their private conversation. He was splendid, with his broad shoulders and long legs. Rachel could not help admitting that. He had the address of an earl—inbred arrogance and wolfish ruthlessness much akin to that of the grandfather he sought to thwart. That stubborn determination may have been inherited, but it had been honed by his life in America. Harry was right about Yankees. They were a breed apart.

And he was the most unique of the lot, Rachel was certain, in spite of never having met any others. Quite simply, he took her breath away. His very height and muscular frame attracted her, she who had always been a "long Meg" in English society. Rachel could never forget the way they had waltzed at their betrothal ball, his large hand pressed so intimately against her back, his steps fitted so perfectly to hers. And that day in the pool, naked flesh to naked flesh, their bodies were an even more perfect fit.

Harry was right. *I have fallen in love with him.*

Rachel no longer denied the fact. She felt drawn to every nuance of his person—the way his hair shone blue-black in the light and curled ever so slightly at the nape of his neck; the midnight darkness of those penetrating eyes as they stripped her naked with one sweep; the deadly white smile that revealed the dimple in his cheek.

Taking yet another breath for courage, she spoke. "I was surprised to learn you were here."

He whirled and pierced her with what she believed was an accusing look.

In fact, Jason was trying desperately not to betray his earlier voyeuristic indiscretion. "I was surprised to receive your note. Indeed, amazed that you would deign to leave Harleigh and come to London to see me." He knew it sounded petty, almost as if he were angry that she had not come to visit him during his convalescence at Falconridge . . . which he was, though he would die before admitting it.

"We have matters to discuss," she replied levelly, closing the door for privacy. The heavy brass knob slipped slightly in her damp hand. She took a calming breath and launched into her prepared speech. "I have been giving our dilemma some thought, and now I believe it best to amend our plans somewhat."

His head jerked up, every fiber of his body on full alert now. "Amend them how?"

"It all hinges on a conversation reported by my sister," she replied evasively. This was not going at all well. "It seems your grandfather has mentioned to my father that he is considering adopting Fox."

167

"Adopting Fox!" Jason echoed incredulously.

"Well, it appears that your mother never did so. The boy is not legally her ward, and she believes it would be greatly to his benefit to receive an education in England. If Cargrave does adopt him, Fox will remain here until his majority . . . forcing you to perform . . . er, your duties as his heir."

She looked delectable when she blushed, damn her. "But that will occur only if I do not steal him away and return with him to America." Was he reminding her—or himself?

"In case you have failed to notice, m'lord, since he learned of the attempts on your life, the marquess has assigned a host of men to guard you every moment of the day. He has Fox at his estate, and there is no way on earth we will be able to reach him without alerting your grandfather. And that does not even allow for the fact that you must somehow convince the boy he will be better off in America than here once Cargrave tells him of his intentions."

Jason began to pace, rubbing his forehead. "This tangle grows more untenable every day. There has to be a way to reach Fox and get him out of Grandfather's clutches." He looked over at her, pinning her with harsh, accusing eyes, as if the dilemma were one of her creation, which he knew it was not. Acute sexual frustration and his own growing emotional attachment to Rachel were proving his undoing. "What new idea have you come up with?"

She bit her lip, forcing herself to meet his penetrating gaze as she replied. "That we go through with the marriage ceremony—'twill make the marquess let down his guard," she quickly added, noting his shocked, scowling expression.

"Pray continue," he said sardonically, with one eyebrow raised.

"The day after the wedding, we will repair to Falcon's Crest for our honeymoon," Rachel said, certain her cheeks were the color of that accursed taffeta gown she had been fitted for earlier. "No one, not even those men the marquess has set to guard you, will be expecting us to slip away then. We can race to Cargrave Hall the following night, using the fastest horses in your stables. Once there, we must convince Fox to leave with us while the marquess is sleeping. By the time he awakens, we will be well on our way to Bristol, where the ship will be waiting."

"You have arranged everything, I see," he said suspiciously. Was this not exactly what he'd feared—that she was trying to trap him into marriage?

Rachel felt her temper rising. Yankee idiot! Why did he have to make everything so difficult? Harry had been wrong. He wanted no part of marrying her, no part at all. "If you have a better idea, I will most certainly entertain it," she snapped.

Jason sighed. As he turned it over in his mind, the plan did have merit. He had no interest in marrying any other woman. With him on one side of the Atlantic and her on the other . . . well, they could both have what they wanted. He would most likely never return to England. Roger could have the bloody titles, and welcome to them. By further involving Fox—not to mention his own mother—in this nefarious adoption plot, his grandfather had finally abrogated their bargain.

"I can see how it might work. You are a shrewd tactician, Countess. The wedding will serve as an excellent smoke screen. The old devil will never dream that we would both defy him after saying our vows." He paced, warming to the idea as his wrath against the marquess grew. "Of course, we will not consummate the marriage, but you will still legally be my countess, though free to live your life as you please. Return to Harleigh and raise cattle, crops . . . hell, anything you wish. Cargrave will be mad as a scalded rooster, but he'll be able to take no reprisal against you for aiding Fox and me in our escape."

"How thoughtful of you," she said in a distant voice, concealing her fisted hands in the folds of her gown . . . the tatty old yellow that she had fretted about earlier.

How utterly mistaken Harry had been. Not only did Jason not love her, he no longer evinced the tiniest bit of desire for her! Had that been a figment of her imagination? Or, being brutally honest, would any female body cast in such proximity have driven him to lust? Once time and distance intervened, his ardor had quickly evaporated. So deep in her own misery was she, it took a moment for his next words to register.

"In the event that you meet the squire of your dreams at some future time and wish to merge your estates, you can always obtain an annulment." As soon as the words escaped his lips, Jason was startled at how greatly the idea of Rachel wed to some portly squire upset him. Of course, he'd been sickened at the thought of Forrestal touching her. What man possessed of one shred of decency would not be? But if she were to find contentment with another farmer, why should he begrudge her a happy union? His mind shut down at the consideration.

Rachel refused to consider her pain, focusing on the practical. Did the double-damned Yankee lackwit not know that once he was gone, the marquess would immediately begin proceedings for that very annulment? Her father would not force her to submit to a humiliating physical examination to prove her virginity, but she knew for a certainty that Cargrave would do so. However, Jason's rejection hurt far worse than the prospect of being placed once again on the marriage block.

Well, she had been bold in the extreme until now. There was nothing to do but face things out. Furious anger stiffened her spine, but she held it tightly reined in as she smiled and said, " 'Tis you, not I, m'lord, who has thought of every contingency. Our plans are laid, then. I shall see you in church."

With that, she spun about and walked from the room, leaving a startled Jason Beaumont staring after her, wondering why his heart hurt.

On the ride back to the city house, Rachel refused to share her feelings with her sister. All she would say was that the earl had agreed to go through with the marriage. She complimented Harry for the idea about embellishing the rumor regarding Fox's adoption by the marquess. When the baroness pressed her about Jason's reaction to the proposal, Rachel pressed her lips together and said nothing further.

That night she lay in her bed, staring at the shadowy frescoes on the ceiling as moonlight bathed her tear-stained cheeks. Sleep was impossible. "I've become a veritable watering pot since I met that thrice-cursed Yankee earl," she gritted out as she climbed from the bed and walked over to the window.

Autumn was fast approaching, and it had begun to rain once more. Her mood was perfectly reflected in the weather. Jason cared nothing for her. Her plan had backfired miserably, making it abundantly clear that he was as eager to rid himself of her as she had at first been to rid herself of him. But she would be damned if she'd allow a broken heart to cause her to give over. After all he had cost her, Jason would be her husband in fact, not merely in name. She swore it.

Never again would she be subjected to her father's persistent wheedling. Nor would she have to endure the marquess's haughty insistence that she prove she was

171

a true wife to his absent heir. The marriage would be consummated in spite of the Yankee's reluctance, and the chambermaids changing the linens the following morning would be her witnesses. The only way a true marriage could be dissolved was by a decree of divorcement, which would require petitioning Parliament. An act which only her legal husband could initiate.

"And Jason will by then be on the opposite side of the Atlantic," she whispered grimly to herself. Damn all men. They sat in control of every aspect of a woman's life. But she would outwit the lot of them. By God, she would be a countess, and *she* would continue to run her own estate. That resolution made, Rachel returned to bed.

She lay in the darkness once more, drifting off in an exhausted slumber, wondering why her heart hurt.

"Leave me the bloody hell alone . . . please, Drum." Jason's words were slurred as he slumped disconsolately in an easy chair, a crystal decanter of brandy in one hand and a snifter just drained of its contents in the other.

Drum stood in the center of the large study of the Cargrave city house, looking down at his friend. A mixture of concern and annoyance marked his expression as he considered how to placate a man who had spent the past week with the worst case of Lombard fever he'd ever seen. "You know full well I cannot leave you unattended after all the attempts on your life."

"Then go out and search for the culprits. I've been cooped up in this prison far too long," Jason replied testily, pouring another drink, then depositing the decanter none too steadily on a turret-top table beside his chair.

"Ah, there's the rub indeed, old chap. I have every

one of my considerable sources in the city engaged in that endeavor. Alors, there is not a trace of evidence linking Forrestal to the skulduggery."

"Then I shall simply have to pound the truth out of him," Jason said, starting to rise from his chair.

Drum placed a restraining hand on his shoulder. "I fear that might not be wise. If you were to find yourself thrown into Newgate for assaulting the son of a royal duke, you would be easy pickings for whoever wants you dead."

"At least 'twould be a change of scene," Jason groused, pouring another draught and glaring at Drum.

"What you require is not a change of scene, old chap."

"And what, pray, do I require?" Jason dared him.

"Rachel Fairchild." Ignoring the earl's snort of disgust, Drum continued, "You've been blue-deviled, not to mention vile-tempered as a badger, ever since you saw her last at the mantua makers."

Jason had explained the quandary he was in regarding his grandfather's plans to adopt Fox. Would it truly be fairer to the boy to allow him to remain in England? If so, would Jason have to wed Harleigh's daughter? Drum suspected that Rachel Fairchild had a deal more to do with his friend's high dudgeon than the situation with his foster brother. "What transpired that afternoon between you and your betrothed?"

Jason shrugged and took another sip. The expensive French brandy tasted like gall to him. "Lud, I'm drinking myself sober."

"I know you don't intend to go through with the marriage, but perhaps—"

Jason's harsh laugh cut him off. "Ah, but you are mistaken. The lady has a *new* plan. We shall go through with the wedding. Then the day after, we shall steal Fox away and I shall return him to America. Jolly old En-

173

gland shall never see me again. And you, my friend, need worry no longer about preserving my thick Yankee hide from assassins."

Drum stiffened, an expression of incredulity narrowing his green eyes. "I say, old fellow, this is a rather drastic step. Marriage." He shuddered, withdrawing his snuff box and placing a pinch on the back of his hand.

"Oh, it will not be consummated. But it will secure the lady's future. Once she is Countess of Falconridge, she will be off the marriage mart. Free to pursue her own life."

Drum digested that bit of information, all the while studying his friend's haggard face. "I've often spoken of my friend Alex, but I have never told you of another very dear friend: Jocelyn . . . his wife."

Jason looked up, surprised at the warmth in Drum's voice as he said the woman's name. To date, he had never heard the acerbic little dandy speak of a female with such fondness.

"Joss is quite . . . unusual for a woman. Not in the same ways as your Rachel—"

"She is not *my* Rachel," Jason interjected emphatically.

Drum waved the remark aside. "Strong woman, willful, determined, lots of common sense. Not at all the thing in the way of fashion or beauty as the ton defines it, but a good heart. She was the only one for Alex."

"Well, Rachel does not have a 'good heart' and she is decidedly not the one for me . . . if I even wanted a wife—which I do not."

Drum looked skeptical. "Don't be so certain. Takes a wise man to see beneath the surface of a gel."

"This from a man who cannot abide the fair sex," Jason said sardonically.

"Don't mean I'm green when it comes to understanding them," Drum replied, deciding that it might be wise to meet Jason's betrothed and take her measure for himself.

When the earl rang for yet another bottle of brandy, the little dandy said good night, leaving his friend to spend the night drinking alone in the library. "At least 'twill keep him out of harm's way while I attend to business," Drum murmured to himself after instructing two trusted family retainers to put His Lordship to bed after he passed out. Everyone in the Beaumont household understood the danger the earl was in and watched over him closely.

Rachel, like Jason, was spending a solitary evening in the city. Her father, Harry and Melvin had gone to see a play at Covent Garden, but she had begged off attending. Everyone there would remark upon the fact that her soon-to-be husband was not escorting her. What the ton whispered was not a flea bite to her, but the fact that Jason wanted nothing to do with her stung deeply.

Although she had remained in residence at the city house until her trousseau fittings were completed, he had not called once in eight days. In spite of the fact that most of the upper ten thousand were in the country for several more weeks, invitations to a number of social activities had piled up on the card table in the entry hall of the city house. Rachel knew she received them only because people were curious about the relationship between an infamous ape-leader and the wild Yankee earl. She loathed being on display and would not have attended most of the soirees even if Jason had been present. But she wanted to know why he refused to at least play his part in this wretched charade. Even Harry, who was wont to put the best construction on any social situation, could make no further excuses for his negligence

Rachel intended to return to Harleigh Hall on the morrow and remain there until the nuptials. Let the ton gossip and be damned. If Cargrave set a dozen guards outside the bridal chamber at Falcon's Crest, it would serve the accursed Yankee right for neglecting her this way.

She was in the midst of selecting what few items of clothing she would take with her on the journey when a maid knocked, bearing a card. The Hon. Alvin Francis Edward Drummond had come calling. Rachel knew of him by reputation. And it was not good. He was from a distinguished old family but was consistently in disfavor with his father, who had recently made noises about disowning him because of his extravagances. He was an inveterate gambler with a fearful reputation as a duelist who associated with Brummel's crowd of dandies, an utter scapegrace.

He was also Jason's companion on many larks, if the scandal sheets had the right of it. What on earth could he want with her? Giving her appearance a cursory inspection in the looking glass, Rachel headed downstairs to see.

She was not at all what he expected. He had heard that Harleigh's eldest daughter was a frightful tabby who drove away every suitor the viscount brought before her. She supposedly preferred the company of horses to society. If not for his aversion to horses, Drum might have applauded that sentiment, since he, too, found many of the diamond squad to be crashing bores.

But he had imagined that Rachel Fairchild would be plain, gawky . . . horsey. She was none of those. Overly tall, yes. So was his friend Joss, but there the resemblance ended. While Joss was thin with mousy hair tied up in a frizzy knot and wore thick spectacles, this female possessed all the curves requisite for her gender.

Rachel's hair was thick and lustrous, draped over one shoulder in a fat plait, and her clear, unsquinting eyes peered at him intently. Although her gown was not all the crack, the aqua mull flattered her complexion and hung gracefully as she moved toward him.

He clicked his heels and bowed, noting that she did not offer her hand for a salute. "Alvin Francis Edward Drummond, at your service, Miss Fairchild."

Rachel inclined her head. "And what brings you here, Mr. Drummond?"

"Please forgive my untoward behavior. I know the hour is late and we have not been properly introduced, but—"

"But you want to see for yourself if I am as dreadful as Jason believes me to be?" she said wryly. At his look of utter consternation, Rachel felt a hint of a smile tug at her lips. She had not smiled often since coming to London.

"I assure you, Miss Fairchild, that my friend holds you in the highest esteem. After all, you are to be wed in less than a month."

"Will you stand as witness?" some imp made her ask.

He paled but nodded. "Yes, if he asks me, I will be honored to do so. But that brings me to a rather delicate point . . ."

When he hesitated, she gestured for him to take a seat on a shield-back chair, then rang for refreshments and sat down on the cabriole sofa directly across from him. "And that point is?" she inquired, looking him straight in the eye.

Jason had indeed drunk himself sober. It was a phenomenon not altogether unknown to him, but those other occasions had been mostly celebratory after weeks at sea. This was different. He was as tense as a coiled wire and angry enough to pick a fight with a

177

tavern full of drunken tars. In fact, the more he considered the latter idea, the better he liked it. He was sick of being under lock and key, watched like a lad not out of leading strings. Sick to death of lying awake night after night for fear of dreaming about Rachel.

Rachel swathed in gauzy silk and lace . . . Rachel whose butterscotch skin he was dying to caress . . . Rachel who proposed this obscene charade of a marriage of convenience. *Her convenience—certainly not mine!* Jason had been the one to jump to the conclusion that they not consummate the union, but he was in no condition to recognize that fact. After all, he did not really wish to be leg-shackled—did he?

But he wanted Rachel in his bed. If it were not for his grandfather's machinations, Jason would have had her by now. And no marriage, convenient or otherwise!

"I have to get out of here before I run mad," he muttered aloud, combing his fingers through his hair. He rang for his valet and ordered a bath and a fresh change of clothing. How excellent that Drum had hied himself off somewhere or other. With luck, Jason would be off before the dandy returned to stand guard.

Within the hour he was dressed and stepping into his coach over the flustered protests of his valet, the butler, housekeeper and a host of other servants. Only the stolid old stableman who had brought the coach around had stood up to him, saying that His Lordship would go nowhere without two of the footmen to watch his backside. Knowing that they could not follow him into any of the gentlemen's clubs, Jason had graciously agreed.

The stars shone brightly after a sudden early-evening storm. The earl stepped down from his coach and made his way past a series of water puddles to the doors of Brooks. When they opened to admit him, his servants were forced to cool their heels outside, assured that no harm could befall His Lordship in one of the most exclusive haunts of the ton. What they did not know was that Jason stayed only long enough to play one hand of whist with Baron Waverly and his sycophants, then slipped out the side entry and hailed a hackney to take him to the East End gambling halls.

If he could not get drunk and did not find any of the ladies of the evening to his liking, he could at least manage to lose some of his grandfather's blunt at the tables. Or better yet, he might win. The money would come in handy on his trip back to America.

Feeling cocky, he leaned back against the musty-smelling squabs and convinced himself that Rachel Fairchild could go to the devil. He did not see the shadowy figure slip onto the boot of the hackney just as it took off.

Chapter Thirteen

"So, sir, have I passed your inspection?" Rachel asked Drum as they sipped their libations. She had called for one of her father's best bottles of port, feeling the need for its restorative powers to face Jason's compatriot. Their conversation had been most . . . enlightening, for want of a better word.

Drum could feel her studying him with the same keen intelligence Joss possessed. "You have passed with colors flying, m'dear."

They had taken each other's measure, at first awkwardly, then as both natural wits flared and clashed, laughingly. It was apparent to Rachel that Alvin Francis Edward Drummond wanted to make certain that she was worthy of Jason Beaumont. At his pronouncement, she felt oddly relieved . . . and yet disturbed. After all, she and Jason were scarcely making lifelong commitments. At least, Jason was not. Rachel knew that if she succeeded in seducing her husband on their wedding night, there would be a lifelong commitment on her part, especially if she became pregnant.

Drum interrupted her troubling ruminations. "In spite of superficial differences, you and my friend Jocelyn Blackthorne have much in common . . . including a well-concealed tendresse for your roguish males."

Rachel almost choked on her port. "As you already know, our marriage will be scarce a day's duration."

"Time enough," Drum replied dryly.

Rachel knew her cheeks had heated and cursed Jason Beaumont for causing her to react in such a missish fashion. *Drummond cannot know what I plan . . . can he?* The deadly duelist had not been what she expected. He was a dandy, yes, even a bit misogynistic as were many of his ilk, but he was fiercely loyal to his friends and altogether too shrewd. She met his level gaze without flinching. How much could she tell Drummond? How much had Jason already told him?

Her swift calculations were interrupted by the sound of distressed voices coming from the foyer. Excusing herself, she opened the door to see what the commotion was about. Drum was immediately behind her, and they both recognized Ames, one of the Cargrave footmen, as he argued with the viscount's butler.

"I say, Ames, why are you raising a breeze?" Drum asked, crossing the floor with a grim expression on his face. He knew this had something to do with Jason.

" 'Is Lordship, sir, the earl, 'e went out, to Brook's, but then 'e give Jemmy 'n Seth the slip. Took a 'ackney from the side door."

Drum cursed, then started to apologize to Rachel, who brushed such niceties aside and asked the footman, "Do you have any idea where he went?"

"The jarvey wot Jemmy talked to, 'e said 'e took 'im to the wharves."

Now Rachel muttered a most unladylike oath. "Does the fool Yankee have a wish to die!"

"I shall find him, never fear, Miss Fairchild," Drum reassured her, although he felt not half so certain as he let on. Just as he turned to go, he felt her hand on his arm.

"I'm coming with you. Only wait a moment while I fetch my pistols."

He stood in amazement as she raised her skirts and sprinted up the stairs with unseemly haste. He was beginning to really like the gel.

Within a quarter hour they were in a hired hackney speeding pell-mell to the rough district lining the Thames. Filled with warehouses and taverns, the area catered to the seamen whose ships lay bobbing on the river. Rachel had donned an old pair of breeches and a man's shirt several sizes too large for her, much to Drum's stupefaction. She carried a brace of Clark pistols tucked in a sash at her waist, and her hair was concealed beneath a battered old felt hat.

As they alighted from the coach at the first grog shop they encountered, she knelt quickly and smeared a bit of filth from the ground over her face. "It may help if I don't look too clean," she muttered.

He nodded in approval, thankful the night was dark, the taverns poorly lit and most of the denizens of the streets well into their cups. In the light of day, no sober man would ever believe she was a boy. But he prayed no one would realize her disguise at night. "Let me do the talking," he said as they entered the Purple Parrot.

After the fifth unsuccessful inquiry in a vile-smelling hellhole no self-respecting tar would even consider, their mood was grim. "Do you suppose he's lying in some back alley injured or . . . ?" She could not bring herself to say "dead."

" 'Tis possible, but Jason has always possessed the

devil's own luck. Those demmed Yankee Doodles usually seem to," he replied, praying it would be true this time.

"Yes, and he's used up three lifetimes of it already, Yankee or no," she said, biting her lip in anger. How dare he risk his life on some stupid drunken lark? Drum had explained during their coach ride how he'd left Jason in an advanced state of inebriation earlier that evening, certain the earl would be safely carried up to bed.

Don't you dare die on me, you great lobcock! What would she do if he were lying in a gutter or alley with life ebbing from his body? Why had he done such a buffle-headed thing after someone had made repeated attempts to kill him? Was the idea of going through with their marriage so repugnant that he would rather die in some sewer than stand before a priest and take her to wife? Rachel had never been so frightened in her life— at least, not since she'd thought he was going to die of that overdose of foxglove.

They trudged through thick fog toward the next grog shop, much dispirited yet still determined.

Jason was just sober enough to realize that he was in trouble. He stood in the corner of the dimly lit tavern with only a table separating him from three menacing strangers. The stench of stale grease and cheap gin melded with the salty smell of rotted wood from the wharves. Torches hung from the walls, and cheap tallow lamps provided the only illumination, casting everything in flickering shadow as the trio advanced on him.

A knife gleamed in the ringleader's hand. He was flanked by two burly tars, obviously recruited on the wharves. One, whose neck bore the suspicious scars of a hangman's rope, carried a heavy cudgel, and the other, a behemoth with his right eye gouged out, clenched his enormous fists, formidable weapons indeed.

That last half-pint of ale had definitely been a mistake. Jason shook his head to clear it, wishing he had more than the small screw pistol concealed in his jacket. Damn it to hell, he had not even brought his boot knife. Perhaps he could take the one from the ringleader, but first he had to even the odds a bit. One shot, and he had best make it count. He decided to use it on the fellow with the cudgel. Withdrawing the gun, he pointed it at the ringleader, a small weasely cutpurse with rotted teeth and stringy yellow hair.

"I would recommend you turn and head for that door," Jason said in a clear voice that carried over the raucous noise of drunken patrons crowded around the tables in the smoky room.

"Then I wouldn't get paid, Yer Lordship," the man said with a mocking grin, revealing diseased gums in addition to his rotted teeth. He made a hand motion to the fellow with the cudgel, and the man began moving to his left around the table while his huge companion with the missing eye moved right.

Jason held the weapon on the ringleader. "You'll be the first to die," he said.

The man appeared undaunted, holding his knife as he watched the barrel of Jason's pistol. He was small and no doubt agile as a cat. Without giving any warning, Beaumont turned and fired at the rope-scarred assassin just as he raised his cudgel. The crowded room erupted with curses and screams as drunken men and their whores scrambled out of the way.

At such close range, the small pistol's bullet struck with enough force to knock the assassin backward. As he crumpled to the filthy floor, his weapon clattered from his hand. Jason leaped over him in an attempt to get away from the giant's fists, but the ringleader was on him from the opposite side, knife flashing.

Jason felt it slash through his heavy jacket but miss his arm as he reached for the assassin's wrist. He tried to pivot away from the killer's next thrust but ran smack into one hammerlike fist that sent him flying. Ears ringing, he stumbled, trying desperately to regain his footing when a second blow to his eye almost snapped his head from his shoulders.

" 'E's mine now." The knife-wielding ringleader stepped in for the kill.

Jason went down on one knee, cursing in no particular order his own stupidity, Rachel's beautiful body, his grandfather's blackmailing schemes and whoever had paid these men. Just as his opponent struck, a shot rang out. The ringleader emitted a high-pitched screech and dropped the knife, clutching his right arm, which streamed blood.

The behemoth shambled back a step, his small piggy eye flashing from side to side, looking for escape. A small toff with a deadly-looking rapier advanced toward him, followed by another taller fellow whose smoking pistol gave mute testimony that he had fired the shot. The one-eyed man charged his smaller opponent, hoping to seize the swell and snap his slender spine. His mistake.

Drum coolly drove the point of his rapier into the man's throat. Meanwhile, Rachel pointed her second pistol calmly at the heart of the babbling assassin who was rocking back and forth holding his shattered arm. Jason gritted his teeth and tried to squint through his one good eye, unable to believe what it revealed as he struggled to stand up.

"You great addlepated, chuckle-headed, maggoty-brained clodpole!" Rachel yelled at her betrothed, so frightened and furious at the same time, she could barely hold the pistol steady on his would-be assassin. "If you wish to kill yourself, kindly wait until after we are mar—"

"Quiet, before you give away that which you want none of our audience to know," he hissed at her, glancing around the room at the now curious and cunning expressions on dozens of grimy, hard-eyed faces. Then, more softly he said, "Fine shooting, Countess."

"Not really. I was aiming for his heart," she admitted before she was able to stop herself.

"Frightened for me, Countess?" he whispered, watching her stiffen in outrage. " 'Tis better you left him alive. He may be reasonable enough to tell us who hired him."

She looked disdainfully at the man she'd shot, then back to the earl. "I have learned not to expect reasonableness in a male. 'Tis enough if they have learned not to drool on themselves."

"Please save your lovers' bickering for later," Drum interjected. "The watch will not venture into this cesspit, and the patrons are getting rather restive."

"Bleedin' swells, comin' 'ere and startin' trouble," the barkeep said, causing a chorus of loud angry curses and mutterings to fill the air. Rachel, who had given her unfired pistol to Jason, quickly reloaded the spent one with practiced efficiency. She leveled the weapon on the barkeep, who quickly subsided.

Ignoring the crowd, Drum stepped neatly over the corpses and seized the wounded man by one grimy lapel, propelling him toward the door. "Watch them and back slowly out," he instructed Rachel and Jason.

His companions needed no further encouragement as they beat a retreat, dragging the howling assassin with them. Hailing a jarvey proved difficult, since none voluntarily came into the area. They had to walk down dark and dangerous streets toward safety while practically carrying the wounded man, who was now slumped in semiconsciousness.

Jason's head felt as if all of Napoleon's artillery had been unleashed inside it. The ache in his ear pounded; and his eye, now completely swollen closed, throbbed wickedly. *A duet! Bloody lovely!* "How the hell can someone so slight weigh so much?" he muttered, bowed down by the assassin.

"He scarce has reason to aid us, now does he?" Rachel replied, her tone too sweet. She was still seething with fury over Jason's foolish brush with death, but damned if she would give him the satisfaction of knowing how terrified the idea of losing him had made her. Changing the subject before he turned his attention toward her, she suggested, "The best course might be to take him to Bow Street and let the authorities deal with him. They know how to extract information from creatures such as this."

"I believe we might have more persuasive means at hand," Drum replied in a soft, deadly voice.

Jason only grunted his agreement. Once safely away from the wharves, Drum backed the killer into an alley, the rapier at the man's throat a pressing reminder of just how deadly the dandy could be.

"Now, old chap, you are going to tell us who paid you to murder the earl."

His injured arm now forgotten as visions of the huge tar's ruined throat seized hold of his mind, the assassin bleated, "No need to be gettin' all grimflashy, Yer Lordship. I—I'd tell if I could, I would. But I dunno who 'e was." When the blade punctured the grimy skin at his Adam's apple, the man tried to swallow down his utter terror. " 'E stops me two nights ago in Whitechapel. Pulls me in an alley just like this 'ere. Dark as a blackamoor's face it were. 'E offered five guineas, but I never seen 'is face."

"Too busy looking at the coin, I warrant." Jason's voice was resigned.

"What else can you remember? Was he young? Old? How was he dressed?" Rachel asked, making no attempt to disguise her feminine voice.

The assassin gaped at her. "Gor, ye be a woman!"

"A woman who will shoot off your wretched nether parts if you do not talk quickly," she replied calmly, raising her pistol and pointing it at the little man's crotch.

He flattened himself against the wall, trying in vain to shield his "parts" with his one functioning hand. He entreated, " 'E were young. Dressed like a swell. Taller 'n me but lean. 'Is clothes was Bond Street stuff. That's all I could tell, I swear on me mum's grave."

"I doubt he knows who his mother is," Drum said contemptuously.

"The description could fit young Mountjoy," Jason replied.

"Or any one of a thousand young toffs about London," Rachel said in frustration.

They spent another quarter hour dissecting his story and asking detailed questions. He begged for mercy, and then fainted from the pain of his shattered arm. When it became apparent that he was telling all he knew, Drum made a decision.

"I shall turn him over to the watch." He looked at Jason and tsked. "You've bled all over your cravat and allowed this ruffian's knife to ruin that splendid kersey-mere I selected at Westin's," he scolded, holding up the slashed jacket sleeve.

"Better the jacket than my arm," Jason replied.

"Most regrettable that tar only struck your hard Yan-kee skull, which seems as impervious to prudence as it is to pain. Had he pounded some sense into your brain, this whole bumble might prove worthwhile," Rachel said.

"You take this sapskull home and tend his wounds," Drum instructed Rachel as he signaled a jarvey guiding his nag down the cobbled streets in the predawn light.

"I can take care of myself," Jason averred, then at once realized the folly of that pronouncement.

"So you have amply demonstrated on . . . let me see . . . how many occasions now, m'lord earl?" Her voice dripped with false sweetness, masking the fear that twisted her belly in knots as they climbed into the hackney.

They started back to the Cargrave city house in absolute silence. Jason was feeling the aftereffects of his over-indulgence, compounded by the beating he had taken. He leaned his head back against the musty-smelling squabs and tried his best to ignore the simmering anger of the woman sitting across from him.

That was impossible. Even dressed in her old riding breeches, baggy shirt and boots, her hair hidden and her face smeared with grime, she possessed a compelling femininity that called to him. Why her? Of all the women he had ever known, why did this swaggering, wasp-tongued female drive him to the brink of madness? Especially considering that he could never make love to her. Perhaps that was it, he tried to reassure himself as he concentrated on the pounding in his head. He desired her because he could not have her.

Forbidden fruit was always the sweetest. Images of her swathed in silk and lace in that fitting room danced in his mind. He tried to focus on the dull ache of his swollen eye, but her presence was still overpowering.

Rachel sat ramrod straight as the coach bounced along, tense as the spring of a tightly wound timepiece, unable to take her eyes off him. What if he had been killed? There had been so many attempts on his life. His luck could not last forever. He would indeed be far better off back in America. She should be glad of the plan for his escape after their nuptials. But she could feel nothing but a bottomless sense of impending loss.

You are a fool. He does not want you. Certainly his folly this night made that abundantly clear, if the prospect of going through with the ceremony had driven him to such drunken recklessness.

He seemed to fill the close confines of the coach. She could smell the familiar male scent of him blended not unattractively with the sharpness of blood, sweat and ale. His long legs were sprawled across the floor, and his head was tilted back against the cushions. At least those mocking blue eyes were closed, not fastened upon her. She could drink her fill of his ruined beauty without being caught at it.

Even drunk, disheveled and bloody, with his eye blacked, he was splendid, damn him. Dark hair hung in rumpled curls around his face, and those thick lashes fanned down over his eyes. She could see the black bristles of beard along his stubborn jawline in the faint light of dawn. His stock and shirt had been torn loose in the fight, and the hairy expanse of his chest was visible. Her eyes moved lower, then abruptly stopped before trespassing into such utterly forbidden territory.

"Are you taking inventory of my remaining undamaged assets . . . or gloating over my misery, Countess?" he asked at length, pleased with her small gasp of dismay at being caught studying him.

Rachel felt the heat rush to her cheeks and pressed herself back against the cushions, trying to ward off his mockery. The insufferable lout! "Continue to bait me, m'lord, and I will make you the same promise I made that little vermin back in the alley. Your *assets* will not long remain undamaged." She caressed the butt of the Clark pistol in her sash.

He leaned forward, elbows on his knees, as he peered at her with his one good eye. "You took as foolish a risk as did I tonight. If those men in that grog shop had discovered you were female, they would have torn you limb from limb."

"Your gratitude overwhelms me," she snapped. "I risked my life to save yours. With half the scum in London trying to dispatch you, why did you slip off alone in a drunken stupor?" The moment she asked the question, Rachel could have bitten her tongue. She did not want an answer, for she knew what it must be.

The earl, however, did not have the slightest idea why he had done what he had. He shook his head, then groaned at the renewed agony the sudden movement ignited. To add to his misery, the jarvey pulled to an abrupt halt in front of the Cargrave residence. Jason cursed and held his pounding head as if it were shattered crystal while Rachel shoved him from the coach.

Once inside the house, she roused the servants, several of whom had fallen asleep in the hallways while awaiting word of His Lordship's return. The servants gaped in horror at the young earl's future countess garbed in male attire. Her face was smeared with filth and her clothes bloody, yet she appeared in complete command as she issued orders. No one dared to question her.

"Fetch me hot water, plenty of it, and a large piece of beefsteak if cook has any," she demanded of the haughty butler. She turned to one of the footmen and instructed him, "Go to my city house and rouse Mistress Yeats. She knows where I keep my poultices. Fetch her here with the satchel at once."

"I do not require nursing, Countess, merely a fortnight or so of uninterrupted sleep," Jason protested.

She slung his arm over her shoulders and guided his stumbling steps toward the stairs. "You will have sleep aplenty after I see that you are cleaned up, sweated out and thoroughly poulticed to draw the blood from your eye and ear."

That sounded ominous indeed. "I have survived far worse injuries in tavern brawls from Florida to the Azores. You need not trouble yourself."

Rachel ignored the idiotic assertion. "Which is your room?" she asked as they reached the top of the stairs.

He glanced down at her, their heads so close together that he could smell the blend of her perfumed hair and street offal. Giving her a slumberous look, he whispered low so the maid scurrying ahead of them could not hear. "Do you intend to have your way with me now that I am feeble and unable to resist, Countess?"

She snorted. "You reek of blood, cheap ale and wharf excrement. Were I to have 'my way with you,' it would be to instruct a groom to scrub you down with lye soap and a stiff brush."

Rachel shoved him through the door the maid had opened into his quarters. A huge Louis XVI bed dominated the room, which was furnished with masculine chairs and a long sofa upholstered in burgundy leather. Jason's valet, Tompson, arose from the deep bowels of leather, wiping sleep from his eyes. He squinted in amazement at the staggering earl, who was being dragged into the room by a tall young fellow . . . who was not a fellow at all! When he recognized the Honorable Miss Rachel Fairchild, Viscount Harleigh's daughter and His Lordship's betrothed, the servant was certain he was having a most outrageous nightmare.

He rushed to her side and took Jason's other arm, unable to say a word as the maid turned back the bed at Rachel's direction.

"Place him in bed and undress him. I shall be back after I freshen up," she said, sliding from beneath Jason's arm at the side of the bed. The earl nearly overbalanced at the sudden loss of support on one side, and Thompson more flung than placed his employer on the mattress as Rachel stalked from the room.

The maid scurried about lighting branches of candles, then fled the chamber without uttering a word. The only sounds were His Lordship's muttered curses as the valet jostled his aching head while stripping off his clothes. "The very least you could do to make up for your cow-handedness is to pour me a brandy, Tompson," Jason said as his valet completed his task.

"Should you not don a nightshirt first, m'lord? Your betrothed will return—"

"We've been through this before, Tompson. I detest bloody nightshirts. Miss Fairchild intends to minister to my head, not my nether parts," he said crossly. Therein lay the reason for his frustration.

"Very good, m'lord."

Jason took the snifter gratefully and swallowed down its medicinal contents in several gulps, then held it out for a refill. The valet complied, and he downed the second glass almost as quickly. "Ah, that's better. I must fortify myself for further abuse when my guardian angel comes to minister to me," he slurred as Tompson took the snifter from his hand and helped him slide beneath the sheet.

The earl was decently covered when Rachel appeared with the cook and a footman in tow. She had washed her hands and face, then donned a shabby gown, obviously a donation from one of the serving women. It was far too short and hung on her like a tent.

"Place the water on the bedside table with the linens," she instructed the footman.

"Wot do ye want me to do wi' this 'ere meat, mum?"

the cook asked, looking almost admiringly at His Lordship's swollen eye and ear.

Rachel took the platter from the old woman and then dismissed all the servants. Tompson hesitated as the footman and cook filed out, wondering if he should protest this most unseemly situation. He took another look at the expression on the face of the noblewoman and thought better of it. After all, she was the earl's betrothed.

When they were alone, Rachel soaked a clean cloth in the cool water, then wrung it out and took a seat beside him on the bed. Good lord, he was naked beneath the covers! Did the man not own a nightshirt? She could see the outline of his long, muscular body beneath the sheet, that body she had so admired in the pool. Rachel blinked and looked away lest he open his eyes and catch her admiring his physique once again. Then she saw the brandy glass sitting on the opposite bedside table.

One sniff told her that he reeked of fresh brandy fumes. "You've been drinking more!"

He stirred and opened his eye. "Purely med-medicinal," he replied, carefully enunciating each syllable of the second word as he brought her into focus.

"You have enough 'medicine' in your body to heal every casualty in the Peninsular Army."

"My head still aches."

"Only wait a few more hours. 'Twill get far worse," she replied cheerfully, setting to work cleaning his injuries.

He tried not to think about that and concentrated instead on her change of costume. "Not the most fetching thing I've ever seen you in, but you could always remove it," he murmured.

"I believe you've created enough scandal for one

night." She gave the cloth another sharp squeeze, then plopped it over his face.

"Ouch! You've the bedside manner of a ship's surgeon." He watched her with his one good eye as she concentrated on her task, leaning over him to better reach his bloodied ear. "And, not to place too fine a point on it, you are the one who created the scandal by going about the city in men's clothing."

"I could scarcely have gone to the wharves in a ball gown, now could I?" she snapped.

Jason considered this for a moment. "I suppose not, but you need not have scandalized Grandfather's servants by coming inside with me." A dim fuzzy part of his brain knew he was being perverse, but he could not seem to help it.

"No, I could have let you crawl up the portico steps on all fours and bark at the front door to gain admittance while I made my escape."

"Could've walked up the steps myself."

"You most certainly could not. I practically carried you up to this room."

"Tompson did that . . . didn't he?" The room was starting to spin a bit now.

The dress she wore belonged to a far heftier female, and the bodice gapped open as she worked over him, affording an excellent view of her breasts, which were covered only by a thin linen shift, leaving little to his imagination. Jason had a superior imagination . . . no, memory . . . when it came to Rachel Fairchild's body. As he focused every ounce of his attention on those luscious pear-shaped mounds, the spinning inside his head abated.

Almost without realizing he did so, he reached up and cupped his hands around them. She froze. The tingling pleasure was so sudden and unexpected that it robbed her of breath. His long, elegant fingers felt as if they were burning her skin through the slight barrier of cloth as they kneaded lightly. Her nipples contracted into hard, aching points just as they had that day in the water.

Damn the man! Even foxed he could bedazzle her out of her senses. Or perhaps a better way of expressing it would be to say that he heightened her senses. Yes, every nerve in her body had grown keenly aware of how close he was. How easy it would be to climb into the bed beside him and pull the sheet over them, to lie with her body pressed to his hot, naked flesh.

Just as suddenly as his hands had touched her, they fell away. Rachel opened her eyes abruptly and looked down at her patient. A loud snore rent the silence. He had fallen sound asleep! Reaching over for the beefsteak on the platter, she plopped it over his blackened eye none too gently, then stood up and glared at him.

"That's what you can do with your meat!" she gritted out and stomped from the room. The bloody hell with poulticing him. Tompson could attend to it when the Yankee clodpole woke up.

Chapter Fourteen

Fox Barlow was very upset. He sat at the big bay window in his quarters at Cargrave Hall overlooking the distant rise of mountains on the Welsh border. He had come to love the bleak and rugged country as much as the forbidding stone monolith of a castle from which the Beaumont family had ruled for centuries. And even more, he had come to love the stern old man who was the present Marquess of Cargrave.

Grandfather.

Fox had sensed with a child's unerring intuition that beneath the forbidding old man's gruff facade beat a loving heart. He missed his wife and had lived a lonely life since her passing. All of their children and grandchildren had also died except for Jace. For some reason, the marquess and Jace could not seem to express their feelings for each other, but Fox knew that the old man loved his heir very much and wanted him to be happy with Rachel. The old man had even shown Fox

197

his marchioness's portrait, hanging in the family gallery, and remarked upon how much Rachel reminded him of his dear Mathilda. The boy had seen the sheen of tears in his eyes even though he tried to hide them.

But now Jace wanted to leave England and return to America. Apparently, it was because of his having to marry Miss Fairchild. Why a man would not want such a beautiful and intelligent lady for a wife, Fox could not understand. But Jace did not, according to what Fox had overheard Grandfather and her father say in the library last week. He had not intended to eavesdrop, but when they'd mentioned his name, along with those of Jace and Rachel, he simply could not resist.

He was distressed to learn that Grandfather was keeping him here and would not allow him to visit Jace until the marriage ceremony, which was to take place in London two weeks hence. It seemed that both the viscount and the marquess were afraid that Jace would take him and sail back to America! But Fox had not wanted to do that for a long time.

How could he hurt Grandfather by running away? Yet yesterday afternoon Jace's friend Mr. Drummond, who was Grandfather's house guest, had met him in the stables. Fox replayed their strange conversation over again in his mind, trying to sort out his thoughts.

He had jumped Little Chief over the tallest of the hedgerows and was feeling jubilant. It had felt just like flying! His riding instructor Bradley had complimented him on how well he had taken to an English saddle and how expertly he had handled the spirited little gelding. The boy walked his lathered mount into the stable, eager to rub him down, something Bradley insisted he do each time he rode. Learning to take care of one's mount was an integral part of fine horsemanship. He had just begun to work with a curry comb when he heard voices.

Then an unfamiliar gentleman, slight of build and nattily dressed, walked down the row of stalls toward him. Fox could see that the man found the horsey aroma distasteful by the flare of his nostrils and the way he held a linen handkerchief to his nose as soon as he set foot inside the door. Putting down his tools, Fox had asked politely, "Is there something I could help you with, sir?"

The stranger smiled uncertainly. "If you are Master Fox Barlow, yes, you may."

Fox nodded, equally uncertain. "I am."

"I'm a good friend of the earl. The Honorable Alvin Francis Edward Drummond, at your service." He clicked his heels smartly and returned Fox's nod as a half bow. Then, checking to see that they were alone, he stepped closer. "I have a message for you from Jason, to be delivered in private. Might we take a brief walk so I may impart it?"

"I suppose so, if it will not take long," the boy replied, knowing that he must finish his chores but curious about what Jace wanted his friend to tell him.

They strolled behind the stables toward a small orchard. Once Mr. Drummond was certain they were well out of sight and hearing of any stable help, he said, "You know your foster brother is betrothed. The wedding will take place in London in a fortnight."

"Yes, to Miss Fairchild. I am to stand for Jace," Fox said proudly.

Drum nodded. "So I have been given to understand— and so you shall." The little man appeared to hesitate, as if uncertain about how to continue. Fox studied him with luminous dark eyes as he cleared his throat. "However, after the ceremony . . . that is, the night after, Jace shall come to fetch you at the Cargrave city house. You are to be waiting for his signal around midnight—"

"Midnight?" the boy echoed in confusion.

"Er, yes. Well after everyone has gone to bed."

"Is that so Grandfather will not know Jace is running away, back to America?"

Mr. Drummond's eyebrows flew upward in surprise. "My, my. What do you know of this matter, eh, lad?"

Fox scuffed the toe of his boot against a rock, then said, "I did not mean to overhear, but Grandfather and the viscount were talking the other day . . ."

"I see," Mr. Drummond said thoughtfully. "Well, the truth of the matter is, Jace don't wish to marry Miss Fairchild and—"

"But she is so very beautiful—and nice, too." Fox felt constrained to defend his angel. "Why would he not want her for a wife?"

The gentleman seemed at a loss for words, something the boy intuited did not happen often. At length his disconcerted companion replied, " 'Tis not her in particular, dear boy. The earl just does not want to be leg-shack . . . er, married—to any lady, no matter how beautiful. And," he hastened to add, "the lady does not wish to marry him, either."

"Is it because Grandfather and the viscount picked them for each other?"

Mr. Drummond tugged at his cravat and muttered something unintelligible beneath his breath, then replied, "You are altogether too wise for your years, young sir."

Fox grinned. "Jace always says that, too."

"Hmmm, I am beginning to see why. But nonetheless, it is imperative that you reveal nothing to the marquess, so that you and Jason can get clean away."

Fox nodded uncertainly. "But why is Jace going to marry Miss Fairchild if only for one night?"

The question appeared to startle the dandy. His face reddened as he cleared his throat. "I have my own theories about that—but never you mind. The thing is to throw Cargrave and Harleigh off their guard. Once the marriage has taken place and they retire to Falcon's Crest for . . . well, after the first night, it will be easier for Jason to slip past those set to watch him and come to fetch you."

"You mean because the marriage will be consummated," Fox said.

Mr. Drummond nearly choked at that rejoinder. "Obviously, they don't teach you that babies come from the cabbage patch in America, do they?"

"Oh, my father's people do, but the Shawnee tell the truth. 'Tis only natural, you know," he said, shrugging at the foolishness of "civilized societies."

Mr. Drummond harrumphed for a moment, then said, "Utmost secrecy is the order of the day if you are to escape. Jason will appear beneath your window at midnight and signal you by making the call of an owl. Then you must dress quickly and climb down the trellis at the garden wall. Do you think you can do that?"

Fox nodded glumly. "I suppose so."

"I sense a certain reluctance, m'boy. Don't you want to go home to your family in America?"

"Some day. But right now . . . well, I don't want to hurt Grandfather's feelings."

Mr. Drummond emitted a sharp bark of laughter. "Can't say I've ever before heard anyone worry about hurting the old boy. Rather, most people fear what he will do to hurt them."

"He has been ever so kind to me," Fox replied with stubborn insistence, feeling a bit of anger at the way this man and so many others judged the marquess.

Mr. Drummond began to pace beneath an apple tree, rubbing his chin thoughtfully. "What a bumble bath this is turning out to be," he said crossly.

Fox did not feel that his visitor's anger was directed at him. He waited patiently for him to continue.

Sighing, the dandy made another approach. "You know about the attempt on the earl's life while you were at Falconridge?" At the boy's nod, he continued, "Well, there have been several others attempts—in London and in the country."

"But who would want to kill Jace?"

"That is precisely what the marquess has charged me with learning. We believe it to be those in the pay of Lord Frederick Forrestal. However, so far, I have been unable to find proof of the villain's deeds. Until I do so . . ."

Fox could see those bright green eyes studying him speculatively and knew what was expected of him. Sighing glumly, he replied, "I will say nothing to Grandfather, and I will go back to America with Jace until it is safe for him to return and be Miss Fairchild's . . . er, the Countess of Falconridge's husband."

"Er . . . well, yes, I imagine you may be more nearly correct than ever the earl or his countess suspects," Mr. Drummond replied with a mysterious chuckle. Then he had winked at Fox.

Sitting in the library, Fox remembered how happy Mr. Drummond had appeared when he was able to take his leave at the conclusion of their talk. But now, after sleeping on it overnight, the boy was still torn. He could not betray Jace. But how could he betray Grandfather?

This Lord Forrestal meant to kill Jace. That had added a whole new dimension to Fox's dilemma. Until they arrested the evil man, it would be better for Jace to return to America. But no one had thought to ask Fox what he wanted to do. He was not sure himself at this point. If only he could talk to Jace before the wedding.

The boy's reverie was interrupted by LaFarge, his master-at-arms. "Young Monsieur Fox, have you forgotten? This afternoon we practice with the foils, *non?*"

*   *   *

The invitation to Sir Roger Dalbert's soiree arrived early the next morning. Fox, who was with Cargrave in the library, listened as the old man read it. "Demned nice of Roger and his wife to keep to tradition this way, having a hunt to celebrate the betrothal."

"A fox hunt?" the boy asked. He had difficulty understanding the English sport which allowed several dozen men and women to use a pack of hounds to hunt down and kill one small fox—especially considering that the fox was his totem animal.

"Yes, m'boy. For generations, although we are distant kin, the Dalberts and Beaumonts have celebrated marriages and births in our respective families by holding a hunt. Brings everyone together for a rousing good time. Last hunt was when Roger announced his betrothal to Mistress Simmons. Of course, her being a Cit and all, some of the family raised their eyebrows a bit, but . . ." He shrugged, dismissing the class prejudices, which he knew a boy of Fox's background would not understand. Neither did Jason, being raised as an American, but that was all to the good. It would bring a breath of fresh air into this stuffy old clan, he decided, chuckling to himself.

"Will I be allowed to accompany you?" Fox asked.

The marquess considered for a moment as he studied the boy's eager face. He knew the lad sorely missed his foster brother. And the Dalberts' country place was only a few hours' ride from Cargrave Hall. Cargrave would make certain that the men he had set to guard Jason watched him like a hawk. With Fox's tutors also in attendance, there would be no danger of Jason spiriting the boy away.

"Yes, I do believe I shall take you with me. Do you good, lad, to participate in a fine old English tradition.

Bradley tells me your riding skills are coming along splendidly."

"Yes, Grandfather. I'm able to jump Little Chief over every hedgerow on the estate now. I am certain I shall enjoy the hunt very much."

The old man did not understand that the gleam of excitement in the boy's eyes had nothing to do with chasing a fox. This weekend would provide the perfect opportunity to talk over his feelings with Jace before the plan to leave England was set in motion.

Frederick Forrestal was more frustrated than ever. He sat in his apartments off Grosvenor Square, drinking alone in mid-morning as he considered his dilemma. Fate had not favored him of late, and that was a masterpiece of understatement. He looked about the opulently furnished room, then took another swallow of fine aged port. There was no way he would give up the life to which birth had entitled him, but he would have to act quickly to avert disaster.

As if all else had not gone to blazes already, now his father, the Duke of Etherington, had disinherited his only son in favor of a puling nephew. To be sure, Frederick would still become the duke and inherit the family's entailed estate. But the vast majority of Etherington wealth was unentailed and would go to the old duke's nephew. Frederick would be land poor, no better off than he was now, while his cousin Marshall would be fabulously wealthy.

Two years his junior, Marsh had been disgustingly easy to bully ever since they'd been in leading strings together. At Eton, Frederick had made his cousin's life pure hell, taking great pleasure in watching the sanctimonious puppy blubber and shriek for mercy as Frederick's friends held him suspended by one ankle from a third-story window. How they had all laughed at him.

But now Marsh would have the final laugh!.

Intolerable. Frederick would deal with that carbuncle-faced fool in time, but for now, even more pressing matters required his attention. Word of his father's decision had spread swiftly through the ton. Unfortunately, it had also spread to the merchants, who now had the unmitigated impertinence to begin demanding that Frederick pay his bills. Considering that he owed his bootmaker alone well in excess of a thousand pounds, he was so far in dun territory as to require a miracle to save him from utter disgrace.

Or a very wealthy wife.

Forrestal smiled chillingly, and his yellow eyes narrowed on the small cloisonné box sitting beside the cut crystal port decanter. He opened it and looked at the embroidered silk bag within, filled with opium. Just a small dose to calm his nerves, help him think. As he pulled the drawstrings open, he considered how he would kidnap Rachel Fairchild. Once he had taken her maidenhead, she would have no choice but to wed him. He would see to her defloration en route to Gretna Green.

A scandal would ensue, of course, and that damned Yankee would be furious. His lips curved slightly in a parody of a smile. Even sweeter than killing that bastard Beaumont would be humiliating him. And as for that haughty Fairchild hellcat? She would be on her knees in front of him before he was finished with her. That would be the best revenge against the earl he could have. And that wretched pop-eyed old viscount would be grateful to call him son-in-law.

Having decided on a course of action, Forrestal put the silk bag back in the box. He could relax later. Now he was impatient to put his plan in motion at once. With one hand he reached for the bellpull while the other picked up his glass of port, lifting it in a toast of self-congratulation.

"To a rich wife and a very angry earl!"

"Do not scowl so. 'Twill wrinkle your face," Harry scolded as Rachel stared across the crowded hall at Jason, who had just arrived for the festivities.

He stood with their host and hostess, Roger and Garnet Dalbert, utterly ignoring Rachel as Garnet introduced him to her son by her first marriage. Evelyn Simmons was slim and wiry, with his mother's sharp dark eyes. Smallpox scars pitted his narrow face. In spite of them, he would be considered handsome. Curious to know what was being said, Harry took Rachel's arm in a sisterly fashion and began strolling closer. They could hear Roger's bluff voice booming over the hall.

"I say, old chap, you look quite the thing now. All recovered from your bout with the foxglove, eh?" Roger said.

"Yes, thanks to you and most especially your quick-witted wife," Jason replied, smiling at Garnet. He turned to her son and said, "I understand you also work at the shipyards at Gravesend."

"Indeed. Mother is most adept at running it, but I am learning the ropes, so to speak." Simmons smiled amiably. "You, too, were in shipping, m'lord, before returning to England, were you not?"

Harry pulled Rachel away from what turned into a boring discussion of Baltimore clippers and Napoleon's embargo, saying, "He does not seem eager to greet his bride. You shall have to do something to rouse his jealousy. Mistress Dalbert's son is unattached, is he not?"

"Don't you dare even think of such a thing," Rachel whispered fiercely.

"Ah, I do believe she doth protest too much. Is that

206

not from something literary?" Harry asked.

"Shakespeare. *Hamlet,*" Rachel replied absently. "And I am not going to make a cake of myself just to amuse that arrogant fool."

"You always were too much the bluestocking," Harry fretted.

"You either accuse me of being too much the hoyden or being too bookish. You cannot have it both ways, Harry," Rachel said, trying to divert the conversation.

"Well, neither is appealing to a gentleman."

"Fine. Jason Beaumont, by his own admission, is no gentleman," Rachel snapped. She had never revealed that she and Drum had joined forces to rescue Jason from his drunken folly the preceding week. She could still feel the sting of humiliation—which she assured herself was really anger—when Jason had passed into snoring unconsciousness with both hands affixed to her breasts. What a vapor her sister would have if Rachel ever confessed that fiasco!

Harry was about to make a rejoinder when young Master Barlow descended the stairs in a boyish rush. Excusing himself from the Dalberts and Evelyn Simmons, Jason bent down and hugged the boy as he flew into his arms. The two black-haired males made a handsome pair, looking as if they were indeed brothers by blood rather than adoption. Harry noted the way Rachel studied them, then commented slyly, "The earl has quite a way with children, does he not?"

" 'Tis his only redeeming trait that I have discerned to date," Rachel replied acerbically. *A pity he will never see the child you may bear him . . . if you are fortunate enough to conceive.* The sudden thought caught her by surprise, and she felt suddenly lightheaded. There was no sense in even thinking about their wedding night. She might well be unable to go through with a seduction. What if he refused her? Laughed at her? How could she bear it?

Harry was speaking to her again, but Rachel could not make out what her sister was saying. Then Jason turned his attention from Fox to her as the lad caught sight of her and dashed excitedly in her direction, dragging his foster brother behind.

"Miss Fairchild, I am pleased to see you again," Fox said in his most grown-up voice, trying in vain to hide his flush of excitement.

Rachel smiled as she and Harry greeted the lad. Roger, Garnet and her son joined the group, chatting amicably. Roger expressed great enthusiasm about the morrow's hunt. As everyone socialized, Rachel felt Jason's mocking blue eyes fixed on her. He had fully recovered from his brush with death in that waterfront tavern. Did he recall anything from their last encounter? She prayed that he had been too drunk to remember.

As he bowed over her hand, looking up into her eyes, she could not resist delivering a barb. "Your appearance is much improved from when last we met. The eye is healed. I doubt the blow to your thick skull caused any injury."

"But of course not. What injury could not be mended by your excellent nursing?" he replied in that lazy American drawl, steering her aside for a private conversation.

Without creating a scene, she could do nothing but allow him the liberty of taking her arm. "If you had remained safely at home to drink yourself into a stupor, you would not have required my excellent nursing."

"I am all the more in your debt for your Christian charity," he replied dryly.

Rachel quickly freed her arm from his grip and placed a discreet distance between them. It was not propriety which motivated her, but self-preservation.

"Actually, I have but a small store of charity, Christian or otherwise. Do not use up any more of my scant supply. The next time, you may be left to the tender mercies of an assassin with no one to rescue you," she replied tartly.

"I shall bear that in mind." His tone was wry. Then, changing topics abruptly just as she was about to turn away and rejoin the rest of the guests, he asked, "Will you go on the hunt, Countess?"

" 'Twould be most impolite for me to refuse."

"Ah, but in polite company you will not be able to straddle your mount and feel him pulsing beneath you, will you?" His voice was an insinuating whisper now, his smile sexually charged. And there was that accursed dimple again.

Damn the man! Rachel knew that any proper English lady should be highly insulted by such a vulgar double entendre. Harry would slap his face, then fall into a dead faint over such unimaginable crudity. In fact, Rachel could see her sister watching them with a bemused expression on her face. Harry was right. She was both too bookish and too hoydenish to ever make a proper English lady, which meant that she could reply to him in kind.

Smiling coolly, she said, "After your bare-arsed ride home from the pool, you certainly must be intimately acquainted with the feel of a horse beneath you."

"That day 'twas not a horse's body beneath me that I had in mind, Countess," he murmured as his eyes swept over the deep rose mull gown that swathed her tall, slender frame like a whispery caress.

Her blood pounded so swiftly she was certain her face must be the same shade as the dress. "If you were thinking of my body, you are doomed to grave disappointment, m'lord for I am always in command . . . when I ride any dumb brute."

He threw back his head and laughed. "Simply because she is astride does not mean that the woman is in command . . . or even wants to be."

"I do." Her eyes dared him, but her knees felt as weak as a newborn foal's.

He met her steady gaze with an appraising one of his own. "When the time comes I doubt the idea of command will even enter your mind. In fact, I doubt very much that you will be capable of thought at all."

Rachel fought back a shiver of anticipation, her mind indeed as incapable of thought as he had boasted.

"I look forward to the hunt, Countess," Jason said, his eyes revealing the hot hunger inside him.

Why was he playing this dangerous game with a woman who would shortly be able to claim his name? he wondered. He needed to avoid her, not pursue her. Yet the moment he had seen her standing in the foyer, glowing like a lush midsummer rose, he had been unable to stop himself. Dim memories of that night she and Drum had rescued him on the wharves flickered through his mind. Something about when she had treated his injuries, leaning over him in a gown that did not fit her.

Quite unlike the feathery soft mull that now showed off every curve. His eyes moved from the angry slash of her lips down her throat to those glorious breasts revealed so enticingly by the low neckline of her gown. Then the memory washed over him like spring rain. He had taken her breasts in his hands and felt the nipples harden, responding to his touch. But then—Jason sighed—he had fallen asleep. Did that explain her acerbic disposition tonight? He grinned at her, wondering if his supposition was correct.

She raised one eyebrow haughtily. "Best beware, m'lord, lest the hunter become the hunted." With that, she swept past him and returned to the safety of her sister's idle chatter.

Fox had observed their exchange from a distance, puzzled by the strange combination of forced smiles and fierce frowns on their faces. They certainly did not act like any betrothed couples he had ever seen before. But his experience was limited to those courting in the Shawnee settlements. Maybe things were different in England. That was something to ask Jace when they talked in private later tonight. He would wait until the whole house was asleep, then slip from his room and go in search of his foster brother.

Chapter Fifteen

If Fox was concerned about Jason and Rachel, Harry was downright vexed. For the past two weeks her elder sister had been blue-deviled to the point of outright surliness. At first Harry had ascribed Rachel's ill temper to the fact that Jason had returned to Falconridge in the midst of the Little Season. Upon further consideration, she realized how absurd that was, since her sister despised social engagements. After Rachel hied herself back to Harleigh, Harry knew they must have had another quarrel. Certainly their behavior here at Roger's country house indicated as much.

But Harry was unable to get Rachel to confide in her, other than making disparaging remarks about the earl's inability to hold his liquor and his possessing the wits of a sand flea. With the wedding less than two weeks away, that did not augur well.

However, Lady Harriet Chalmers was a consummate matchmaker. And a hopeless romantic. By the time the

soup course had been served at dinner that evening—
with Rachel and the earl still exchanging barbs—she
determined on a course of action. It was apparent to
anyone with *half* the wits of a sand flea that the earl
passionately desired Rachel. And she, too stubborn to
admit it, was quite in love with the rogue.

Those were just the right ingredients to turn a moonlit
night in early autumn into the setting for a perfect tryst.
Excusing herself after the trifle was served, Harry
slipped upstairs and had her maid fetch paper and ink.
After dinner the guests retired to their assigned rooms
for a good night's rest before the early-morning fox
hunt.

Rachel stood by the window, looking out at the
bright moonlight bathing the gardens with a silvery
glow. The fresh country air beckoned her. She was certainly too restless to sleep after an evening of verbal
fencing with Jason. He had to be the most infuriating
man she had ever had the misfortune to meet. One
moment he was devouring her with his eyes as if he
could not wait for their wedding night. Such desire
would make her humiliating plans for seducing him
utterly unnecessary. But then he would reverse himself
and appear supremely indifferent, teasing her as if she
were a spoiled child wanting a lesson in manners.

Ha! He was the one wanting for manners. She looked
down at the note, crumpled, smoothed out, then crumpled once again and tossed into the fireplace. Of
course, with the warm weather, there was no fire set,
so the cream vellum just lay there, taunting her almost
as much as its author would if she went to the rose
garden to meet him. Which she would not.

Would she?

"Oh, bugger it," she muttered angrily and stormed to
the door. The tall case clock struck the quarter hour.
Still thirty minutes before he'd asked her to meet him.

That would give her time to enjoy the fresh air and compose herself to do battle with Jason Beaumont, Earl of Falconridge. She strode down the hall as if daring anyone to question what she was doing out alone at this time of night. But not so much as a chambermaid appeared as she made her way downstairs, intending to let herself out one of the French doors in the dining room. Heavy puce-colored velvet draperies were drawn partially closed.

The interior of the house was furnished quite expensively, if not in the best of taste. Hideous gilt-encrusted tables and chairs squatted on claw feet with wings down their sides, rather like sinister beasts about to pounce on the unwary. Murals depicting classical mythology—Garnet's choice—and hunting scenes in gory detail, a sop to Roger's taste, filled every wall with clashing colors, mercifully muted now by dim moonlight. Huge Egyptian urns and cloisonné bric-a-brac filled every corner.

She picked her way through the costly obstacle course and slipped out the door onto the patio. Walking across the uneven stones, Rachel surveyed the grounds. In contrast to the interior, the exterior of the Dalberts' country estate looked quite down at the heels. Thick ivy vines worked their way up the sides of the brick walls and thrust impatient fingers into the mortar, loosening the masonry dangerously in many places. The late-blooming roses were sadly neglected, blighted and weed-choked. In the distance the moonlight glistened off puddles in the deep ruts of the drive. Rachel's coach had nearly broken a spring while making its way to the front entry.

"I suppose Mistress Dalbert is more interested in running her shipping business than an estate," she said softly to herself. Roger, whose antecedents had lived on this land for hundreds of years, appeared blissfully unaware of how poorly the servants and tenants tended his grounds and fields. It seemed to Rachel that he should be concerned, but it really was none of her affair. The couple appeared quite devoted to each other.

She and Jason were just the opposite. Of course, after the war he could resume running his shipping interests and she could manage their combined estates . . . if they had a real marriage. What was she doing, wool-gathering such a fantasy! He would be gone, and she would be alone for the rest of her life. Just as she had always wished to be.

Then why are you so miserable at the thought of it?

Rachel shook off the insistent inner voice and stomped down the well-worn stone staircase to the rose garden. Just like the lobcock to be late after summoning her. Was he hiding behind an overgrown hedge somewhere, laughing at her for being taken in by his joke?

Jason stood bemused in the shadows of the big house, watching Rachel move among the roses, stooping now and then to pull a weed or smell a bloom. *'Tis the farmer in her,* he thought with a smile as he watched the way her lush hips swayed when she straightened up. Being here was not a wise idea.

He had almost decided to remain in his room and ignore her message, but then he'd reconsidered. The mule-headed chit was just nervy enough to come rapping on his door in the middle of the night. He had delayed approaching her for half an hour, hoping that she would grow impatient and give up. But she had not given up.

And here he was, making, as Drum would say, an utter cake of himself. He watched with a grin when she squatted in the dirt and used a twig to dig out a particularly recalcitrant vine menacing one of the rose bushes. No prim vaporing miss, this one. The thought occurred to him that they could rub on rather well with her in charge of the estates and him overseeing his shipping interests and the marquess's investments. He snorted at the daydream. Within a week's time together, they would be at each other's throats—when they were not in bed.

Ah, yes, in bed they would do quite well together. Of that he was certain. For all her protests, Rachel Fairchild was a passionate woman who might know the mechanics of animal reproduction, but had only the slightest inkling of the pleasure a man and woman could give each other. Without undue vanity, he knew he could initiate her successfully. That would take care of the nights. But what about the days?

And what about the scheming old marquess who cared only that the Beaumont name and Cargrave titles were carried on? No, he would not fall into that trap, no matter how beauteous an enticement she presented. Why the deuce had she written that note asking him to meet her this way? Since his arrival at the Dalberts', they had taunted and sniped at each other until his nerves were raw.

Their plans for the escape were finalized. What more was left? A moonlight tryst. Keeping his hands off of her had become increasingly difficult with every meeting. If he weakened and seduced her, all would be lost. Did he have the willpower to resist her?

"Only one way to find out," he muttered grimly and stalked across the terrace to the rose garden.

Harry sighed, wringing her hands. She had been unable to sleep, eager to learn what had transpired in the garden between Rachel and the earl. Would they have succumbed to passion right out in broad moonlight? On a bed of roses? She was not certain if her English sensibilities found that romantic or merely very uncomfortable. It would certainly be imprudent, but then at least they would realize that they were meant for each other. Far past time for that to be settled. She simply had to find out what delicious results her machinations had wrought.

Opening the door to her room, she peeked up and down the long hallway. As usual, there were no servants about. Sir Roger and his lady were decidedly niggardly in hiring staff, she sniffed. The light was dim but sufficient to allow her to make her way to Rachel's room. Turning the lock, she slipped inside and closed the door, calling out softly, "Rachel, dear, 'tis Harry. Are you asleep?"

No answer. Harry moved cautiously toward the bed. At times her sister could sleep like the dead after spending hours riding around Harleigh and mucking about with the tenants. Harry pulled back the heavy satin bed hangings and squinted in the faint moonlight. Empty.

"Well, I shall just have to wait." She stepped on the footstool and climbed onto the bed, letting her feet swing over the edge of the mattress. It would be far more comfortable to lie back on the pillows than to sit in that uncomfortable chair by the window.

Before long she dozed.

Moments later the door opened and two figures slipped inside, closing it behind them. The taller carried a heavy woolen blanket. His slighter companion held a small truncheon in his hand. "Yer wants me to cosh 'er first?" he whispered to his accomplice.

"Let me throw this over 'er, then see," the big fellow replied as he stepped deftly to the bed. Shoving the curtains aside, he looked down at the sleeping woman. Learning which room belonged to Rachel Fairchild from the drunken footman had been as simple as taking a coin from a street urchin. Now all they had to do was deliver her, relatively unharmed, to the toff waiting at the edge of the woods.

With a practiced hand, he threw the heavy, vile-smelling blanket over the sleeping woman and rolled her inside it before she awakened enough to make one small, muffled cry. She wriggled and coughed, but he held her easily, then tossed her over his shoulder. Turning to the fellow with the truncheon, he said, "Now give 'er a tap, light 'un—careful not to damage the goods."

Chuckling, the smaller man did as he was bade and Harry's struggling ceased.

Fox stood at the end of the hallway, looking from Jason's room, which was mysteriously empty, toward the room into which two ill-dressed and hard-looking strangers had just slipped. They did not seem to belong here. Certainly they were not guests, and he was almost positive they were not servants, either. At best they might be stablemen, but what would stablemen be doing in the house in the middle of the night?

They looked more like the sort of toughs he'd seen from carriage windows as he and Grandfather rode through the streets of London. Instinctively, Fox did not like them. He darted back into Jace's room and looked about for the carved pecan case in which his hero always carried his pistols. Seizing one, primed and ready, for Jace never allowed them to be any other way, he slipped out the door and crouched behind a pier table in the hallway.

Within a moment the men reemerged from the room. The taller one was carrying what looked like a rolled-up carpet over one shoulder. Cracksmen stealing rugs from the guest rooms? Puzzled, Fox began to follow as they made their way stealthily down the servants' stairs.

They moved through the kitchens, where the cook-fires were banked and deserted, and made their way out a doorway as if they had been given an architectural drawing of the old manor house. The two thieves walked down a gravel path leading to a ramshackle dairy barn. Bypassing that, they headed toward the woods, where another man emerged from the shadows.

This one was even taller than the man carrying the rug and he was dressed like a toff. Just then the rug began to move, wriggling like a centipede on a stick. Fox's eyes grew huge as he watched the man toss his burden on the thick, dew-wet grass and yank it up, unrolling the figure of a woman, who cried out. The baroness, Miss Fairchild's sister! The boy would have recognized her pale golden hair and high, sweet voice anywhere. The blackguards had kidnapped her, and now the smaller one reached down and struck her before she could cry out again.

Fox dashed closer, using the overgrown brush and weeds for cover as his Shawnee uncles had taught him. Now he was ever so glad he'd brought Jace's pistol. There would be no time to summon help. He would have to rescue her all by himself. Fox could overhear the angry exchange between the gentleman and the cracksmen now.

"You utter idiots! This is not Rachel Fairchild but her sister."

"She were in the Fairchild woman's room, asleep in 'er bed," the tall man protested.

"And were no one else in the room neither," the one who'd struck her averred.

"You had the wrong room, you incompetent louts. The gel recognized me. Someone may have heard her cry. Get rid of her quickly," he said.

"We don't do nothin' 'less we gets paid, gov," the little man said nastily.

With a snarled oath, the nobleman tossed the pouch

of coins he had at his waist to the taller of the pair. "Kill her and throw her body in the woods."

With that icy command, he turned on his heel and stalked toward the big, blaze-faced chestnut grazing unconcernedly a few yards away. Jumping on its back, he vanished into the darkness, leaving the two thugs with their prey.

Fox swallowed hard for courage and moved in closer, clutching the pistol in one small, sweaty hand.

Rachel heard the soft echo of footfalls and turned with a stifled gasp as Jason loomed behind her. "Must you always make it a habit to sneak up on people?" His hair was rumpled and glowed blue-black in the moonlight, framing that harshly beautiful face, now made even more menacing in the shadows. He had shed his formal dinner clothes and wore a soft shirt, open at the throat as was his wont. Her eyes skimmed over the hard planes of his hair-sprinkled chest as was her wont.

"You were expecting me. My arrival should scarce be a surprise." He could smell the faint essence of her perfume blended with her unique female scent, a fragrance more enticing than all the roses in England. His hands ached to touch her, and he found himself stepping dangerously close. Her breasts were barely an inch from his chest. If either of them took a deep breath . . .

Rachel tore her eyes away from that muscular chest and stepped back before she did something utterly stupid. Her heart hammered and the blood all seemed to rush from her head, leaving it swimming, fuzzy and confused. Every instinct in her body cried out that she fall into his arms and let him kiss her, for that was certainly what it seemed he wished to do. She swayed ever so faintly toward him without realizing it.

That was all the encouragement Jason needed. One hand reached up, taking a fistful of the shiny dark hair cascading down her back, pulling her against his chest. "I'm glad you did not plait it," he murmured as he tilted her head backward and lowered his mouth to hers for a kiss. She tasted sweet and tart all at once—a fitting match to her personality, he thought ruefully. Then her lips parted with a soft moan and he could not think at all.

His tongue was fierce, commanding and hungry, just as his eyes had been when he had taken her aside in the foyer before dinner. This was madness, but such sweet madness that she could never deny him. A dim part of her brain was telling her that this was the perfect solution to her fears about seducing him on their wedding night. But what if he took her now?

That sudden thought snaked its way past the excitement as he rained kisses across her eyelids, cheeks and throat, then once more centered on her mouth. Rachel struggled to make her body obey the commands her mind was frantically sending. *Do not let him have you here! It must be on your wedding night. The servants must see your virgin blood on the sheets so that they swear it is a true marriage that cannot be annulled.* But a deeply buried fear lay like ice in her heart. What if in refusing him now, she so infuriated him as to kill his desire for her? How could she deny herself the intense pleasure of his caresses? What if this were her only chance to have him?

Her jumbled thoughts finally crystallized when his hands once again cupped her breasts, just as he had that night in his bed . . . before he lost consciousness. She had been grateful he did not appear to remember it, but humiliated by her own disappointment when he was unable to go further. Letting him come near her before the wedding was insanity. She had to get away. Biting back a cry of anguish, she turned her head and twisted from his embrace.

They were both breathless, dazed as they stood look-ing at one another. His hands fisted at his sides, and the tendons in his jaw twisted when he gritted his teeth in frustration. Rachel dared not lower her eyes, for she knew what would be revealed by his tight-fitting britches. Her first impulse was to turn and run away, but she had never been a coward and her nature was too set to change now, even for the likes of this Yankee earl.

Fox watched the two men as they considered how to carry out the ghastly assignment they had been given. He could hear the shorter one saying, "I say we 'as a bit o' sport w' 'er afore we kills 'er."

"No. Remember wot 'Is Lordship said. She may 'ave raised the alarm. We got no time," his tall companion replied, reaching inside his raggedy jacket and produc-ing an evil-looking knife.

Fox saw the gleam of the blade as the killer knelt over the unconscious form of the baroness. Stepping out from behind the shrubs where he had been hiding, he aimed Jace's pistol and said in the steadiest voice he could muster, "Drop the knife and step away from the lady."

"Whot 'ave we 'ere, eh?" the short fellow said, moving menacingly toward Fox.

"No bigger 'n a minute, is 'e?" the tall one said, re-leasing the baroness. "You better go back ta yer stables whilst ye can still walk away."

"You are the ones who will leave—without harming the lady."

"Now, lad, there be brave 'n' there be foolish," the knife-wielder said, signaling his companion to outflank Fox.

Knowing he had but one shot, the boy decided the knife was the most immediate danger. Just as he prepared to fire, the baroness began to stir, giving out a moan that caused all three to glance down at her as she struggled onto all fours.

Rachel inhaled to calm her pounding heart, trying desperately to think of something to say to Jason. "This is an ill way to apologize for your churlish behavior at dinner. I believed you'd written that note for a better purpose than seduction," she finally managed.

"I'd written a note?" he echoed incredulously. "You were the one summoning me, Countess."

"I—?" Suddenly realization dawned. "You received a note, too?"

"From you. I recognized your handwriting." He looked at her with narrowed eyes. What game was she playing?

Rachel was uncertain whether to laugh, cry or sink into the ground with embarrassment. "Harry. My sister is quite an adept penman. She used to forge all sorts of notes from parents for the other girls at school when we were young. Once she's seen a sample of anyone's handwriting, she can copy it."

"But why . . ." He cut off his question, not altogether certain he wished to know the answer.

Rachel supplied it anyway. "She's taken the notion that you and I are quite the perfect match and did not like how we behaved this evening."

He smiled grimly, almost seeing the humor in it. "So I've gone from dastardly rake from whom she must rescue you to shining knight she must aid so that I win you."

Before Rachel could reply, a shot rang out in the distance. "Where did that come from?" she asked.

"Behind those outbuildings near the woods, I think. Stay here," he commanded, turning to run toward the sound of voices yelling faintly. One was a woman's.

"Are you beetle-headed? Someone's trying to kill you, and you intend to run into the darkness all alone!" she cried out, picking up her skirts and dashing after him.

Jason stopped long enough for her to catch up and seize hold of his arm. He pried her fingers away, saying, "Go to the house for help. Someone's in trouble. I haven't time to argue."

With that, he took off again. She followed him, cursing the mule-headedness of the male of the species, and reached into her pocket to produce her Clark pistol. "I always carry a weapon when I go out at night alone. A precaution you would be wise to emulate, m'lord, especially considering present circumstances."

He turned and saw the pistol. "Give it to me."

" 'Tis mine, and I know how to use it, as you would recall if you had not been so foxed the night I saved your arse," she replied, passing him at a swift run.

Cursing beneath his breath, he followed her. "I wasn't *that* drunk," he replied, catching up as they approached a small cluster of dilapidated buildings.

As they drew nearer, the sounds of a fight became clear. Rachel heard the woman's voice again and instantly recognized it, as well as a second high-pitched voice. "Harry and Fox!"

Jason's longer strides carried him around the shed first, with Rachel directly on his heels. The sight they beheld was almost comic. The body of a tall, thin ruffian lay stretched out on the ground while nearby another hard-looking fellow battled with two opponents. Harry was hanging like a leech on his back, while Fox gripped the man's wrist with one hand and flailed away at his kneecap with Jason's empty pistol.

Just as the man succeeded in clubbing the boy to the ground, Harry bit his ear and he let out a piercing oath, whirling around in a vain attempt to punch her. Rachel leveled her pistol, unable to shoot until her sister was out of the line of fire, but Jason waded in, seizing the man by his grimy shirtfront and smashing in his nose. The sound of bone breaking was audible even over the shrieks and yells of Harry and Fox.

The intruder dropped like a stone. Harry jumped away. Rachel lowered her pistol, about to rush to her sister's side, when she caught a flash out of the corner of her eye. The attacker who had been lying on the ground had rolled to his knees and was raising a knife over Jason's back as the earl knelt beside Fox.

"Jason, behind you!" she cried as she aimed and fired. The sound of a second shot blended with her own, and the would-be killer fell sideways and backward, struck simultaneously by two pistol balls.

Both Rachel and Jason turned to see LaFarge lowering his smoking pistol, only to be almost trampled as two of the marquess's "special" footmen came crashing through the shrubs. The stocky little Frenchman held up his hand, and the two beefy footmen came to heel as obediently as Paris and Adonis.

Jason turned from his examination of Fox and flashed Rachel a genuine smile of gratitude. But his words were teasing. "My darling, I soon may be the only man in England whose wife is his bodyguard."

"M'lord, you may be the only man in England whose wife need be his bodyguard." Rachel was amazed at the steadiness of her voice.

Jason crouched beside Rachel as she attempted to comfort her sobbing sister. But when Fox would have joined them, his way was blocked by his master-at-arms, who held out his hand. The lad knew what was coming. He handed LaFarge Jason's spent pistol.

"A Hawken sixty-five caliber, is it not, *mon petit?* A very fine example of American craftsmanship. Your brother, the earl's?"

Fox nodded in misery. "Yes, *monsieur.*"

"Hmm," the stocky little man continued. "Then, *mon petit,* why were you abusing it by using it as a club against that worthless wretch's knee?"

"Well, sir, I had already shot the one man . . ."

"Ah, yes," exclaimed LaFarge, in the manner of one to whom a great secret has just been revealed. "You of course refer to the dead man who was just about to stab your brother in the back."

"Well," admitted Fox, "I suppose I did not shoot him as well as I thought. I aimed for the center of his chest."

"However, it appears, *petit monsieur,* that you hit him in the hip." LaFarge sighed and muttered to himself, "Less time on foils, more time on pistols."

Harry sat sprawled in the grass with her skirts up above her calves, hiccuping and sobbing. " 'Tis all right, dear heart, just calm yourself," Rachel said, placing her arm around her hysterical sister's shoulders. "You were very brave."

"Oh no, I was not. I was frightened to death. And I bit him! Ugh," she said, covering her mouth with her hands to keep from gagging. "I shall probably get the plague from the filthy blackguard. Oooh!" she gasped, suddenly realizing that her legs were sticking out for the whole company to see. She struggled to pull down her skirts so they were decently covered, all the while sniffling and coughing.

"Will someone please tell me what in blazes is going on?" the marquess gritted out as he arrived on the scene. Soon everyone from Roger Dalbert to the upstairs maid was milling about.

"I was w-waiting in Rachel's room," Harry hiccuped miserably, "when I was set upon by these two kidnappers. But they were not after me. They must have been after Rachel."

At that, Jason and Rachel exchanged startled glances.

Fox eagerly interjected, "The baroness is right. The two cracksmen carried her to this tall, thin man, who became very angry. He said, 'This isn't Rachel Fairchild.' Then, he ordered them to kill Lady Harry because she recognized him."

Rachel embraced her sister. "Good God, my darling. Who was it?"

Harry hiccuped, "It was Frederick Forrestal. I will swear to it."

Chapter Sixteen

" 'Twould appear our quarry has taken French leave of the ton. Not a soul knows aught of his whereabouts. I do believe young Mountjoy was quite shaken when I informed him of the gravity of the charges against his hero," Drum said dryly as he poured himself a glass of Roger Dalbert's excellent port.

Jason had dispatched a special messenger to London to summon his friend to the Dalberts' country house after the bungled abduction attempt. His missive indicated that Etherington's son was every bit the blackguard they had thought him to be, and at last they had eye-witness evidence regarding Forrestal's character. If he would stoop to kidnapping Rachel to force her into marriage, Jason reasoned, he would also have hired assassins to kill his rival.

"What about the duke?" Jason asked. "Might he have any ideas about where his son has gone?"

"None. Etherington left no doubt whatever that the

young scoundrel has now made forfeit his chance at the title as well as the bulk of the Forrestal family money."

Jason lifted an eyebrow in curiosity.

"You left London just before the gossip mills began to whirl with the news. Quite a delicious scandal. Seems the old man has bestowed all the unentailed lands and investments on his nephew Marshall. Fed up with dear Frederick's debts and dueling. Never gave a fig about his dissolute vices but couldn't abide a loser. Left his son with an empty title, some paltry estates, and no way to maintain them or himself."

"Unless he found a rich wife," Jason supplied.

"Exceedingly foolish of him to try for Rachel. As a future duke, even an impoverished one, he could have found some Cit with more money than sense who'd be willing to supply a handsome dowry to make his daughter a duchess. Now old Freddie ain't even got that chance." Drum's expression revealed more than a hint of relish.

"If he is convicted of a capital felony, Lords may deny him the succession?" Jason asked, already pretty sure of the answer, which Drum's nod confirmed.

"With the blessings of his esteemed father, who shall bring the matter before that august body forthwith. Unfortunately, I've been unable to catch even a whiff of where Forrestal's run to ground."

"Sooner or later he'll be caught. In the meanwhile, I'm considerably reassured that no one will be taking shots at me or trying to poison me before I depart Albion's shores," Jason said, draining his glass.

"I would not be all that certain," Drum cautioned. "The danger is—"

"What's endangered, eh?" Roger asked as he burst through the door to his library, still dressed in dusty riding clothes from his daily outing. He made his way

229

to the Pembroke table and poured himself a drink as Drum explained.

"Jason feels Forrestal will give over his attempts to kill him. I disagree. The way a chap such as he reasons, his disgrace, the loss of everything from Rachel Fairchild to the dukedom, will be the earl's fault. He'll want revenge."

"Now the blighter has nothing to lose, eh, what?" Roger nodded his head in agreement. "We'd best see that Forrestal's brought before the bench, and that right soon. Can't have him popping up at the church with pistols blazing!"

"Ah, no. We certainly would not want anything to disrupt your cousin's marital bliss, would we?" Drum asked slyly, watching Jason with a glint of amusement in his eyes.

Through the open door, Rachel had overheard the conversation after Roger barged into the library. Before making them aware of her presence, she stood quietly, waiting to see what Jason might reply to Drum's sally.

"Since the wedding is scarce a week away, I doubt that my *marital bliss*—" he paused to emphasize the words—"is in any danger."

The irony of his tone spoke volumes to Rachel. He could not wait to escape the odious prospect of marrying her. "Forrestal is accounted to be quite an excellent shot," she said coolly as she swept into the room. "If he deigns to come after you himself this time instead of hiring incompetents, I would not dismiss the idea that he could kill you before the week is out."

Jason was surprised to see her. He turned, striding over to take her hand and press a kiss on it as Roger and Drum made their bows. After the botched kidnapping two days ago, the fox hunt had been canceled and all the guests had returned home. "I understood you were off for London to collect your trousseau this morning, Countess."

His lips felt warm and hard, sending a shiver of desire coursing straight up her arm to her heart. Could he see how his touch affected her? She prayed not. "Harry insists on accompanying me. 'Twould seem I'm not to be trusted for a final fitting without her present to oversee it. But before we are off to London, she must wait for Melvin, who is arriving tomorrow from their estate to accompany us."

Rachel withdrew her hand from his and turned to practical matters. "Now, what is to be done about Frederick Forrestal?"

Jason grinned at her straight-to-the-point manner. "At times you are as tactlessly blunt as a Yankee, Countess."

"There is no need to insult me, m'lord."

Coughing to cover his delight at the chit's cheekiness, Drum replied to her question about Forrestal. "I have Bow Street runners searching every haunt which the villain favored in London, and other agents dispatched to seaports from Gravesend to Brighton. If he's taken ship abroad, we shall know it in a few days. Meanwhile I'm off, headed back to the Great Wen to assume my role as master-of-the-hunt. We shall run Forrestal to ground, have no fear."

"I have every confidence you will, Drum," Rachel replied.

He nodded gravely to her.

Jason watched the exchange between the two with interest. He had been quite certain that his misogynistic companion and his sharp-tongued bride would instantly detest each other. But that had not proven true at all. For some reason, which utterly eluded him, they appeared to genuinely like each other. That sent warning bells clanging inside his already troubled brain.

They had apparently discussed him at some length

prior to rescuing him from those waterfront thugs. Such collaboration did not augur well for his plans to escape leg-shackling. What if Drum took it into his head to join Harry at matchmaking? Uneasily, Jason walked with Rachel and the little dandy to the side portico, where Drum's curricle awaited.

As they waved farewell to their friend, Garnet's son Evelyn strolled out into the bright morning sunshine, holding a hand over his eyes as he strained to see who was departing. He smiled flirtatiously at Rachel as he bowed over her hand, saying, "Miss Fairchild, you make the sunlight more bearable."

"A fulsome compliment indeed, coming from one who toils in dank warehouses," Jason interjected.

Sensing that his purring remark held a hint of jealousy, Rachel could not resist another jab. She smiled at Evelyn. "My thanks, sir, for such a gallant compliment." Then turning to the earl, she said, "Not that you would know aught of compliments, gallant or otherwise."

"Yankee clodpole that you have named me, I do not deal in Spanish coin, Countess." Jason gave her a sharkish grin and then said to Roger's stepson, "I assume you must return to the shipping business soon." He did not give a fig about Evelyn's commercial affairs, but he found the way Garnet's son watched Rachel to be most irritating.

"My mother has been chiding me for working too hard. She insisted that I rest in the countryside. I am finding it quite refreshing here," Evelyn replied as his dark eyes fixed warmly on Rachel.

The upper ten thousand might be fools, dismissing her rare beauty because it did not fit the current mode, but Jason knew that Simmons was anything but a fool. In fact, the young Cit appeared quite smitten with her. And the earl did not like it one bit. Would she one day ask for that annulment so she could wed a man such as Evelyn? Surely not, he assured himself. Garnet's son was a creature of the city, and she was a woman of the countryside.

"I say, was that Mr. Drummond taking his leave?" Simmons inquired.

"He's off on the trail of Forrestal," Jason replied.

"Hope he catches the blighter. Odd fellow, your friend Drummond. The manners and dress of a peer, but he seemed quite interested in the effects of the embargo. Is his family in trade of some sort?"

Jason could not help chuckling at the thought of Drum as a man of business. "Scarcely. The nearest Drum has ever come to work is cleaning the blood from his foil after a duel."

Just then Evelyn's mother waddled out the front door with a wide smile pasted on her chapped lips. This morning she was dressed in a day gown of bright pumpkin orange with deep lavender ribbons trimming the bodice and sleeves. Garnet patted her son's arm affectionately, saying " 'Tis so good to have you take a few days to visit here in the country, Evelyn. But you know how important our business is in Gravesend."

Jason could not resist a wry grin at catching his erstwhile rival in a lie. Obviously, Evelyn's mother did not consider him in need of a rest.

"Time enough to return to work, Mama. I find the country air quite salubrious." Simmons's eyes swept over Rachel before returning to his mother's face.

"Yes, 'tis pleasant here, but we have work to attend to at the warehouses," she replied.

Rachel thought she detected a flash of irritation on the older woman's face; but it quickly vanished, if indeed it had been there at all. She was certain that, as an only son, Evelyn was the apple of his mother's eye. He was certainly attractive, but Rachel could not help

233

comparing his pale, slender body with Jason's sun-bronzed muscularity. Angry at her own treacherous thoughts, she turned her attention to Evelyn, asking, "I do hope you were not disappointed by the cancellation of the fox hunt, Mr. Simmons."

He laughed in a husky baritone, replying, "Quite the opposite, I must confess. I'm really a terrible rider. I end up eating everyone else's dust, and the broom has always been awarded by the time I catch up."

"Too bad we were denied the opportunity to witness my bride's riding skills," Jason interjected. "Rumor around Harleigh has it that she can outrun the hounds and strip the fox of his tail before anyone else rides onto the scene."

Evelyn looked startled at the pronouncement, but Garnet chuckled.

Rachel could feel Jason's mocking gaze send a warm flush to her cheeks. Fighting it down, she turned to him with a less-than-genuine smile. "I take no pleasure in the kill, but you should be grateful that I am an excellent rider, m'lord earl." The moment she spoke, she could have bitten her tongue.

"Oh, I am, Countess, I am," he replied innocently.

Only Rachel appeared aware of the double entendre. Would she have the courage to go through with her plans for their wedding night?

Just after luncheon, Rachel received a message from her steward, who had ridden hard from Harleigh to deliver it as soon as it arrived, per her instructions. Passage was arranged for two, leaving Bristol the Friday after the wedding. She needed to share this vital information with Jason, but somehow could not bring herself to do it. She held the sheet of paper in one hand, staring down at the tangible evidence that he would soon be out of her life forever.

234

"Perhaps a good hard gallop will make me feel better," she murmured to herself, folding the missive and slipping it in her bodice. She dashed upstairs and quickly changed into her old riding togs. A fancy habit and sidesaddle might have been necessary in the presence of Roger and Garnet's guests, but now she intended to be alone. After making certain no one was about, she slipped out a side door and strode toward the Dalberts' stables.

Rachel had tossed and turned in her sleep for weeks now, unable to rest for thinking of that . . . that Yankee clodpole. He'd even admitted himself that he was one. Arrogant and overbearing and used to getting his way. Of course, many people said the same of her, including her own family!

"Well, all the more reason we could never suit. We'd be at loggerheads every hour of the day," she muttered to Sugar, the small white mare she was saddling.

But insidious thoughts about the hours of the night intruded as they had ever since she'd first met Jason Beaumont. She led Sugar from the stable and swung into the saddle, then cantered off. Why did she have to care for the loutish earl so very much? To be blindly attracted to a man so utterly unsuitable? It simply was not fair.

You only say that because he does not return your tendresse.

The unbidden thought stung her bitterly. But it did not signify. She knew it would be a disaster for them to attempt a real marriage. Building a companionable relationship and raising children together required that two people have things in common and dispositions that complemented each other. All she and Jason Beaumont seemed to do was ignite each other to maddening fury . . . or maddening desire.

The best she could hope for was to use the latter to

her advantage and have the marriage consummated. If a child came of it, well . . . Rachel could not allow herself to hope for that. At the very least, she would be free of the marriage mart, and that was no small matter, she reminded herself as she urged Sugar into a hard gallop, letting the cool autumn wind brush her face.

And dry away the tears.

Jason reined in Araby behind a buckthorn bush and watched Rachel from a distance. She seemed to float with the breeze, utterly graceful, one with the smooth-gaited little mare. He had never seen better horsemanship in his life. She wore her usual scandalous men's britches and loose shirt. He grinned, wondering how she'd managed to leave the Dalberts' house without anyone seeing her. Or perhaps someone had. Rachel Fairchild would most probably not give a fig if a butler or a baron fainted dead away from shock.

He could see the way her slim thighs hugged the horse's sides, and he imagined her riding *him* instead. The wind picked up as she raced across the meadow, scattering bright patches of orange and gold leaves and molding the sheer linen of her shirt over her breasts. He had touched them, felt the nipples harden. She was a passionate woman who denied her nature. Why did it have to be so?

"Dangerous thoughts, old chap," he murmured to himself and started to turn Araby away, but just then the wind tore the ribbon from her hair. He watched transfixed as the plait came unbound. Her thick waist-length hair streamed on the breeze, gleaming like a brown satin banner. All he could think of was burying his fists in the rich dark curls, immobilizing her head as he lowered his mouth to hers.

Madness. He turned his stallion and rode as if all the hounds of hell were after him, back to Roger's stables. Unlike most of his cousin's staff, the stablemen were competent, doubtless because Roger was an avid horseman and hunter. But today Jason felt the need to do some hard physical work. He dismissed them and began to rub Araby down himself. Anything to keep his mind off Rachel.

The horse barn smelled of hay and manure mixed with the tang of liniment and sweat, equine and human. Not an unpleasant blend, to Rachel's nostrils. She walked her lathered mare around the paddock a few times to cool her, then headed inside to rub her down. She hoped the smirking stablemen were in the kitchen having dinner. The mood she was in, she would most likely take a pitchfork to the first one who provoked her with another leer.

Whickering and snorts greeted her as she pulled open the side door of the barn and led Sugar in. She could hear a male voice humming. Probably one of the stableboys, she thought—until the fellow began singing a sea chantey. And a most ribald one at that. What else would she expect from a Yankee privateer?

His voice was a deep baritone, clear and strong. Rachel hated to admit that he could carry a tune exceedingly well. She paused by the doorway of Araby's stall and froze, unable to turn away from the sight of Jason, stripped to the waist, plying a coarse cotton cloth to the big black brute's lathered coat.

She was not certain which of the two, man or horse, was more soaked with perspiration. Suddenly the low-ceilinged barn seemed stiflingly close indeed. She felt a tingling warmth spread from her face to her throat, then move over her breasts and settle low in her belly like liquid fire. By contrast, her throat felt dry and scratchy, and the normally soft, much-washed fabric of her chemise abraded her suddenly swollen and tender nipples, causing them to burn.

237

She knew the reason. He stood before her, completely unaware of her presence. Rivulets of perspiration glittered like diamonds as they ran down his broad back and vanished tantalizingly into the low-slung waistband of his trousers. His skin was bronzed from hours spent under a relentless sun. With his every movement, lean, sinewy muscles rippled and tensed.

Rachel bit her lip to steady her breathing. Memories of that afternoon in the water came rushing back, tantalizing her with images of his wet, naked body. Somehow seeing him partially clothed, so compellingly male, aroused feelings in her that matched or even exceeded what she had felt that day. It seemed that every time they met, her desire for him intensified.

Was this truly love? Or merely lust? Considering that she had always been impervious to male charms, Rachel knew the answer. She needed to get away from him as quickly as possible.

Jason suddenly felt a prickling along the back of his neck and knew someone was watching him from the stall door. Frederick Forrestal's sneering face flashed into his mind, along with Drum's dire warnings about how dangerous the disinherited nobleman might be. Without allowing himself time to consider anything further, he spun around, using the heavy cotton rubdown cloth as a weapon, snapping it sharply into the face of the intruder. Then he dived forward, tackling his prey and throwing them both to the straw-covered ground.

Both Araby and Sugar started prancing and whinnying in fright, trying to avoid stomping on the crazy humans rolling around beneath their hooves.

Rachel tasted the pungent musk of horse sweat as the wet cloth smacked her face with a sharp sting. Before she could do more than grunt, her breath was knocked from her and she found herself lying on the stable floor with Jason on top of her. As soon as she could take in sufficient breath, she let out a volley of strident curses.

By the time they had hit the ground, Jason knew he had made a mistake of monumental proportions. And he also knew the shape and contours of the body beneath him. "Rachel?" he croaked stupidly, blinking straw and dust from his eyes as he stared down into her startled face, which by now was taking on the rosy hue of fury.

He tried to scramble off her. She assisted him with a sharp punch to his lower abdomen and followed through with a kick that landed wickedly close to his private parts. Thank heavens it only grazed his thigh as he rolled to his side. He put up his hands to ward off further mayhem, trying to grunt out an apology over her shrieks.

Soon a stableman came running into the barn, just in time to be knocked down by Sugar, who having had quite her fill of human escapades, bolted out the open door into the paddock. Araby continued to snort, but once his master and the other human ceased rolling around on the floor, he stood still, as if waiting to see what would happen next.

"You beetle-headed, hell-bent, cow-handed Bedlamite! My mouth tastes as if I swallowed a horse blanket. What on earth were you about? You could have broken my neck," she yelled, gathering wind for another diatribe as she rolled up on her hands and knees, glaring at him through a tangle of straw-matted hair.

Regaining his own breath as he climbed to his feet, Jason could see the humor of the situation. "I believe this is called déjà vu, Countess," he said, extending his hand to assist her up. "The first time we met . . . er, collided, you were positioned just so."

"And 'twas you, you great buffoon, who occasioned what is becoming an habitual posture in your pres-

239

ence," she gritted out, slapping his proffered hand away and scrambling to her feet unassisted.

"At least consider that straw is more easily removed than mud," he replied with a cheeky grin.

"Yes, I am so fortunate. Why on earth did you attack me?"

"Why on earth did you lurk behind me without making a sound? I've grown overcautious since Forrestal began trying to have me murdered."

Knowing her face was red, and not all of it from anger now, she shot back hotly, "I was *not* lurking."

"Yes, you were. I can always sense when someone is contemplating my backside with hostile intent."

"A pity your instincts work only when you're sober or you might have sooner noted those thugs encircling you in that tavern."

"Touché, Countess. But just what were you doing spying on me, anyway?" he asked as he took up his shirt from a peg on the wall and deliberately began rubbing his chest with it.

She wished he would not do that. It quite destroyed her concentration. Now what had he just asked her anyway? Bits of gold straw glinted in the black pelt as he dried perspiration with the shirt, then started to slip it over his shoulders. Her mind whirled for an instant before she blurted out, "I have a message from Bristol."

The instant the words escaped her lips, she gasped, realizing they were not alone. So did Jason, who raised his finger to his lips when the young stableman came stumbling down the long corridor toward them.

The lad was more than a little curious to see an earl and a viscount's daughter rolling about the stable floor and frightening the horses. The Quality really were a different breed, a bit drafty between the ears. "Everythin' all right, m'lord?"

"Quite all right, thank you," Jason replied smoothly

240

as he patted Araby's neck and crooned to the big black, who instantly quieted. "Would you be so kind as to see to the lady's mount?"

"Yes, m'lord." With a short bow, the youth left, still rubbing the shoulder that he'd slammed into the barn door when he leaped out of Sugar's path.

"Now, what news from Bristol?" Jason asked after the servant left the stable.

"I just received word this afternoon. Your ship sails the Friday after the wedding," she said, trying in vain to ignore his strong brown hands smoothing his shirttails below the low-riding waist of his britches.

He took the missive from her and glanced at it, trying in vain to ignore her outthrust breasts as she ran her slender fingers over them, brushing away bits of straw clinging to the sheer fabric of his shirt. "Ah, the *Mirabelle*. Not as fast as a clipper but a good craft all the same. 'Twill be good to feel the pitch of a ship's deck beneath my feet again."

"Do you miss the sea?" she could not help asking.

"Aye. At times I do," he replied thoughtfully. " 'Twas an adventuresome life."

"I have never been aboard anything larger than a packet going from Gravesend to Brighton. What is it like to sail across an ocean?"

His blue eyes took on a faraway expression for a moment as he remembered the past. "There is a sense of boundless freedom when you face that endless rolling blue horizon where sky meets sea. The keen salt scent of the air, the sharp sting of the wind are all unique when you're in the middle of the Atlantic. And the ports . . . heavens above, the sights and smells, so alien, so alluring."

"To where have you sailed?" Rachel had given little thought to his life before he became the earl.

"Where have I not? The West Indies, South America.

There is a lushness to the tropics that scents the air like nothing else. The sweetest fragrance blended with decay. The sky is so blue it blinds one, and the trees groan with exotic fruits just waiting to be picked."

"You've been many places," she murmured.

"Once I rounded the Horn and crossed the Pacific to the Sandwich Islands, then went on to China. Quite a lucrative trade in the East. If not for the war with England, I would've made a second voyage."

"Far Cathay. I read about Marco Polo when I was a girl. Are the inhabitants really yellow-skinned with oddly shaped eyes?"

He chuckled. "Their complexions vary just as ours do. The more time they spend in the sun, the more they appear yellow, but 'tis not really yellow—more like golden brown. And many are as white as the palest Englishman. As to the eyes, they believe ours most peculiar, being what they call rounded."

Rachel nodded. "That makes sense. Every race judges others by their own peculiar standards of beauty. Have you ever sailed to Africa?"

"No, but one day I would like to. There are ebony-skinned races with ancient civilizations and whole tribes of people no taller than children. Perhaps now I shall have the opportunity to see all of that for myself," he said pensively.

"I had never considered how much you gave up to become an earl."

The earnest tone of her voice resonated deep within him, surprising him. Jason could see that she understood, even sympathized with, his torn loyalties. "Being a ship's master is not unlike being an earl. In both cases, the man in charge must place the well-being of those under his protection above his own. Not an easy task, with some of the rowdy fellows who sailed with me." He grinned fondly, remembering long-ago adventures.

242

"Once I had to bluff my way through an audience with a Chinese warlord to secure the release of two boatswains who had gotten . . . er, boisterous in a Shanghai brothel."

Rachel returned his smile, feeling suddenly sad. "How narrow our world must appear to you. Balls, plays and routs, senseless frivolity. Gossip and social position are all Englishmen think about."

"Considering the situation with Napoleon, I imagine the War Office and Admiralty have a few other things weighing on their minds," he said, feeling oddly touched. He had always known that she was intelligent, but she could be surprisingly intuitive and sensitive as well. "Thank you, Rachel."

She looked at him, bemused. "Whatever for?"

"For understanding that I did not wish to be an earl. Even had matters worked out with my grandfather, part of me would always have been a simple American sailor."

"There is nothing about you that is simple, Jason Beaumont," she murmured.

While twirling her parasol absently, Harry studied her sister across the seat of the caleche. Since it was such a lovely morning, they had decided to ask the driver to let down the top. Harry protected her fair complexion, but Rachel made no effort to keep the sun off her face as they journeyed back to London. Wanting to get some exercise, the baron rode his horse ahead of the conveyance.

"You were splendid with young Simmons, Rachel. I could not have handled the matter more adroitly . . . well, perhaps I might have lingered a bit longer when he bade us farewell. He is quite interested in you, you know. 'Twould appear you appeal to unconventional males."

243

"Utterly unsuitable males, you mean. Father would have apoplexy if I showed interest in a Cit, even though he is a decent and intelligent man. Besides, I have no intention of using Garnet's son," Rachel replied.

"More fool, you. Especially considering how often you've remarked on the arrogance of your betrothed. Nothing takes a man down so handily as seeing the lady of his heart being attended by another man."

Rachel snorted. "I am not the lady of the earl's heart. According to him, I am no lady at all. Nor do I claim to be," she quickly added.

Harry did not snort but instead gave a delicate cough, which served the same purpose. "Balderdash. I marked the way Falconridge scowled when Mr. Simmons took your hand before we boarded the caleche."

"Jason always scowls . . . unless he's in a towering rage, in which case he screws up his face and bellows."

"And you love him to distraction—never deny it."

Rachel sighed at her sister's tone. "You are positive that Jason desires me and that such physical longing will lead to genuine affection. But I know better. He desires nothing so much as to return to his sailing ships and resume his old life. Nothing else will make him happy. Nor would I be happy playing dutiful wife. No, I don't want him to remain here after the marriage has been consummated . . . if it is consummated," she added softly.

"You do not doubt Jason. You doubt yourself," Harry admonished. "All men—"

"Jason Beaumont is not like any man alive," Rachel blurted out impatiently.

"Indeed he is not. That is why he is your perfect match. I must give credit to the marquess for seeing it first, but I now quite agree with his decision."

Rachel looked at her sister as if she'd grown a second

244

head. "Cargrave saw his grandson and me as a love match?"

"Do not look so incredulous. Raising your eyebrows thus causes wrinkles. And yes, His Lordship did point out to Father that a gel such as you required a firm hand—and," she hastened on, forestalling Rachel's angry retort, "a wild young rapscallion such as Jason required a woman of spirit to gentle him."

"How did you learn such a preposterous thing?"

Harry's pink lips plumped up in a self-satisfied grin. "How do I ever learn what Father and his friends are plotting? I eavesdropped on their conversation the other afternoon in Cousin Roger's study. The two of them thought no one else was about. Anyway, I'd made earlier inquiries about the marchioness."

"Lady Mathilda?" Rachel risked more wrinkles, frowning in concentration. "Fox once mentioned something about his grandfather showing him her portrait at Cargrave Hall."

"Theirs was a famous love match, according to the Dowager Duchess of Chitchester."

"She is certainly old enough to remember," Rachel replied dryly. "But even if 'tis true, Jason and I are not Cargrave and Lady Mathilda."

"I suppose we shall have to wait until the wedding night to find that out, shan't we?" Harry said impishly. "I do believe the cream silk nightrail with bronze lace will do the trick . . ."

Chapter Seventeen

As Rachel and her sister and brother-in-law made their way back to London, Jason prepared to depart for Falconridge. His marriage was less than a week away. And he was more confused than ever about Rachel Fairchild. They had played at cat-and-mouse, taking turns bedeviling each other, taunting, teasing, and in the process discovering that there was physical desire between them. But was there something more?

The question haunted him day and night, never more so than after their encounter in the stable yesterday. Did Rachel also dream of the kind of freedom he craved when he set sail? She had said she did not wish a husband because she wanted to run her estates without interference. But had she ever imagined more than a prosaic existence as the spinster mistress of Harleigh? Did she long for someone to share her life?

There he went again, delving into mysteries best left unsolved . . . unless he wanted to fall in with his grandfather's schemes and spend the rest of his life leg-shackled. The idea of life with Rachel did not bring the shudder it had when they had first hatched this scheme to outwit the marquess and the viscount. In fact, there were moments when it held surprising appeal. How did Rachel now feel about his leaving?

Before he could give further consideration to the thought, a knock sounded on the door to his room. Expecting it to be Roger, who had promised to stop and bid him farewell before heading out to hunt stag with a neighboring squire, he called out, "Come in, Cousin." He was surprised to see Fox slip inside and quickly close the door.

"I was going to ask you to ride later this morning after my valet finished packing," Jason said, smiling at the lad, who looked decidedly grave.

"That would not serve, Jace. Bradley and the new bodyguard Grandfather hired would only ride with us, and I need to speak privately with you before we return to Cargrave Hall."

"I must confess, with all the excitement here the past few days, we've had little chance to visit," Jason replied, sitting down in a large comfortable easy chair and inviting the boy to take the one across from him.

"Grandfather has had me guarded ever so closely," Fox said.

"Yes," Jason said uneasily. Drum had reported with great relish the lad's questions about why Jason would not wish to remain married to Rachel. "Mr. Drummond explained everything to you, did he not?"

"One thing he could not explain . . ." His voice faded and he squirmed nervously.

Already Jason did not like where this conversation seemed to be headed. With a sigh, he said, "Go on, Fox."

"Miss Fairchild—Rachel," he corrected himself, re-

247

membering that she had given him leave to use her Christian name, "is such a beautiful lady . . . and she's smart and nice and ever such a good horsewoman. She can even shoot as well as LaFarge, and she knows lots and lots about everything from medicine to farming."

"The lady is a veritable paragon," Jason interjected dryly. No, he was not going to find this easy at all.

"Then why don't you want to stay married to her?"

There it was. How could he answer the boy when he did not know himself any longer? "Fox, we . . . er, Rachel and I did not have a choice in the matter. We were both blackmailed into agreeing to wed because the marquess and the viscount wished to merge their lands and families. We simply do not suit."

"You don't want to do it because you're being forced," Fox said with a nod of his head.

The boy said the words as if they made perfect sense in twelve-year-old logic. Somehow that sort of agreement did not make Jason feel better. Indeed, it sounded rather churlish when put so baldly. "Fox, choosing a wife—or choosing a husband—is a very personal matter that should be decided mutually between the two participants. 'Tis not something to be done just because their hereditary lands happen to adjoin. Surely you remember the Shawnee way."

"Yes, Jace, I do. And Grandfather has chosen the Shawnee way, although he does not realize it." Fox sighed, impatient with the density of his older and supposedly wiser brother.

"Pray, enlighten me," Jason asked.

"Rachel reminds him of his marchioness, and you are just like him. They were very happy. He told me so."

"Whether or not Rachel has anything in common with our sweet grandmother is highly dubious, but saying that I am 'just like' Grandfather is downright insulting!" Jason snapped, leaning forward in his chair and pounding on the wide wooden arm.

Fox smirked. "See! Just like him."

Jason quickly leaned back and took a deep breath. "Well, be that as it may," he equivocated, "the fact remains that Rachel and I do not wish to wed. However, if you would prefer to remain with Grandfather, I will not ask you to leave." As he spoke the words, Jason prayed that if he left Fox behind, the old man would not turn away from the lad. But gut-deep instinct told him that George Beaumont would never use Fox that way.

Fox slumped back in the chair. Sometimes adults were impossible to understand. As soon as Frederick Forrestal was apprehended, they would no longer have to worry about someone trying to kill Jace. To Fox's way of thinking, that left no reason for them to leave England. Except Jace's stubborn insistence that he did not want to marry Rachel. And Rachel's claim that she did not want to marry him. "If you run away after you're married, won't Rachel still be your wife?"

Now Jason was beginning to understand how Drum had felt when he'd had that talk with Fox. "I would not use the term 'running away,' "

"What would you call it, then?" Fox shot back innocently.

Jason combed his fingers through his hair and prayed for patience. "I have responsibilities—business in America."

"But you were going to stay here and be the earl until you had to get married. And now you're going to get married anyway. You might as well stay here and be the earl, too, as far as I can see."

"Out of the mouths of babes," Jason muttered, now the one squirming in his seat. "Going through with the ceremony is the only way we can hope to outsmart

Grandfather and escape. As I said, if you wish to remain here with him, I'll understand."

Fox's expression grew even more troubled now. He could not desert Jace. "I'll go with you, but do you think Grandfather will be angry with me?" he asked in a small voice.

"No. I think he'll understand."

"I don't wish to hurt him. He's been so good to me, Jace."

"You are a fine young gentleman, Fox," Jason said fondly. "You could write him a note and invite him to visit you in America," he suggested. "Or you could come here on visits as I did while I was growing up."

"That might make him feel better," Fox conceded. "Mama Beaumont understands about my being here, but my Shawnee family may not. I'll write to Grandfather and explain that, too. And I will promise to return some day." That would be the way to get Jace to return as well.

"Well, if that's settled, what say we go for that ride so I can gauge whether or not you've become as expert as Bradley reports, eh?"

As they galloped across the rolling hills of the Dalbert estate, Jason could not get their conversation out of his mind. Was he doing the right thing, taking Fox away from all the advantages he would have here in England? The boy mentioned nothing about the marquess's plan to adopt him. Perhaps he did not know about it. If he told Fox, would it make him reconsider staying behind?

What a moral conundrum this had become. No matter which way he turned, Jason felt trapped, frustrated and guilty. If the old man's feelings for Fox were genuine, and Jason was beginning to believe they were, was it also possible that more than a dynastic alliance had influenced Cargrave's selection of Rachel? Did the old fool actually believe they could make a love match?

A voice inside his head reminded him that the ninth Marquess of Cargrave was many things, but a fool was not one of them. That explained why the issues Fox had raised about Rachel continued to plague him. She would be his wife, at least in the eyes of the law.

How do you feel about an unconsummated marriage? About leaving her behind? He forced the unpleasant considerations from his mind and challenged Fox to a race—this time over flat, safe terrain.

"I feel ready to faint."

" 'Tis merely bridal vapors," Harry said dismissively, arranging the long lace train of her sister's wedding gown.

"No, 'tis the weight of this dress," Rachel snapped back. "The seed pearls alone must weigh three stone. Lord, I feel as if I'm outfitted in chain mail." She tried to move her shoulders and grimaced in discomfort.

"Why is it I think the gown has little to do with your taking and your groom much more, hmmm?"

"I am *not* in a taking!"

Harry only chuckled as she adjusted one of the pale pink hothouse rosebuds in her sister's elaborate coiffeur. "Ah, I hear the music. Come, dear sister. 'Tis time you became the Countess of Falconridge."

She took Rachel's hand, which was icy cold in spite of the warm autumn morning, and led her out of the small anteroom into the large narthex of St. George's Church. "You are a most beautiful bride," she whispered proudly. And it was nothing but the truth. The color of the gown was not at all what Harry would have selected, but thanks be to heaven that she'd been able to talk Rachel out of black! There were times when Harry thought her sister's sense of humor bordered dangerously on the macabre . . . or the deranged.

Their sister Sally, the middle gel of the trio of Fairchild siblings, waited with their father. When he saw his eldest, an expression of pleasure wreathed his face—or was it relief? He walked quickly across the stone floor, worn smooth by the pious and the politic who had worshiped here during the church's four-hundred-year history. Bowing before Rachel, he took her hand and tucked it around his arm, as if making certain she could not escape at the last moment. "You look smashing, m'dear. Don't she, Harry? Sally?"

Sally, petite and blond like her younger sister, nodded, faintly surprised that the tall, hoydenish Rachel could be turned into such a bridal vision. "You shall do us proud, dear sister," she said a tad jealously. Sally had only managed to snare a viscount. Drat, her ape-leader of a sister would one day be a marchioness!

Just then the organ music swelled, giving them their cue to start down the aisle to the altar where Jason Beaumont, sixth Earl of Falconridge, waited. The moment she saw Jason standing beside the priest, Rachel found herself clutching her father's arm for support. Her groom looked grim and forbidding and more handsome than any man had a right to be. His cutaway jacket and trousers were made of the finest kerseymere and accented the breadth of his powerful shoulders and the length of his legs. He had chosen black, a dramatic complement to his deeply tanned face and inky hair. Rachel feared it might also be a statement regarding the marriage. The deep blue brocade of his waistcoat perfectly matched the color of his eyes. Eyes that pierced her with hunger . . . or anger. Sweet God, she could not discern which.

Rachel swallowed and held her head high as the music swelled in a crescendo, breaking the spell which held her in Jason's thrall. She looked away from him to

Drum and Fox, who smiled warmly at her. Her lips curved in a faint attempt to return their encouragement, but her heart was not in it. *Damned if I let him see how shaken I am by this charade,* she vowed and forced herself to assume a veneer of serenity.

If only he were not so heartstoppingly handsome that she wanted to reach out and stroke his harsh, dark jawline, to brush her hand over his blue-black hair. But he stood ramrod-straight with his hands clenched rigidly at his sides, remote and cold. There was no hint of the laughing, teasing man who had dared to kiss and caress her. The man who had boldly exchanged risqué double entendres with her. The wild Yankee who cared as little for the sensibilities of the ton as did she.

What are we doing here? This is a terrible mistake. Yet she kept walking steadily down the endlessly long aisle toward the man she loved, whose name she would carry, perhaps whose child she would bear. The man who would leave her. She felt as if she were going to the block.

Jason stared at Rachel, unable to tear his eyes away from the vision of loveliness dressed in shimmering silk and lace. The deep, clear rose color of the gown was a perfect foil for her rich dark hair, which was piled high on her head and entwined with a garland of rosebuds. Hundreds of seed pearls covered the bodice of the dress in intricate patterns, woven lovingly around the gentle swell of her breasts. A heavy lace overskirt fell from the high waistline of the gown. A Watteau train worked with lace and seed pearls swept from her shoulders.

She was simply the most beautiful woman he had ever seen. God, how he desired her! And he was honor bound not to touch her. He had given his word. Now, standing before the altar in this old church, he wanted desperately to recant; but knew he could not.

Her wide hazel-green eyes were dark with unhappiness. She held her head high, her face grim as she walked toward him. She could be facing the gallows. And perhaps, to the wild, free Rachel Fairchild who loved riding astride and working in the dirt with her tenant farmers, this was a fate worse than hanging. But he would leave her free to return to her old life, unencumbered by a husband she did not want. Was that not enough? he thought pettishly. What else could he do except hold to their devil's bargain?

He willed her to meet his eyes as she drew near, but she did not. Thick sable lashes lowered, shielding her inner emotions from his probing stare. When Harleigh gave her over to him, she stepped forward like a sleepwalker. Jason took her hand, shocked by its coldness. She was numb with shock. He should have remained angry with her. But he could not.

A wave of protective tenderness swept over him as he enveloped her slender hand in his and they knelt before the priest. At last she met his gaze. His fiercely independent, boldly unconventional countess was terrified by all this pomp and circumstance.

They went through the exchange of vows, making all the appropriate responses in the appropriate places, but neither registered a word that was said. At the appropriate time, he placed the ring on her finger, a large square-cut pink diamond surrounded by tiny rubies in a heavy gold setting. The ring had been in the Beaumont family for a dozen generations. Every Marchioness of Cargrave had worn it. Now it rested on Rachel's long, slender hand.

When the priest gave the benediction and pronounced them man and wife, Jason helped her rise as her sisters fussed with the heavy lace train. Before they knew it, the bridal couple was surrounded with beaming well-wishers as they walked slowly up the aisle and made their way out into the bright sunlight.

The marriage of any peer drew a crowd of London's "great unwashed," but since Jason Beaumont was the infamous Yankee earl and Cargrave's heir, interest was especially high. A phalanx of footmen held the throng at bay as Falconridge guided his new bride down the steps of the church. Cargrave's most handsome carriage, pulled by a set of matching grays, awaited to whisk them to the wedding breakfast at the marquess's city house.

Jason assisted his bride into the carriage as Harry oversaw the arrangement of Rachel's train, scolding a footman who dared to let one corner of the lace touch the ground before it was carefully folded on a velvet cushion. Once the bridal couple was seated side by side, the driver cracked his whip, starting the horses off at a smart clip.

Once they were alone, Jason and Rachel became acutely aware of each other. On several occasions when they had been this close together, they had nearly given in to the fierce desire that always hummed between them. Both thought of that now. Neither said a word. At length, desperate to take his mind off the alluring scent of roses and the feminine bounty that was Rachel, Jason broke the silence, blurting out the first thing that came to mind.

"Does the ring fit? When I inquired of your sister as to size so the jeweler could adjust it, she said she had no idea because you'd never worn a ring in your life."

" 'Tis a perfect fit," she replied, glancing down at the heavy diamond winking brilliantly in the bright sunlight.

"You have never favored jewelry. What a rarity in a female. My mother and sister collect baubles with utter glee."

"It feels as if it weighs two stone at the least. Of

course, I shall return it to the marquess after . . . you are gone," she added awkwardly. Not wishing to dwell upon that, she said, "I have worn some of the Harleigh jewels when occasion demanded."

"Such as emeralds and tiger's eyes? I remember how the tiger's eyes set off your unusual coloring." He remembered altogether too much of that first night when he'd learned about his grandfather's machinations. He noted that she looked away as if she, too, was recalling how they had plotted to avoid this day back then.

Change the subject, he urged himself. "Do you suppose my grandfather chose St. George's as a sop to his vanity?"

Rachel looked up into his face then. His expression revealed nothing but the cocky grin back in place. She felt on safe ground now, smiling back. "Although I do not doubt that George Beaumont believes the patron saint of England is named after *him* and not the other way about, 'twas my father who selected the church. Generations of Fairchilds have wed there."

"He did seem pleased when we passed him after the ceremony."

"More like relieved to have me safely wed. I'm certain he harbored a suspicion that I would bolt at the altar and leap astride a carriage horse to make my escape," she replied, trying to keep the tone light.

He frowned for an instant, then said, "When I watched you walking down the aisle, I had that fear myself."

"Well, it would certainly have solved your problems. And you looked no happier than did I, all grimflashy with fists clenched as if I were an opposing pugilist," she said crossly.

Jason forced himself to laugh. " 'Tis an apt comparison, considering how we have sparred ever since we first met." He would never allow her to know how accursedly difficult it would be the next two nights to have her sleeping in the room beside his and not enter it.

"Rather more like wrestling in the mud than merely sparring, if memory serves me," she replied.

"Ah, yes, I do seem to recall your lovely body covered with mud . . . and water," he said in a husky voice, unable to stop himself.

Rachel's heartbeat suddenly speeded up and her mouth went bone dry. She moistened her lips with the tip of her tongue before she was able to speak. Then some bold imp made her reply, "I should not talk of water were I you, m'lord earl, after your sojourn in the pool with Paris and Adonis."

"And with you. You were an infinitely more agreeable companion. Smaller fangs." His tone matched the dark fires leaping in his eyes as they gazed intently at her mouth.

He is going to kiss me! Rachel was powerless to look away even though she feared her very soul must be bared to him.

Jason leaned closer, his lips drawn like a magnet to hers as he took a silky tendril of hair trailing over her shoulder and wound it about his finger.

Just then the carriage came to an abrupt stop, breaking the spell and throwing them both back against the seat cushions. "Sorry, m'lord, m'lady," the driver said, turning toward them in red-faced embarrassment. "That ale wagon near run me down." His eyes narrowed on a heavy dray laden with barrels that had pulled in front of them from a side alley.

As the flustered driver attempted to calm his skittering grays, Jason and Rachel struggled to compose themselves. Silently Jason watched as she smoothed imaginary wrinkles from her gown. How the hell had that happened? they both asked themselves.

The carriage started up again as the marquess and viscount in the second vehicle pulled close behind them. The two old men exchanged conspiratorially gleeful looks. Since both carriages were open, they had avidly watched the interlude between bride and groom. Cargrave rubbed his hands together. "I would wager they'll produce an heir before the year's out."

Harleigh smiled, his pop eyes wide with pleasure. "I would not care to bet against you on that one, my friend."

Fox, who was riding with them, listened and said nothing, feeling guilty over what was to transpire in two days.

The scent of roses teased Jason's nostrils as he pictured again the way her tongue had darted out to moisten those lush lips. What man alive could have resisted kissing her? He vowed to be very careful. And honest. "If our plan is to set you free of me, Countess, then we had best beware the next few days."

Rachel had been fussing with the yards of train now tangled at her feet. She sat back and turned to look him in the eye. She could not dissemble, damn the Yankee clodpole. He knew that she understood his meaning. " 'Twas you who started playing games again, m'lord. Not I." She was proud of her level tone of voice.

Jason shrugged in good-natured concession. "We do strike sparks from each other, Countess." His eyes studied hers, trying to gauge her reaction.

Rachel willed herself to return the insouciant gesture with a smile. "Nay, nay, m'lord, 'tis you who are the fiery one; but if you will recall, I know well how to use water to douse your . . . spark."

He shook his head. "Alas, we're back to water again. My downfall." Suddenly he began frantically lifting the folds of her voluminous train, attempting to peer underneath.

258

She slapped his hand. "Woodcock, what, pray tell, are you doing?"

He looked at her with feigned suspicion. "Where have you hidden those damned dogs?"

They grinned at each other, not for the first time realizing how much they enjoyed such verbal sparring. But it was the first time they were both willing to let it show. Jason was sure it was a mistake, but one he seemed powerless to stop. Rachel considered it a good omen for the night ahead.

Best not overplay her hand yet. She nodded, then leaned back primly against the squabs and said, "We shall be saved from our own tempestuous natures by our audience, m'lord earl. Might I remind you that your grandfather and father-in-law are watching every move we make?" She smiled mischievously. "Of course, we could come to blows right now. That would teach the meddlesome old buggers."

Jason threw back his head and roared.

The wedding festivities at Cargrave's city house went on interminably to Drum's mind. He was eager to resume the search for Forrestal. When one of his runners from Bow Street arrived just as they were being seated for the wedding breakfast, he was relieved to make his excuses with regret, then depart on the chase. Some of the guests murmured about the mysterious errand, while others noted the satisfied nod of the old marquess's head when the dandy conferred with him and the earl. Something was afoot, but speculations about the matter were quickly eclipsed by those regarding the new bride and groom.

What a splendid, striking couple they made. Whoever would have imagined that the hoydenish Rachel Fairchild would be such a regal countess? The bold Yankee earl must be responsible for the miraculous

259

change in her volatile nature. He had indeed tamed a shrew. Several gentlemen were said to remark that they wished they knew the secret American men possessed.

"A toast, ladies and gentlemen," the marquess said, bringing the happy chatter in the room to a sudden halt as he stood up with a glass of champagne raised. "To my grandson, who has chosen most wisely, and to the magnificent new Countess of Falconridge."

To shouts of "Here, here!" and "Congratulations!" Jason and Rachel nodded, smiling as was expected of them. Everyone urged him to propose his own toast. Slowly he stood, then took Rachel's hand and pulled her up beside him.

"To you, Countess," he said gravely; then to break the solemnity of the moment, he added, "And this time I hope you will drink the wine, and not dispose of it as you did when our betrothal was announced." He linked the arm holding his glass around her arm holding her glass, then raised his to his lips. Rachel paused for a moment, as if considering. The guests held their collective breath. When there was complete silence, she drank. Everyone burst out with applause and relieved chuckles.

"Now you are my countess indeed," he murmured softly to her.

No, she would only be his countess if tonight went as she planned, but Rachel schooled her face to reveal nothing of that.

They stared at each other over the rims of their glasses, arms still linked, each contemplating the night that lay ahead. And how they would get through it.

Chapter Eighteen

Because the city house was filled with servants bustling about and guests demanding attention, the bridal couple were able to go their separate ways during the interminable afternoon. Rachel closeted herself with her sisters, who insisted she take a revitalizing nap before the ball that evening. She was grateful to shed, even briefly, the cumbersome wedding gown and all that it symbolized, though she could not relax sufficiently to catch even a moment's sleep.

Jason retreated to the library, where he perused the hastily scrawled note Drum had left for him, explaining in more detail the reasons for his hasty departure. A ship departing for Italy the following morning from Gravesend was said to have a tall, fair-haired peer as a passenger. With luck, the culprit might be apprehended before he vanished on the Mediterranean. Drum also alluded to some other mysterious leads which he had been working on, although he gave no clue as to what he hoped to learn.

By early evening, there was nothing to do but go on display again. At least this would be the last time Jason and his countess would have to play out the charade before a large assembly of family and guests. They would be forced to smile and pretend they were looking forward to a lifetime together. They would have to look into each other's eyes and join hands. Worse yet, they would have to lead off the dancing.

Jason was not certain if he could get through that part without losing control. He had never been able to forget the night of their betrothal ball when they had waltzed together. He had never before danced with a woman of her uncommon height. She had fit so naturally in his arms, matched her long strides so perfectly to his as they swept about the floor. That was the first time the insidious idea of keeping her by his side permanently had flashed through his mind.

Of course, the thought had fled once she informed him that they were to be wed. But during the course of the summer he had dreaded taking her in his arms in front of an admiring audience, for fear the madness would come over him again. Although he refused to admit it, that had been one of the principal reasons for his hiding at Falconridge instead of squiring her about the obligatory round of London social events.

But tonight he must dance. For the very last time, thank heavens. He tried to hold that thought as he walked down the hall to the retiring room where he was to meet his bride so they could make a grand descent of the curving staircase to the applause of the assembly below.

Rachel was once more done up in her wedding finery, with her massive train now carefully pinned up so that she might carry it on her arm during the dancing.

She resisted the urge to pace as she waited for Jason and instead contented herself by staring out the large oval window at the inner courtyard garden below, now turned russet and gold with autumn foliage. At her sister's exclamation of delight, she turned to face her husband. The earl stood filling the doorway, resplendent in black kerseymere and deep blue brocade. The sapphire studs at his cuffs and on his shirt winked like a dare. He bowed to her and extended his hand with what seemed like forced politeness.

"Countess," he said very formally. "Our guests await us."

"You mean my father's and your grandfather's guests," she replied as she placed her fingers lightly over the back of his hand, which was warm to her touch in spite of his cool demeanor.

"True, but Fox is also at the foot of the stairs, waiting to view his 'angel' as she descends from on high to mix with mere mortals." His smile when he mentioned the boy seemed more genuine.

"I shall be honored to dance with him."

"I suspect he'll be so thrilled that he will quite forget every step his tutors have had him practice." His murmur was drowned out by applause as they reached the head of the stairs and the herald announced them.

Rachel kept her gaze fixed on Fox's beaming face as she made her way down the wide, carpeted steps. She smiled and murmured greetings to family friends in the press while Jason led her into the huge ballroom. The orchestra played softly, and hundreds of candles blazed from two huge chandeliers at opposite ends of the room.

The marquess, wearing a smug smile of satisfaction, gave a signal to the leader of the musicians, then nodded to his grandson and Rachel. As the guests fanned out around the perimeter of the polished walnut floor, the bridal couple made their way to the center. The orchestra struck up a waltz.

Just as he had that first night in this very room, Jason swept Rachel into his arms and whirled her around the floor. "The old devil selected a waltz on purpose," he growled. "He told me that we were a perfect match on the dance floor."

"A pity we are not so perfect off it," she replied with feigned humor, fighting the light-headedness that came from her heart's wild thrumming.

His hold on her waist tightened, drawing her more closely to him than was seemly, even for a newly wed couple. "I can recall a number of occasions, Countess, when we did very well off the dance floor . . ."

His breath was warm against her ear as his suggestive whisper trailed away. "A good thing there were no witnesses at those occasions, else the scandal would rock the ton," she replied breathlessly.

"I've never given a fig for scandal, nor have you, Countess," he reminded her.

Why was he leading her on this way? Would he come to her tonight? Testing the waters, she said, "Ah, but I was not your countess then, nor had either of us intended that I should be."

"We agreed on a plan of your making," he said stiffly. "You will be my countess until Grandfather is forced to give over and disinherit me. But then you'll have Harleigh and possibly even Falconridge, with no one to say you nay ever again, just as you always wanted," he reminded her.

Just as you always wanted. The words tore at her heart. The unfairness of it angered her. 'Twas he who had made the ridiculous stipulation that they have a marriage in name only. He had set his course for America. He would not come to her room tonight.

She would have to go to his. . . .

* * *

"You must wear the cream silk with the bronze lace this evening. Hold the gold satin for the morrow at Falconridge," Harry said as she unfastened the myriad buttons from their loops at the back of Rachel's wedding gown. The heavy train lay spread across the bed in the chamber adjoining the earl's. An elderly upstairs maid carefully rolled it for storage, listening unobtrusively to the conversation whispered between the sisters.

The old woman had overheard the gossip concerning the match and knew a bit about how her crafty employer had forced his wild American grandson to wed Harleigh's scandalous daughter. She sniffed to herself. Riding astride, indeed! A most unnatural female, but then His Lordship the earl was scarcely less of a scapegrace. Would the younger sister, who had been wed a year ago, explain what was expected of the countess when he entered her bedchamber tonight? She smiled inwardly, drawing out her chore, waiting.

"Now you must not be nervous, pet. It will not be—"

"Thank you, that will be all, Mistress Adair," Rachel said with a perfunctory smile as Harry started to launch into what Rachel knew would be a euphemistic assurance that this was all for the good of England.

"Oh, I had quite forgotten she was here," Harry said after the brittle old woman departed, taking the train and gown for storage as she had been instructed to do earlier. "Now, as I was saying, you—"

Rachel sighed, forcing herself to admit the humor in the situation. "Harry, you may be the natural flirt who can coil men about your pinkie finger, but I am a country wench." She paused, remembering the phrase from her earlier conversation with Jason, then continued, "I know what men and women do in bed to procreate."

Harry's head snapped back in shock. "Honestly, Ra-

265

chel! That is too forward by more than half." Then she could not help giggling. "But I fear 'tis the truth. Would that I had been as well prepared on my wedding night as you."

"You would have been, had you allowed me to discuss the matter with you," Rachel said wryly.

Chewing her lip thoughtfully, Harry dismissed that sally, concentrating on the night ahead for her beloved sister. "Of course, being such a reckless . . . er, American, the earl may be considerably bolder than Melvin was. Yes, I suspect he will be. Hmm, but I do believe you will be able to handle him."

Rachel snorted. "I'm gratified at your confidence in me, but not all that certain he will act so boldly. Remember, he has never intended to consummate the marriage."

"Are you still prattling on about that? Why, the man's been unable to keep his hands off you."

"He blows hot and cold, I fear. One moment I believe he intends to disregard our scheme, the next that he thinks of nothing but escape from England . . . and from me." Rachel positively hated the woeful sound of her voice. Snatching up the filmy lace night rail, she yanked it over her head.

"Once he sees you in that, there is not the slightest doubt that he will totally forget aught else," Harry said dryly.

"The only way he shall see me in it is if I go to him," Rachel murmured, steeling herself for what she must do.

Harry only chuckled dismissively, reaching for the heavy sterling hairbrush on the dressing table. "Here, sit," she commanded.

"We used to brush each other's hair when we were girls," Rachel said with a sigh of pleasure as the bristles massaged her scalp, then gently tugged through the heavy masses of dark hair falling about her shoulders.

"Yes, but usually 'twas you tending to Sally and me. You were our rock after Mama died, Rachel. I only wish we had been able to do something for you in return."

Rachel smiled up at Harry. "You have, more than you know, dearest. You accept me in spite of my oddities. Now, 'tis best if you leave me to consider how I shall lure the earl to my bed."

Harry almost snorted. "Only stand in yon doorway clad in that and he will fall upon you like a ravenous wolf! Oh, dear, I did not intend that to sound—"

Rachel stood up and took the brush from her sister's hand, then hugged her. " 'Twould solve my problems neatly to have Jason 'fall upon me' in such a manner, but I don't think it will happen quite that way."

"I only want you to be happy, dear Rachel."

"I know," her sister said, shooing her out the door with a fond smile.

Rachel needed time alone to compose herself for what lay head. Methodically she placed the brush inside its mahogany case, then went about snuffing the branches of candles scattered around the room until only one fat white one flickered on the bedside candlestand. Holding out her hand, she looked down at the magnificent Cargrave ring. Even in such soft light it winked back at her as if this whole sad situation were naught but an enormous jest.

"I am his wife," she whispered softly to herself. "I have the right to this . . . and to him." Ignoring the chill of the polished wood floor, she paced back and forth in her bare feet, working up courage for what she intended to do. Was it merely to secure her future so that she would never again have to face another marriage? Or was it for love?

Either way, it did not make her feel good. If she seduced him for her own gain, she would be no less scheming and manipulative than the old marquess. But the second alternative stung far worse yet. Did she truly love a man who wished only to be quit of her? Would she spend the rest of her life regretting what might have been?

What was wrong with her that Jason could not return her love? In that instant she knew the answers to the other questions.

Then she heard the sound of his door opening and closing.

Jason could see the faintest flicker of light from beneath the door adjoining his room. She was still awake . . . or not. Perhaps she preferred to sleep with a candle or two left burning. Either way, she was *there*, so close by. All he had to do was open the door and walk inside. She was his wife. He had every legal right to take her. But no moral one.

"I gave my word," he ground out, reminding himself for what seemed the hundredth time that day of their accursed bargain. In his wildest nightmares, he could never have imagined how difficult it was to avoid what he had spent his whole life avoiding. With a snarled oath, he stalked over to the tea table and poured himself a generous slug of his grandfather's fine aged brandy.

He'd instructed the butler to send it up earlier in the day. After seeing Rachel at the church, he had known he would need help in getting through the night. He swallowed down the first glass like medicine, then poured a refill.

A soft tap on the door was followed by his valet Gentry's voice. "Are you ready to disrobe, m'lord?"

Jason's first impulse was to tell the man to go to hell, but he quickly reined in his temper. No sense creating a scene everyone on the floor would overhear. He jerked open the door so quickly that the valet practically fell inside. "I will not require your services tonight, thank you, Gentry," he said, taking a second swallow of brandy.

"But, m'lord, you'll require that I see to brushing and pressing of such superb kerseymere. We wouldn't want to ruin your wedding finery. Now, m'lord," the little man said, reaching for the brandy glass with the practiced air of an upper servant, "if you'll permit me, I'll have you properly prepared to perform your marital duties in short order."

Jason snatched back the glass and drained it defiantly, then affixed Gentry with a look that had made hardened tars quiver like a bowl of blood pudding. "For your information, I have been dressing and undressing myself since I was a stripling. I have even managed to accomplish the feat aboard ships pitching sharply on stormy seas."

"But, m'lord, you were not the earl then," Gentry replied, only slightly daunted.

"As memory serves me, I still remove my britches one leg at a time, title or no title, dammit!" Jason snapped.

"But—but—"

"I will see to my own needs. Is that clear, Gentry?" He bit off each word in a quiet, deadly voice that finally penetrated the valet's huffy indignation. As he spoke, Jason backed him toward the door, towering over the diminutive servant, who fumbled behind him for the knob and with a sputtering apology quit the room.

"Marvelous. Just bloody, buggering wonderful," Jason muttered, draining the glass. Tomorrow he would have to soothe Gentry's ruffled feathers. He had no right to take out his frustrations on an elderly servant.

Tugging at his cravat, he let his eyes stray in the direction of Rachel's room. Had she overheard the petty outburst? Would she know that she was the cause of it?

Probably so, he concluded glumly as he tossed his shirt onto the growing pile of clothing strewn across the floor. Briefly he considered pouring a third brandy, then dismissed the idea. The morning would come early enough, and they had to ride to Falconridge. It would serve him ill to have a pounding headache to match the evil throbbing in his nether parts.

Doggedly he took a seat on a chair and tugged off his boots and stockings. Barefoot, he padded about the room with the brass candle snuffer. When the last little flame was doused, he threw himself disconsolately across the bed and stared at the canopy overhead. A bright shaft of moonlight trickled in from a slit in the draperies, striking his face. Jason did not notice. With eyes closed or open, all he could see was Rachel as she had looked that morning walking down the aisle toward him, as she had looked at the wedding breakfast with her arm entwined with his, as she had looked when they waltzed that evening at the ball.

He could not have said how long he had lain staring fitfully when a soft tapping issued from the inner door connecting his room with that of his countess. Startled, he swung his legs off the bed and stood up in one swift motion, causing a slight dizziness that reminded him of how quickly he had downed two generous brandies. If ever in his life he required a clear head, it was now.

He walked over and pulled open the door. Rachel stood limmed by the golden glow of a lone candle. She was clad in the sheer cream silk confection she had worn that day at the modiste's when he had spied on her. She clutched a pitcher in both hands. He was speechless.

Rachel forced herself to look into his dark blue eyes as she blurted out her well-rehearsed fabrication. "Mistress Adair forgot to fill my water pitcher in all the confusion this evening." In fact, she'd poured the contents into the potted palm by her bedroom window. She pressed on, "I'm thirsty, but I hate to ring for her now that she's asleep. All the servants have been frightfully overworked because of the wedding . . . but . . . could I trouble you to share some of your . . . water."

He groaned inwardly. *Sweet Jesus! Water shall truly be my downfall.*

Her mouth was so dry that the lie must be convincing. Still he made no reply. She thrust the pitcher toward him and he took it but did not move. He was barechested and barefoot but still wore his trousers. She'd hoped to find him in bed, drowsing, calling out for whoever it was to enter. He did not look sleepy at all. In fact, he looked fiercely wide awake. "I . . . I could not sleep . . . for thirst," she added quickly. Now she was blathering. "I'm terribly sorry to disturb you." Rachel turned away, humiliated beyond imagining.

But before she could beat a cowardly retreat and close the door, he had shoved the pitcher on a table and seized her by her wrist, pulling her around and into his arms. "You have disturbed me from the first moment I met you, Countess," he said harshly as his mouth descended to hers.

He tasted of brandy and sex. Hot and hungry, his tongue plunged deeply, twining with hers. She dug her fingers into his shoulders, holding on to him in despair . . . and in joy as his lips continued the onslaught to her senses. Rachel kissed him back with all the fervor her untutored lips and tongue could muster, remembering the other times when his kisses had taught her what to do.

She must be doing it well because as he pressed her closer against his body, she could feel his heart slamming beneath the thick muscles of his chest, and that male part of him grow hard and demanding. When he buried his fist in her hair and pulled it, she let her head

271

tilt back, giving him access to the slender column of her throat. He bent her supple spine, raining kisses over her jawline and down to the pulse at the base of her throat.

Without knowing she did so, Rachel raised one leg and rubbed the inside of her thigh against the outside of his. He muttered a muffled oath as his mouth followed the heavy folds of lace down the deeply plunging neckline of her night rail, pressing fierce, wet kisses to the tender skin exposed until he reached the vale between her breasts. When he nuzzled there, she moaned and raised her knee higher.

His every instinct urged him to sink to the floor with her as they had almost done in her room at Harleigh Hall. *No, do this in a bed, properly,* some voice deep in his head commanded firmly. He swept her up into his arms and carried her into his room. The pale moonlight from the window combined with the flickering of the candle through the open doorway, bathing her in silvergilt as he laid her on the bed.

Her hair spread around her, like a heavy dark cloud on the white pillows. The sheer silk of her night rail molded to the slim curves of her hips and those deliciously long legs. Her breasts were accented by the thick ruffles around the neckline. Rose nipples peeked through the lace. He placed one knee on the mattress and stared down at her, letting his hand caress her arm, running his fingers skittering over her collarbone.

Then he paused just short of touching her breast. Marshaling his thoughts, he swallowed and said hoarsely, "If we don't stop now . . . I won't be able to stop, Rachel."

"We have both wanted this for a very long time, I think . . ." She raised her arms in entreaty, welcoming him.

That was all the invitation he required. There would

be no further thought, or self-recrimination about what they were doing . . . at least not tonight, not while his brandy lubricated brain and body thrummed with desperation to have her to the exclusion of all else. His grandfather and the vast inheritance of Cargrave, the old man's scheming manipulations, even his belief in his and Rachel's utter incompatibility—all evaporated in the passion of the moment.

Jason swung his other leg over her and lowered his body on top of hers, supporting his weight on his elbows. He buried his hands in her hair and cradled her head, positioning it for his kisses, raining them across her eyelids, brow, temples, then on to each ear, using the tip of his tongue to graze the small curves until she shivered with delight. His lips moved over her high cheekbones, past the hollows below to the strong lines of her jaw, nibbling small, swift kisses around the edges of her mouth.

To Rachel, it felt like butterfly wings, soft, warm, moist, brushing and teasing, delighting her yet leaving her hungry—no, starving. She framed his face with her palms, guiding his lips back to hers, opening her mouth for that sweet invasion. Eagerly he devoured her just as she wished, moaning low into her mouth as she arched up against him and let her tongue answer his.

His arms and back were corded with hard muscles that bunched and flexed as he moved over her, slanting his mouth to kiss her even more intensely. She ran her hands over his naked upper body, exploring it as she had wanted to ever since the first time she'd seen him with his shirt hanging indecently open. Her fingers curved around his biceps and then glided over the smooth, heavy muscles of his shoulders. She used the tips of her fingers to touch his spine.

Rachel could not get enough of his powerful male body. She could feel the tickle of his chest hair as it brushed the tender skin bared by her low-cut night rail. Her breasts ached, the nipples distended and tingling beneath their cocoon of silk and lace. He tugged on the neckline and freed one milky globe, teasing the nubby tip until she cried out with startled pleasure.

Then his tongue traced keen little circles around the aureole before taking the nipple deep into his mouth and suckling on it. She dug her fingers into his hair and urged him on, whimpering when he released his prize, moaning deeply when he pulled the other one free and repeated the process. Rachel clung to him, arching her head backward to raise her breasts for his feasting. She had never imagined anything like this, she who had watched hundreds of foals and calves nurse at their mother's teats.

Jason had never tasted anything so sweet. He felt like a starving man brought to a banquet table. Her skin was like silk, her flesh firm and smooth as he loosed the tie of the night rail and peeled it open. He lowered his mouth from her breast and traced a wet pattern with his tongue down to her navel, letting the tip dip into the tiny depression as she writhed beneath him.

When his large warm palm flattened against her lower abdomen, Rachel gasped with a wanting so intense that it robbed her of breath. She ached in her woman's place, feeling the pounding of her blood as it pooled low in her belly. The bodice of her night rail was open and the long silk skirt had ridden up high on her thighs. Unable to stop herself, she arched her hips against him, opening her legs and entwining them with his, only dimly aware that they still had the impediment of clothing separating them from the final culmination of their desires.

He raised himself up on straight arms and looked down at her, studying the lush curves of her breasts with their rose-brown nipples, the slim indentation of her waist and sleek flair of her hips, which now undulated in unschooled, unconscious invitation. His own body was heavy with wanting, his blood pounding, his breathing harsh as he pulled away from her to remove his trousers.

She cried out at the loss of his weight, his heat when he moved. But then she could see that he was unbuttoning his fly. It was quite unseemly of her to watch, but Rachel was far past being aware of propriety. Her eyes fastened on the huge bulge in his breeches as he released the last button and began to peel the tight pants down long, hard legs. When he straightened up and stood before her, she had the first unimpeded view of his naked body.

This time he made no attempt to turn away from her curious and hungry eyes. He let her observe the jutting proof of his desire. His heated gaze swept over her as she sat up on the bed, letting the lacy night rail fall free of her shoulders and bunch around her hips. Rachel studied him as boldly as he did her, noting the pattern of black hair that ran from the thick pelt on his chest and narrowed as it descended over his flat, hard belly to bloom once again around his thick staff.

Wanting to let her hands travel the same course as her eyes, she knelt up and buried her fingers in the hair of his chest. His breath caught sharply when she ran a nail over a tight male nipple. Experimentally she used her other hand to do the same, then ran them together and let them move lower. When she had almost reached her final destination, courage suddenly deserted her, until he spoke in a broken whisper.

"Touch me, Rachel."

Chapter Nineteen

Rachel did as he commanded—no, more as he pleaded. She could hear the catch in his voice, the roughness of his entreaty, and a part of her gloried in the fact that he desired her with such desperate hunger. But desire was a double-edged sword. The instant her hand encircled his shaft, the heat of it scalded her. She almost pulled back but could not bear to lose contact with the male essence of him.

Jason drew in a deep, shuddering breath and knew that she could feel him trembling, but he was powerless to stop his hips from rocking forward, showing her the motion his body craved. Her smooth hand glided down the slick, hard length, then back up. Excitement inspired inventiveness as her other hand found his sac and cupped it tenderly. His breathing accelerated.

She was lost in the wonder of discovery, glad of the small golden pool of candlelight augmenting the moon so that she could see the outline of his body as it moved with such sinuous grace. His hands covered hers, guiding her ever so slightly for a moment, but then his grip tightened over her wrists.

"You must stop else I'll not be able to control myself, love," he gasped.

Rachel was uncertain if she had done something wrong, but before she could speak, he knelt facing her on the bed. His hands glided over her body, peeling the rumpled night rail lower, pausing to caress and kiss each inch of silky skin. He drew her into his arms after sliding the night rail over the curve of her hips until it pooled around her legs.

When his hands cupped her buttocks and gently squeezed, molding her lower body to his, she could feel the hardness of his staff. It felt so hot, so hard, so wonderful that she could hardly wait as they exchanged fierce kisses. Rachel knew the dueling and plunging of their tongues was but an intimation of what was to come.

Jason took time to recover his control, which this passionate woman had nearly shattered. How long had he wanted her? Seemingly endless months had fed this madness . . . a ravening madness that he was powerless to resist. "Lie back," he whispered raggedly, still raining kisses on her throat and shoulders as he pressed her down into the softness of the mattress. Moonlight and candlelight bathed her body in silver and gold. Its curves and hollows were shadowed and mysterious, beckoning his eager hands as he pulled the silk night rail from her legs and sent it floating to the floor.

He traced tiny circles about her nipples with his fingertips, praising the way they tightened into sweet dark rosebuds, begging for his mouth. He obliged, suckling them once more as she buried her fingers in his hair, urging him to continue. A soft keening rose from deep in her throat as he moved from her breasts to her navel, using his tongue and lips to delight her. Then he moved lower yet into the lush dark curls at the apex of her thighs. His mouth was hot and seeking, nuzzling her mound as his fingers found her pearly moisture.

"Your nectar is sweet," he murmured as he touched his index finger to his lips. "I would taste more."

She had never imagined this! When his lips brushed the soft, wet petals, her hips arched. He gave a low growl of satisfaction, settling in between her thighs. Rachel whimpered as his tongue touched the very center of her desire, then began to stroke and draw on it with utmost gentleness. The sweetness was fierce beyond her ability to describe. He continued his magic, drawing her to greater and greater heights of pleasure.

Her fingers dug into the bedsheets, clutching linens, kneading in frantic counterpoint to the pulsing joy of his ministrations. Before she realized it, her hands were once again buried in his hair, cradling his head, urging him onward. Gradually the pleasure grew so keen that it was almost pain. An urge for some unnamed yet desperately needed surcease spiraled up in her. She cried out his name as the splendor burst, sending her hurtling through time and space for this one perfect moment.

He could feel her crest, hear her cries and taste the heady richness of her body as he raised himself up over her, positioning her for his entry. Her head thrashed from side to side, tangling her hair in a great silken skein across the pillows while he was poised at the brink of her welcoming heat. She was slick and swollen, still pulsing from her release. The pleasure of giving her this gift was even greater than that of being the one to breach her maidenhead.

Rachel felt the heat of his staff as it slowly began to penetrate her body. The slowly subsiding contractions pulled him deeper, welcoming him into her most secret place, a place that seemed to ache with emptiness, needing to be filled with him. She felt a great stretching, then a small twinge of pain. So this, then, was the culmination of their marriage vows, the mystery revealed when two became one flesh. She arched into his first slow, careful stroke, encircling him with her arms, wanting to hold them joined like this forever, never having to face tomorrow.

Give me your child, Jason.

The plea was quickly overpowered by renewed hunger as his big, muscular body labored over hers, fanning the gently cooling embers into flame once again. With each strong thrust her hunger grew. He murmured endearments to her, instructing her to wrap her legs around his hips. She did so, arching up to meet him. Her fingers dug into his back, pulling his chest to flatten her tender breasts and press her deeper into the mattress. This time as the ache grew, Rachel knew why the pressure was building inside her and how it would be released in glorious explosion. She urged him on.

Jason could sense her renewed desire and let slip some of the careful control holding his own passion in check. His strokes grew longer, harder, swifter as the ecstasy spiraled out in ever widening circles. Where did he stop and she begin? He could no longer tell. All was such intense desperation, such intense pleasure, that he gave in and murmured her name against her throat over and over as they rode to the crest together.

He held off at the very last moment, waiting for her body's signal, which mercifully came quickly. Then the culmination began and continued, longer than he had ever experienced it before. Not even after months at sea had he felt this searing, all-powerful release while he spilled his seed deep into her womb, shuddering in fulfillment.

His staff, already so large and hard inside her, seemed to swell even more as he cried out and began

279

to shake like a patient with the ague. It would have startled her if she had not been so caught up in a second shattering climax of her own, this time gloriously melding with his.

Slowly they descended from the heights of that ethereal place only lovers can know, sweat-soaked in the still coolness of the night. His weight pressed her into the soft mattress, yet she would not relinquish her hold on him. Her arms and legs were wrapped securely around his. Her fingers contentedly kneaded in the slick muscles of his back as his lips nuzzled her throat. She slipped one hand up to cradle his head against her on the pillows, then dropped off to sleep, too satiated and exhausted to think of the morrow.

Jason, too, felt a deep sense of peace and lethargy overtake him. Rather than face the consequences of this irrevocable act, he gave in to unconsciousness. Did he perchance murmur her name once again as he was falling asleep?

Rachel awoke in the early-morning chill, alone in Jason's big bed. A sheet partially covered her. She flung it aside and sat up groggily, feeling a sudden twinge between her legs. Untried muscles cried out in protest as she slipped her legs over the side of the mattress and stared down at the smears of blood on the snowy linens of her husband's well rumpled bed. The marriage was accomplished, indissoluble by her father or the old marquess without an act of Parliament.

And only the absent Jason Beaumont could initiate such an act.

She had done what she'd set out to do. Why, then, did she feel so unutterably sad? So guilty? She was every bit as manipulative, as scheming as those two old men. Was that what her husband now realized? Surely it must be the reason he had fled the scene of her deflowering.

"Oh, Jason, my love, please do not hate me," she whispered brokenly as she slipped on her silk robe.

Before she could fasten the belt, the door to her room opened and her maid called out a cheery greeting, then gingerly approached the open door to the earl's adjoining quarters. "Oh, Gretchen, please draw me a bath," Rachel instructed in as level a voice as she could muster.

The servant approached the doorway, her eyes huge as she peered nervously into the room as if expecting His Lordship to leap out from behind the armoire with a cutlass in his fist like the privateer he had once been. "Very good, m'lady," she murmured with a bobbed curtsy, starting to back away, then hesitating. "If you wish, I'll send the upstairs maid to change the linens." Her face was as scarlet as the sunrise.

Well, was this not what Rachel required? Before noon every servant in the city house would know the marriage had been consummated. Woodenly the Countess of Falconridge nodded, but just then the door to the hallway opened and Jason entered, clad in a pair of old britches and an open shirt, his "country uniform," as Rachel had come to think of it. Her knees grew weak, and she struggled to stand upright and face him in the bright morning light.

The maid vanished, leaving the earl and his lady alone.

"Good morning, Countess."

His expression was unreadable. He had used her Christian name last night. Somehow she forced her vocal cords to work. "You were gone when I awakened." That was not what she'd intended to say. What had made her blurt out an accusation as if she wanted him to stay by her side? But she did, Rachel realized with a sinking feeling. It was too late to undo what had happened. If he regretted it, he must share at least a part

281

of the blame . . . no, that was not strictly true.

Until she had knocked on his door, he had been content with their agreement. She had seduced him for her own devious ends, and now she would have to pay the price.

"I had a deal to think about," Jason replied neutrally to her remark. He observed her tight expression, the guilty way she met his eyes, then let her gaze quickly slide past him. This was not virginal vaporing after doing one's duty for England. While he tried to gather his scattered thoughts, he moved closer to her. Damn, even the scent of her intoxicated him! She smelled of feminine musk, that soft honeysuckle perfume she wore . . . and now, of him.

"You can still sail home to America, Jason," she said softly, unable to keep her eyes from a fleeting glance at the tangled bedcovers before she willed herself to meet his gaze once more.

"If you are so eager to be rid of me, why did you come to me last night?" he asked before considering the rashness of the question. The instant he asked it, the answer became apparent as his eyes followed the course of hers to the bed and its incriminating evidence. She had used him. But he admitted to himself that she had scarcely forced him to perform against his will.

He'd awakened with her clinging softly to him, still deep in sleep. She had looked so innocent and lovely in the morning light that he had almost succumbed to the overpowering urge to make love to her again. No woman had ever had such a hold on him, and it had frightened him into a swift retreat. He'd ridden across the city without finding any answer but to return to Rachel . . . his wife.

Before she could say anything in response to his remark, two footmen carrying pails of hot water followed his valet into the dressing room on the other side of his quarters, creating a commotion. Damn Gentry's efficiency!

Then her maid returned, calling out that the countess's bath awaited in her quarters. Stammering, Rachel said only, "We'll speak later," then beat a hasty retreat to soak her aching limbs in heavenly warm water.

As she lay against the fan back of the tub, Rachel reviewed the events of the preceding night. Everything had gone according to plan . . . as long as that plan only included proof that theirs was a valid marriage. So much for Harry's silly fantasy about his being in love with her and wishing to remain by her side! He'd hied himself away from her before the sun even peeked over the horizon, leaving her alone in *his* bed, the rotter!

Now he would be angry with her. And truly, she could not blame him. She had broken their agreement by seducing him last night. Well, she supposed if he were ever inclined to wed a sturdy American woman, they could divorce. The thought of him in another woman's arms, murmuring another woman's name, made her heart ache. She rubbed her fingers in tiny circles on her temples, trying to soothe the matching ache in her head. How could he ever think to share with any other woman what they had experienced last night? How could he dare?

But Jason Beaumont had been a sailor. No doubt a womanizer with a willing wench in every port from Baltimore to Bali. His considerable skill in making love certainly attested to a surfeit of practice. She'd overheard enough whispered conversations among country wives and ladies of the ton to know that they often went miserably unfulfilled in the marriage bed. Until last night she had no idea of what that fulfillment was. Ignorance had indeed been bliss. Once initiated, how could she live without his touch?

"Well, I shall simply have to," she murmured to herself, trying to be practical as she ran a soapy sponge down her leg. Even the soft brush of the sponge made her skin tingle. Damn the man, she wanted him again in spite of her soreness. Well, there were still several days before they parted company. Could she lure him again en route to Bristol? Perhaps with his freedom in sight, he might feel assured enough to dally a time or two.

Or three . . .

Jason made his morning toilette quickly and hurried downstairs to break his fast before anyone else was about. He had not reckoned on the early-rising marquess, who was tucking into a plate heaped with kippered herring and scones slathered in clotted cream. The earl chastised himself for not realizing that the old man would certainly be up and about to learn the outcome of the preceding night.

The thought affronted him greatly. What had passed between him and his wife was too intensely personal for servants' speculations. Or his grandfather's inquisition. Glowering, he walked to the sideboard and began filling his plate.

"I see you've an appetite," Cargrave remarked smugly, wiping a bit of cream from the side of his mouth. "Good night's exertions will do that for a man," he added, chuckling.

Jason dropped the serving fork back onto the tray of bacon and glared at the old man coldly. "I went riding this morning before breakfast."

"And last night after dinner, too, I warrant," the old man shot back gleefully.

Jason cursed his stupid tongue. "What manner of riding I may or may not have done is not your concern."

"Mayhap not, but it is the concern of your countess."

Even his grandson's sharp ill humor could not dampen the marquess's jolly mood.

"Then let us settle the issue," Jason replied, depositing a spoonful of clotted cream on his plate with a nasty splat.

Cargrave waved his napkin dismissively. "No need to act the frustrated swain. I know full well what transpired between you and your countess."

"And so, I imagine, does all the staff of the city house and half of London!" Jason bellowed, setting his plate on the sideboard with sufficient force to crack the Sevres china. Suddenly all appetite had fled. He spun on his heel to quit the room, but the marquess stood up, his expression abruptly changed.

"Wait, my boy. I did not mean to make light of your wedding night, nor in any way to denigrate your lady, whom I hold in the highest regard. Surely you know that."

Jason studied the imperious old man, startled by a flash of vulnerability on his face. Or had he imagined it? As quickly as it appeared, it was schooled away and the marquess's arrogance was back in place. "How could you not hold the Countess of Falconridge in high regard, since 'twas you who chose her for the title?" Jason said scathingly.

"And you, of course, found her so utterly unattractive that I'm certain you closed your eyes and thought of England all the while you were performing your duty!" Now it was Cargrave's turn to bellow.

"My duty! My bloody, damnable duty! Yes, m'lord, as I'm sure every footman and laundress in this mausoleum has informed you, I've performed my duty. Now, by your leave, I will collect my countess and repair to Falconridge for two weeks of uninterrupted *duty*."

The marquess watched his grandson storm from the room, then sat back down at his plate, a thoughtful expression on his face. Then a slow smile warmed it after he recalled how very possessive he had felt about Mathilda when they first were wed. Damnation, he'd felt that way about her every day of their lives together. It was a good sign that Jason exhibited the same proprietary air. Humming to himself, he dipped another piece of scone in clotted cream and popped it in his mouth.

By coach the journey to Falconridge took the better part of a day. Normally, Rachel rode one of her horses, but owing to her current tenderness, she made no protest when the marquess sent word that he had ordered up his most luxurious carriage for the bridal couple. Of course, she would have to sit in close quarters with Jason for hours. Would he glower at her . . . or could they find more pleasant ways to pass the afternoon? She was becoming positively incorrigible!

Unnerved by the thought, she finished dressing while Harry oversaw the packing of her trousseau. Then her sister shooed the gaggle of maids from the room and faced her sister. This was a moment Rachel was not anticipating with any relish.

"Well, I have heard the servants' gossip," Harry said with a smug little grin. "Do tell me, are American men all they are said to be?"

"If you have heard the servants, then you know that I succeeded in seducing my husband. That is all I required." Her tone was waspish to put Harry off, but it did not deter her sister.

"The servants only know that the marriage has been consummated—in his bed. You went to him. He did not come to you, so you are in a taking, I see, hmmm," Harry said, tapping her fingernail against her cheek.

"I am *not* in a taking! Honestly, Harry, there are times when I could—"

"Tut. See? You *are* in a taking, never deny it." Harry's grin widened. "Of course, I'm quite certain you had to tie your earl to the bedposts, then ravish him utterly against his will."

The image of Jason bound spread-eagled on his huge bed flashed into Rachel's mind, and she could not hold on to her ill humor in spite of her guilty regrets. "Scarcely that. Once I opened the door . . . well, you were right about his"—she groped for the word—"virility."

"Ha! Did I not tell you so? The man's mad for you."

"Then why did he quit his own bed before dawn and go riding about the city like some lost soul?" Rachel shot back, her mood mercurially shifting once more.

"But he returned, did he not?" Harry countered.

"Yes, only to take one look at the evidence of our consummated marriage and retreat. He knows what I did and why, and he does not like it. We're still going to steal Fox and ride for Bristol on the morrow," she said forlornly.

"Well," Harry said, undaunted, "you still have from now until you reach Bristol."

Jason was confused and uncertain of what he should say to Rachel. Perhaps they could sort matters out when they reached Falconridge that evening. He needed to get away from the Cargrave city house, that was certain. His grandfather's smug satisfaction reminded him anew of exactly why he must thwart the old man's plans. Not that he should require reminding, he thought crossly.

Why had she come to him last night? He vaguely recalled something about annulments being easier to obtain than divorces under English law. Was that her reason? She had certainly appeared as eager to have him make love to her as he had been to oblige. He needed time to think about it, and spending hours confined in a coach with his quick-witted wife would not allow him that luxury. He went to the mews and instructed the head groom to saddle Araby as soon as he had the carriage horses hitched up and ready to go.

When he made his way back to the house, Fox waylaid him on the brick pathway through the garden. "Good morning, Jace."

Jason could deduce by the boy's fidgeting that he had something on his mind. Looking about to be certain no one was within earshot, Jason asked, "Grandfather has not decided to leave for the country before the first of the week, has he?"

"No. He and the viscount are going for dinner at their club tomorrow night," the boy reported, shuffling from foot to foot anxiously.

"Good. Then they'll be too well occupied to cause any difficulty. Be ready to ride by midnight."

Fox's expression was crestfallen. "Then you haven't changed your mind . . . about deserting Rachel?"

Jason muttered an oath beneath his breath. "And why should I?" The instant he asked the question, he wanted to withdraw it, but it was too late.

"I thought after last night . . . well, that is, everyone knows—"

"You may discuss country matters when they pertain to ship's mates and serving wenches, but you are not to utter one syllable about the Countess of Falconridge. Is that clear?"

Fox's eyes grew round as he observed Jace's fierce expression. No, it was not clear at all, but he knew better than to say so. "Yes, sir." Adults were even more impossible to understand than he had believed a scant few weeks ago. Well, they had at least three days' ride to Bristol. Who knew what might happen between now and then? he thought with renewed optimism as they resumed their walk to the house.

Rachel came downstairs accompanied by her sister, who was busily instructing a small army of footmen how to stow the myriad of trunks and boxes in the baggage coach which was to follow them. Jason could not help admiring the way his bride's emerald velvet traveling dress flattered her rich coloring, bringing out the green in her hazel eyes. A matching spencer trimmed with black satin piping emphasized her slim waist. She moved with such elegance that Jason could not imagine any man being immune to her cool beauty.

He certainly was not. "Countess," he said, taking her hand as she reached the bottom of the stairs.

She could see he was dressed to ride, but surely he did not intend to leave her alone in the coach for the long journey. Or did he? He'd abandoned his scandalous old shirt in favor of a cutaway coat of tan twill and beautifully polished Hessians. The doeskin riding pants fit like second skin, and she remembered how powerful his thighs had been in bed last night. Grateful that the rim of her bonnet hid her flushed face, she tilted her head away from him and concentrated on saying goodbye to the gaggle of well-wishers gathered on the front steps to see them off.

Fox seemed preoccupied as he made his bow. The marquess, her father and Harry were all smiles, as was Melvin. Always early risers, Roger and Garnet offered cheery good wishes. Evelyn stood back, studying Rachel with brooding dark eyes. Then when all the others had said their goodbyes, he kissed her hand with a courtly flourish which she knew drew Jason's ire.

"I'll be toddling along to m' country place in a few days, but Garnet and Ev have to return to work," Roger said, giving Jason a hearty slap on the back, oblivious to the jealous interplay between his stepson and his cousin. "Perhaps we'll get together in a week or two

289

after you've had time . . . well, er, in a few weeks, then," he harrumphed with a red face.

"I shall look forward, coz." With thinly veiled hostility Jason turned to Evelyn and said, "How unfortunate you won't be joining us in the country."

"Yes," Garnet's son replied smoothly. "A pity we must attend to matters at the shipyard. I shall look forward to seeing you at Christmas." His eyes moved from the earl to the countess when he made the promise.

Rachel could practically hear Harry titter in satisfaction. She knew Jason was furious as he took her hand and assisted her into the coach. She took her seat and waited for him to join her.

He stepped back, saying, "Araby is restive when he's tied behind a carriage. I'll ride him to Falconridge."

With no further ado, he nodded to the driver as he closed the carriage door. Startled and embarrassed at the abrupt announcement, Rachel leaned back against the squabs and seethed silently as the coach started up with a lurch. Jason swung up on Araby and trotted beside the window, as if devotedly keeping company with his bride. Only Rachel knew that he intended no such thing.

Well, once they arrived at Falconridge, there would be an accounting.

Chapter Twenty

As he rode beside the closed carriage, Jason could not keep his thoughts from the woman inside. Thanks to her magnificent enticement in that cream lace night rail, they were well and truly married. There could be no annulment. Not that he had ever wanted one. No, bugger it, he reminded himself, it was that he never wanted a wife in the first place!

Or did he?

He trembled at the question, startling Araby into a skitter. As he calmed the big black, he considered what it might be like if he remained in England with his countess. Would life truly be so terrible? Not so long ago, he would have yelled from the rooftops a resounding "Yes." But in thinking about the past few weeks with her, Jason was no longer so sure. Certainly the delights of the marriage bed had been as marvelous as he had imagined they would be. He had no cold and prim English icicle for a bride!

Had Rachel begun to change her mind about him as he had about her? Or had she merely been making certain her father could not annul their marriage? Suddenly another thought came to him like a bolt from the blue. What if she had conceived a child of their passion? The thought of using a French letter with Rachel had never occurred to him, even though he had never failed to take that precaution with a woman before.

Well, once they arrived at Falconridge, there would be an accounting.

That, however, was far easier vowed than achieved. By early afternoon the overcast skies opened up with promised rain, drenching them in a deluge of biblical proportions and turning the country roads into quagmires of muck. Then Rachel's carriage became stuck in a deep rut, breaking a wheel during the arduous attempt to pull it free. By the time Jason and one of his men returned with a wheelwright from a neighboring village, it was growing dark.

The rain still had not abated when they were once again on the road. Jason was drenched through his heavy cloak, as well as covered with so much mud that it provided him an additional excuse for not climbing inside the coach with his wife. Moreover, he had always shared his men's privations aboard ship and saw no reason to change his style of command just because he had been elevated to the peerage.

When the coaches finally reached the entrance to the sprawling estate, it was nearing midnight. The final indignity was provided by a tenant's cart overturned in the middle of the road. Bushels of turnips were scattered in huge piles, now smashed into slimy pulp by the skittering horses' hooves and coach wheels.

The rain had relented to a slow, cold drizzle as Jason dismounted from Araby to supervise the cleanup of the mess. He ordered more lanterns lit to expedite the work. With the aid of his footmen, they quickly had the cart righted and shoved off the road. He instructed his servants to gather what tools they could from the coach, then shovel away the wreckage.

Rachel pulled up the hood on her cloak and climbed from the carriage to investigate all the commotion. After taking a few steps in the wretchedly uncomfortable slippers which Harry had insisted went so well with her outfit, she nearly fell into the noisome mess before grabbing hold of the harness on the carriage team. The horses were snorting and prancing nervously in the confusion. She decided to make herself useful and calm them, since the driver had tied off the reins and joined the cleanup.

As she soothed the matched grays, she watched Jason, imagining that this was much the way he must have looked aboard his ship, giving orders and putting his own strong arms to work beside his men. "He was born to command," she murmured softly, rubbing the muzzle of the lead horse.

Seeing her standing in the drizzle with the horses, Jason was struck by how calm and practical a female she was. He could well imagine most ladies of the ton wringing their hands and vaporing inside the carriage. He walked over to her, picking his way with considerable care across the road. As he drew near, her expression in the dim lantern light was obscured by the hood of her cloak. "You seem to have matters well in hand as always, Countess," he said.

"I was thinking the same of you, m'lord," she replied. " 'Tis a pity you will not be Cargrave's heir after all. You would've made a splendid marquess."

Before he could reply to that disturbing compliment, one of his footmen interrupted, saying, "The coaches can pass now, m'lord."

"Good. Leave two of the lanterns so the servants can see what they're doing. Damnation, what a night," he muttered, shivering in misery. "If it continues raining like this, we'll never make the ride to Bristol without breaking our necks," he added in a whisper.

Hearing his angry words, Rachel felt a chill that owed nothing to the raw night air. He still intended to go through with their plan. She had failed to deter him. Perhaps her scheme had even contributed to his resolve. There was nothing she could say to him that would change a thing. *How wrong you were, Harry.*

Within minutes they pulled up to the front entryway of Falcon's Crest, where Jason assisted his new countess from the carriage. "We are almost as muddy as our poor servants," he said as he took her hand.

Even through the damp thickness of leather separating their fingers, she could feel a frisson of heat when he touched her. "Considering how we met, mud seems our destiny." His smile twisted her heart when he nodded.

A full array of household servants were now lining the front steps to welcome the bridal couple. The chief housekeeper, a portly woman of indeterminate years but possessing a very determined jut of chin, began issuing orders for hot baths and a lavish supper to be laid out in spite of the ghastly hour.

"I believe a simple pot of hot soup and some warmed bread would suffice, Mistress Mallory. Do you not concur, m'lord?" Rachel asked, turning to Jason.

When he gave a bone-weary nod, she smiled at the harried older woman and said, "Have the food brought to our rooms after we bathe."

Jason lay back in the tub of steaming water and closed his eyes. His valet gathered up his ruined clothes, which he had stripped off the moment he reached the dressing room. Bloody hell, would he ever be warm again? His muscles ached in ways they had not since he was a stripling lad first shipping out on one of his father's schooners. Life as an earl had made him soft. Best that he leave it and return to the sea.

But that would mean leaving Rachel. Why did that bother him? She was a schemer almost to match his grandfather. Small wonder the old man had chosen her. He could see her standing by the frightened horses in the rain, calmly patting the nose of the leader, crooning to them, oblivious of her muddy hems and slippers. When visions of her beneath him followed, he shifted uncomfortably in the water. Just thinking of her made him as hard as an oak stake.

He cursed aloud in the empty room. Splashing water over the sides of the tub, he rose and stepped out, reaching for one of a pile of snowy towels on the stool beside the tub. Seizing it, he began to dry himself with considerable vigor. At least he had finally made it clear to his personal servants that their services were not required unless he specifically asked for them. He had never learned to be comfortable with valets and footmen hovering.

Striding across the small dressing room, he pulled a brocade banyan from a hook on the wall and put it on, tying the sash as he searched for carpet slippers to keep his feet warm on the cold wooden floor. Rachel had instructed the housekeeper to bring up hot soup. His stomach gave a sharp rumble when he remembered that. Donning the slippers, he strode silently from his room through the door adjoining hers, expecting to find servants laying out the simple meal.

What he found instead was his wife, reclining naked in a tub of water right in front of a roaring fire in the fireplace. One slender golden arm was raised languidly as she plied a dripping sponge to it with the other hand, affording him an excellent view of her breasts. Soap bubbles kissed the rose-brown nipples which rode just above the water line. Her eyes were half closed, and her expression was one of utter contentment.

She raised one impossibly long leg to apply the sponge to it, beginning with the high, elegant arch of her foot. Great masses of chocolate hair were piled in gleaming curls on top of her head, secured helter-shelter by heavy pins as if she, too, had performed the task without help from servants. Another of many things about her that he admired.

But right now, it was her magnificent body that he admired most of all. Every wet, glistening inch of it. And he would have it. His hunger for soup and the pain of his aching muscles were utterly forgotten as he walked silently across the room and took the sponge from her hand.

Rachel looked up with a startled gasp as his large, dark hand covered hers. "Allow me," he said softly. Then he bent to his task, skimming the soft sponge over her leg, lowering it to the full curve of her hip, then raising it to circle her breasts until the nipples stood up, puckered by the delicate stimulation.

She moaned low in the back of her throat and closed her eyes in bliss. If she could not have him forever, at least there would be these few precious days before he left her. Then his voice, low and urgent, broke into her thoughts.

"Please, Rachel . . . I need you."

She sat up, her eyes wide open now as she studied his face in the firelight. He looked grim, his dark blue eyes shadowed by fatigue . . . or wariness. She could not tell which, nor did she care. Without saying a word, she stood up in the tub, letting the water run in silvery rivulets from her body as he took a towel and enfolded her within it, then began massaging her dry.

296

"That will have to do," he rasped out after a moment of feeling the sweet, feminine heat of her body. Sweeping her into his arms, he carried her to the turned-back bed on the other side of the fireplace and laid her on it, throwing the towel on the floor.

She watched in avid silence while he shed his banyan and climbed beneath the covers with her. In spite of the chilly rain outside, the room grew toasty warm as they lay side by side, caressing and exploring each other's bodies. They kissed with a drugging hunger that made them both breathless. His tongue plunged into her mouth, twining with hers, then withdrew. She rimmed his mouth with the tip of her tongue and then nibbled at his lower lip.

He raised himself over her and began to suckle on her breasts as she ran her hands across the breadth of his shoulders and down his back. The pull of his mouth on her nipple seemed to cause a tightening deep in her belly, an ache which only he could assuage, an emptiness only he would ever be able to fill. She arched up, letting her hands find his hard buttocks and squeeze. He growled low in his throat, and she could feel the heat of his erection pressing against her thigh. She reached for it with both hands.

He stilled. She imprisoned it, her fingers boldly plying the velvety length. When he thrust against her hand in desperation, she held him fast, cupping his sac with her other hand as she stroked. Then she guided him to the portal that ached for his entry. He felt her wetness and knew there would be no barrier now. But might she be tender from last night? He hesitated for an instant, but when she arched up and clenched his hips between her thighs, he was lost.

She felt the power of his first thrust and moved with him, urging him onward. They coupled fiercely, mating like two starved wolves feasting on a fresh kill. He rolled them over until she was riding on top of him. Rachel looked startled for an instant, but when his hands kneaded her buttocks and guided her movements, she quickly took over like some wild Valkyrie. The new position gave her more control, and she began rotating her hips in deep, rolling plunges that made them both cry out with the wonder of their joining.

The pins from her hair had long since been lost, and the rich chocolate-colored curls streamed over her shoulders, burnished in the firelight. His hands moved upward, brushing the dark locks away, taking a breast in each hand, cupping them and teasing the distended nipples with his thumbs as she pressed her palms against his chest. She could feel the hard thrumming of his heartbeat match her own. The intensity of this joining made it too uncontrolled to last. Now she understood what was to happen, and happen all too soon.

Rachel wanted to go slow, to make the moment last, but she was as powerless as Jason to stop the wild rush to fulfillment. When it began, she arched her back and cried out his name, feeling his shuddering response.

His body seemed to buck off the mattress as the explosive orgasm engulfed him. Beyond the incredible pleasure, he could hear the keening cry of his name on his wife's lips. He did not hear himself as he rasped out, "Rachel!"

They lay, arms and legs entangled, the heavy coverlet twisted at their feet. In the fireplace, the flames leaped brightly, casting long shadows over their bodies. He raised his head and played with a curl of dark hair that lay over her breast, rubbing it back and forth across the nipple until it tightened once again. He could feel her begin to move her hips restlessly, turning her head into the tangle of her hair spread across the pillows. She kept her eyes closed.

Jason considered that he might be wise to do the

same, but he could not get his fill of looking at her. Thick lashes fanned down over her high cheekbones. Those wide, eminently kissable lips parted ever so slightly as her breathing became erratic. Her face was strong, the nose and jawline straight—bold for a woman yet utterly pleasing to him. Slim dark eyebrows arched perfectly over those changeable eyes. What shade would they be in the firelight? He rolled her onto her back.

"Look at me, Rachel," he commanded, taking a curl and tickling her chin with it until she turned and opened her eyes.

"Gold. I thought so," he murmured as he lowered his mouth to hers.

This time they went slowly, taking the time to caress and kiss, rebuilding the inner fires even as the one on the hearth began to subside. Neither said a word but only made soft exclamations of pleasure. She traced the pattern of hair on his chest downward in its vee to his navel, then applied her mouth to a flat male nipple, eliciting a growl. Taking that to be good, she applied her skills to the other one and was likewise rewarded.

When she reached for his phallus this time, he allowed her complete freedom to touch and explore, caressing experimentally. Now that he had been once sated and could maintain control, he was able to indulge her curiosity. His hand found her woman's place, warm and wet for him. He cupped it, then used his fingers to massage the swollen bud of her passion ever so softly until she cried out, arching her hips in supplication.

He turned her on her side, facing away from him, nibbling on her neck as they spooned together. His staff pressed between her thighs until he gripped her hip with his hand, then entered her in one long, slow thrust.

"This way it will last much longer," he murmured in her ear.

She shivered with the pleasure of his slow movement, catching the rhythm and pressing her buttocks back into his thrusts. This was pure, mindless delight. Rachel thought of nothing but the man holding her so intimately against his big, hard body. She lived in the moment—this moment and those few precious ones to come on the road to Bristol.

I have made my peace with his leaving. All I ask is this, now. After that . . . well . . . She blotted the consideration from her mind and concentrated instead on making this golden time last.

Slowly they ascended the heights. Whenever they drew too near, he would stop and clamp his hand over her hip to still her movement, then resume. At last, when they were both panting and desperate for surcease, he stroked swiftly until her body began to contract in tight little spasms around him. Burying his face in the silky fragrance of her hair, he let go and joined her.

They lay that way for several moments afterward, unwilling to let reality once again intrude. Jason wanted nothing more than to hold her close and sleep for hours, then make love to her again. What did Rachel want? She certainly had learned to enjoy bedsport quickly enough. A fine quality in a wife . . .

Just then a knock sounded on the door. It was the housekeeper, wanting to know if she should have the soup served in the countess's room or the earl's. Pulling a cover over them, Jason called out, "Serve it by the fire in my room."

Rachel watched as he calmly rolled from the mattress and reached for his banyan as if without a care in the world. Well, he was certainly sexually appeased, the lout! And altogether so splendid-looking that just watching the play of muscles on his long, lean body made her heart speed up. One lock of hair fell across his forehead as he looked down to belt the robe, and she could see his profile in the firelight. That hawkish nose, powerful jaw and those heavy eyebrows furrowed together made him look as fierce and forbidding as the privateer he had been. A stranger and yet her lover. *My husband,* she reminded herself sadly.

She sat up, suddenly shy now that the passions of the evening had been spent. How wanton and needy she must have seemed to him. Yet she knew in her woman's heart that she had pleased him well, just as he had her. But he did not wish the encumbrance of a wife any more than he wished to be an earl.

He walked around the bed and picked up a deep gold satin robe lying across an easy chair, holding it out for her. "Our supper awaits," he said simply.

She could do nothing but let the covers fall and slip from the bed, allowing him to fit the robe over her shoulders as she slid her arms into the sleeves and belted it, all the while keeping her back to him. Then resolutely she turned and met his eyes. "I don't know about you, m'lord, but I am famished," she said boldly, even though her stomach was twisted in knots.

He smiled and took her hand. "Then let us eat."

They walked through the adjoining door into his quarters, where the fire had been newly stoked to a roaring blaze. A small table with a tureen of soup placed upon it was situated in front of the hearth. A kitchen maid waited nervously to serve them, but Jason dismissed her with thanks, then began ladling fragrant vegetables and beef chunks into their bowls while Rachel set to slicing thick pieces of bread from a crusty loaf and slathering them with butter.

He pushed in her chair as she took a seat, then sat down opposite her and tucked into the food like a starving man, which she imagined he must be after all his physical exertions during the long day just past, not to mention those more recently in her bedroom. She began to eat, finding to her surprise that she, too, was genuinely hungry once she tasted the first spoonful of rich broth.

Soon they had used hunks of bread crust to soak up the last of the soup in the huge tureen. Taking a sip of tea, he studied her over the rim of his cup. "Why did you come to me last night, Rachel?" he asked softly.

She straightened in her seat, startled by the direct question. How could she answer? That she loved him and wanted them to have a real marriage? That she wanted at the least to have a child by him to keep for her own? Such words might weaken his resolve, causing him guilt enough to stay with her. But she did not want him that way. He was like his namesake, the falcon. And he deserved to be free.

Swallowing for courage, she decided upon a half-truth, one that would at least allow her to confess the guilt that she felt, whether or not he forgave her. "An unconsummated marriage would satisfy neither the marquess nor my father. They would have me back on the marriage mart within the year."

He nodded. "And divorce is far more difficult to come by than annulment." Her forthrightness should not have surprised him. She had ever been a bold and outspoken woman. He had come to admire that quality in her.

"I did not mean to use you ill, Jason." She struggled to keep her voice from breaking. "I am sorry."

He smiled infectiously. "You used me quite well, Countess. And for that, I am not sorry."

"But now . . . if you ever wish to marry a woman of your choosing—"

"There is no woman in America waiting for me, Ra-

chel," he said impatiently. "But there might be a squire
hereabouts who will take your fancy one day. Have you
ever considered that?" He did not want to consider it,
but damnation, it was her life—provided, of course,
that she was not carrying his child!

He looked angry all of a sudden. The guilt caused by
her scheme washed over her again. She had bound him
when it was apparent that he did not want her—at least
not for more than a few nights of passion. "I have no
more interest in English squires than you do in American women. I've explained my dreams regarding Harleigh, just as you have told me yours of far Africa. We
shall both be content, shall we not?" Her voice sounded
brittle to her own ears. She pasted a smile on her lips
and took a fortifying sip of tea.

It had grown cold.

He stared into the flames, debating whether or not
to inquire about the possibility of pregnancy. What purpose would it serve? They were wed. She bore his
name, even though his grandfather would probably de-
earl him. In any case, it would be a simple matter to
have Drum keep him apprised of her condition after he
was gone. If there was a child, he would return to take
responsibility for its upbringing. What more could he
do?

"Yes, Countess, we shall both be content indeed," he
replied thoughtfully.

Chapter Twenty-one

What more could I do? The thought haunted his dreams as he slept alone in his big bed, tossing restlessly through what remained of the night. Dawn found him out riding Araby breakneck across the soggy countryside, taking his last look at the birthright he was leaving to Roger Dalbert. The day was sunny. Lingering raindrops clinging to trees and shrubs glistened magically in the bright light. Odd, but he had grown to love the rolling hills and rich farmlands, the trickling streams and quiet pools. Best not to dwell on pools, he thought grimly, remembering the interlude in the water with Rachel.

Try as he might, he could not get her out of his mind. Their conversation last night had settled nothing. To the contrary, it had been most unsettling. Yes, she had had an ulterior motive for consummating their marriage, but that did not account for her succumbing to his entreaty last night. Yesterday had been a long and exhausting day, and they faced another long ride tonight. She could have told him no.

Instead, she had risen from that tub like Venus from the sea and met his passion with her own. Was there more to Rachel's feeling for him than mere expedience? He patted Araby's neck and murmured, "Well, I suppose I have three more days . . . and nights to find out.

"Yes, indeed, we must not forget the nights." He grinned and kicked the stallion into a gallop once more.

Fox was worried about LaFarge. The canny Frenchman seemed to know something was afoot. He was always one step ahead of his pupil. Take tonight, for instance. He had insisted on playing a second round of whist after soundly beating Fox in the first one, saying that a gentleman must always give his opponent the opportunity to win back some of his losses. Never mind that they played for only a pence a game, a sum which Fox could easily afford because his allowance from Grandfather was quite generous.

Grandfather. The boy swallowed a lump in his throat. He had labored for days over his farewell letter to the old man. If only Jace and Rachel would decide to remain married. But as of yesterday, their plans for flight remained in place. All he could do was to leave the message for the marquess in his room and slip out when Jace signaled him. If only he could first get LaFarge to go to bed!

He gave a mighty yawn, one of several he had been forcing the past hour, even though it was only nine. Since tomorrow was a Saturday, he would be allowed to sleep later, the reason his master-at-arms was indulging him.

"You seem tired, *petit,* eh?" La Farge said as he looked at his cards.

Not wanting to be too obvious and arouse suspicion, Fox shook his head. "I'm fine." He fanned out a winning hand. "You were right. I have won back what I lost. *Merci, monsieur.*"

LaFarge looked at his pupil, considering his overly-bright eyes. What devilment was he up to? Well, boys were boys, after all. He vividly remembered his own childhood mischief in France. "Tomorrow we shall work with foils again, eh? You still parry like a shepherdess using her sheep's crook."

Fox yawned again and grinned. "I do not," he said stubbornly.

When LaFarge had departed, Fox sat down at his desk and composed another note for his beloved tutor. He was certain the Frenchman had let him win that last game.

The night was moonless but dry and clear. Jason and Rachel's journey back to London would be infinitely swifter than the one to Falconridge the day before. They dared not depart before dark because it would raise suspicion, but Jason ordered the housekeeper to send another private dinner to his room early in the evening. Then he dismissed the staff for the night. Everyone was pleased, since no one had gotten much rest in the previous twenty-four hours. How considerate the earl and his new countess were. And how much in love!

They ate quickly, saying little, making last-minute plans and packing what gear they would need for the swift journey they had to make. When she entered his quarters dressed in her disguise, he chuckled. "You make a fetching Gypsy wench indeed, Countess."

"You always did believe me a wench from the first

time we met." *I will always have these memories to hold after he's gone,* she reminded herself.

"A most beguiling wench," he murmured, observing her brightly colored skirt.

"I filched this from a kitchen maid at Harleigh last week." Raising her wrist to reveal several glittering gold bangles that matched those around her throat, she said, "The jewelry I bought at a country fair this summer."

"You plan well. Now if the ship is in the harbor, naught can go wrong."

"Oh, quite a bit can go wrong before that. The watch may arrest us before we can even reach Fox, not to mention the risk of raiding your grandfather's stables."

"Stealing horses is a fine old tradition among my blood brothers."

"Then you and Fox should be quite at home galloping over the countryside on the marquess's finest mounts."

Their bantering concealed the misgivings both had about their enterprise. Rachel was determined to go through with the accursed plan. She really had no choice. It had been her idea in the first place, and now she would have to pay the price for her pride and folly . . . a life without Jason Beaumont.

As for Jason, he had decided to wait until they were en route before deciding his course of action. With three nights ahead of them and a boy who would be exhausted and sleep soundly . . . well, he could test Rachel's resolve quite a bit more before he sailed away— if he sailed away. Just exactly what did the countess want? Damned contrary female!

He saved Araby, riding another excellent mount from his stable, and leading the stallion by his reins. When they reached the Cargrave city house, they slipped quietly to the marquess's mews. While Rachel stood guard, Jason rubbed down their spent horses as the stableboy

307

slept in a stall behind the tack room. The earl selected two new mounts apiece for her and Fox and another for himself. Then they led the six horses out into the street.

Nervously she watched for any wandering charleys, rehearsing in her mind what they had planned if anyone tried to stop them. Jason was still dressed as a gentleman and would have to bluff, playing the role of arrogant earl. 'Twould take little effort, Rachel thought. The damned lout was born to it. Once they were clear of the city and on the road to Bristol, the earl would metamorphose into a Gypsy horse trader, traveling with his wife and son.

With their dark hair and a few smears of dirt, no one should question their identities, although some observant sheriff might wonder at the quality of the horseflesh they rode. Jason carried a sizable pouch of gold to bribe their way free if the need arose. If they were accosted by real thieves, they were both well armed. He carried his Hawkens and she her brace of Clark pistols. The earl also had a wicked knife concealed in his boot. They would make a good accounting of themselves if any bully ruffians thought to relieve them of their gold or their horses.

She shivered in the chilly night air, peering into the dark street. "Are you certain Fox is awake?"

"Only one way to find out," Jason replied, cupping his hands over his mouth. He made a low, eerie bird call that she did not recognize. Then after waiting a beat, he repeated the call of an American horned owl. "Fox was trained to sleep lightly by his Shawnee family. If only English life hasn't made him soft."

"We English are not a soft race, m'lord Yankee. Ask Napoleon," she whispered sweetly.

Just then a figure holding a candle waved from the window above them. Fox! As the boy vanished, Jason instructed Rachel, "I'll bring him. Take the horses and wait for us down the street in the shadows of those trees."

She did as she was bade. When a group of drunken young toffs came weaving around the corner, Rachel held her breath. If they saw her here, there would be the devil to pay. She crooned low to the nervous horses, keeping them silent until the danger had passed. Well into their cups and raucously loud, they passed by on the opposite side of the street and vanished into an elegant house halfway down the block.

When Jason and Fox came dashing toward her, she could see the boy was armed as well. Eyeing the small Manton pistols in his sash, she asked, "Have you learned how to fire those accurately? If not, they'll be a greater danger to you than to anyone else."

"LaFarge is a fine teacher, Rachel," the lad replied with bravado. "And I am a very good pupil. Though my aim was a bit off, I did stop that cracksman from hurting your sister. And since then, LaFarge has made me practice even more."

"We can discuss the merits of Fox's marksmanship once we're out of the city," Jason hissed as he swung up on Araby's back. "Mount up and let's ride. The sooner we're out of this neighborhood, the less attention we're likely to attract."

" 'Tis a good thing Grandfather's such a sound sleeper," Fox replied as he leaped nimbly onto Little Chief. He would really miss his horse and new puppy, but not nearly so much as he would miss Grandfather. . . .

The trio of "Gypsies" rode hard to the west, avoiding crowded roads in favor of back country lanes. Rachel was familiar with the countryside and knew ways to trim hours from the arduous ride without sacrificing

309

their safety. An hour or so before daybreak they changed horses, deciding it was best to place as much distance between themselves and London as possible before finding a place to sleep.

After an expensive encounter with a Berkshire sheriff at midday, they decided to veer to the south and find a place to camp before they roused any more curiosity. A heavily wooded swale near a stream on Viscount Moreland's land provided the perfect spot. Knowing the old man was currently in the city with only a minimal staff left behind, Rachel assured Jason and Fox that they would likely not be detected if they spent the evening there.

"How long have you planned this route?" Fox asked her as they unsaddled their horses and began to rub them down. "You seem to know a lot about the countryside and who's in residence and who's not."

She shrugged. "I spent my childhood riding about the Berkshires, attending markets and fairs with my father's cooks and stablemen and other servants. As to which members of the peerage are in residence at their seats this time of year, Harry was my source of information."

Fox's eyes grew round. "Your sister knows what we're doing, and she has not told her husband or her father?" he asked incredulously.

Rachel stopped rubbing down her big bay gelding and looked at the boy. "Difficult as it is for the male of the species to believe, women do act independently of their husbands and fathers every now and again," she said drolly, casting a meaningful look Jason's way before resuming her task.

They dared not make a campfire as the chill of evening settled over the land. After devouring a meal of cold meat pies and cheese that Rachel had packed, they laid out their blankets for sleep. She noted that her husband made his pallet a distance away from hers. If

Fox noted that arrangement, he said nothing as he crawled beneath the covers and fell instantly into an exhausted sleep. It had been an arduous journey for a twelve-year-old boy, even if it was a splendid adventure.

Rachel lay listening to the low trill issuing from the stream nearby. A thick stand of sedge shielded their camp from the stream. Her body was tired, but her mind raced, leaving her unable to sleep. Only two more nights and she would never see Jason Beaumont again. Had his desperate behavior last night been but an aberration, perhaps brought about by seeing her naked in her bath? She admitted to herself that the decision to have the tub in her dressing room moved before the fire owed more to her desire to entice her husband than to a need for warmth.

But how could she entice him tonight?

Having the boy with them did complicate matters. If she went to Jason's blankets, most likely Fox would not awaken, but her pride was stung when she realized that such a brazen move appeared to be the only way she would gain her husband's attention. *Great Yankee clodpole!* She tossed off the blanket, then walked down toward the sound of the swiftly moving water. Perhaps it might soothe her.

Jason lay staring up at the starry sky, recognizing the familiar constellations he had studied all his life at sea. On the midwatch he had always loved walking to the bow of his ship and looking at the grandeur of the night. Soon he could be at the helm of another swift Baltimore schooner. Tonight the thought afforded him cold comfort. All he could think of was his wife, lying so near yet so far from him. He had waited to see if she would come to him, but she had not.

Suddenly he heard a soft rustle and saw her a short distance away. Hope surged in his breast until she began walking toward the stream. In an instant she vanished into the darkness. He assumed that she was simply answering a call of nature. But when she did not return, he became concerned. Damnable woman, did she have no idea how difficult this was!

Then the thought occurred to him that she might have fallen or somehow injured herself. Of course, she most certainly would have cried out and he would have heard, but Jason ignored that realization as he went in search of her. He found her sitting by the water's edge, her head resting on her bent knees as she hugged her arms around them. She looked small and lost and ineffably sad.

He knelt beside her, and she raised her head with a startled gasp. "I did not hear you approach," she said, making a show of shoving the stubby Clark pistol back into her sash.

"I lived with the Shawnee, remember?" he said lightly, sitting down beside her.

"How did you get to be a ... what did you call it? Blood brother? Is there some sort of ceremony?"

" 'Tis very solemn. Once an outsider is judged worthy by tribal elders, the warrior who wishes the blood bond with the outlander cuts his own wrist or sometimes palm and the outsider cuts his. Then they press the wounds together, allowing their blood to mingle."

"William Harvey might dispute that," she said, oddly miffed at Jason's willingness to follow her lead and speak of inconsequential things.

"Always the bluestocking," he teased, lifting a heavy mass of dark hair away from her face so he could study it in the moonlight. " 'Twas not your Englishman Harvey who first discovered the circulation of the blood, but a poor benighted Spaniard a hundred years earlier. Michael Servetus."

Rachel shivered at his touch. "Now who is playing the bluestocking?"

312

" 'Tis no fault in a man to be erudite." Again he lifted a heavy curl, stroking it between his fingers.

" 'Tis a fault in a man to talk when actions are required," she said, reaching up and seizing his ears to pull his face to hers for a fierce, hungry kiss.

Jason was startled by her voraciousness and tumbled back against the soft, damp moss of the riverbank, taking her with him. One hand cupped her buttock, pressing her closely to him, as the other caressed her breast through the grimy peasant chemise she wore. For convenience as well as modesty around Fox, they had retired to bed fully clad, removing only their boots. Now all that clothing seemed an impediment as they rolled across the ground, frantically tearing at buttons of trousers and shirts.

He buried his hands in her hair and savaged her mouth as she did his, kissing her with all his pent-up hunger. Her eager fingers had his fly unfastened before he could do more than cup a splendid white globe of breast in each hand after pulling down the low neckline of her chemise. When her hands touched his already rigid staff, he muttered a curse, muffled against her breast. He reached down and tried to gather her skirts in one fist, raising them to reach the treasure beneath.

She helped him, seizing the other side of the full skirts from the front and bunching them at her waist to accommodate his entry. Shadows veiled his face as he peered down on her with glowing eyes, watching her intently as he sank slowly into her wet, eager flesh. Rachel arched up to quicken his thrust, biting her lip to keep from crying out and awakening Fox.

Silent and swift it was, rapacious yet tender, too. Each gave and took as they rode to the crest together, their bodies now attuned to subtle signs of impending release. He knew when she neared her peak and struggled to hold off his own fulfillment. Perversely, she would have none of such control. Her legs locked around his hips and her pelvis arched upward. The ecstatic contracting of her sheath drove all possibility of slowing from his mind.

He drove hard into her repeatedly until the world seemed to spin away and the universe contained only the two of them, male and female, locked in the most ancient and beautiful of all rituals . . . and battles . . . and bonding. She was flesh of his flesh now. How could he ever leave her? Jason slumped over her body, damp with perspiration in spite of the cool night air. Cradling her in his arms, he vowed that he would never let her go.

"Bugger our bargain," he murmured as an exhausted sleep claimed him.

His voice was muffled in her hair so that Rachel could not make out the softly slurred words. She held him tightly for a moment, treasuring the closeness that all too soon would end. But there was tonight. And tonight she would sleep in her husband's embrace. Her eyelids grew heavy and she, too, drifted off in contentment.

Jason awoke at false dawn, stiff from the chill given off by the stream and damp bank, but grateful that at least the moss was soft, for he had ended up on the bottom, cushioning his wife with his body. His wife. How natural the sound of that was now, he considered as he untangled their limbs. She awakened with a small cry that he muffled with his hand, whispering, "Fox," as a reminder.

Like two conspirators evading the law, they put their clothing to rights, retrieving Rachel's Clark pistol, which had been lost in their amorous struggle. They slipped silently back to the camp, where the boy still slept soundly. "Poor lad's exhausted," she said as she rummaged through their saddlebags for more of the food she had packed.

"We could let him sleep." Jason waited to see what she might reply to that pregnant comment, but just then Fox stirred.

Sitting up and rubbing his eyes, he asked, "Is it time to ride again?"

Faint streaks of red were lighting the eastern sky as he climbed dutifully from his blankets and reached for a hunk of cheese Rachel offered. He ate with the appetite of a growing boy on the brink of puberty. After their night's exertions, Rachel and Jason also found themselves starving.

She eyed the remaining food supplies dubiously. "I fear I may not have packed enough to last us until we reach Bristol."

"Then we can go on a raid, can't we, Jace?" the boy responded brightly, looking at his mentor.

"A raid?" she echoed with an arched eyebrow. "Is this another of your Shawnee customs?"

Jason shrugged. "There is a bit of intertribal . . . er, competition—"

"We steal each other's horses," Fox put in with a grin. "It's considered a great honor for a warrior to return to his village with many enemy ponies."

"Well, in case it has escaped your notice, young sir, we are still in England and there are no enemies from whom to steal. Besides that, we English do not eat horses," Rachel scolded. Soon she would lose not only her love, but also this wonderful boy.

Jason laughed. "As a general rule, neither do the Shawnee. In fact, right now we have too many horses. I believe it would be wise to release the ones we've ridden the hardest. They'll be of no further use to us, and if we leave them to graze on Moreland's estates here, they'll soon be found by his gamekeeper. Having

315

served our initial needs, they'll only slow us down." He watched Rachel, wondering if she would argue to keep the remounts in order to make her party more vulnerable to capture. What did the little witch really want? However, her reply gave him no clear answer.

"That sounds practical but still does not solve the issue of food," she said.

"Well, since we can't go raiding, Jace has money enough to buy food from some farmer," Fox supplied helpfully. "Unless you had to give it all to that sheriff yesterday to get him to let us go," he added. The thought had suddenly occurred to him that if they had no food or fresh horses, perhaps they might call off this whole foolish plan and decide to be married after all.

Fox and Rachel both looked expectantly at Jason, but before he could reply, the sound of a hound baying echoed across the hills. "That might be Moreland's gamekeeper. Best he not find us on the viscount's land," Jason said, gathering up his saddle and throwing it on Araby's back.

Rachel and Fox did the same, and their meager camp was quickly packed up. Jason released the three remounts, giving them sharp swats on their rumps to send them running in the direction from which they had heard the hound. They rode cautiously out of the swale and skirted the woods for half an hour or so, looking for a safe place to climb up onto the road. Seeing a clearing, Rachel motioned for them to follow her and started out.

She had no more than kicked her gelding into a trot when a shot whistled by her head and a voice called out, "There they be—the thievin' Gypsy bastards!"

Another man fired, yelling, "We know you stole them horses from Quality!"

"Stay low on your horses and ride like hell," Jason commanded, assuming the rear guard position as he urged his charges forward. "This is no time to try explaining who we are!"

Chapter Twenty-two

They rode madly down the twisting mud-rutted road with Rachel in the lead. If any of the horses stumbled, they would be doomed, but Jason trusted her knowledge of the surrounding countryside. Fox's horsemanship had improved considerably, he noted, giving silent thanks to poor Bradley.

Jason considered returning a shot or two, but decided against it since the gamekeepers were only doing what they considered right in apprehending a trio of horse thieves. He'd made a bad misjudgment in releasing the horses. At least they appeared to be widening the distance between themselves and Moreland's men. Rachel and Fox turned at a sharp bend in the road. Just as Jason was about to follow, he felt the sting of lead biting into the flesh of his thigh.

Gritting out a curse at the pain, he nevertheless gave thanks that it was he and not Fox or Rachel who had been hit. He wheeled Araby around, determined to hold off their pursuers until she and the boy could escape. "Keep riding," he yelled as he guided the black into a dense stand of elm. "I'll meet you at the ship."

Before he could jump from the stallion's back and set up a line of fire, Rachel had turned her mount, as had Fox. Both of them followed him into the brush. "Get the hell out of here while I distract them," he whispered furiously to her.

"Even a fierce Yankee privateer cannot hold off three men with a brace of pistols," she hissed as the riders came thundering into sight.

Fox watched as the men kept coming, riding at breakneck speed. "I don't think they've seen us, Jace," he whispered.

"Keep your mounts quiet," Jason replied. Perhaps a bit of luck was coming their way after all the ill that had befallen them since they began this wretched misadventure.

Sure enough, the gamekeepers continued down the road and vanished around the next curve. "I would have considered this evasion a stroke of considerable cleverness on your part, m'lord, if you'd not given all away with your foolish heroics," Rachel said with a chuckle.

"Jace, you're bleeding!" Fox cried, noticing the gash in Jason's britches oozing dark red.

"Let me see that," Rachel said, moving her horse closer, her amusement vanishing.

" 'Tis nothing. Soon those men will figure out that we've left the road and double back. We need to ride hard and fast now." Jason urged Araby out of the brush and then turned to Rachel. "Which way now, m'lady pathfinder?"

Shaking her head at male stubbornness, she sighed. "We should reach Chippenham by midafternoon . . . that is, if you do not bleed to death before then."

319

"I shall endeavor not to inconvenience you, although you'd be a right wealthy widow, Countess," he said in a teasing, lazy drawl.

"I did not wed you for your money, m'lord," she replied with a cheeky grin.

Fox watched them exchange a gaze that spoke volumes. As they resumed riding, he considered once more how utterly irrational adults often seemed. Especially when they were in love.

Rachel's prediction about Chippenham was conservative. By dusk they were well to the west of it, nearing Bristol. "We could keep riding and get a room in a waterfront inn for the night," Jason said, eyeing her speculatively.

Rachel met the hot, dark fire in his gaze, wondering for the hundredth time since their wedding night just how to assess his true feelings for her. "I think it would be wiser to camp somewhere off the road and let me see to your injury before we ride any further. If 'tis as slight as you insist, we can press on to Bristol. Otherwise, we will spend the night and ride at dawn . . . if you are able."

Would the ship sail without them if they did not arrive in time? The thought tantalized her as she watched his reaction to her proposal.

"I'm well able to ride, Countess," he said in a husky murmur that suggested an entirely different sort of activity. "But if 'twill ease your mind, I'll let you tend my wound while Fox sets up camp."

Rachel snorted. "How magnanimous of you, m'lord. Let us search out a hidden spot off the beaten paths. I do not know this countryside as well as that back east."

Within a quarter hour Fox was building a small fire while Rachel took medical supplies from her saddlebags. Jason watched her lay out bandages and various

vials of herbal ointments and other mysterious reme-
dies. "Good lord, were you anticipating a battle?"

She met his slumberous gaze and knew they would
not be leaving this place until they had made love
again. Swallowing to moisten her dry throat, she replied, "Just so. And since making your acquaintance, I
have yet to be disappointed."

"And to think only half a dozen or so of the dangerous encounters I've survived were caused by you,
m'dear," he said with a husky laugh.

"Remove your britches," she instructed in as steady
a voice as she could muster. At his wickedly cocked
eyebrow, she added, "I must cleanse the wound of any
bits of fabric embedded by the shot." She was grateful
that the fading light concealed her scorched cheeks.

Fox was concentrating on rubbing down the horses
and seemingly paid no attention to what the adults
were doing. Rachel knelt by the fire beside Jason, who
peeled his pants down, then sat on a blanket with his
shirttails covering strategic parts of his anatomy. He
stretched out one long leg, revealing an ugly gash running diagonally across his thigh.

" 'Tis shallow. That is the good part," she said, inspecting the wound with a practiced eye.

"I told you 'twas but a scratch," Jason said with an
indrawn hiss of breath when she applied a warm wet
cloth to the injury.

" 'Tis also clotted with dried blood. That is the bad
part," she replied sweetly as she soaked the blackish
tissue away. "I think it best if I stitch it to keep it closed,
since we must ride again soon."

"Then stitch away, Countess, since we must ride
again . . . soon." Each word was like a caress.

She knew he was not referring to reaching Bristol.
Her hands trembled as she threaded the needle. "I
might as well monogram my initials on your thick Yan-

kee hide, I've stitched so many other places on you already," she said, attempting an acerbic tone.

His hand reached out and steadied hers, large dark fingers wrapping gently around her slender wrist. "I'll bear your mark for the rest of my life, Rachel . . . deep inside here," he replied, placing her palm against his chest.

"You truly are a buffoon, sir. Courtly protestations! With your breeches pulled down around your ankles?" Still, she could feel his heart beat, feel the heat of his body through the thin cloth of his shirt; and suddenly she longed to have no clothing between them, nothing separating naked flesh from naked flesh. As if reading her thoughts, he guided her hand through the gaping opening, burying her fingers in the crisp black hair on his chest.

Fox broke the spell when one of the horses began dancing sideways and the boy had to scold and tug on the gelding's bridle to get him to obey.

Without another word, Rachel set to work, willing her hands to perform the task of closing the ragged wound. Once it was done, she smeared more of the healing ointment on it and then bandaged it carefully. "You rest by the fire. I'd best help Fox finish with the horses."

"You set out our food. I can help Fox." Jason pulled up his pants and stood. With a slight grimace, he walked over to where the boy was working.

"Yankee lobcock," she said fondly, too softly for him to hear. He was incredibly tough. And to date, he had been quite lucky, considering all the attempts on his life. What would his future on the high seas bring? She could not bear to think of that, so she began rummaging about in the saddlebags for the meager remainders of bread and cheese.

By full dark, Fox was sleeping soundly and Rachel and Jason sat facing each other from opposite sides of the fire. Wordlessly he stood up and stepped around the flames, reaching his hand down to her, palm open. She placed her hand in it and felt his strong fingers close over hers as he drew her up into his arms. She pulled the blanket with her while they made their way from the fire into the darkness to seek out another kind of heat.

This time they stripped off their clothes before coming together and wrapped themselves in the heavy blanket, bodies pressed closely, legs entwined as their kisses grew fierce and then, by turns, gentle, exploratory. He rolled on his uninjured side and spooned her against him, then entered her very slowly while his fingers played delicately with her breasts. She bit her lip to keep from crying out, moving with the keen pleasure that had now grown so dearly familiar and necessary to her.

They went slowly, murmuring indistinct love words, climbing the summit together and finding that ultimate peace that was at once fierce and yet ever so tender. Jason held her to his body, kissed the nape of her neck, then buried his face in the dark masses of her hair. At length, he murmured softly, "Do we need to continue on to Bristol, Countess?"

Uncertain if she had heard him aright, Rachel turned in his embrace, trying to see his face by moonlight. "What do you—"

His hand suddenly covered her mouth and he whispered, "Be still. I hear something."

As he quickly pulled on his pants, she searched frantically for her scattered clothing. Before she could do more than draw the blouse over her head, he knelt beside her, covering her with the blanket as he whispered in her ear, "Wait here and do not move or make a sound until I say 'tis clear."

With that, he vanished silently into the night. His life

323

among the Shawnee had certainly taught him much that she wished she knew in a dangerous situation such as this. She was left to fume as she struggled into her skirt, heeding his admonition to make no noise. But she would not huddle idly beneath a blanket while danger threatened him and Fox.

Jason circled the dying campfire and saw that Fox was awake, lying tensely beneath his blanket, feigning sleep. The boy had a keen ear. His Manton pistols lay close beside him, ready to fire as LaFarge had taught him. Good man, that Frenchie. Jason heard another snap and a guttural curse from the opposite side of the camp. Grateful that Rachel was safely out of harm's way, he made the low call of an owl, signaling Fox, who threw off his covers and seized his weapons. As he rushed toward Jason's hiding place, a shot whizzed past his head, missing him in the darkness.

"Follow me and don't make a sound," Jason whispered, taking one of the pistols from the boy. With his other hand he removed the knife from his boot.

"Your pistols are by the fire," Fox whispered back, adding in a frightened tone, "So are Rachel's. Where is she?"

"Safe," was all he replied.

He could hear them, doubtless clumsy street toughs who might be adept in back alleys but cow-handed, or rather, hoofed, in the woods. Keeping them from Rachel was his paramount concern. They must be more of Forrestal's minions, paid to kill him and most likely kidnap her so the disgraced lordling could drag her to Gretna Green. He cursed the man as they moved swiftly toward the sounds of faint thrashing. Then he heard the distant wicker of horses and turned to Fox. "Let us see how many mounts."

"Then we will know how many are in the woods." Fox followed his hero.

Five horses were being held by a skinny fellow who had the smell of the London streets upon him. After motioning Fox to stand still, Jason slipped quickly up behind the thug and coshed him on the skull with the butt of his pistol. The man slumped to the ground unconscious.

"Get to their mounts and send them flying when I signal you. Then find cover and wait until I call you. Fire only if you are attacked, and then shoot to kill. Understand?"

The boy nodded calmly. Jason's heart would have burst with pride if their situation were not so dangerous. He retraced his steps toward the other four, knowing that only one shot and his blade stood between him and death. He had to shoot at least one man before he signaled Fox. That would leave three who would, he hoped, rush toward their horses and thus allow him to ambush them in their headlong escape. If he could take out another with his knife, he hoped Fox could handle at least one of the survivors. Then, with luck, he could take out the last man from behind. He shivered. Too much of his strategy seemed built upon hope and luck.

Above all, Rachel must not be taken. Rachel. His wife. His love. How would she have answered his question if he'd not heard that distant sound of horses and stopped her from speaking?

He had no time to consider it as he waited behind the trunk of an oak, freezing at the sound to his right. Twenty yards? The sound of snapping twigs came closer, and Jason raised his pistol.

Rachel reached the rim of faint light cast by the campfire, then stopped. She could detect no sign of Jason or Fox. Where in blazes were they, and who or what was out there that so concerned them? Fools. She knew how to shoot as well as they, in fact probably better; and her

Clark pistols lay clearly visible beside her saddlebags. She cursed herself for not taking one with her when she had slipped off with Jason, but considering the passion of that moment, well . . .

"No help for it," she murmured softly as she made a dash toward her weapons, only then seeing Jason's Hawkens also lying in plain sight. Something was definitely wrong! Just as she stepped forward, leaves crunched behind her, and a big meaty paw covered her mouth, muffling her scream.

Even before she heard his voice, the acrid stench of Mace Bings signaled her attacker's identity. After that day in the stables, she would never forget the way he smelled.

"Well now, sweeting, wot 'ave I got 'ere?" he whispered, then gasped as her elbow connected wickedly with his gut.

She kicked, twisting in his arms for better leverage, but his brawny arms held her tightly in spite of the blows she dealt. Then his fist smashed into her jaw, and all went dark as her head snapped backward. He threw her over his shoulder with a grunt and began running to the horses.

As long as they had the gel, they could get Beaumont in time. Besides, it was safer this way, since the earl and that boy were lurking somewhere in the woods. Just then he heard the sound of a shot nearby, almost immediately followed by a struggle beyond the thicket of buckthorn off to his right. Murray? Or was it Percy engaging Beaumont? One of them must be down.

He did not wait to find out.

Fortunately, Jason's shot had hit its mark and the lumbering assassin was flat on his back and not moving. Unfortunately, the second brute behind him was twice the size of the one stretched on the ground. He was also much more agile than any human his size had a right to be. Jason grazed the thug's throat with his blade, but the man ducked swiftly enough to avoid being cleanly sliced, then raised his own blade.

With their hands locked over each other's knife hands, the two antagonists fought with the viciousness of men schooled in combat on waterfront wharves. When his foe slammed Jason against a tree and almost succeeded in kneeing him in the groin, the earl decided it was time for a diversion. He took a quick breath and made the call.

Almost at once, the sound of horses whinnying and galloping in all directions filled the quiet night. His opponent's momentary distraction provided Jason the opening he needed to land his own blow, which connected sharply between the thug's legs. The instant his knife hand was freed, Jason plied his weapon and disposed of another enemy.

Where in bloody hell were the other two?

He stood still for a moment, waiting to hear sounds of footfalls over the receding noise of pounding hooves. Instead, he heard a familiar voice yell out, "Meet at Beckworth's, lads!"

Bings! As Jason raced toward the sound of the man's retreat, he remembered that day in the stables when he and Rachel had discussed Bristol, believing Mace to be unconscious. "The bastard is more cunning than I would have credited," he muttered as he ran.

Suddenly he realized that Mace's voice came not from the direction where Fox had scattered their horses, but from where his own mounts were tethered. He whistled for Araby just as a shot rang out. "Fox!"

"I got him, Jace," the boy yelled, obviously pursuing his prey even though he was now unarmed.

Jason could hear Araby's frantic cry as the big stallion tried to break free, mingled with the sounds of the other two horses stamping and jumping in distress. He ran blindly now as a sense of impending doom surrounded him like the heavy night air.

Where was Rachel? He'd heard not a sound from her throughout all the fighting. Suddenly Araby came thundering through the brush toward him. Without a thought, he swung up on the black's back and turned him toward his wife's hiding place just outside the dying coals of the campfire. All that remained there was the blanket, lying in a twisted heap on the mossy earth.

"Rachel!" he yelled as he wheeled Araby around and headed toward the sound of two horses galloping away over the hill.

She did not reply.

Fox came running from the trees just as Jason reached the spot where their horses had been. "Mace Bings has Rachel," he said as he swung down from Araby and scooped up his brace of Hawken pistols as well as her Clarks. "Reload both of your weapons and wait here," he instructed, tossing one spent Manton to the boy.

"Jace, wait. Araby—"

Jason could see the blood on the horse's neck in the dying firelight. "The bastard must have tried to slash his throat when he couldn't get him to go with the other horses," Jason snarled with an oath. Already he could feel the big black shuddering in pain. He slid down, knowing that Araby could not carry him fast or far enough to overtake Mace and retrieve Rachel.

"What are we going to do?" the boy asked, his voice breaking.

"Reload the guns," he said grimly. "We'll have to run down two of the horses you scattered."

"But how will we find Rachel?" Fox was fighting tears now.

"Mace knew how to find us, following the road from

Bristol east. He's working for Forrestal, who wants me dead. That's why he virtually gave us an invitation to this Beckworth's."

"A trap? Aye," Fox said, with evident relief in his voice. "Then we can save her. If Forrestal wants to marry her, he won't allow her to come to harm."

Jason nodded, but thought to himself, *Frederick Forrestal had better pray that bastard he hired does not touch her before we reach them . . . else he as well as Mace Bings will learn how the Shawnee kill their blood enemies.*

In the dying firelight the Yankee earl's face looked demonic.

"So, m'boy, thought you'd take a bit of warm Mediterranean air, did you? Could you possibly be so dense as to think the scandal over your botched kidnapping attempt would simply evaporate like fog in Florentine sunlight?" Drum tsked at the sullen-looking Frederick Forrestal, who sprawled his lanky frame over a splintery wooden chair in a private room of what could most charitably be called a modest inn in Gravesend.

Forrestal's yellow eyes narrowed, catlike, on his diminutive captor. "You have no right to threaten your betters."

Drum made a show of looking around the spartan room. "I see none such hereabouts."

"I will one day soon be Duke of Etherington, you son of some back country baronet," Forrestal said with a sneer.

"Give me leave to doubt that, considering that your beloved pater was in the process of filing a petition with his closest companions in Lords to relieve you of the burden of succession. He's already divested you of his unentailed wealth. I shall still be the Honorable Alfred Francis Edward Drummond when you are naught but

329

another inhabitant of Newgate. Oh, and by the by, my father is a baron, not a baronet."

With fury contorting his features, Forrestal attempted to lunge at Drum. The dandy flicked his wrist with blurring speed and the razor-sharp tip of his foil made a prick directly beneath Forrestal's chin, drawing a trickle of blood.

"Now be a good chap and sit down. The sheriff should be here anon. I do hope the fellow is prompt. I so detest missing my morning tea. It puts me quite out of sorts."

He did not add that he still had other business to attend to at the shipyards nearby.

The fellow Jason had coshed on the head was still unconscious as they started the search for the kidnappers' scattered horses. Fox's deadly Manton had dispatched one tough. Jason had disposed of the other two during the earlier fight, so he knew that Mace was alone with Rachel. The earl did not like it, but said nothing to the boy. They would both need their wits about them when they reached Beckworth's.

It did not take them long to find the horses grazing peacefully in a meadow a half mile across a small stream just off the road. They quickly caught the best two and set out, armed to the teeth with three sets of pistols as well as Jason's knife. Fox even carried Rachel's small stiletto, which she had left in her saddlebags along with extra ammunition for her Clark pistols.

As soon as they reached the outlying portions of the bustling port city, they learned that Beckworth's was a dilapidated warehouse somewhere on the Bristol wharf. Rumor had it that the building had recently been sold by its owner. As Jason and Fox neared the waterfront, the smell of dead fish and rotting wood blended with the choking stench of coal smoke, which poured from every chimney.

A light rain began to fall as they made their way through the muddy streets. Thick ocean fog masked every building in swirling mist. The wet cobblestones were slick and the footing as treacherous as the denizens of the waterfront taverns along the way. When they passed by one called the Blue Whale, an ancient sailor hobbled out, his peg leg tapping an uncertain rhythm on the street.

Approaching the bent form, Jason inquired, "Do you know where Beckworth's warehouse is located?"

The old man squinted through the fog-laden air, trying to make out the face that went with the cultivated voice. Dressed in bloody, torn Gypsy clothes and armed like a brigand, the Earl of Falconridge was not exactly a reassuring sight, even to one with impaired vision. "Why d'ye want to know?" he asked cautiously, lobbing a large mouthful of phlegm onto the already noisome bricks.

"I'm second mate signed on with the *Seasprite*. Jason Beaumont. This is our cabin boy, Cam Barlow. Our friend Ruben Fairchild was to meet us at the Mermaid," he said, gesturing to another tavern at the opposite end of the street. "But he was taken by crimps. Someone told us they hold their 'cargo' at a deserted warehouse around here. Beckworth's. You ever hear of it?"

"Ye don't talk like no tar. Ye're not with the Customs, are ye?"

Jason laughed. "Believe me, the last thing me and my mates want to do is run afoul of those fellows! But we do have to rescue our mate from Beckworth's." He produced a coin, letting it wink enticingly in the dim light emanating from the Blue Whale.

The old man seemed to relax slightly. "Ye'd best 'ave a care, then. Crimps in Bristol er like roaches in a cargo hold. I be able to guide you to the ware'ouse," he said, eyeing the shilling.

"If you can take us there and then do us another service, I'll see you get a sack of these," Jason replied, handing over the coin.

"Wot do I 'ave to do, guv?" the old tar asked, taking the shilling in one filthy, gnarled old hand and stuffing it into his sash.

Rachel strained against the bonds biting into her hands and feet. Useless. They had lashed her to a huge oak chair wedged into a corner. It was far too heavy for her to move—even if she had been able to get her feet on the ground, which she could not. Each ankle was securely bound with coarse hemp to a chair leg. She could not even chew at the ropes binding her wrists, because they had lashed her upper body against the back of the chair and stuffed a foul-smelling gag into her mouth. She could barely breath.

She was alone now, in utter darkness but for the slim line of light coming from beneath the door to the adjoining room. Thank God they had finally left her. Rachel Fairchild had never been so frightened in her life, not only for herself, but far more so for her husband and his young brother who were riding into a trap.

When she had awakened and attempted to cry out as they neared this hellish destination, Mace had laughed at her, then struck a blow to her head which had rendered her unconscious again. The next time she awakened, she was in this ghastly room, tied and gagged. Relieved that Bings had some reason for keeping her alive, she had puzzled over who would pay him to abduct her and had concluded it must be Forrestal.

How mistaken she had been. . . .

Chapter Twenty-three

Jason explained to the old sailor what he wished him to do as they walked toward the end of a deserted pier on which sat a large two-story building. After they left the old man in front of the ugly structure and made their way through a narrow passage to the alley behind it, Fox whispered, "Do you think we can trust him, Jace?"

"Greed's a universal incentive. He wants that sack of shillings. I expect he'll do as he's told," Jason replied as he eyed the tall structure consideringly.

"It seems to be deserted," Fox volunteered as his gaze swept over the darkened windows in the upper story.

"Appearances can deceive, though. See that faint glow from the far window," his mentor said, pointing to the broken glass panes about forty feet above where they stood concealed in shadows.

"How can we get up so high?" the boy asked.

"How, indeed," Jason replied as they made their way

closer, moving like two wraiths under cover of the fog.

They found a rusted old pipe for draining some sort of noxious substance, which cut through an adjacent wall. When tested, it proved sturdy enough to hold Jason's weight. Then the duo waited until a loud brawl broke out on the previously deserted street.

"Our peg-legged friend is earning his coin, I see," Jason whispered as he began climbing the pipe. His injured thigh ached abominably, but he ignored it as he used his legs to grip the rough surface of the rusted metal.

Fox followed closely behind him until Jason reached the top of the pipe. From there he could lean over, precariously, and reach for the rotted edge of a windowsill. Although it would never have supported his weight, it could hold Fox. Jason boosted the lad past him and held him as the boy hoisted himself agilely over and unlatched the pane, then swung the window out and climbed inside.

The noise of the disturbance in front of the warehouse covered the squeak of rusty hinges and Fox's voice as he whispered, " 'Tis an empty hallway, Jace. Can you swing across now that the window is open?"

"No other choice," Jason replied, trying not to look down at the bricks below. He reached for the open sash, then leaped from the pipe to grasp the rotted wood by the inside edge. After swinging by one arm for a moment, he was able to lever his other arm over the sash with help from Fox, then hoist himself through the small window, at some considerable expense to his now throbbing leg.

Both man and boy drew pistols from their sashes and began creeping down the long, dark hallway. Along the way Jason very carefully opened each door to see what lay inside. The first two rooms were deserted, but upon opening the third door, he could hear muffled sounds in the far corner. Motioning for Fox to be silent and stand guard inside the doorway, Jason made his way toward whomever was shrouded in the darkness.

The moment he drew near, he recognized her scent. Rachel! His hand found her hair, a tangled mess, then felt the tight gag binding her mouth. "Close the door, Fox," he whispered as he knelt at her feet. His heart pounded and his head grew light with relief that she was alive. Pray God she was unharmed! As he drew his knife from his boot, it was all he could do to keep from raining kisses all over her beloved face.

At once she stopped struggling. "Shhh, my love," he crooned as his eyes became accustomed to the darkness. Once he could see enough, he was able to slice away the kerchief holding the gag in place.

"Jason, this is a trap," she croaked, her voice hoarse and weak.

"I know," he whispered. As he worked to cut her arms and legs free, he rubbed the cruel abrasions to restore circulation where the rough hemp had cut into her wrists and ankles.

"Jace, someone's coming up the stairs," Fox whispered.

"Give me a pistol," Rachel hissed, as she stood up.

Jason handed her one of her own Clarks. "How many men does Forrestal have besides Bings?" he asked as he and Fox stationed themselves on either side of the door Jason had quickly closed.

"There are four more of them . . . but 'tis not Forrestal," she murmured, making her way toward them just as the door swung open.

Garnet Dalbert's face was framed by the light of the candle in her hand. The instant she stepped inside, her expression shifted from a malevolent grin to twisted rage. "How did you—"

Before she could complete the sentence, Rachel

moved as swiftly as a Whitechapel cutpurse. Raising the butt of her pistol, she struck the older woman a hard blow to the head. Mistress Dalbert crumpled to the floor in an ungainly heap as Jason deftly seized the candle from her nerveless fingers.

"She's been amusing herself with me, describing how they were going to drown me in the harbor, tightening that gag until I almost blacked out from suffocation. She's a Bedlamite, Jason, utterly mad! 'Twas she and her son who've been trying to kill you, not Forrestal."

"Explanations will have to wait," Jason whispered, silencing her with a kiss. "We have to get you to safety before our diversion out front ends."

He pulled her behind him and led her and Fox from the room, leaving the candle on the floor with the unconscious Garnet Dalbert. They got no further than the stairwell leading to the ground level of the big warehouse when they heard Evelyn's voice.

"Back to your posts, you imbeciles! 'Tis only a bloody pack of drunken tars wandered onto the pier. You'd better not let them see light in here or they might mention it in an alehouse and bring the watch to investigate."

"I don't know, guv," Mace replied, scratching his greasy hair. "Wot made 'em come 'ere so far from the taverns ta start a fight. I says I take me a look."

"We do not dare attract attention. Remain inside and keep a careful watch for Beaumont and that boy," Simmons said curtly, turning on his heel. "I'm going to check the perimeter of the warehouse, then go see how Mother is doing with our bait."

Mace spat on the filthy wooden floor and muttered beneath his breath, "I knows wot ye'd like to do wi' 'er, even though ye wouldn't let me 'av 'er." He motioned for the three men Simmons had hired to slip back to their posts, watching the other door and windows around the big cluttered warehouse that Simmons Shipping had purchased only a few weeks ago and had not yet had the time or money to refurbish.

As the men shambled off, Mace's eye happened to stray to the rickety open steps leading to the second floor. He caught a flash of movement and at first assumed it was either that old hag coming down or her bastard of a son going up. But Mace Bings had been raised on the streets and his instincts were well honed. Whoever it was was moving far too stealthily to belong here.

Disobeying Evelyn's orders, he bellowed, "Wot's goin' on 'ere?" He started to run toward the stairs, pulling out his pistol and aiming it at the figure who slipped behind a half-collapsed wood crate on the landing. One of Evelyn's other men darted in from the opposite direction, also armed and ready to shoot the intruder.

Fox took careful aim and fired at the fellow nearest him. Rachel aimed at Mace, aching to repay him for her throbbing head and jaw. Fox hit his target cleanly, but Rachel's shot was off since Mace moved with amazing speed. He dived behind a pile of rubble, emitting an oath as her ball tore a deep gouge across his shoulder.

Jason used the confusion to vault over the railing and take cover beneath the stairs. He was just in time to send a shot dead center into another of the thugs, dropping him in his tracks. "Stay down and cover me," he yelled up at his wife and brother, aware of the headstrong natures they both possessed. He knew that the truly dangerous adversary was Evelyn Simmons, who had vanished silently somewhere in the dark shadows of the vast, debris-filled warehouse.

Moving silently from crate to crate, he searched for Garnet's viperous offspring, wondering in dull amazement if his cousin Roger, too, was a part of this monstrous conspiracy. He did not see Bings until he smelled his blood and whirled to face the big ruffian's upraised knife blade. Before Jason could aim, Rachel fired.

This time she did not miss.

The last of the hirelings, desperate to escape from the trio of armed enemies, made a dash for the front door. He got no further than yanking it open before Fox fired his second pistol and the man crumpled whimpering to the floor, dropping his gun as he cradled his injured right knee.

Rachel peered into the darkness, looking for her husband, who had vanished into the bowels of the warehouse in search of Garnet's son. Cautiously she began descending the stairs with Fox beside her. Both were reloading their spent pistols as they moved. Then Rachel heard the sound of steel ringing on steel and knew that Jason had found his quarry.

"Guard that one," she ordered Fox, who coolly aimed his pistol at the miscreant groveling on the floor. She clutched one reloaded Clark in her hand and stuffed the second one into the waistband of her skirt as she headed toward the fight.

Jason had the advantage of height, being taller than Simmons, but Garnet's son had a decidedly greater advantage in that he was using the blade from his sword cane. Both men were lightning-quick to thrust and parry, but it was, Rachel knew, an uneven contest. She wanted desperately to shoot Simmons, but the two men circled each other rapidly and the light was poor in the warehouse. She feared hitting Jason or distracting him.

"A crude weapon, perfectly suited to a former pirate," Simmons sneered at Jason as the Yankee's knife deflected a thrust aimed at his throat.

"No," Beaumont grunted as they disengaged. "I would prefer to have a true pirate's cutlass, but I will settle for this Shawnee skinning knife to take your scalp."

Jason knew that it was dangerous to prolong the uneven contest, and he could see Rachel from the corner of his eye, trying to find a good shot. But that was too dangerous, and his sensible wife realized it, thank the Lord. He went on the offensive. Lunging under Evelyn's foot and a half of steel, Jason nicked his foe, then retreated beyond the reach of the deadly blade. The tactic necessary for victory was difficult but not impossible, considering that he'd learned to fight aboard the pitching deck of a ship on the high seas. The problem was his thigh. The wound Rachel had stitched so carefully the day before was torn open again and bleeding.

If only there were some way I could help him, Rachel thought desperately, scanning the rough wooden planks of the floor, littered with empty packing crates and other debris. Then she looked higher. Dangling from a high beam was a length of rope with a nasty grappling hook attached to the end of it. Wasting no time, she made her way around the crates, keeping out of sight of the combatants until she reached the hook.

It hung enticingly about ten feet above her head. How to reach it? She shoved two crates together, then piled a third on top of them and used it as a crude stepladder. Seizing hold of the hook, she gave a mighty yank, and the rotted rope gave way from its mooring at the top of the beam. Perfect. Graceful as a cat, she jumped down to the floor and approached the two men, gripping the hook.

Although Jason had bloodied Simmons superficially, it was his own thigh wound that now soaked his trousers with gore. *He'll begin to tire, and then his reflexes . . .* She refused to let her thoughts dwell on that as she inched closer to the two men, still using the crates as cover so as not to distract them. Just then

Evelyn made a desperate thrust, knocking aside Jason's blade. The earl pivoted and avoided a mortal wound as the ribbon of steel sliced cleanly across the front of his shirt.

Unfortunately, he had been forced to turn on his injured leg and it began to buckle. Rachel could see him going down, but his blade once again engaged Simmons's, holding it in check—barely.

"Now . . . I . . . do believe . . . I have you," Simmons gritted out, struggling to free his weapon for the killing thrust.

Hold on, my love! Rachel slipped behind Evelyn. With one mighty swing, she embedded the hook in his throat, yanking backward with all her strength.

The rapier clattered to the floor as he raised both hands to his ruined throat, gurgling an oath as he turned murderous eyes on Rachel . . . eyes that quickly filmed over while he crumpled to the floor. Without sparing Simmons another glance, she knelt beside her husband, who was struggling to his hands and knees.

He looked up at her with a grin. "If you can use a grappling hook that efficiently, perhaps I shall take you with me next time I go privateering." He looked down at the widening pool of blood surrounding Evelyn Simmons's dead body. "Then again, given your temper, perhaps not."

"You've bled almost as much as he. Come, let me get you into the light so I can see how much damage you've done to yourself." Rachel shuddered, deliberately ignoring the corpse and her horrible handiwork.

"I had a bit of help, love," he replied, allowing her to place his arm about her shoulder for support. He was able to walk without it but said nothing, wanting to hold her as close as he could.

She looked up into his face, studying it. "Thank you for saving my life, Jason," she said gravely.

"Rachel, my love, just before Mace and his brigands interrupted us, I asked you a question."

" 'Twas devilish difficult to answer with your hand clamped over my mouth," she replied lightly, but there was a question in her eyes. Did he mean what she hoped he did?

Before he could say anything more, Fox's voice rang out excitedly, "I got two of them, LaFarge!"

The little Frenchman walked through the open door, his keen eyes taking in the scene of carnage. Just then, before Rachel's and Jason's horrified eyes, he raised a pistol from his side and aimed it at Fox. *Oh, God, another of Garnet and Evelyn's minions?* Neither could do anything as the boy stood frozen. The ball whizzed past him cleanly and struck its target.

Knife still clutched in her hand, Garnet Dalbert fell back against the stairs, landing in a most undignified heap with a small red stain widening over her black heart. While Jason and Rachel were still in shock, the little Frenchman rushed to Fox and clutched him in his arms, scolding angrily.

"*Mon petit*, how many times have I explained that you must never gloat until you have made certain all your enemies are buried, lest they rise up and slit your throat while you crow?"

Fox nodded, chastened, as Jason and Rachel approached. Neither the fight master nor the boy took note of the cutthroat who sat behind the doorway still clutching his injured knee and moaning softly. Just as Jason prepared to secure their prisoner for the watch, the ninth Marquess of Cargrave rushed through the door, breathless from his unsuccessful attempt to keep up with LaFarge. Several watchmen followed closely behind him and took charge of the lone prisoner, as well as seeing to the bodies of the others.

"However did you find us, m'lord?" Jason asked, not bothering to suppress his amazement.

"You owe it to your friend Drummond. 'Twas he who sent word from Gravesend that although Forrestal was a bounder, he was not the assassin. He also alerted me to the danger of allowing you to gallivant about the countryside en route to Bristol while that fool Dalbert's wife and stepson remained unaccounted for."

"They were going to kill both of us so that Roger could inherit," Rachel said.

"But Roger never wanted the titles," Jason murmured, perplexed.

"Your cousin knew nothing of what his wife and her son were doing. Ironically, Garnet cared nothing more for the titles than did her husband, since Roger could not pass them down to Evelyn. She confessed everything while she was tormenting me," Rachel said. "They wanted the money."

"Needed it quite desperately, in fact, for their business ventures," the marquess added, having been apprised of that fact by Drum's message.

"Drum always was suspicious of the Dalberts, but I dismissed the idea as preposterous because I couldn't imagine Roger as a villain and Forrestal seemed so likely a candidate. I never thought about the Simmons shipping business being in trouble," Jason said.

"Well, 'tis a good thing your cynical friend did," Cargrave replied testily. Then with hearty approval, he added, "Dandy he might be and a wastrel to boot, but the Honorable Albert Francis Edward Drummond has risen sharply in my estimation over the past few days."

"Didn't Garnet save Jace's life when he was given the foxglove?" Fox asked, puzzled.

"She explained it," Rachel replied. "Remember when she told us how her father was afflicted with a heart condition and she tended him? She knew all about the drug. Knew that if the dosage is not sufficient to be lethal, it can cause the victim to suffer paralysis and brain damage but possibly live for months, even years. Then her hired killers would have had no chance to get close enough for another attempt on your life."

"I hadn't drunk enough of the punch. She couldn't chance that I'd not oblige her by dying. Thank God good old Roger accidentally spilled most of my drink," Jason said.

Rachel nodded with a grim shiver. "She used foxglove to kill her own father because he had uncovered some of her son's unsavory business dealings."

"The woman was a bedlamite," Jason replied. "Poor Roger. He will take this hard."

"Then we shall not tell him." When everyone looked at Rachel with amazement, she shrugged. "What need to hurt the poor man? We can with complete justification blame the whole thing on Evelyn and say that Garnet learned what he was doing and came here to stop him. She was accidentally killed in the confusion by one of her son's men."

"Countess, you are a marvel," Jason said with a tender smile.

As the watchmen were carrying the last of the bodies away, Fox tugged on the marquess's coat sleeve and whispered something that caused the old man to roar with laughter, then shake his head.

"No, m'boy. Must I keep reminding you that this is England."

"No scalps!" Jason admonished, knowing at once what the boy had asked.

Everyone burst into laughter, even LaFarge. Then Cargrave turned to Jason and said, "May I have a word in private with you, Grandson?" His expression had turned suddenly somber.

Nodding to the others, Jason stepped outside into the

343

chilly night air with the old man, who turned to him with what was now a wistful smile. "I have always gotten my way, Jason. Played to win. Yes—" he put up his hands with a sigh—"and I cheat when necessary. I wanted you for my heir and Hugh's daughter for your wife, but this time my scheming almost cost you both your lives, not to mention the lad's. I played you false.

"And now I intend to make what amends I can. There is still time for you and Fox to sail with the morning tide. I will not interfere. The decision is yours . . . and perhaps Rachel's. All I ask is that neither of you think too ill of a conniving old bastard." He reached out and embraced his startled grandson before Jason could utter a word, then walked slowly back toward the lighted doorway.

"Grandfather, wait." When the old man turned around and faced his grandson, Jason said, "I have heard stories about you and Grandmother. That yours was the greatest love match of the last century."

Cargrave nodded with what Jason would have sworn were tears gleaming in his eyes. "Aye, it was that, lad."

"And you wanted the same for me with Rachel. Fox told me, but I was too blind a fool to see the truth."

"As I was too stubborn to explain it to you honestly. From the time Hugh first brought her around, and she almost broke her neck trying to jump a pony over a hedge, I knew you were right for each other."

" 'Twould seem, m'lord, that you and the viscount are far wiser than your offspring," Jason said ruefully.

"We damn well should be, considering we are three times your ages!" the marquess roared, once again his old imperious self.

Jason hugged the old man hard, then said with a wink, "I think that in the fullness of time I shall be able to convince my bride of that fact."

* * *

344

They all rode in the marquess's coach to a better district of town and took lodgings in a comfortable inn. With the innkeeper's wife assisting her with warm water, medical supplies and bandages, Rachel restitched Jason's thigh by the light of a blazing fire in the common room, which was empty at that late hour.

When Jason was once again decently clad, Cargrave, Fox and LaFarge came in to assure themselves that the earl was all right, then bade good night to the bridal couple and retired. Jason and Rachel remained behind.

"You never did have the opportunity to answer the question I have asked you twice now." He looked at her expectantly.

Rachel had been uncharacteristically quiet since they'd left the warehouse, but now she cleared her throat and said, "I know you and Fox can return to America if that is your wish . . . and I would not blame you . . . for you see"—she paused to swallow her tears—"I have been every bit as conniving as your grandfather."

"You mean because of the need for consummation of our marriage?" he prompted, holding back a smile.

"That and more. Your grandfather never intended to adopt Fox as a means of forcing you to produce heirs. He loves the boy well, for I've heard him bragging to my father about how bright the child is and making plans for his education, and for seeing him established as a well-to-do English gentleman—but that's all. I lied."

"Just as your body lied when you came to my room on our wedding night? For a woman intent only on effecting a consummation, you went considerably beyond the, hmmm, necessary. I seem to recall the nature of your responses—on our wedding night, then at Falconridge and twice while we were on the road to Bristol. Now, unless you have an unusually elastic

345

maidenhead, Countess, naught but once was required."

He was grinning at her, the great Yankee lobcock!

What else could she do? Rachel threw herself into his arms and kissed the arrogant smile off his lips. She dug her fingers into the thick black hair of his scalp and tugged on it as he deepened the kiss.

"What's a poor Yankee earl to do?" he asked between kisses. "Here I am, beset by a savage little brother, a devious grandfather, and a wife with a bizarre animosity toward maidenheads. Duty demands that I remain in England and set all aright."

"Oh, and how, m'lord earl, do you intend to do that?" Rachel asked, tightening her arms around his shoulders.

"I shall begin with a compromise. Falconridge, Harleigh and, eventually, all the Cargrave lands are yours to administer as you wish. You may plow the earth; but I, my darling Countess, will see that you are well plowed also."

Rachel laughed, a rich bubbling sound of overwhelming joy as she said, "A delicious bargain, m'lord earl, but even for a Yankee, you are vulgar."

"Yes, Countess, but a damn good plowman," he replied, slanting his mouth over hers once more.

Epilogue

Snow fell softly across the rolling hills surrounding Falconridge. Soon it would be Christmas, the first one celebrated together by the earl and his countess. And it would be a very special occasion for a number of excellent reasons. His entire family had come from America for an extended holiday visit, via a most circuitous route through Canada. Drum had agreed to forgo the pleasures of the Great Wen for the privations of the countryside just to spend Christmas with Jason and Rachel. Fox had just completed his first term at Harrow with gratifying results. Grandfather, breaking his decades-long holiday exile at Cargrave Hall, had come to Falconridge instead. Hugh and his other two daughters and their families were also expected to join in the festivities. Even a still-bereft cousin Roger had been coaxed into spending the holiday with the rest of the family.

"This house will be Bedlam shortly, when everyone awakens," Jason said to his wife as he raised himself up on one elbow, resting his head on his hand. His tone indicated not the least perturbation as he looked down into Rachel's sparkling eyes.

"I cannot wait to see Fox's expression when he opens the package Mama Beaumont brought him from his Shawnee cousins," she murmured as his free hand reached out and cupped her breast, thumb teasing the nipple of a ripe, full breast.

"Much as I look forward to Christmas morning, this morning I have other joys in mind . . ." His voice trailed away as he let his hand glide down the voluptuous curve of her hip. "You are filling out most lushly, Countess. It must be all the holiday feasting," he murmured as he trailed kisses across her breasts and down to her navel.

"Not precisely that, Jason. There is something I must—"

Her words were interrupted by a sharp little gasp of pleasure as his mouth found the dark curls at the apex of her thighs and nuzzled them, causing her to arch up into his caress. Her hands cradled his head, guiding him up beside her. Bracketing his face with her fingertips, she said breathlessly, "No, first I must—"

"Later, my love," Jason murmured as his lips took hers in a slow, lazy kiss. He slanted his mouth across hers and let his tongue persuade her.

Rachel acquiesced, dueling with him as she wrapped her arms around his neck and pulled him over her. His big body pushed her into the mattress as they continued the kiss, fiercely, then gently, then with renewed hunger. At length, he moved his lips from her softly swollen mouth to plant moist caresses across her eyelids and cheeks, then let his tongue trace the delicate curves of her ear. His hand seized a mass of her hair, spreading it out across the snowy pillow.

"Like spilled chocolate, glistening, warm and inviting." He held a fistful up to his face and rubbed it across one beard-stubbled cheek.

Rachel caressed his stubborn jawline, murmuring, "Until you, I always thought of it as plain brown."

"No imagination." He feigned a sigh of regret as he lowered his head to her breasts, feasting on one, then the other as she writhed beneath him, offering herself joyously. When her nipples contracted into wet, shiny little nubs, he raised his head in satisfaction, allowing her access to his chest. Clever fingers trailed through the thick pelt of black hair and sought out his own hard male nipples, circling them with her nails until it was his turn to gasp with pleasure.

He rolled onto his back with her in his arms, one hand buried in her hair, cradling her head, while the other roamed lower, skimming the delicate vertebrae, moving down her spine past the deep valley that led to the sweet mounds of her derriere. "You are smooth and firm," he said, kneading one buttock, then the other as he kissed her throat.

"No soft English lady's rear . . . too much riding," she murmured, wriggling provocatively under his ministrations.

"You haven't been riding lately . . . on horseback, that is," he whispered with a teasing grin.

She kissed it from his mouth, then used her tongue to dip into that delicious dimple at its side. He was utterly beautiful, unshaven, his hair tousled, his sea-blue eyes heavy-lidded with a mixture of sleep and passion. How she loved him! Rachel slithered down his body, causing a growl of satisfaction when she brushed over the hard evidence of his desire. Sliding from atop him, she took his phallus in her hand and glided up and down, observing with keen pleasure the single pearly drop perched at its tip.

Slowly, deliberately, she lowered her lips, licking them in anticipation as he watched her through half-closed eyes. When her tongue darted out and swept the drop into her mouth, he cried out her name. Then she opened her mouth and took him inside, tasting and teasing as he arched his back in ecstasy.

After a few moments, when he could bear the pleasure no longer, he pulled her up and rolled her over, kneeling between her spread thighs to taste of her. She was glistening wet now, utterly enchanting as the essence of her unique female musk blended with the soft fragrance of her bath perfume. They'd had quite a time of it in the tub last night, he thought fleetingly as his mouth closed over the portal of her sweetness, finding the tiny nub that made her whimper with joy.

Her body bowed up as he tongued her in that intimate caress, her hands curving around his head, guiding him and urging him on until she could feel the crest nearing. Then, by supreme will, she tugged him away, gasping, " 'Tis time . . . well past time for plowing . . ."

Breathing hard, he towered over her, cupping her buttocks in his hands as he buried himself to the hilt in her hot, wet sheath. Rachel looked up through pleasure-glazed eyes to feast on the magnificence of her Yankee, so lean and dark and sinuous, with his night-dark hair obscuring his face in shadow. His blue eyes glowed, shining down on her, meeting her own, turned hazel-gold with passion.

They communicated silently with each gliding stroke as he plunged in, slowly withdrew, only to plunge once more. They moved in perfect sync, like dancers in a beloved and familiar ballet, each intuiting the other's slightest intent. Prolong the incredible pleasure. Rush breathless and heady toward the ultimate completion.

And at last that was what they did.

Rachel signaled the beginning of her spiraling ecstasy with the tiny tremors that began to build deep inside her. Jason responded to her cue, swelling rigidly and pulsing his seed in rhythm with the contractions of her body until neither could distinguish one's culmination from the other's. Finally, he collapsed onto her and she held him fast in her arms as they both panted in satiation.

After several moments joined in that tender embrace, he raised his head and smiled down into her glowing face. "I seem to recall you had something of great import to say before I . . . distracted you. Would you by any chance happen to recall what it was?" he asked smugly.

Now it was her turn to grin. "As a matter of fact, I would. You mentioned that I have not been riding for the past week or so . . ."

He looked puzzled. "I assumed 'twas because you've been so busy with all our guests." His expression turned to concern. "Rachel, you are not ill—"

She pressed her fingers to his lips, shaking her head. Her whole body was tingling with the joy of what she had to say. "I have never been in better health in my life. I only wanted to be certain before I told you that you are to be a father in the late spring."

At once Jason rolled off her and took her in his arms as if she were the most fragile china. "I should have let you speak, not fallen on you like a ravening wolf. Could I harm—that is, can we—I mean—"

Rachel's laughter pealed like Christmas bells across the vast space of the master suite. "I am breeding, my love, not an invalid. My mother and both grandmothers birthed children without the slightest difficulty. I come from hearty stock, and given my predilections toward vigorous exercise, I should do even better, since I am tough as a badger and strong as a plowhorse. Speaking of which, there is not a reason on earth that I should stop my work on the estates. Neither will I allow you to shirk your duties as a plowman, m'lord."

Jason threw back his head and laughed with sheer joy. "Have you not heard what fools for work we Yankees are? I would not dream of shirking. 'Tis but a small way for me to become acquainted with our offspring before he or she enters the world."

She caressed his face. "I did not tell you after we came home from Bristol, but . . ."

"But?" he prompted.

"When I feared I was going to lose you, 'twas not only my joy in coupling with you that led me to seek you out repeatedly. 'Twas also the hope that you might give me a babe before you sailed away."

He kissed her reverently. "What prideful fools we were. I worried that such might happen and I would not be here for you and the child. I spun all sorts of improbable plans to have Drum inform me the moment he learned you were breeding, but all the while, what I really wanted was to remain here as your husband."

"If nothing had impeded us, you would not have sailed, then?"

"Never," he replied simply. " 'Tis you, only and always you, whom I shall love, my countess, Madame Beaumont."

She smiled. "You make that sound seditiously French, Monsieur Le Comte."

Jason returned her smile. " 'Twas a French surname in the distant past. The Normans may have conquered

England, but their victory was short-lived. 'Tis home
and the heart that always conquer in the end."

"I will love you, only and always you, Jason Beaumont, be you earl, marquess or Yankee privateer, I care
not." Rachel sealed their tender words with a kiss.

Acknowledgment

The idea for a Yankee privateer who makes a devil's bargain with his ruthless grandfather to inherit an earldom came from my husband, Jim, who wrote me a whole plot synopsis of Jason and Rachel's story. The idea so intrigued me that I decided it might be the first in a series of books about bold, reckless American men who inherit titles and meet their matches in clever, resourceful Englishwomen who teach their hearts to love.

Thus the concept for the American Lords series was born. However, since I had already written two books set in Regency England, *Wicked Angel* and *Wanton Angel*, I decided to move ahead in history after *Yankee Earl*. *Rebel Baron* will be set in Victorian England just after the American Civil War, and *Texas Viscount* in Edwardian England at the very opening of the last century.

Because my reader mail indicated that Alvin Francis Edward Drummond, "Drum to his friends," was so popular in the *Angel* books, I gave him an encore in *Yankee Earl*. For anyone interested in the research I used to create the world which Drum and his friends inhabit, please check the author's notes from those stories for references.

I sincerely hope you enjoy the love story and share in the laughter as Jason and Rachel are drawn against their stubborn natures to build a life together. Originally, there was only to be a trilogy of American Lords, but the character of young Fox Barlow began to fascinate me as the story developed. A Shawnee Lord ... hmmm, now there's an idea. Let me know what you think. After all I can't rely on Jim for all my ideas. He might become as full of himself as Jason Beaumont!

Happy reading,
Shirl Henke